VEIL Online

VEIL ONLINE
Book 3

An Epic LitRPG Series

Written by John Cressman

ISBN: 978-1-7351302-1-7 (Paperback)
ISBN: 978-1-7351302-2-4 (Hardcover)
ISBN: 978-1-7351302-0-0 (Amazon Kindle)
ISBN: 978-1-7351302-3-1(Audiobook)

Any references to historical events, real people, or real places are used fictitiously. Names, characters, and places are products of the author's twisted imagination.

Front cover image by Karen Dimmick from ArcaneCovers.com.
Book design by Rebecka Yaeger of Becka's Best Author Services.

Printed by Maverick-Gage Publishing in conjunction with IngramSpark, in the United States of America.

First printing edition 2020.

Maverick-Gage Publishing
Allentown, PA
info@maverick-gage.com
www.maverick-gage.com

John Elijah Cressman
www.johnecressman.com

Prologue

Jace, or Jynx as he was now calling himself, climbed onto the deck and stretched. They'd been on the ship for three days now and Jace was restless. The ship wasn't exactly small, but the cabins were tiny. And apparently, being a Baronet meant nothing on the ship. Other than the captain who got her own quarters, and the crew who slept in a large open room below, all the passenger cabins were the same size.

This was one of the few times he missed his old apartment, back in the real world. Though now, it was something he could never see again. He'd found out that he wasn't the real Jace Burton. Rather, he was a copy of the mind of the real Jace Burton, uploaded into the most sophisticated virtual reality world ever created, VEIL Online.

The real Jace Burton was in a coma after a car accident in which the paramedics had pronounced him dead. Even though the real Jace had later been revived, the paramedics had inadvertently triggered Jace's last will and testament that specified that his last "brain backup" was uploaded into the system.

But things didn't go as planned. Instead of waking up in his VEIL Online character, a level 95 vampyre assassin named Mordred, he had been inserted into a monster body. Every time he had died, he had jumped into a different monster body, unable to communicate with other players.

Before being inserted into the game, Jace had worked as a computer programmer for WorldCog and had managed to "hack" his way into a player body. He'd made his way to the capital of the land he'd spawned, a city called Whitecliff.

In Whitecliff, he'd located an artifact called the *Help Desk*. The *Help Desk* was left over from the beginning of the game when VEIL Online support was handled solely in-game. The company soon realized this was impractical and had moved support to their website. But the *Help Desk* had remained, if you knew where to look for it.

In reaching the *Help Desk*, Jace had discovered that his old co-worker, Damian, had been the one who had created a bug that was causing people to appear in monster bodies. The bug also relieved them of any money they willed into the game.

Jace had told support about Damian and about the bug which turned out to be less of a bug and more like malicious code created by the senior programmer for his own good. But, Damian had discovered what he was doing and moved the *Help Desk* before he'd finished his conversation with support.

Worse, Jace knew that a player controlled an epic, raid-level dragon. Whatever player now controlled the dragon, he or she was systematically destroying cities. It had been heading for Whitecliff, forcing Jace and his friends to leave right after talking to the *Help Desk*.

It was Midweek. That was three days ago. The dragon would have reached the city two days ago, which was Monday, or Moonsday in the game. Since they'd been at sea the entire time, heading north to the gnome homeland, they'd heard no news of whether Whitecliff had survived.

Jace hoped it had. He had earned himself the in-game title of Baronet, which came with a manor and some vineyards to the south. It would be nice if they still existed. Noble titles were purchasable in the game - for the right price. In Jace's case, it was probably a million gold, or the real world equivalent of 100,000 US dollars. If it were gone, it would take him a long time to earn back that money in the game.

Looking around the deck of the ship, he spotted Mika and Diana at the bow of the ship. Both women were players he'd found trapped in monster bodies and had freed. Somehow the ability to talk with monsters had stayed with him through his "hack" to human player form.

He'd helped others as well but hadn't run into them yet. It was no surprise since VEIL Online was an enormous world. He'd once heard that the virtual planet that made up VEIL Online was almost twice as large as the real Earth.

The company claimed no one had seen it all, plus there was an entire world underneath the world and even creatures and monster civilizations that lived on the bottom of the ocean. It really was an enormous game, run by the world's most powerful supercomputers. And now, it was his permanent home.

He walked over Mika and Diana. Mika was a Japanese woman who had never come right out and told Jace her age, but he guessed she had been in her early twenties when she had died. She looked beautiful, but that's how the game worked. The game put you in your genetically perfect body permanently set at age 25. But more than that, Mika had an enthusiasm and optimism that had helped keep his spirits up.

The woman next to him was equally stunning. Taller than Mika, Diana was a raven haired woman with a more voluptuous figure. Unlike Mika, Diana had lived a full life and was in her mid-90s when she had died and been inserted in the game. A former romance writer, she was now in the genetically perfect body of her 25-year-old self.

"There you are, dear one," Diana said as she spotted him. "And Luna too, I see."

Jace looked down to his familiar, an orange tabby cat he'd named Luna, after his dead sister. Luna was his familiar, but as he'd discovered quickly, his speak-with-monsters ability extended to her. She had become his companion and he couldn't imagine not having her around.

"Any sight of land," he asked.

"No land," Mika replied and gave Jace a bright smile. "But the ocean is clear."

Jace smiled weakly, remembering the first night, when they'd encountered a storm and Jace learned that he could get seasick in a virtual ship. It had not been pleasant.

"Four more days to Nynymmost," he stated. "That's depressing."

"Well then," Diana said. "We may have some pleasant news."

"Oh?" Jace raised an eyebrow.

"We are stopping at a port tomorrow," Mika grinned.

"Really?" Jace asked excitedly. He could really use a break from the ship at this point. Plus, they might get some news about Whitecliff and whether the city remained.

As if reading his mind, Mika reached out and took his hand. "Maybe Whitecliff killed the dragon."

Jace gave her a smile but neither of them really believe it. In the hands of a player, a raid level monster like a dragon was nearly impossible to kill. Especially if that player knew the game mechanics. While a normal dragon AI might have the dragon land, making it vulnerable to attack, a player could rain down destruction from high above, never coming close enough for any weapons to touch it.

When he'd been at the *Help Desk*, he'd warned support that a player was controlling the dragon, but he wasn't sure if they believed him or if they would wait until they did some investigation before they would act. And even though the person he'd talked with had said they would contact Jace in-game, he'd had no word from them.

"I just want a hot bath," Diana said. "All this salty air and lack of hot water is making me feel all dirty." The older woman gave him a wink. "And I don't mean the good kind of dirty."

The old Jace might have blushed at the woman's blatant flirting but Jace had gotten used to it. He'd realized Diana was an incorrigible flirt, at least with Jace. That and knowing she was old enough to be his grandmother also helped him to ignore her advances.

"We have enough money," Jace said. Along with the title of Baronet, Jace had inherited over half a million gold from the previous Baronet. He'd helped the royal guard to uncover a plot by Baronet Tiebaut to steal the princess' tiara. The king had executed the former Baronet and given his lands and titles to Jace as a reward.

Unfortunately, they'd burned through much of the money so far getting to the *Help Desk* and then more money changing their name to hide them from Damian. They had split the remaining money between the three of them.

"True, dear one." Diana smiled. "Hopefully we're in port long enough that I can actually get a hot bath."

"Do we know how big the city is? Is it a human city or gnomish city?" Jace asked.

Diana turned to Mika, who just shrugged. "She didn't say."

"I'll go talk to her. If it's a larger city, maybe we can get some news about Whitecliff," he told them. "Plus, it might be possible to send a raven message to Charlena."

"Raven message?" Diana asked.

"It's a type of... Um… certified letter, for lack of a better analogy," Jace explained. "It's expensive but the raven will find whoever you send the message to and delivers the message. Then it flies back to you and tells you it was delivered."

"That's very modern," Diana said.

"Except for the raven," Jace offered. "It costs like a thousand gold to send a message to someone in the same faction and even more to the other factions. Plus, it's not instant. The raven has to actually fly to the target, though it has a special tracking algorithm. As long as you give it the character name, it will find them."

"Is that what Damian will use to try to find us?" Mika asked.

Jace nodded. "Something similar. But since we changed our names, it shouldn't work now. Theoretically. Honestly, that wasn't a part of the game I really had a lot of exposure too. It was more of the support side where I was on the troubleshooting team."

"Let's hope he can't find us," Mika said and then she frowned. "What are you going to tell Charlena?"

Jace knew Mika didn't care for Charlena and that Charlena's affection for him was part of the reason. Mika seemed to care about him, and they'd shared a few kisses but he wasn't about to start something serious with her when he might not be around.

He'd told support that he was Jace's twin brother, something that would explain the same DNA. If they discovered the truth, that he was the consciousness of a live person who had been inserted accidentally, they'd be forced to delete him. He'd simply cease to exist.

Even knowing that the real Jace was out there, in the real world, didn't make him feel any better. He felt real. In every aspect, he was the same as any other person who had been inserted into the game. With only one difference, his real self was still alive.

He realized Mika was still waiting for an answer. "I'm not sure. There's only so much I can tell her. Even sending her the message is dangerous. If Damian is monitoring her, this could lead him back to us."

"You can at least warn her about Damian," Diana said. "That's not something Damian can use against us. And let her know we contacted support."

Jace nodded. "That's what I was thinking. I can't mention the real Jace or the fact that I'm just a copy. I'm not sure what he would do with that information, but it wouldn't be good."

They lapsed into silence then as they considered Jace's words. None of them knew exactly what Damian was capable of, and none of them wanted to find out either.

Chapter 1

They arrived in Lasthaven around 6am on Tavernday. Jace and the girls had watched from the bow as the ship approached the town. From what Jace could tell, it wasn't even half the size of the capital. It was closer to the size of Crossroads, a town he'd visited on his way to Whitecliff.

"Do you think it will have a raven messenger?" Mika asked.

Jace held his hand above his eyes, shielding them from the glare of the morning sun. "I can't tell. I'll have to ask around."

"As long as there's an inn with a bath, I'll be happy," Diana stated.

"Be careful," he told them. "And avoid using your name whenever possible."

"Do you think Damian is looking for us too?" Mika asked.

"I don't think so. But Damian's smart," he replied. "He could have questioned some of the people at the party and found out that I came with two women. He might even have checked with the patents office and found our name changes."

"But I thought you framed him for theft of the princess' necklace," Diana cut in.

"Me too," Jace admitted. "But I just don't know what resources he might have. Who knows how much gold he has at this point?"

"Stolen gold!" Mika argued.

"Yes. Stolen gold. But if he has tens of millions of gold at his disposal, he might just be able to buy a pardon. For that matter, he might be able to pay off another member of nobility to ask the questions for him," Jace said.

"You aren't exactly inspiring hope," Diana told him.

Jace shrugged. "Sorry, but I don't want any of us to let our guard down. Damian had me fooled. Had everyone on the team fooled - for years."

"You assume the team members were fooled. Is it possible they were in on it?" Diana asked.

He thought about it for a moment before answering. "I don't think so. Damian kept to himself and he wasn't the trusting sort. I doubt he would have shared his plan, or the money, with anyone."

"Do you think support is investigating him?" Mika asked.

"I hope so," Jace told her. "But we won't know for sure unless they contact us."

"Couldn't Damian just delete the evidence or what he did? The code or whatever it is he created?" Diana wondered. "Cover his tracks. That sort of thing."

Jace frowned. He'd been thinking the same thing. Would Damian cut his losses and wipe out any trace of the code he created? Damian might be many things, but he wasn't stupid. He probably had a contingency plan. Or maybe not.

Then again, maybe Damian was too arrogant to assume he'd ever get caught. After all, from what Jace knew from talking with the other players he'd rescued, some of them had been in monster bodies for over two years. That meant Damian had been stealing people's money for years without getting caught.

"Let's hope not," he told Diana. "If he dumps the code, it might be years before they figure out what he did and are able to fix it."

"Years?" Diana and Mika said at the same time.

"Hopefully that's an exaggeration." He smiled but then let it slip. "There are literally billions of lines of code that make this game work. Without knowing exactly what he did, they'll need to reverse engineer it. That could potentially take months or years."

Diana let out an exasperated breath and turned to stare Lasthaven.

"Does this mean we will be running from Damian for years?" Mika asked. Diana turned back as well, waiting for the answer.

Jace looked between the two girls. He wanted to give them a good answer, but he didn't have one. So, he lied. "I'm sure support will resolve it before then."

Diana smirked. "Dear one, you are a terrible liar."

They lapsed back into silence as the Sea Tyrant maneuvered up to the dock and then tossed over mooring lines.

"Looks like we're here," Jace observed. "Anyone for shore leave?"

***

It took another fifteen minutes before the gangplank was lowered and the captain allowed them to leave the ship. Jace and the girls were the first in line but it looked like the other passengers were ready for some time on solid ground as well, including his staff from the manor. He hadn't seen much of them on the cruise, although Fimipp Wisesworn did occasionally check in on him to see if there was anything he needed.

"4pm," Captain Yehmee bellowed. "We sail with the tide. If you aren't aboard, you'll be left behind. Savvy?"

Jace and the rest of the passengers either nodded or made sounds of acknowledgement and the captain let them proceed. Before Jace or the girls could even step onto the gangplank, Luna darted between them, down the ramp and onto the docks.

Luna reached the bottom and stopped. Now on the dock, the orange tabby used her special ability to grow to the size of a tiger. Her sudden transformation caught a few dock workers by surprise, but they quickly resumed their work. Now huge, his familiar turned and sat down, wrapping her tail around her. She looked up at them as if to say, "I'm waiting."

"Someone's happy to be on land," Diana commented and the three of them followed the cat's example and walked down the gangplank.

"Yes," Jace said. "I think she likes that growth ability a little too much."

Jace had told his familiar not to use her ability on the ship, due to the confined quarters and limited space. She'd whined until he relented and allowed her to grow large up on the deck. Unfortunately, it was only for a few minutes a day, when there were no other passengers on deck. Now, it seemed she was making up for lost time.

Once on the dock, they walked over to where Luna was waiting for them and discussed their plans. After the constant motion of the ship on the ocean, walking on stable land felt odd and Jace almost felt like the world was still moving.

"First, we need to find the graveyard and rebind," he told the girls. "If Whitecliff was destroyed, we'll each have random spawn points if we die. After that, I'm going to go check on a raven messenger."

"And then I'm going to find a bath to soak in," Diana said, stretching her arms above her head. The motion drew attention to her already large breasts and Jace smirked as he saw several dock workers stop what they were doing to admire his companion.

Mika looked at Jace. "I will go with you."

"Okay," Jace nodded. "Let's agree to meet back here at noon and we'll find some place to get some real food."

"Oh yes, please," Diana agreed.

"Waffles?" Mika asked hopefully.

"At this point, anything is better than salted fish," Diana complained.

"True," Jace agreed. "But, first let's go to the bind point."

He asked one of the dock workers where the cemetery was, and the man muttered something under his breath before pointing in what Jace thought was west. After thanking the man, the four of them went the direction he'd pointed.

While smaller than Whitecliff, Lasthaven was still a decent-sized city. Jace kept a wary eye out for anyone paying them too much attention. Damian could already have players or NPCs looking out for them. They couldn't afford an ambush until they changed their rebind spot.

They passed all manner of shops and Jace noticed that many of them were specifically for adventurers. He wasn't sure exactly where Lasthaven was, other than north of Whitecliff, but it must be on the frontier. That meant, the monsters in the area were probably higher level.

They walked for twenty minutes before they came to the city gate. The guards gave them only a cursory look as they walked out of the gate. The trio were dressed in their armor again and their weapons were plainly visible, but Jace knew the guards were used to players coming in and out of the city. Just part of their programming.

He'd noticed that, like in Whitecliff, NPCs didn't seem to notice or pay any attention to the oversized cat walking with them and the only reactions he received were from other players. It must be some sort of AI routine that caused the NPCs to simply accept familiars.

In a way, Jace was glad since it might have otherwise drawn unwanted attention from the NPCs. As it was, he realized that if Damian knew Luna could grow large, it might be an easy way to keep track of them.

After all, that ability was something unique she had gained when he'd used some ritual blood on her. He didn't know of any other familiars who could grow large. He'd need to think about it and, if necessary, convince Luna not to use the ability in public. Most likely it would mean lots of chicken and fish bribes.

Once outside the city, they spotted the cemetery on a hill to the south and immediately headed for it. When they reached the cemetery, they each changed their bind point. Now, if they died, they'd respawn here in Lasthaven.

"We're all bound here now. We'll see each other at the docks at noon," Jace told them. He turned to Luna. "Can you go with Diana? Watch over her and relay any messages."

The cat's only reply was to grace him with a bored expression.

"Do that," he offered. "And we'll get you something special for lunch."

"Chicken?" Luna said, looking hopefully. Normally she asked for fish so perhaps even that cat was growing tired of the salted fish they served on the ship.

"Whatever you want," Jace told her.

Luna considered their deal for only a moment before getting to her feet and rubbing up against Diana. "Chicken."

"I guess we know what she wants." Diana smiled, stroking the cat's soft fur.

Because Mika and Diana had been monsters like Jace, they had the ability to speak with monsters as well. This included familiars like Luna. Since Jace and Luna could communicate telepathically over long distances, she made a great walkie-talkie. But he was sure Luna would be offended if he called her a walkie-talkie.

The four of them walked back to the city gate before parting ways. Just inside the city gates, he put a hand on Diana's shoulder. "Be careful. Use Luna to send us any messages."

"Yes, yes, dear one," Diana reassured him. "I've written some spy novels, you know. I know how to lie low. Come on kitty, I'll buy you a chicken to eat while I soak in the tub."

Jace smiled as he watched her go and then turned to Mika. "Let's go see if we can find the raven messenger. Maybe he'll have some news about Whitecliff too."

"Sounds good!" she responded and reached over, took his hand in hers. "Let's go!"

Chapter 2

It took them only a few minutes to find the raven messenger. Jace had stopped a guard to ask about it and, because of game logic, the guard had immediately recognized him as a Baronet and had been only too eager to direct them. Apparently, rank had its privileges. Did that mean Whitecliff still stood? Or did his title as Baronet last as long as Ardor lasted?

The building was located on the north side of town, near the docks. Other than the large raven sign in front of the building, it was recognizable by the aviary on top of the building and the squawking of the ravens it contained. And the smell. At full sensory levels, there was a very pungent odor around the entire area and even Mika wrinkled her nose.

Jace had only used the raven messengers a few times, most to communicate with potential raid leaders and setup times to meet them. Occasionally, he'd seen the messages delivered, but it wasn't often.

One of the reasons they weren't used as often was the cost. If he remembered correctly, a raven message cost 5,000 gold. Even for a high level character, that wasn't cheap. When questioned on the forums, WorldCog has explained that players are playing for a magical service and that the price was fair.

Despite a small outcry, the company had left the price as is, claiming that it was a luxury service and that players could always communicate in person for free. Just one more way for them to make money. As if they needed another way.

Entering the building, their senses were assaulted by a much stronger version of the odor outside. Jace quickly saw why. In the back of the small building was a spiral staircase that led directly up to the aviary. The staircase and floor below it were caked in bird droppings of varying ages.

The rest of the room was a cluttered mess of bookshelves, papers and a large wooden desk. Behind the desk was a gnome, sitting in a chair that was obviously meant for a human. As he got a better look, he could see that the gnome was sitting atop of several stacked books so that he could better work on the overly large desk.

"Gleergaklis Quirkpipe at your service. How may I help you, milord?" the gnome asked as he looked up. The gnome had bright orange and blue hair that burst from his head as if he had recently stuck his finger in a light socket. Interestingly, his clothes seemed to match the hair, with Gleergaklis wearing a bright blue shirt under an equally bright orange jacket, trimmed in lime.

The entire image of the gnome seemed like an assault on his visual senses but that was the way some gnomes dressed. And while NPC gnomes were sometimes flamboyant in their clothing choices, some players took it to an entirely new level.

"We'd like to send a raven message," Jace told the little gnome.

"You've come to the right place then, milord!" Gleergaklis replied cheerfully. Again, Jace had been recognized as a Baronet. It was a bit anachronistic, but like the name change, all NPCs simply "knew" Jace had a new name and "knew" that he was a Baronet.

While the old Jace would have found that very convenient, right now he only considered how that might work in Damian's favor. His old friend was undoubtedly looking for him at this very moment and Jace saw these little conveniences as ways that he might use to track them.

For a minute, he almost changed his mind about sending the message. But, they would be leaving Lasthaven in a few hours and Damian should be working right now, so he wouldn't have time to act on the information until after they'd left.

"Milord?" the gnome asked, giving Jace a curious look. "You wanted to send a message?"

"Yes." Jace smiled. "I do."

Gleergaklis smiled cheerfully and pulled a long strip of parchment from a nearby stack and, after smoothing it out, looked up at Jace expectantly. "Your name?"

Jace he had no choice but to give his actual character name, since the raven messenger worked off of those names. "Jynx Knightly."

"From Jynx Knightly," the gnome wrote down his name on the slip of parchment. "And what would you like your message to say?"

Jace already knew exactly what he wanted to say. "Charlena, found *Help Desk*. Damian discovered us. He doesn't know the last thing you told me before you left. Keep it that way. He might go after what you told me about. There is money in the bank that you can get out with your signet ring. Change your last name to something else. He is tracking us. If you can, meet us in Nynymmost. Same thing we told the others about Whitecliff."

The gnome scribbled furiously with his quill until Jace was finished and then picked up the paper. He seemed to read it to himself and then nodded. He looked up at Jace and repeated the message back. "Is that correct?"

Jace nodded. "Yes."

Setting down the parchment with his message, the gnome brought out a ledger and jotted some information down before looking up at Jace. "That will be 5,000 gold please."

Sighing, Jace pulled a small bag of gold from his inventory and handed it to the gnome. They were burning through money at a fast rate and he feared that if they were forced to do another name change, they'd really be in trouble.

"Thank you, milord." He smiled, and the money disappeared one of the desk drawers. When it was gone, the little gnome hopped down from his chair and scrambled up the spiral staircase. He disappeared up into the aviary for several minutes before coming back down with a large raven clutched between his hands.

"Milord," the gnome said apologetically. "If you would be so kind as to hold the raven while I attach the note. Normally, there are two of us, but my co-worker was drafted into the militia after troops were sent down to combat the dragon."

That reminded Jace that he had intended to ask the gnome about the situation in Whitecliff. Gingerly taking the raven, he looked down at Gleergaklis. "What news of Whitecliff? Did the dragon destroy it?"

The brightly dressed gnome looked up with a huge grin. "You haven't heard, milord?"

Jace gave the gnome a questioning look as he shook his head. "Heard what?"

Gleergaklis took a step closer to Jace, his tiny body seeming to vibrate with excitement. When he spoke, his voice was a mixture of awe and elation. "Tholtar himself appeared and cast the dragon down. He might have killed it but the dragon fled. Whitecliff still stands!"

"Tholtar?" Jace repeated incredulously. Tholtar was one of the gods of VEIL. They rarely made appearances, though Jace knew of at least two instances where avatars of the evil gods had appeared as raid bosses.

He remembered that Tholtar was the patron god of Whitecliff, but to have his avatar directly intervene to save Whitecliff was something Jace would have never expected. He wondered if his message to support had caused the developers to intervene directly. Or, maybe there really was an in-game reason for the god to appear.

Either way, it meant Whitecliff was safe, as was his manor. In fact, if Damian wasn't looking for them, Jace might suggest that they return back right now. But considering their situation, he thought it was safer if they kept on the move.

"Who is Tholtar?" Mika asked next to him.

The gnome looked aghast but had the decency and good judgement to not say anything to the wife of a Baronet.

"Tholtar is the god of truth, duty and honor," Jace told her.

"And promises," Gleergaklis supplied and then realizing he had interrupted a Baronet, quickly looked chastised. "Um, sorry milord."

"He's the patron god of Whitecliff and especially the royal guard," Jace continued, ignoring the gnome's interruption. "Normally, he doesn't intervene in mortal affairs. In this instance, he did."

"He is a god. But he didn't kill the dragon?" Mika asked in confusion.

"The gods don't appear in their natural form," he explained. "They form avatars, or vessels for their power. Because the avatars exist in the physical world, they can have certain physical limitations. In this case, my guess is the two were fairly evenly matched."

The gnome looked shocked but kept his mouth shut this time. Jace knew that the NPCs didn't understand game mechanics and while Jace was stating things from a game mechanics perspective, in the mind of the non-player characters, the gods were all powerful.

"I'll explain more later." Jace smiled and gave a subtle, but meaningful glance at gnome.

"Okay." Mika gave him a wink.

"Was there anything else you needed from me to send the message?" Jace asked Gleergaklis.

The gnome seemed to snap out of whatever thoughts he'd been having and hurried back around to the desk. He retrieved the strip of parchment and rolled it up much smaller than Jace would have expected. Then he came back around and attached the paper to a small metal band on the raven's leg.

"The band is enchanted," Gleergaklis explained. "When the raven finds his target, the message will disappear, and the raven will speak it to the recipient. Once the message is delivered, the bird will fly to you and tell you it was delivered, before returning home to me."

"If you come this way," the gnome said and ushered Jace towards an open window near the stairs. "Simply speak the name of the recipient and let the bird fly out this window."

Still cupping the bird in his hands, Jace brought it to his mouth and whispered her name, "Charlena Burton." Then, he opened his hands while pushing the bird towards the window.

The raven went a few feet before its wings unfurled and it flew off to the south. Jace watched it go until it was out of his field of view and then stepped back from the window.

"Do you wish to send any other messages?" the gnome asked.

"No, thank you," Jace told him and moved to the door.

"Always a pleasure, milord" the gnome called after him.

Opening the door to the small office, Jace was about to step through when he felt a massive pain in his chest. He looked down just in time to see a crossbow bolt embedded in his chest, before his body collapsed and he was in spirit form.

Fayanna Bane uses Surprise Attack on YOU for 471 damage.
You have died.
Do you wish to respawn at your last spawn point? (Yes or No)

As had happened in Whtiecliff, Jace had been assassinated. He looked around for the assassin but couldn't see much as people on the street ran screaming. Then he saw a female fox-kin appear as she slid a dagger into Mika's back.

His companion stiffened and then her body dropped to the floor as well. Even though he knew Mika was in spirit form too, they wouldn't be able to see each other. He watched morbidly as the fox-kin bent down, sliced off Jace's ear, and then disappeared.

There was no question about it. He had been assassinated by someone in the assassin's guild and that had cut the ear off his body to prove the assassination had been succesful. Along with the ear, the person who hired her would know where the kill took place. And that person was undoubtedly Damian.

They had no time to waste, they needed to get out of town as soon as possible. Choosing Yes to respawn, he felt a momentary disorientation before his awareness reappeared into a new body in the Lasthaven graveyard.

Unconsciously, he reached for the ear that the assassin had cut off and was happy to feel it. Thank the developers that you got a brand new body every time you respawned. His new body was naked except for his loincloth and his soulbound saber. He heard a gasp next to him and turned to see Mika's mostly naked body as she too respawned. He'd rarely seen her without armor and he found himself staring at her flawless body.

Looking over at him, she caught him staring at her. She blushed but made no attempt to cover herself. Not that she needed to. Like him, she was wearing a loincloth but she was also wearing the equivalent of a bra or bikini top.

He might have stared long but a new message popped up and he groaned.

You have died recently.
Your experience gain has been decreased by 10%
for 10 hours.
Your skills have been decreased by 10% for 10
hours.
Your maximum health has been decreased by 10%
for 10 hours.
Your maximum mana has been decreased by 10%
for 10 hours.

"What is it?" Mika asked as she saw his pained expression.

"Death penalty," he answered, getting to his feet. He reached down and helped her feet. "Once I reached level 10, I became subject to the death penalty."

"I hate that," she said and Jace remembered that she'd played a cat-kin before she had died and had been around level 50. No doubt she was familiar with the "pleasure" of the death penalty..

"Come on," she said. "Let's loot our bodies and find someplace safe."

Chapter 3

Jace and Mika raced through the town naked except for their loincloths and her bra. As they ran, Jace realized that with his death, Luna would have been dismissed and he'd need to re-summon her. Unfortunately, it also meant they had no way of communicating to Diana what had happened.

"How did the assassin find you?" Mika said as they turned to run down an alley.

"Unlike players," Jace frowned. "NPCs instantly know about name changes."

"What?" Mika gave him a confused look..

Jace sigh. "In the game, our characters have a unique identifier that links back to our character record. Players NEVER see it and even developers rarely, if ever, bother with it. It's just a long hexadecimal number. Instead, developers and support people will look up a player by name. After all, that's what players know - their character name - so all the lookup tools look it up based on the character name. With me so far?"

Mika furrowed her brow but nodded, "I think so."

"But NPCs remember their interactions with players via that unique identifier. So even if you change your name, they internally look you up by that unique identifier and then pull the name from the record," Jace explained. "That's why all the NPCs addressed us by our new names when we changed our name during the marriage ceremony. None of them even noticed the change or commented on it."

Mika nodded. "Ok, that sort of makes sense. So NPCs can find us even if we change our names?"

"Yes," Jace admitted. "Unfortunately. And Damian knows this. I suspect he sent the assassin after us right before we did the second name change. The assassin's guild took the contract and they're searching for me based on that unique id."

"So he can't find you anymore?" Mika asked hopefully.

"Not exactly," Jace replied. "Did you see the assassin cut off my ear?"

Mika made a face. "Yes, that was disgusting." He saw her glance at his restored ear and smile. "At least you got it back when you respawned."

"Yes, well, the assassin will deliver that ear back to Damian as proof the assassination had been carried out. When he gets it, it will say 'Ear of Jynx Knightly'. So he'll have my name."

"But you can change it again, right?" Mika asked worriedly.

"I can. The problem is, it costs me 50,000 gold each time. That's a big deal for us right now. But as soon as I do it, Damian can just hire another assassin. Because I'm so low level, it won't cost him much and even if it did, he has more than enough money to keep sending assassins after me."

"So then what do you do?"

"I'll have to wait. We're leaving in a few hours and then we'll be out at sea. We'll be much harder to track since there won't be assassins to find us. When we get to the next port, I can change my name," Jace replied.

He purposefully didn't mention the fact that Damian was a high level warlock who had access to the teleportation spell. With it, he could travel to any city he'd been to before. That meant, he was much more mobile than they were.

But the teleportation spell was also a limitation that they could exploit. Since Damian could only travel to cities he'd been to, he might be limited to the major cities. It also meant he couldn't just teleport to them once they were out on the ocean. But they couldn't stay on the ocean forever. And when they finally reached a port, would Damian be waiting for them?

Jace and Mika reached the raven messenger shop to loot their bodies but had a surprise waiting for them. Surrounding the shop were a group of people. In the real world, it might not be surprising to see a crowd of people around a double murder scene. But this wasn't the real world.

Normally, NPCs didn't really react to player deaths, just like they didn't react to players running around in loincloths after they had died. It was something that was programmed in. There were exceptions, but generally the NPCs ignored them. So why were they gathered around the shop?

Pressing their way through the small crowd, he saw why. Not only were Jace and Mika's body lying in the doorway, but just beyond them, still in the shop, was the body of the little gnome who had helped them.

The assassin had killed all three of them. That was odd. Very odd. Normally an assassination only targeted one person. Instead, this one had killed all three of them. But why? Had the assassin simply been covering his tracks.

"Jace!" Mika said, grabbing his arm. "Look!"

She was pointing to her body and Jace instantly saw what she was referring to. After they had respawned, the assassin must have cut her ear off as well. He strained his eyes to look into the room and saw that the gnome was missing an ear too.

"Geez," he breathed. "All three of us had our ears cut off."

"But why?" Mika asked. She moved in close to her body and a moment later, her old body disappeared.

His mind whirling with possibilities, Jace bent down next to his body and looted all of his items. As soon as he removed the last item, his body dissolved away without so much as a stray glance from the NPCs.

Apparently, they were all here because of the gnome's death.

Jace motioned for Mika to step back from the crowd and once they were clear he frowned. "This isn't good."

"What does this mean?" she asked, clearly rattled by the assassinations.

As he tried to think of a response, Jace considered donning his Infiltrator's Hat and his Mountebank's Cloak. The hat allowed him to change his shape into a similarly sized humanoid shape, while the cloak allowed him to remain hidden in most situations. But the hat wouldn't disguise his name, so it wouldn't prevent an assassin from finding him. And unless he wanted to stay hidden the entire time he was off the ship, the cloak wouldn't be of much use either.

Jace had years of experience playing VEIL Online. Yet despite this, he'd never been in a situation when he was being hunted by another player. Were there items that would obscure his name? There wasn't a player auction area in Lasthaven, but he could always look in Nynymmost when they arrived.

He looked back at Mika who was still waiting for an answer. "I'm not sure exactly what it means, but I think Damian might be even more devious than I gave him credit for. Not only did he assassinate me, but I think he must have given them instructions to kill everyone with me.

"Why?"

"Well," he started. "If he talked to anyone at the ball, he knows I came there with two women. He probably knows you're my wives at this point. But he may not have your names. He probably had the assassin kill everyone around me so he'd get the ears of all of my companions. Then, he'd know your names."

Mika furrowed her eyebrows. "Does this mean he can track both of us?"

"Unfortunately, yes." Jace frowned and nodded. "Once those ears get back to him, he'll know both of our names."

"Now what?" Mika asked.

"I think we should go back to the ship and wait for Diana," Jace told her. He saw her disappointed look. "But you can probably look around some more if you want. I was the assassin's target, not you. He won't know about you until he gets your ear."

She considered that and then a big grin spread across her face. "I will bring you waffles!"

Jace chuckled despite the grim circumstances. "Waffles actually sound excellent right now."

"Okay," she said. "You go back to the ship and I will get waffles."

"See if you can find the servants, especially Fimipp," now that we know Whitecliff still stands and probably will keep standing, ask them to return. Give them enough money for all of them to catch a ship out of here and back to the manor. They're just NPCs, so Damian won't bother with them."

"Are you sure?" Mika asked.

"They don't really know anything," he said. "And they're probably in more danger with me."

Mika considered his words, probably thinking about the assassin attack. They'd both respawned, but the gnome hadn't. Had any of their servants been with them, they'd be permanently dead. "Okay. I'll find them and tell them. And get waffles!"

He smiled and she moved forward then and kissed him, quickly but softly, before turning and disappearing into the crowd. He could do nothing but stare after her as the mass of NPCs swallowed her up.

He looked down, expecting to see Luna but remembered he needed to summon her. Alone, he walked back to the docks and found the Sea Tyrant. He could see that there were only a few people on deck and guessed most of them, crew included, had disembarked. That was fine. He needed some time to think, anyway.

Jace went below deck to his cabin. Once inside, he closed the door and braced himself for summoning his familiar. He was stuck at full sensory input, with no way to dampen the sensations from the game. From everything he had read, it meant he and the girls were experiencing everything at 110 or 120% of normal.

While heightened senses might be great when eating waffles or indulging in virtual sex, it wasn't very welcome when experiencing pain. And tremendous pain was what he felt every time he summoned Luna.

The pain of summoning a familiar was so bad that Diana had refused to summon her own. She'd tried it once and had instantly given up. He didn't blame her. It felt like his very soul was being sucked out. And yet, if he didn't go through the pain, he couldn't summon Luna. And the little cat had been his companion since he first became human in the game.

Sitting down and steeling himself for the process, Jace summoned his familiar. He recognized the ripping feeling as it felt like his insides were being pulled out. Jace saw the blue and red glowing orbs that came from him and then merged to form his cat familiar.

In a few moments, it was over and it left him sweating and breathing heavy. He looked down at the cat who had appeared and she looked back at him. "Summoner die?"

"Yes," he told her. "Summoner die. Assassins."

"Bad assassins," she hissed.

He chuckled as he got his breath under control. "Yes, bad assassins." Jace remembered Diana's promise to get the cat something other than fish. "Did Diana buy you some food?"

"Yes," Luna meowed. "Good chicken."

"Glad you liked it," he told the cat. "Once we leave, it will be back to fish."

His cat gave him a dejected look and then began licking her paws. Recognizing her actions as a dismissal, he sat back in the chair and looked around the cabin for something to do. Unfortunately, there was nothing. Other than the bunk, the chair and a small nightstand, there was nothing else in the room.

Jace began looking through his inventory for something he could do or work on and saw the logbooks he'd taken from Captain Drakkar. He'd taken them when he'd slipped aboard the *Wyvern's Tail* and retrieved the princess' crown as part of a thieves guild quest. He'd caused a fiery explosion when he'd left but he knew it hadn't killed the pirate.

He snickered. He first met and defeated Dainard Drakkar when he was the guildmaster of Crossroads. They had dueled and Jace had nearly killed him when the guildmaster had used his *Vanish* ability and *Backstabbed* Charlena, killing her. The scoundrel had then fled and Jace thought he had seen the last of him.

But that wasn't the case. Somehow, the former guildmaster had become the captain of a pirate ship that had been involved in the theft of the princess' tiara. Once again, Jace had faced him and lived to tell the tale. Hopefully, that was the last he'd seen of the man.

Eying the logbooks, Jace wondered if they would shed some light on how the former guildmaster had come to be the captain of a pirate ship. If nothing else, at least it was something to do while he waited for Mika to return with waffles.

Chapter 4

"Waffles!" Mika announced as she threw open the door. The Japanese girl was grinning broadly and carrying a parchment wrapped bundle in one hand and a small bottle in the other.

Jace, who had been reading the logs, was startled by her sudden appearance and the logbook he'd been reading went sailing to the other side of the room. Unconsciously, he began to scramble for his weapons before he realized who it was.

Luna had been lying on his bunk napping, but the sudden noise and motion had caused her to screech and spring straight up into the air. The moment the cat's feet hit the bunk, they windmilled for several seconds before she launched herself against the far wall, bounced off, hit the floor and then darted underneath the bunk.

Recognizing the figure as Mika, Jace slumped back and tried to slow his rapidly beating heart. "You scared the bejesus out of me!"

Having witnessed the sudden flurry of movement from Jace and the bouncing cat, Mika's grin slipped a bit and she looked chagrined. She gave him an apologetic shrug. "Sorry."

"It's okay," Jace muttered. "If I actually aged in the game, I think you would have just scared 10 years off my life."

"But I brought waffles," she offered, holding up the wrapped package. "And syrup!" She held up the small bottle.

Jace smiled despite himself and motioned her to sit on the bunk. She did so and handed him the waffles and syrup. He caught a whiff of the food and with his enhanced sense of smell, he suddenly found himself feeling famished.

He ripped through the parchment surrounding the waffles to reveal still thick, warm waffles that were still steaming. Mika chuckled and handed him the syrup, which he poured over the waffles.

"Sorry," she told him. "No utensils. They were not willing to give away their silverware."

Jace shrugged. Reaching down, he picked up a sticky waffle and bit into it. After days of salted fish, he moaned in pleasure at the delicious, syrupy waffles. "Oh, this is so good."

Mika giggled at him and gave him a cheshire cat grin. "I ate two orders!"

Jace took another bite and barely chewed before swallowing it. "I don't blame you. These are really good."

"And I found the halfling and the other servants at a tavern," Mika said. "I told them about Whitecliff and they will take the next boat back. They're getting their luggage now."

"Excellent," Jace said. "Thank you. I really think they are safer away from me."

Mika bent down and picked up the logbook he'd been reading when she had surprised him. "What's this?"

"It's one of the logbooks I took from Captain Drakkar when I stole the tiara," he replied between bites.

"Logbook?" she looked at him questioningly. She thumbed through the book and furrowed her brow. As she did, he took another bite of waffles and enjoyed the warm sweetness. Mika looked up at him. "Can you read this? Is it in a special language?"

Jace took the book from her and smiled. "It's coded. At least, the first part of it is."

"A code?" she raised an eyebrow. "And you figured out the code?"

Grinning broadly, he nodded and took another bite of the waffles. "One of my college courses was on cryptography. It was mostly on computer cryptography, but the first part of the course was a history on codes. Plus, I've played the game for years so I'm familiar with some of the ciphers they use."

"So, you figured it out?" she asked excitedly. "You know what it says? Does it have secret information?"

Jace nodded knowingly. "As it turns out, the logs are written by two people, as I said before. The most recent is Drakkar and his entries aren't encoded. But the previous entries are from a Captain Burchard Southey. I've never heard of him, but from the logs I read he was quite the pirate."

Luna came out from under the bed at that moment. She looked around the room and, seeing nothing scary anymore, hopped up on the bed and began rubbing herself against Mika. She picked up the cat and set it in her lap before starting to pet it. In only a few moments, his familiar was purring loudly.

"Anyway, Captain Burchard used a Caesar shift cipher..." he said.

"Caesar shift cipher?" Mika interrupted, looking perplexed.

"It's one of the simplest ciphers there are," he explained. "Basically, you shift the alphabet by a certain number of characters. Say your number is four. That means whatever the letter is, you count backwards that many characters. When you decode it, E becomes A and R becomes N. Encoded, Mika would be Qmoe."

"That is pretty neat. How did you figure out the number to shift the letters by?"

Jace took another bite of the waffles before answering. "I almost didn't. I thought he either memorized the number or maybe there was something in his room or on his person that would remind him of the cipher."

"So how did you…"

"It's the day of the week," he said proudly. He was actually proud of that. He'd figured out other game codes before but this one had been tough. Until he figured out the cipher key. "I kept wondering why the date on the log entry was always unencoded. And once I looked through more and more entries, I noticed that on each one, he always put the day of the week first. I converted the day of the week to a number and volia! Each entry has a different cipher based on the day of the week: 1 for Sunday, 2 for Monday, etc.."

"Very clever." She smiled at him. "So you know what it says?"

"I do." He smiled. "And it's actually very interesting. It seems Captain Burchard was raiding up all over the Sea of Daggers. He accumulated all sorts of treasure."

"Treasure?" Mika's eyes lit up. "Pirate treasure?"

"Yes." He grinned. "Literally. In fact, he was extremely paranoid that his crew would eventually mutiny and he'd be killed for the treasure."

"Killed by pirates is good," Mika interjected.

Jace just looked at her. He'd heard that line somewhere but couldn't place it. She looked down shyly. "Or so I heard."

He tried in vain to remember where he'd heard the line but gave up and continued. "What the paranoid captain decided to do was to accumulate treasure for several months. Then, he'd pay his crew, send them ashore and take on a brand new crew. The first thing he'd do is tell them the story of how he had to kill his treacherous first mate and they'd stop off on some island and bury his 'remains.'"

"It was his treasure!" Mika said excitedly. Her excitement disturbed Luna and the cat hopped out of her lap, kneaded a place on the far end of the bed and curled up.

"Yes," he acknowledged. "And apparently, he'd been doing that for years until he went up river to lay low after a particularly big heist."

"Up river?" she asked.

"Yes. He went up the White Run River to a town called Crossroads," he told her. "It's particularly deep from the ocean to a little past the town."

"Crossroads?" Mika asked.

"Crossroads is a medium sized town about a week from Whitecliff," Jace said but then remembered it had been destroyed. He thought back to his first run in with Drakkar back in Crossroads and catching the caravan with Charlena.

Jace shook his head to regain his train of thought. "At least, it was. The dragon destroyed Crossroads before turning towards Whitecliff. Anyway, according to the log, the captain decided to lie low and make repairs after stealing the princess' tiara from a heavily armed merchant ship."

"So Captain Burchard was the one who stole the tiara?"

"Yes. And he was about to get a major payday from the thieves guild when he made the mistake of taking aboard a couple of hands at Crossroads."

"Drakkar?" Mika hissed.

"Yes," Jace nodded. "Drakkar was one of them. Apparently, Burchard had a bad feeling about him but they were short-handed after the fight with the merchant ship. Against his better judgement, he brought him onboard."

Jace finished up the last bite of his waffles. "The next entries are unencoded and written by Drakkar."

"Drakkar killed him," Mika said.

"From Drakkar's scribblings," Jace confirmed. "He challenged the captain to a duel - he probably got that from me - and killed him by poisoning his blade and using his *Backstab* ability along with his *Vanish* skill. He killed him the day after we left with the caravan."

"He is sneaky," Mika said.

"Very true." Jace smiled. "I can't exactly begrudge him using his skills to defeat the man but at this level, depending on what poison he had, that could really turn the tides. And speaking of which, now that I'm level 10 and get the death penalty when I die, I should probably go buy some antitoxin and a few health potions. Not that we'll be doing any fighting until we get to Nynymmost."

"So now we know how Drakkar became captain," she said. "Did you learn anything else?"

Jace gave her the biggest grin he could. "If by 'anything else' you mean the locations of all of Captain Burchard's buried treasure, then yes. I found something."

Mika's eyes went wide. "You know where all of his treasure is?!"

"Shhh!" Jace put his fingers to his lips. "Considering what happened to Burchard, we should keep this to ourselves for now."

Mika looked around conspiratorially. "Yes, it will be our secret! Ours and Diana's!"

Jace looked down at his timepiece and swore. "Darnit! We were supposed to meet Diana." He started to get up but Mika held up a hand.

"No!" she ordered. "You stay here. No more assassins! I will go."

Jace relaxed back into the chair. "Thanks. I guess it's safer for all of us if I stay here for now."

As Mika turned to go, Jace called after her. "Do me a favor. While you're out, see if you can find a cartographer and buy some maps of the Dagger Coast."

"Maps?" she asked.

"Try to find ones with the coordinates on them," he told her. "I want to see if I can see where some of these treasures are located. I mean, if there's one on the way, maybe I could talk the good captain into stopping."

Her eyes lit up. "A treasure hunt! Okay! I will find you a map!"

She opened the door and started to leave but then stopped. Mika turned around and gave Jace a kiss, then, grinning, skipped out the door and down the hall.

He listened to her bound up the steps and then heard her footsteps disappear. Getting up, he closed the door and sat back down in the chair. He still had log entries to read. And some more treasure to discover.

Chapter 5

According to Jace's gnomish timepiece, it was 3:45pm when the girls knocked on his door. Over the past hour, the ship had been a flurry of activity. Even though he remained in his cabin, he heard the sailors getting the ship ready to be on its way. He also heard the passengers as they clamoured back on board and shut themselves away in their own cabins.

A half hour ago, Fimipp and his other servants had appeared at his door and bid their farewells, well as thanking him for paying for their trip home. The halfling butler stressed that the manor would be immaculate when he returned.

He wished them all a safe journey and then went back into his cabin. He hadn't really talked to any of the other passengers since they mostly kept to themselves. Other than the occasional trip to the mess hall and a walk around the upper deck, they stayed in their cabins.

Considering that the guildmaster of the thieves guild, Webley the Snake, had arranged for this ship, Jace guessed the other passengers were members of the Whitecliff underworld. Or at least, associates of it. He doubted they wanted any more attention than Jace and the girls wanted.

The door opened and Mika peeked in. She looked at Luna, asleep on the bed. "See, I didn't throw open the door this time!"

"Luna and my heart thank you." Jace smiled.

"We brought you fish and chips and some mead from the tavern," Diana told him. "They're a bit cold, but still better than the salted version. Oh, I brought some vinegar too."

"Hey…" Jace smiled. "Vinegar is like the English version of ketchup."

"I got you something too," Mika said and held out several vials. Jace recognized them instantly. They were potions. "Three healing, one mana potion and one anti-toxin. All level 10."

Taking the vials from her he gave her a genuine smile. "Thank you! I'm sure these will come in handy given our situation."

"I thought so," Mika grinned. "I also have the maps."

Diana was smirking at them, but then closed the door, making Jace realize exactly how small the cabin was with three people inside. He was also very conscious that the other two were very attractive women.

The older woman leaned against the door and folded her arms over her large chest. "Mika told me you found something interesting in the logs. And they were encrypted?"

Jace nodded as he slipped the vials into his inventory. Once his hands were empty, Mika produced several maps and handed them to him. He took them and set them on his small table. "I did. And I think it might be a small - possibly a large - fortune. I'm not sure why the captain wasn't a raid level boss or something with this much treasure."

"Oh, dear one," Diana tsked. "You realize that all the treasure is probably guarded by monsters and traps."

Jace raised an eyebrow. "Writer's intuition?"

Diana gave him a wry smile. "I don't just write books, I read books too. And I used to watch things called movies. What you youngsters call vidstreams. There's always something guarding the treasure. Giant boulders ready to roll over you. Giant Anacondas. Dinosaurs. Zombies. There's always something."

Jace chuckled. "I've watched a good number of the retro vidstreams, sorry, movies. And you're probably right. Nothing in this game is just given away."

Mika nodded grimly. "So we must fight monsters to get this treasure?"

"Probably," he admitted. "Or very nasty traps. But we'll cross that bridge when we get to it."

"Do we even need the treasure?" Diana asked. "Isn't WorldCog going to fix us up now? Aren't they supposed to fix us up and give us back our assets?"

Mika and Diana were both looking at him expectantly and Jace sighed. "That's the plan. At least, I hope that's the plan. But we don't know how long that will take." He leaned back in the chair and sighed. "Plus, if they don't delete me, I'm going to need some money."

"Oh, dear boy," Diana said. "Once I get my assets back, I think I can help you out. You certainly have done more for me that anyone else in the last few years. Except for maybe my publicist."

Mika nodded. "Yes, you have helped us. Once I get my money, I can help you too."

Jace frowned and shook his head. "I'm not going to be a charity case. I can take care of myself."

Diana rolled her eyes. "Dear one, I know the feeling. I haven't taken a man's money for about sixty years. Quite the opposite. And I wouldn't have taken a dime, or gold, from you if I didn't have the intention of paying you back once I had my money."

"Yes," Mika agreed. "I will pay you back too!"

"Yes, but…" Jace started to object but Diana held up a hand.

"No buts," Diana said, putting her hands on her hips. "You've been helping us, paying for us and leading us. You're the one who told us how to get out the monster bodies. You're the one who got us together in Whitecliff. You're the one who found a way to contact the help thingy…"

"*Help Desk*," Mika supplied.

"...*Help Desk*," Diana continued, "so that we can also get put straight again. I will pay you back. End of discussion."

Mika nodded firmly. "Yes, I feel the same way."

"Besides," Diana said, giving him a sly grin and a wink. "We're married. You're entitled to certain marital… assets."

Jace was about to reply when the ship lurched as it began moving. The girls, who had been standing, staggered as they reached for the cabin walls to steady themselves. Luna, who had been sleeping on his bunk, opened her eyes wide for a second, looked around, and then promptly closed her eyes and went back to sleep.

Up on the deck, Jace could hear movement and shouting as the ship began to move away from the dock. Glancing at his timepiece, he saw that it was 4:05pm. Captain Yehmee hadn't been joking.

Looking back to the girls, Jace opened his mouth to speak but seeing the glares from both women, he shut his mouth. He realized there was no point in arguing with them at the moment.

Still, he didn't feel right taking money from them. Or anyone for that matter. He wasn't used to needing or asking for help from anyone. He wasn't about to start now. At least, not in a financial way.

"We can talk about this later," Jace told them. "Right now, I want to see if I can actually see if the coordinates I took from the logs actually correspond to real places."

"Can I help?" Mika asked, beaming at him.

Jace smiled at her enthusiasm over such a mundane task. "Sure. That would actually work out well. One of us can look at the map while the other goes over the coordinates."

Diana made a dismissive gesture and turned towards the door. "In this case, three's a crowd. I think I'll go up top and get some fresh salty air."

Once Diana had left, Jace and Mika laid out the maps on the bunk and on the floor, careful not to disturb the sleeping cat. Then, the two of them took turns going through Jace's notes and marking what they thought were the locations on the map.

Although he had been worried that there would be a different cipher on the actual coordinates, apparently neither the devs nor Captain Burchard thought to encrypt them. Jace was thankful for that at least.

It was harder than Jace thought since the coordinates were in nautical coordinates and not just gps style coordinates he was used to. Luckily, after a short conversation with Captain Yehmee and her navigator, they were able to figure out how to reach the coordinate system.

By the time night had fallen, they had plotted out all eighteen of the treasure hoards the late Captain Burchard had documented.

Jace turned to Mika. "Good job! We know where to look for the treasure."

"We have a treasure map!" she said excitedly. "We are treasure hunters!"

"At some point we will be," he said. "But in the meantime, we need to protect our knowledge of the treasure. I want to divide up the information between the three of us. Let's go to find Diana."

The two of them left his room as Luan hopped off the bed to follow them, apparently unwilling to be left alone. Her cabin was empty so they checked on deck. It was dark, but they found her on the stern of the ship with the captain and several other crewmen. All of them were looking out to the ocean. Jace followed their gaze to a point of light on the dark horizon.

"What is it?" Jace asked, startling some of the crewmen.

The captain turned around, a grim look on her face. "Ship on the horizon. It's been there for an hour or two."

"Is that unusual?" Jace asked, unsure what that meant for them.

"Not necessarily," she told him, the racoon-kin's striped tail twitching. "But I've altered course three times. Each time they match us on an intercept course."

Jace wasn't a seaman by any stretch of the imagination, but even he knew what that meant. Given that they were in what was possibly a stolen ship, it was possible it was the authorities. He glanced back at the spot of light and then to Yehmee. "Navy?"

The racoon-kin's ears went back a little but she shook her head. "No, there'd be at least two of them. Those navy types don't like a fair fight."

Unfortunately, in his limited experience, that could mean only one thing. "Pirates?"

The crew members all turned to regard the captain, worried expressions on their faces. Yehmee glared briefly at Jace. He guessed she would have preferred if Jace hadn't asked that question in front of the crew. She glanced at the crew and then back to Jace.

"Aye, Baronet," she told him. "My guess is, it be pirates."

Jace suddenly got a really bad feeling about it. He happened to know a pirate. A pirate he'd bested twice and the last time had set his cabin on fire - with him in it. Captain Drakkar. But how would Drakkar have found him? Or was it coincidence?

He shook his head to clear his thoughts. He didn't even know if it was Drakkar. It could be any pirate ship or it may not even be a pirate ship.

"Can we outrun them?" Mika asked the captain.

"This is a merchant ship. Not even a particular new or fast merchant ship," the captain shook her head. "We're built for hauling cargo. We can barely outrun our own wake."

"So what do we do, captain?" asked one of the crew members. He was a skinny, tanned man with a shaved head and tattooed arms.

"We pray I'm wrong," the captain said. She locked eyes with Jace. "And if I'm not, we pray we can repel them."

Chapter 6

As the sun rose on the eastern horizon, Jace and the girls watched as it illuminated the ship following them. It was much closer now. The ship had been far enough away earlier in the night that they had tracked it mostly by its lights. But the pursuing ship had gained on them. Now in the daylight, it was easy to see.

"How long before they're on us?" Jace asked the captain, who was staring off at them with a leather bound spyglass.

The racoon-kin didn't look away from the spyglass. She muttered something to herself, maybe numbers or speeds and then looked at Jace. "They'll be on us by nightfall."

Jace frowned. "What about heading into shore?"

Captain Yehmee looked at him like he was out of his mind. "Run the ship ashore? Are you mad? Besides, what makes you think that would make you any safer?"

"What do you mean?" he asked.

"We're not carrying any goods, except maybe some personal goods from the passengers," the racoon-kin said, her tail twitching from side to side. "It seems much more likely they are after someone on the ship."

Mika looked at him, but Jace kept quiet.

The captain chuckled mirthlessly. "I heard about the assassin attack. You managed to survive but the shop owner was not so lucky."

Jace's hand unconsciously fell to his saber and the action did not go unnoticed by the captain. He noticed that Mika and Diana had come to stand beside him. Both of them seemed to sense his sudden tension.

She smirked. "Don't worry, if I put you off the ship, Webley would have my head. I was hired to deliver you bunch safely to the gnomish homeland and that's what I will do."

He and the girls relaxed at Captain Yehmee's words and Jace heard the truth in them. Webley ran the most powerful thieves guild in the good faction. He had a long reach for anyone who crossed him.

"But to answer your previous question, even if I ran the ship ashore, there's no guarantee they wouldn't follow us," " the captain continued and then gave him a pointed look. "Especially if it's one of the passengers they're interested in."

"You don't think we would stand a better chance on land?" Diana asked.

The captain shrugged. "Maybe. Maybe not. But there are more of them than there are of us, judging from the size of the ship. Because of the way Webley acquired the ship and the urgency of the voyage, we left short-handed. If I had to guess, we're outnumbered two to one and you three are the only passengers who might have a chance of helping. Assuming you're willing."

"If pirates come aboard," Mika said, fingering the hilt of katana, "we will stand beside you."

"Good," the racoon-kin nodded, her tail flicking left and right. "Let's hope it doesn't come to that. There are still a few tricks I can try before they catch up to us."

Jace nodded and looked at the captain's spyglass. "Can I borrow that for a second? I just want to get a better look at the ship."

Yehmee gave him a knowing look. "Think you might see someone you recognize?"

He sighed. The story of him stealing the tiara from Drakkar had made the rounds in the thieves guild. Since she knew Webley, the chances were good she'd heard about it. "You already know, don't you?"

The captain just smiled and handed him the spyglass. Jace took it from her outstretched hand. He turned and, putting the glass up to his eye, pointed it at the pursuing ship.

The ship was still far away and he could make out very few details but it was enough to let him know that he was right. Turning around, he handed the spyglass back to the captain. He locked eyes with her and kept his voice low. "It's the Wyvern's Tail. Drakkar's ship."

"Aye," she whispered back, her face a grim mask. "And we have no chance at outrunning it. I wasn't lying. I have some tricks but even if Drakkar is new, his crew won't be. But you never know." Yehmee looked around at the crew manning their stations. "But let's keep morale going as long as we can."

Nodding, he turned to the girls and motioned them back to the railing, away from the crew. The girls' expressions were as dark as the captain's. He wished he had good news to tell them, but he didn't.

The problem with travelling over the ocean, either in a normal ship or in an elvish airship, was that if a player died, their body was basically unretrievable. Once it sank, there was nothing short of high level spells that could retrieve it. And those cost money. Lots of money.

He might be able to afford to have one body recovered, but not all three of their bodies. That was especially true since they had split the remaining money between the three of them. And then there was the treasure map too.

They'd split the map, the logs and his notes between the three of them. As long as one of them survived, he could recreate the map and find the treasure later. If none of them survived, the information would be lost forever.

Jace thought he could defeat Drakkar. After all, he'd done it once. But he couldn't defeat an entire crew of pirates. Especially if they did coordinated attacks. There would just be too many of them.

He looked to the girls, who were waiting for him to say something. He took a deep breath and then let it out. When he spoke, he kept his voice low so none of the crew should hear him. "It's Drakkar, the pirate I stole the tiara from. And the captain says there's no way we can outrun him. That means, we'll have to fight."

"Can't we abandon ship?" Diana asked. "You know, take a lifeboat and head to shore?"

Jace turned and looked towards the shore in the distance. "We'd never make it. And we'd make easy prey in a little lifeboat."

"We can fight them!" Mika said. She said it with enthusiasm, but it sounded forced to Jace. He gave her a smile.

"I don't think we'll have a choice. But there's too many of them," he told them. "Especially since they'll attack at once. It would be like the grolls, only times four or five."

"Can't you duel him or something?" Diana asked. "Isn't that how you said you defeated him in Crossroads?"

Jace shook his head. "I doubt it. I bested him last time, or would have if he hadn't backstabbed Charlena and then run off. There's no way he'll do that again. Plus, I'm not a pirate. I have no standing to challenge him."

"You need to make him fight you then," Mika said.

"He'll never agree to it," he replied. "And he doesn't have to. This time, he'll just order his men to kill us."

"Wait," Diana said, looking thoughtful. "These men, they're mostly the former captain's men, right?"

"Burchard's men?" Jace asked, letting the confusion show in his voice. "I'm sure most of them are. Maybe he picked a few new ones here and there. Why?"

Diana smiled. "I'll bet you they know about at least one of the captain's treasures."

"So?" Jace retorted. "All the more reason for them to kill us. Or kill me at least."

"Except…" Diana smiled. "You have the treasure. Or rather, you know where it's at. And how much do you think one of his stashes is worth?"

Jace was beginning to see where she was going with her line of reasoning. He thought back to the notes in the log. "Each one is probably worth a hundred or two hundred thousand gold."

Mika whistled.

"So, I'll bet you they would like to get their hands on that gold," Diana said. "Maybe enough to force Drakkar to fight you…"

"If I offer them the treasure?" Jace proposed.

"Exactly." Diana smiled.

"But they'll just kill us and take the logs and the maps," Jace said. "At least, that would be their plan. But they won't be able to loot the maps or the logs off our bodies. But they won't know that."

"Right." Diana smiled. "But if you threaten to destroy it, say by burning it with a spell, that puts you in a position of power. Theoretically, of course."

"Of course. That's risky," Jace said dryly. "But it might work. It's certainly better than facing all of them at the same time."

As he thought about Diana's idea, he suddenly had some inspiration. A way to up the stakes. But he needed some items. "Quick, give me my notes and the logs."

The girls retrieved the items from their inventory and handed them to Jace. Taking them, he went to Captain Yehmee. "Captain, I have a plan that might prevent a wholesale slaughter."

He explained what he needed and part of his plan to the racoon-kin while she nodded and finally smiled. "Webley was right. You're a bold one, I have to give you that. But since I don't have any better ideas, it's worth a try."

"And you think his crew will force him to fight?" Jace asked.

"The word among the other captains is," she replied. "They don't much like him, but he's doing alright and no one else is man enough to challenge him.

If you defeat him, they'll accept you as captain. But they'll expect that treasure."

He nodded. "So, if I pull this off, the girls and I will have to go with them. But you'll be able to continue on unmolested."

"Assuming they don't cripple my ship." The captain smirked.

"Won't they only attack if you don't surrender?" he asked her.

She furrowed her brow at him. "You want me to surrender?"

"Didn't you just tell me we couldn't outrun them?" he retorted. "And that your crew was outnumbered?"

Yehmee nodded cautiously. "I think I see where you're going."

"Surrender," he told her. "Let them pull up alongside us and then I shout over my proposal."

"Blast you," she said, but there was no real venom in her words. "Fine! But this harebrained scheme of yours better work."

"If it doesn't," he looked at her, "will we really be in any worse trouble?"

The racoon-kin stared at him for a long time, her expression unreadable. Finally, she sighed and her shoulders slumped. "You're right. The result will be the same. I just don't like to go down without a fight."

"Me either," he told her. Then more quietly, mostly to himself. "Me either."

Chapter 7

Captain Yehmee spent the next few hours trying to outrun and outmaneuver the approaching pirate ship. She ordered her ship to navigate over reefs and to come uncomfortably close to the shore into shallow water she thought the Wyvern's Tail couldn't match. Each time, the pirate enemy ship kept pace with them. They might not follow them close to the shore, but they kept a parallel course.

"They're calling our bluff," Yehmee sighed. "They can keep that parallel course until we either run to ground or hit reef. It looks like we're going with your plan."

Jace let out a breath. The captain had told him this would be inevitable, but now that he knew it was about to happen, he felt the virtual butterflies stirring in his virtual stomach. If this didn't work, they were going to lose everything. All their money and equipment. They'd end up naked back in Lasthaven. And they might even find Damian waiting for them.

He looked at the girls. Both wore worried expressions. He smiled and tried to pretend he was confident. "This'll work."

Mika gave him a genuine smile, the trusting expression on her face nearly causing him to falter. She seemed to have much more confidence in him than he had in himself. At least, more confidence that he had in his plan. After all, Drakkar had already cheated once, during their first duel. He couldn't be trusted.

He looked over to Diana who also wore a smile, but it didn't reach her eyes. She was the cool voice of reason and experience. She had already pointed out the many things that could go wrong with his plan and obviously didn't share Mika's blind confidence. Good. The older woman would keep him from getting too cocky.

"Do it," he told the captain with as much confidence as he could muster into his voice. "Hoist of the white flag. Let's get this done."

"Aye," she said. "Time to see what the tides bring us."

Yehmee barked the order and the sailors reluctantly hoisted the white flag. Then they changed course to bring them back into deeper waters to Drakkar's ship. It was time to see whether or not his plan would work.

It took another half hour before the Wyvern's Tail pulled alongside the Sea Tyrant. Drakkar's ship had circled the smaller ship several times, allowing his crew to taunt, jeer, and threaten them before finally throwing boarding ropes over and pulling the two ships together.

Pirates lined the deck of the Wyvern's Tail, still jeering at the cowed sailors aboard Jace's ship. It was clear they enjoyed toying with their prey. After several minutes of jeers, the pirates parted, and a gangplank was put between the two ships. Through the gap in the pirates, an imposing figure appeared. It was Drakkar.

The ex-guildmaster had changed much from the last time Jace had seen him. The most noticeable difference was the scars that marred the left side of his face and the eyepatch he wore over his left eye. Besides the scarring, he was dressed in what appeared to be a very anachronistic outfit that looked like it belonged in a pirate movie.

"Jynx Knightly," Drakkar snarled as the man caught sight of him. "I've been looking forward to this for a long time."

The pirate captain turned to his crew. "Men, this is the one that stole the tiara and your big pay day."

His crew erupted in angry threats and jeers, working themselves into a frenzy. Drakkar had probably been flaming their feelings of anger and resentment the entire time. It seemed like the old guildmaster may have been stroking their anger since he'd lost the tiara and now it was at a fever pitch. Jace started to wonder if his plan would actually work.

Taking a deep breath, Jace summoned up every ounce of bravado he could and laughed. His laughter caught them all, including Drakkar, by surprise. For a long moment, his laughter was the only sound.

"Stealing it away from you was so easy, Drakkar," Jace *Taunted*, trying to sound as cocky as he could. Roleplaying was one thing but roleplaying when a mistake would cost him all of his gold and items was much harder. "Like taking candy from a baby kobold."

There were some jeers among the crew, but also some angry muttering and even some laughter. That was a better sign. Some of them might be bitter enough to turn on Drakkar once Jace made his offer.

"I am going to kill you slowly, boy," Drakkar growled, his face white with rage. The pirate captain drew his sword and motioned. "Come on men. It's time to get our revenge!"

Drakkar and the other pirates began to move onto the Sea Tyrant. Jace was against the opposite deck railing and took out the map he'd prepared. At the top of his lungs he yelled out. "Stop! Or I throw this overboard!"

Drakkar hesitated, as did the rest of the pirate crew. They looked at Jace and then at each other in confusion, obviously unsure what to make of Jace's stange threat. Confused, they looked at Drakkar. "Captain?"

Drakkar's good eye narrowed. "Go ahead, boy. Throw over your piece of parchment. You're still going to die slowly. I've had a long time to think about how I was going to..."

"You didn't tell them about the treasure Drakkar?" Jace bellowed, interrupting the captain. As he hoped, the word treasure got the crew's attention and he could hear them muttering.

"There is no treasure!" Drakkar spat. "He's bluffing to save his hide. But it won't work. I'll skin you and..."

"You forgot to tell them that I didn't just steal the tiara, I stole the logbooks too!" Jace yelled, addressing the crew more so than Drakkar. "The ones that had the location of Burchard's hidden treasure."

This time there was much louder muttering and some of the crew was casting angry glances at Drakkar instead of Jace. Drakkar seemed to realize he was losing control of the situation and opened his mouth to speak. That was exactly what Jace had been waiting for.

"Or had you planned to keep the treasure all to yourself?" Jace said loudly. Drakkar's face grew livid and he started toward Jace. A nod to Mika and she held up the logbooks over her head. "Those are the logbooks, right there. The only record of where Burchard hid his treasure!"

With his second nod, Mika threw them overboard, into the sea below. There was a collective gasp from the pirate crew as she did but Jace didn't give them time to think about it. "The logs are gone! The captain is dead! The only copy of the treasure's location is this map!"

Jace dangled the map further over the rail. "Keep coming and it goes into the sea. Gone forever! If you thought the tiara's payday was big. You should have read what the late captain wrote about how large his hoard was!"

"Captain wait!" shouted several of the crew and then more joined in. Drakkar, who was halfway across the deck to Jace, looked back over his shoulder at his crew. Jace could see the man working it out in his head.

He just hoped the former guildmaster's sense of self-preservation was stronger than his need for revenge.

Now that Drakkar was closer, Jace could see the tell-tale green tint of poison on the captain's blade. Many players might have missed it, but Jace had played an assassin character. He knew what to look for. After reading how the former guildmaster had used poison to turn the tide of the fight with Buchard, he wasn't surprised.

While the pirate captain was considering his options, Jace also took the opportunity to examine him with his HUD.

Dainard Drakkar
Race: Human
Class: Rogue
Level: 21

Jace grimaced as he saw Drakkar's new stats. The former guildmaster was now 10 levels higher than when Jace had faced him last. That put him in the tier 3 class, as far as weapons and armor. A higher tier, meant more damage and high *Defense*. Those things made him much more dangerous and Jace was suddenly unsure whether or not he might be able to win a fight with him.

Unfortunately, it was too late to change the plan. Even if he were to offer Drakkar the map in order to let them go, he didn't trust the captain to honor the deal. He'd just take the map and then kill Jace and the crew. For better or worse, Jace was locked into his course of action and he'd have to see his plan through, regardless of the outcome.

"So," Drakkar said, lowering his sword. "What do you want? A deal? The map for your lives?"

His crew snickered but there seemed to be enough dissension that Jace thought his plan would work.

"No deal," Jace bellowed. "I don't trust you and more than your own crew trusts you. There's only one way you are getting this map."

"And what's that?" Drakkar hissed through clenched teeth.

"You and I fight," Jace called out. "One on one. Winner takes all. If you win, you get the map and then you can do whatever you want to the crew of this ship. If I win, your crew gets a real captain… me. Either way, the crew gets the treasure."

The crew muttered among themselves as Drakkar watched them but Jace already knew he'd convinced them. Within a few moments, the crew began chanting. "Fight him! Fight him!"

Drakkar looked around at the faces of his yelling crew and a look of resignation settled on his face. He held up his sword to get the crew's attention. "Alright! Alright! We fight. One on one! No help from our crews." The captain's eye flickered to the extremely large cat sitting near Jace. "Or familiars."

"Fair enough," Jace said. He hadn't really counted on Luna helping. The pirates wouldn't know it was a familiar so they wouldn't think it was a fair fight if he got help from a giant cat. "But as long as we're laying out the ground rules, how about: No backstabbing women who aren't part of the duel."

"That's right," Drakkar snickered. "How is that redheaded elf doing?"

"Better than you'll be in a few minutes," Jace said. He handed the map to Mika, who made a show of dangling it over the edge of the railing.

The girl darted forward and kissed him. "For luck! Don't die!"

Jace heard the pirate crew cat calling and making other rude comments but he ignored them. He took a mead bottle from his inventory and downed the entire contents. He threw the empty bottle at Drakkar's feet and then put a mockingly apologetic look on his face. "Oh, I'm sorry, did you want a last drink?"

He gave the pirate captain a genuine smile, but not because of his *Taunt*. The smile was from the system message that had accompanied him drinking the antitoxin he'd put into the mead bottle.

You use Mild Antitoxin.
You are immune to poison for 5 minutes.

"Let's dance, you and I," Jace taunted, drawing his own blades. He enjoyed the look of disgust Drakkar gave him when he unsheathed the Kraken's Claw. "Oh yeah, I'm sure you remember your sword. Or, should I say, MY sword."

Snarling in rage, the pirate captain launched himself at Jace and the fight was on.

Chapter 8

As soon as he'd seen Drakkar rush forward, Jace had cast his *Air Armor* spell, bringing his *Defense* up to 17. He wore level 10 chainmail shirt, leggings and coif. The rest of his armor was leather. Unfortunately, none of it was magical, but just armor he'd looted from the orcs he'd fought in Whitecliff. The combination gave him the best armor value while also utilizing the *Deft Warrior II* and the *Stalwart Defender II* abilities.

Kraken Claw was in his right hand, humming with power. In his left hand, was a non-magical saber he'd looted. As he'd leveled up rogue to level 10, he'd gotten not only his hide skill up to rank 20, but also most of his other combat skills as well. While he hadn't needed those in the palace, it seemed like they would be put to good use now.

Just before Drakkar reached him, the former guildmaster disappeared. Jace guessed he had used *Vanish* to get into position for a *Backstab*. At level 21, the pirate's *Backstabs* were going to hurt. He quickly blew 4 mana and used his *Evade*, just as Drakkar appeared behind him.

Dainard Drakkar Backstabs YOU but you Evade.
Dainard Drakkar Backstabs YOU for 0 damage.

His evade had managed to prevent the damage from Drakkar's saber and the man's dagger hadn't penetrated his *Defense*.

Jace used another 4 mana to use his own *Vanish*. He intended to do his own *Backstab* on the pirate. As he did, he realized he'd forgotten that his *Backstab* was still only *Backstab I*. It did three times the damage, which was the same amount of damage as his *Critical Eye II* ability he'd gained with Rogue level 10. He could have just done a *Feint*. Instead, he'd just wasted 2 mana.

Then Jace noticed that Drakkar was turning with him, as if the man could see him rolling. That shouldn't be possible since Jace should be invisible to him for the next couple of seconds. As he came out of his somersault, instead of facing the pirate's back, Drakkar was facing him. It was so unexpected, Jace didn't even follow through with his attack.

Drakkar just grinned and gestured at his eye patch. "Even though my left eye can't see normal things, with the patch, I can see things that are hidden."

With that, the former guildmaster grinned and disappeared again. Getting over his shock, Jace blew another 4 mana on *Evade*.

Dainard Drakkar Backstabs YOU but you Evade.
Dainard Drakkar Backstabs YOU for 0 damage.

Jace dodged the pirate's first attack with his *Evade* only to see that Drakkar had switched up his attack order. He had attacked first with the dagger to eat up Jace's *Evade* and then attacked with his saber, which did much more damage. Luckily, it had skidded off his chain mail shirt but next time he might not be so lucky.

"I know your tricks, boy!" Drakkar mocked. "This time will be different!"

Considering that the man was adapting to his technique, Jace was actually getting even more worried than he had been about being able to defeat Drakkar. He didn't usually leave opponents alive and learning that if he did, they learned from their mistakes was troublesome on many levels.

Ignoring the pirate's taunt, this time Jace did a *Feint*. He guessed that Drakkar might try and *Evade* as well, so he switched up his own attacks. After all, turnabout's fair play.

You critically hit Dainard Drakkar but he Evades. You critically hit Dainard Drakkar for 33 damage plus 18 acid damage.

"First blood goes to me Drakkar!" Jace taunted.

The pirate captain grimaced in pain as Kraken's Claw caught him in the gut. "I see you've learned some new tricks too. But they won't help you!"

Once again, Drakkar disappeared and Jace had no choice but to use his *Evade* again. He could have used *Block*. It effectively did the same thing as *Evade*, but force of habit with his assassin made using *Evade* second nature.

Dainard Drakkar Backstabs YOU but you Evade. Dainard Drakkar Backstabs YOU for 0 damage.

Once again, his *Evade* caught the dagger strike but also he lucked out again and the saber bounced off his buckler. He had been lucky. But could his luck hold out?

Jace used his Feint, intending to *Critically Strike* the pirate but as he did, Drakkar grinned and blurred. Jace recognized the rank 30 ability, *Shadowy Double*. It was something he'd used when he'd played Mordred. He didn't much care to see it used against him.

Where Drakkar had stood a moment ago were now three Drakkars. The two doubles moved to intercept Jace's blades, and neither hit the pirate.

You critically hit Dainard Drakkar but Shadowy Double absorbs the blow.
You critically hit Dainard Drakkar but Shadowy Double absorbs the blow.

"Still think you're going to win, you little upstart?" Drakkar sneered. "Today I pay you back for Crossroads and Whitecliff!"

Drakkar *Vanished* but Jace didn't even bother using *Evade*. He didn't think the dagger could penetrate his *Defense*, so there was no point in wasting the mana. He was down to almost half mana now and he needed to conserve.

Dainard Drakkar Backstabs YOU for 0 damage.
Dainard Drakkar Backstabs YOU for 0 damage.

As he thought, the dagger hit him but couldn't penetrate while Drakkar's saber slid off his chain mail again. Jace smiled as he realized the pirate captain was having a bad day with the random number generator. Too bad for him.

Feinting again, Jace lunged at the Drakkar again but the pirate managed to get his Shadowy Doubles up in time to absorb both the blows.

You critically hit Dainard Drakkar but Shadowy Double absorbs the blow.
You critically hit Dainard Drakkar but Shadowy Double absorbs the blow.

That earned a growl of frustration from Jace but Drakkar just gave him a smile. When he spoke, the pirate's voice dripped with condescension. "Problems hitting me… BOY?"

Once again, the pirate disappeared and Jace tried to turn to meet his *Backstab*, but without being able to see him, it was impossible. Drakkar appeared behind him and once again switched his tactics and attacked with his saber first. Unfortunately, this time it penetrated his chain mail and glanced off one of his ribs.

Dainard Drakkar Backstabs YOU for 18 damage.
You are Poisoned.
Dainard Drakkar Backstabs YOU for 0 damage.

Poison damage suppressed.

Jace gasped in pain as the point of Drakkar's saber punched through his armor. Seeing his agony, Drakkar snickered. "Finally got through your defenses I see. Then you're in for a very special treat!"

No doubt, Drakkar expected the poison to turn the tide in his favor. Little did he know Jace had taken Antitoxin. He considered taunting the captain with the knowledge but decided to keep it to himself for now.

Using the pirate captain's moment of gloating against him, Jace *Feinted* and struck out with both sabers. Unfortunately, Drakkar was still fast enough to get his *Shadowy Doubles* up.

You critically hit Dainard Drakkar but Shadowy Double absorbs the blow.
You critically hit Dainard Drakkar but Shadowy Double absorbs the blow.

"You're beaten," Drakkar mocked. "You just don't know it yet."

Drakkar disappeared and this time, Jace did use *Evade*. He guessed that had been the captain's reason for switching it up. To keep Jace using *Evade* and keep him using his mana.

Dainard Drakkar Backstabs YOU for 18 damage.
Dainard Drakkar Backstabs YOU for 0 damage.

Poison damage suppressed.

Drakkar had gone back to striking with the dagger first and managed to catch Jace's *Evade* with the dagger strike, while leaving him open for the saber thrust. Luck, or the random number generator, was with Jace and the blow slid off his chainmail leggings.

Jace started to attack Drakkar but stopped as soon as the *Shadowy Doubles* appeared. He cast a *Flame*

Bolt, that was absorbed by one of the doubles, then *Feinted*. With his regular saber, he took out the other double. Then he lunged with Kraken's Claw.

You burn Dainard Drakkar with Flame Bolt but Shadowy Double absorbs the blow.
You critically hit Dainard Drakkar but Shadowy Double absorbs the blow.
You critically hit Dainard Drakkar for 42 damage plus 18 acid damage.

His magical saber penetrated his chest and Drakkar screamed, but it wasn't enough to kill him. The pirate captain danced back and spat. "You have learned some new tricks."

He meant to press the attack, but Drakkar *Vanished* and Jace was forced to use another *Evade*. This time, he had to draw on Luna's mana. She was his familiar and he had the ability to pull mana from her when needed. But he needed to be careful. If he pulled all of her mana, she would be dismissed, and he'd need to resummon her.

Dainard Drakkar Backstabs YOU but you Evade.
Dainard Drakkar Backstabs YOU for 0 damage.

Poison damage suppressed.

Jace silently thanks the random number gods as Drakkar's attack didn't generate enough damage to penetrate his *Defense*. The captain snarled and Jace began waving his hands like he was going to cast another *Flame Bolt*.

This time, Drakkar didn't immediately cast his *Shadowy Doubles* and Jace *Feinted* and attacked, hoping to get his attacks in before the man could get them up.

You critically hit Dainard Drakkar for 27 damage.
You critically hit Dainard Drakkar for 33 damage plus 18 acid damage.

A shocked look came over Drakkar's face as he looked down at Jace's two sabers sticking out of his chest. Then Jace saw the system message.

Dainard Drakkar dies.
You gain 210 experience.

The life faded from Drakkar's eyes and his body slumped to the deck of the ship. Jace had done it. He'd beaten Drakkar. Finally, the man would haunt him no longer.

A cheer went up from the crew of the Sea Tyrant but Jace barely noticed. Instead, he was captivated by a series of new system messages that popped up on his HUD.

Congratulations! You have killed the captain of a pirate ship in one on one combat and unlocked a special class.
Prestige class Swashbuckler has been unlocked.

A Swashbuckler prestige class? Jace had never heard of that prestige class before. But prestige classes were more powerful versions of classes. There were the base classes, or original classes as they were called. Then, there were the newer premium classes which were slightly more powerful versions of the base classes.

Prestige classes were the next level. They were generally more powerful than premium classes and offered some abilities that couldn't be found with any other class, like the assassin's *Assassinate* ability. Whatever Swashbuckler was, it was most likely stronger than any of the classes he currently had access to.

Unfortunately, he would need to reach level 11 in Rogue before he could switch classes again, so Swashbuckler would have to wait.

Jace looted Drakkar's body and got several items but didn't take the time to look at them. Instead, he turned to the crew of the pirate ship and held up his swords. "I am now the captain of the Wyvern's Tail. Are there any who wish to challenge me?"

The crew looked around, seeing if there were any who dared, but no one came forward. "Make ready to set sail. We leave soon to go find your treasure!"

With that, a chorus of hoots and cheers went up from the pirates and they began to scramble around the deck.

Luna and the girls came over to stand behind him as he turned to address Captain Yehmee. The racoon-kin was looking at him and shaking her head. "I honestly didn't think it would work."

"Oh, ye of little faith," he replied and smiled.

"I knew it would work," Mika chimed in from behind. "Jace is awesome!"

The captain held out her hand and Jace clasped it. "Good luck, Captain."

"Watch yourself with those pirates," she told him.

"I will," he said and released her hand. He turned to the girls and motioned towards the pirate ship. "Come on girls. Our crew awaits."

Chapter 9

Jace started across gangplank to board what had been the enemy ship just a few minutes ago. He had defeated Drakkar, and he thought doing so made him captain. But with a crew of pirates, he would have to watch his back. Luckily, he had Diana, Mika and Luna to help him with that.

As his foot touched the deck of Wyvern's Tail, new system messages and prompts appeared on his HUD.

Vessel Wyvern's Tail is unbound.
Take possession of Wyvern's Tail? (Yes or No)

He'd never owned a ship in the game, or anything other than a horse really. A ship cost hundreds of thousands of gold and he'd always found it easier just to pay for a teleport - faster too. So this prompt was new to him, yet seemed obvious. He answered Yes.

Wyvern's Tail is now bound to you.
Title gained: Captain
New menu available: Vessels

Wyvern's Tail is currently designated as a pirate vessel. Do you wish to change the designation? (Yes or No)

That was an interesting development. Jace had only thought briefly about the implications of becoming the captain of a pirate ship. Honestly, he'd been more concerned about not dying at the hands of Drakkar. But now he was forced to think about it.

Would he inherit the crimes the ship had committed? Or would he only be guilty of any future crimes? He also wondered how this would affect his title as Baronet. If the authorities found him guilty of piracy, would he have it stripped away? Or, because he was a player, would he keep it?

He wished he had access to the forums. Someone would surely know. For the moment, Jace was just going to take his best guess and hope for the best.

Jace chose Yes to change the designation.

Choose designation for Wyvern's Tail:

1. ***Cargo (Unavailable)***
2. ***Passenger (Unavailable)***
3. ***Pirate (Current)***
4. ***Privateer***

It didn't appear he could turn a pirate ship into a cargo or passenger ship, so those options weren't available. He wondered if other players had fleets of passenger or cargo ships and made a passive income with them. He guessed you had to have money to make money.

The only option available to him, other than leaving the ship as a pirate ship was privateer. He focused on the option and a description appeared.

Privateer - attack enemy ships for crown and country. Your ship may attack and be attacked by enemy factions but not by friendly factions.

Warning: Your ship is still subject to attack by pirates, sea monsters and natural disasters.

He considered the two options. One, he could remain a pirate and prey on ships from the good faction, or any other faction for that matter. Or, he could switch to privateer and only attack, and be attacked, by enemy ships.

Considering their current predicament, the last thing he needed was to be chased by navy ships. Privateer seemed the safer option. Hoping he was making the right decision, he chose to switch to privateer.

Wyvern's Tail now designated as Privateer.

Choose Faction:
1. Eastern Alliance
2. Central Coalition
3. Western Syndicate

It surprised Jace that he could choose a faction he wasn't a member of. The Central Coalition was the rough confederation of the animal-kin islands nations considered the neutral faction. The Western Syndicate was a tense union of the evil nations. It was the faction that Jace's old character, Mordred, had been a part of. Since he was part of the Eastern Alliance, he thought that was the safest choice.

Wyvern's Tail now designated as Privateer with the Eastern Alliance.

"You okay, Jace?" Mika asked from behind him and he realized he had stopped mid-stride on the gangplank. Since neither Mika nor Diana could see his prompts, to them it must seem that he had stopped for no reason.

"Sorry," he turned and gave them a smile. "Apparently, I just gained the vessel, and the game was prompting me for some information."

"Oh?" Diana raised an eyebrow. "What kind of information?"

"For one," he replied. "I just changed us from pirate to privateer."

"What does that mean?" Mika asked, a look of confusion on her face.

"It means Jace just turned us from all from regular pirates and cutthroats to discriminating pirates and cutthroats." Diana smirked.

"Basically," Jace nodded. "We can attack other factions but not our own."

Stepping onto the ship's deck, Jace moved out of the way and let the two girls come aboard. Once the three of them and Luna were on the ship, a sailor came over and took the gangplank away. Other sailors on both ships then removed the lines connecting the two boats.

With a wave, Captain Yehmee ordered her sailors to hoist their sails, and the wind began to slowly move the Sea Tyrant away. Jace wished them well. Belatedly, he realized he should have asked Yehmee to keep things quiet about him and the Wyvern's Tail.

Chances were good that Damian would be waiting for them at Nynymmost. After all, he'd sent the assassin and once he got the ear back, he'd know where they'd been. He could just teleport there and interrogate the people until he found out they were aboard the Sea Tyrant. His former coworker would then just need to find out the ship's destination and he could watch for the ship's arrival in the gnomish capital.

"What's the heading, captain?" yelled the pirate behind the wheel, breaking Jace out of his thoughts.

Turning, he saw it was a dark-skinned woman with short-cropped hair and large, gold hoop earrings. A quick glance at his HUD told him her name was Colette Nash. According to the information, she was first mate. Jace moved close to Mika and lowered his voice to a whisper. "Tell Colette the coordinates to the closest treasure."

Mika nodded and climbed up the stairs to the wheel. She spoke briefly with Colette and then the dark-skinned woman began barking orders. The other pirates hurried to obey and soon the ship lurched into motion.

"She said it would take at least a day," Mika told them when she returned. "Maybe a day and a half. Something about currents and winds."

"We probably need to take her word for it," Jace admitted. "Since none of us know anything about sailing."

"I don't enjoy being at their mercy," Mika said, casting a sideways glance back at Colette. She lowered her voice to a whisper. "They are pirates. We cannot trust them."

"It's a good thing none of us sleep," Diana commented. "Or we might not wake up."

"You may be right," Jace told them. "But now that I technically own the ship, through the game mechanics, I'm not sure that any of them could dispose me as captain. Drakkar could do it because he was one NPC doing it to another NPC."

"And you don't think they could do the same thing to you?" Mika asked.

"No," Jace said. "Well, maybe. I'm not sure. This is the first vessel I've owned in the game - even as Mordred."

"That's comforting," Diana said.

"Normally," he retorted, "I'd just look up the information on the forums or ask someone at work. But neither of those things are options at the moment."

"So, what do we do now?" Mika asked.

"Whatever it is we decide to do," Diana said, looking around at the many crewmen on deck. "We should do it somewhere else."

Seeing the curious glances they were getting from the sailors, Jace agreed. "Let's go into the captain's quarters and talk about what's next." He looked up and Colette. "I'll be in my quarters if you need me."

"Aye, captain," she called down. "Your quarters are downstairs, towards the bow."

Jace motioned to the door that led into the room where he had confronted Drakkar the night he'd stolen the crown. "Wait. I thought that was the captain's quarters."

"Aye." The dark-skinned woman smiled. "It was. Till some scurvy thief broke in and torched the place. Now it's just storage." She punctuated her words with a knowing smirk.

"Fine," Jace told her. "I'll be below deck then."

He, the two girls and Luna went downstairs, through a long narrow hallway to a large wooden door. Pushing it open, Jace could see that many of the things he'd seen in the captain's cabin were now in this new room.

The bed, the desk and several of the bookcases littered the new captain's quarters. They moved to the back of the cabin where the bed was. The bed and end tables hadn't been touched by the fire, though they all smelled of smoke.

There was also a desk, though the front of it had been badly singed, as well as three wooden chairs. The trio moved into the room but Luna bounded past them. The cat, still in her giant form, leaped atop the bed and caused the thing to give out a pained groan. She walked around in a circle and then settled into a spot near the head of the bed.

"Luna," Jace scolded. "Same rules as the other ship. Inside, you have to be normal size."

The cat looked dejected but shrank back down to the size of a regular cat. Jace could have sworn she huffed at him before putting her head down on her paws and closing her eyes.

"So now we're all here," Diana said, falling back into one of the chairs around the desk. "Now what?"

Both girls were looking at Jace for his plan but Jace hadn't really planned beyond defeating Drakkar. He wasn't even sure his plan would work and that the pirates would force the late captain to fight him. But he had won and now he was struggling to figure out their next steps. He'd have to make it up as he went.

"First thing," he told them. "We need to watch each other's backs. No one goes up on deck alone. I don't think they'll attack us, but let's not take chances. It's a long way from here back to Lasthaven for respawn."

The two women nodded.

He flopped down in the leather-bound chair on the opposite side of the deck. "Second, we need to keep the number of treasures to ourselves. I'm guessing that if we get the first one and pay off the crew, we can dock somewhere and take on a new crew. Then go get another one, but without telling them what it is."

"You think that will work?" Mika asked.

"I'm not sure," Jace replied. "But if we start going treasure hunting, the crew's going to want a large cut of it and right now, we need that money if we're going to stay ahead of Damian."

"Can we even do that?" Diana asked. "Stay ahead of him, I mean."

"I don't know," Jace told her. "And even if we can stay off his radar for a time, eventually he'll figure out a way to track us."

"What can he really do if he finds us?" Mika asked. "He is a character too, right? He can kill us, but we just respawn. He can't kill us for real. Right?"

"Theoretically, that's true," Jace nodded. "But theoretically, he shouldn't have been able to put us into monster bodies either. And there are worse things than death in the game."

"Worse?" Mika asked.

"There are spells and items that can imprison people," he told them. "Indefinitely. If you get caught in one, someone has to release you in order for you to escape. Either that, or you create a new character."

"But we can't create new characters," Diana pointed out.

"Exactly," Jace said. "It's like being thrown in prison. Most people will either log out while they serve their sentence or create a new character. We can do neither."

"So basically," Diana summarized. "We're screwed."

Chapter 10

The first mate had been right. It had taken them just over a day to reach the island the late captain's log had pointed them to. It was near dark, but Jace could see the twin volcanic peeks peeking through the dark jungle canopy.

"The charts don't have an official name for the island," Colette told them as they all looked out towards the island. "But it looks like Buchard had the words 'Kroaker Island' scribbled next to it though.

"Did you say Kroaker Island?" Jace asked worriedly.

"Aye," the first mate nodded. "I take it you know what they are?"

"I do," Jace nodded grimly. He'd faced them before as Mordred. They were bipedal frog people, primitive but cunning. Some higher level kroakers were even poisonous. They used poison from their own bodies to coat their weapons, making them very dangerous.

"I too have faced kroakers," Mika said quietly. "They are common among the islands of the Coalition."

"Kroakers?" Diana turned and asked with a confused look. "Dare I ask what kroakers are?"

"Amphibious frog people, or maybe toad people, I don't really know the difference," Jace replied. "They are strong and, as you can imagine, extremely good jumpers. One of their favorite techniques is to leap at their enemies, spear first. It does a ton of damage. High level ones use poison so it's even worse."

"Sounds painful," Diana said.

"I'd recommend avoiding it," Jace nodded. He looked out at the island. Even with the *Cat-Vision* granted to him by his familiar, he couldn't see past the initial trees of the jungle. "Let's wait until morning. I don't think it would be a good idea to go into the kroaker's territory at night, when only I can see."

"According to your coordinates," Colette said. "The treasure can be found somewhere near the volcanoes."

Jace smirked. "Of course it can," he said sarcastically.

"You taking the entire crew?" the first mate asked him.

"I wasn't planning to take anyone," he replied and saw the woman's eyes narrow.

"Why wouldn't you take the crew?" she asked accusingly, her voice louder than it needed to be. "Planning to run off with the treasure?"

That got the attention of some of the nearby crew mates and it got suddenly quiet on the ship. Jace looked around and saw that the crew had stopped in their tasks and had all turned to stare at him. They were pirates. They probably suspected he was going to double cross them.

Jace sighed. "If you think I'm planning to run away with the treasure, I want you to take a good hard look at the ocean around you. Do you see any other ships?"

Several of the crew did actually look around and shrugged. Colette kept staring at Jace. "Maybe you plan on hiding some of it. Keep it for yourself so you can come back for it. Maybe with that racoon-kin captain."

Jace shook his head at the paranoia but considering their former captain had been an idiot like Drakkar, he couldn't blame them.

"Listen," he told them. "I promised I'd give the treasure to you and I'll keep my promise. You're owed it. But, I don't know what's in that jungle. There could be an entire army of croakers. But even if there's just a single tribe, how much noise is the entire crew going to make trampling through the jungle? They'll be on us in a heartbeat!"

"Then we fight them!" yelled one and several more joined in. "Yeah! Fight them!"

"Have you ever seen a poison kroaker arrow?" Jace asked. "Have you ever seen someone skewered by one? Do you know how long it takes them to die, screaming in agony? Or have to watch their body contort and watch them bite off their own tongue?"

Jace hadn't actually seen anyone other than players get hit by a kroaker arrow and their necromancer had purged the poison from them before it could do much damage. Plus, like most players, their sensory input level had been turned down. So maybe he was embellishing it a bit. For all he knew, that's what COULD happen to NPCs.

True or not, his words had the desired effect. The pirates looked much less sure of themselves and even Colette's glare waivered. They began muttering among themselves. Good. He let them. But only for a minute.

"My companions and I will go through the jungle, get the treasure and bring it out," Jace told them in a loud, firm voice. "And then you all can split it. I won't take any of it. Each of you will get what you're owed."

"But," Jace said, trying to put as much iron into his voice as possible. "I'm the captain now. If anyone feels like questioning me again." Jace glared at Colette. "They can do so with steel. But I'll warn you, I held back with Drakkar. I wanted you to see me beat him on his terms. But make no mistake. If anyone mutinies, I won't hold back."

He continued to hold Colette's gaze until the woman finally looked away and nodded. "Aye, Captain."

"Oh," Jace said. "And in case anyone thinks they can plan something on this ship without me knowing about it…"

Jace sent a mental command to Luna. Thankfully, she listened to him and padded over to him. The tiger-sized cat rubbed up against him but looked menacing. At least, as menacing as a giant sized orange tabby could look.

"This is Luna, my familiar," he said. "She can hear everything that happens on this boat. Not only that, because she's a familiar, she understands what you're saying. In case you don't believe me…"

"You!" Jace directed his gaze at someone on the far side of the ship. The man went white, probably unsure what his new captain was going to do to him. "Whisper a word. Now!"

Everyone turned to the sailor and Jace could see the man's lips move nervously.

"What did he say?" Jace asked Luna, using his Monster Speak skill to speak her language. He could have just used telepathy with her, but he thought speaking in a cat language might appear more magical.

"Bollocks," Luna meowed, the boredom in her tone evident.

"He said the word bollocks?" he asked. Hopefully, it was the sailor's words and not the cat getting cheeky with him.

"Yes," she responded.

"Thanks!" he meowed back to her. "Remember, looking frightening. You're a giant-sized, killing machine now!"

Luna did seem to puff up a bit at his words and glared around at the crew members. Jace looked back to the sailor. "Bollocks!"

"Plautia's Mercy!" the man blurted out. "That's what I said. He's not lying."

"Now that we've established that," Jace told the assembled pirates. "Let's get back to the treasure. My companions and I will go fetch it. You lot will stay here and guard the ship. Remember, kroakers are amphibious. They can stay submerged for a long time. I want everyone on their toes tonight and tomorrow while we're gone. Colette, organize them into shifts and keep watch. They may already know we're here from our lanterns."

"Should we put them out?" Colette looked around at the half dozen lanterns on deck.

"No, we need to be able to see," Jace shook his head. Just knew some of the crew were dog-kin and he'd spotted a racoon-kin as well. They'd have better eyesight than the humans and at least he could use that. "Set at least one of the kin with each watch so they can use their better eyesight. I don't know if kroakers can see in the dark, but let's assume they can if they can see underwater."

"Aye Captain," Colette said. "Will you be retiring to your quarters?"

"No," Jace replied. "I'll be keeping watch too."

"What shift?" asked the first mate.

"All night," Jace replied and suppressed a grin at the woman's surprise.

"Aye captain," she said and Jace thought he detected a little more respect in her voice. Whether it was from taking watch or his earlier speech, he didn't know. But he hoped he wouldn't have any trouble with the pirates. He, the girls and Luna could probably kill every last one of them but if he did, he'd have no one to crew the ship.

"I will keep you company," Mika offered.

"Oh great," Diana said. "I guess I'll be walking the decks too then. There's nothing to do down in the captain's quarters. It's not like I can sleep." The older woman turned to Jace. "Is that a permanent thing? The not sleeping? I mean, if they fix us up, will I be able to sleep?"

Jace considered her question. He realized he really didn't know. It wasn't like he had planned on dying anytime soon. Even though he'd willed himself into the game, he hadn't really done the research to find out what that meant when he actually died. For him, it had been enough that he'd live forever inside the game. He shrugged and gave the older woman an apologetic look. "Sorry, I really don't know.

"I hope so. God, I miss dreaming," Diana told him. "Plus, the days just all blend together after a while with no sleep to break them up."

Although he hadn't really paid attention to it, he did know what she meant. Since he'd appeared in the game, his primary concern had been on getting to the *Help Desk* and contacting support. He had just wanted to get things fixed at first.

Then, when Charlena had thought he was alive, the situation had been a bit more urgent since he believed he was stuck in a medical pod while he was in a coma. At the time, he had thought he would need support's help to safely wake up.

Once he'd learned the truth, that he - or rather the real Jace - was alive and in a coma but not in a pod, things had changed. He realized he was just an error. A copy of the real Jace's consciousness and was inserted by accident when he was declared dead at the scene of that car accident.

WorldCog would erase him from the system if they found out the truth. And he honestly wasn't sure how long his story of being Jace's twin brother would hold up. How ironic would it be if he managed to elude Damian, only to get deleted from the game. Damian might just be able to sit back, relax and wait. Soon, Jace might get a long, never ending sleep.

"Are you waxing philosophical?" Diana asked him and he realized he had been lost in his own morbid thoughts.

"Just thinking about the jungle, the kroakers and the treasure," he lied, forcing a smile. They were his friends and, technically, his wives. That didn't mean he needed to burden them with his worries. Especially since there was nothing they could do to help him. There was nothing anyone could do.

Chapter 11

No attack came that night and when the morning sun rose in the east, they took one of the small rowboats to shore. Diana and Mika insisted on rowing while Jace and Luna kept watch. The water here was a crystal clear blue so seeing anything underwater was easy. The only issue was Luna rocking the boat as she followed the schools of colorful fish as they swam beneath them.

Fifteen minutes later, they were pulling the boat onto the shore and then they each swapped their clothes into their inventory and then back out to dry them. It was an old trick most players knew. Items in inventory didn't keep their status. Put a wet or dirty piece item into your inventory and when you brought it back out, it was clean and dry.

"Are you seeing this?" Diana asked, staring at the mist rising up from the jungle in front of them. The mist seemed almost unnatural to Jace. It rose from the moist ground and lingered in the air like a thick fog.

Jace nodded. "That's going to make spotting kroakers very hard."

"Luna can hear them," Mika said, walking over to the cat and rubbing behind her large ears. His familiar purred contentedly.

"I don't feel good about going in there," Diana frowned. "This is the part in the movie or book where the hapless people wander into the fog and get killed."

Looking into the fog, Jace couldn't help but agree. He didn't like the idea of trying to navigate through it. He doubted they'd even be able to make out the peaks of the volcanoes through the thick mist.

"I think it might be better if we go around," Diana said, gesturing to the island.

"I'm not sure we can," Jace replied. "The volcanoes are in the middle of the island and the treasure is between them."

"How do you know for certain?" Mika asked.

Jace smiled. "Each of the coordinates had notes too. But I wasn't about to tell the crew. They would have been searching for days or weeks, if they found it at all. It's not like there's a GPS in this game."

"And when were you going to tell us?" Diana glared at him.

"Well," Jace said sheepishly. "I was going to wait and try to look like the hero, but I guess I've let my secret slip."

"Hmm," Diana clicked her tongue. "Keeping secrets from your wives. That's no way to be a good husband."

"So, it's a good thing we didn't throw the real logs overboard," Mika said thoughtfully.

"Exactly," Jace agreed. "But I wasn't sure whether or not Drakkar had figured out the code, so I wanted him to think the only way he could get the map was to fight. And I paid the good captain well for her logs books."

"Just so you could throw them over," Mika observed.

"I had to sell my performance," he said in his best diva voice. "I am an… artist."

Mika giggled but Diana just rolled her eyes and motioned to the mist. "Are we seriously going in there? We'll get lost for sure."

"No!" Mika said and produced an object from her inventory and held it out for them to see. It was a crude, but working compass.

"A compass?!" Jace exclaimed happily. He had been planning on relying on Luna's sense of direction but he hadn't been completely sure whether or not she could maintain it surrounded by dense fog. "Where did you get that?"

The Japanese girl beamed at him. "I found it in your bedroom. I thought it would come in handy."

"You were right!" he said as she dropped it into his hand. "With this, we can keep our heading."

"So we're really going in there?" Diana was looking into the now impenetrable mist.

"Yeah," Jace said with a resigned shrug. "We don't really have a choice. But first, I want to tie us together."

"So we don't get lost?" Diana said with a furrowed brow. "I think I've seen this in a movie. The rope gets cut and we get separated and then killed one by one."

Jace looked over at the older woman as he retrieved the rope from his inventory. "Yeah. I recommend we keep one hand on the rope in front and back. If it goes slack, we yell out and stop in place. Then we move towards each other until we're together."

"I guess it beats the alternative." She shrugged. "We could wait, you know."

"We could," Jace agreed. "But then we risk getting caught at night. And unless you've decided to summon your familiar so you can see in the dark, that means only I would have night vision."

Diana hugged her arms to her body and shuddered. "I tried that again. I felt like I was dying. I don't know how you can do that. And do it more than once."

"You're right," he gave her a sympathetic look. "It's painful. The first few times were rough, but I think I'm used to it now. Well, as used as I can be to feeling like my insides are being ripped out."

The older woman shuddered again. "Yeah, that's exactly what it feels like. Like someone is ripping my soul away or something."

"So let's just stick to daylight," Jace changed the subject and held out the rope. He took a few minutes to tie the thin rope around each of their waists.

Once they were tied together, he motioned Luna to come up next to him. The cat seemed to sense their tension and padded over without comment. "Stay next to me and let me know if you smell or hear anything. Especially anything like a giant frog."

"Froggy?" she asked hopefully. Jace remembered she enjoyed chasing frogs and butterflies back in Whitecliff.

"Not the small ones," he explained. "Giant ones. The size of orcs."

Luna seemed to consider his words for a moment before responding. "Yes."

He glanced back at the two girls tied to him and then down to Luna. "Let's go."

The group entered the fog then, with Jace and Luna in the lead. Diana was next in line and Mika took the rear. Once they were actually in the fog, visibility was reduced to a matter of feet. Any hope he'd had to navigate by looking up at the volcanoes was gone. He couldn't even see the sky.

The initial minute or two was slow going since he could barely see the ground and finding sure footing became an issue. Several times he or one of the girls stumbled and, since they were tied together, almost took them all down. But after several minutes, they seemed to find their grove and the odd procession began to make some progress.

A shrill cry sounded in the distance to their left but there was no way to know what had made the sound or exactly where it was. Then another sound answered, slightly deeper, from the opposite side of them. He prayed they were just large birds or some other harmless animal and kept moving.

Jace checked their direction and then continued to check it every few minutes to make sure they were on course. He also checked in with Luna, who was constantly sniffing the air. She seemed to catch the scent of things from time to time but only paused once to sniff a patch of ground before continuing.

Screeches and other sounds continued to sound around them, keeping their nerves on edge. As they walked on, each was looking around, trying to penetrate the thick mist. But it was no use. Not even Luna's acute *Cat-Vision* could see through the swirling fog.

After an hour of walking, Jace called a halt and the three humans huddled around Luna. "How are you two doing?"

"Hot," Diana said, and he could see that she was sweating. "I've done the trick with the clothes a few times when they got sweaty."

"Me too," Mika admitted. "It is very humid too."

"Yes," the older woman agreed. "I feel like I need a drink."

"I don't think you're sweating," he told them. "I think it's the mist or fog. It feels damp and I think we're just picking up condensation or something on our skin and clothes. Like walking through the mist of a waterfall."

He thought about Diana's comment regarding feeling like she needed a drink. They shouldn't be feeling thirsty since they had eaten rations before they'd left. The game didn't keep a strict track of a character's food and water consumption as long as they ate every 6 or 8 hours. After that, they'd get a hunger debuff that would gradually get worse until they ate.

If they were feeling thirsty, it was because of something else. He checked his HUD but found no debuffs. That meant it might be something with the environment. Something the devs added to the island on purpose to make this area more difficult. Like the fog. Was the fog here for no other reason that the developer who made the island thought it would be cool or spooky?

"Keep an eye on your HUDs," he told them. "Let me know if you see any debuffs or weird messages. Maybe this fog has some other effect. Something the devs built in."

Both girls nodded their heads.

"How much further?" Diana asked. Of the three of them, she looked the worse for wear.

Jace wished he could see the sun or some point to mark their progress but that was impossible. He had pointed himself at the left most volcano and once they reached the base, he was going to turn west. But he had no idea when that would be. "Sorry Diana, I don't know."

She nodded and he could see her head beading with moisture from the fog that surrounded them. "It won't be soon enough."

He gave them another minute or two before getting his bearing and continuing their trek. He guessed they needed at least another two hours to get to the base of the volcano. Yet, without a point of reference he couldn't be certain.

Walking and checking his compass, Jace nearly didn't see the edge of the lake in time to avoid it. Luckily, Luna had seen it and nudged him with her head just in time for him to see the water's edge and avoid stepping into it.

He turned around and saw Diana nearly blunder into him before catching sight of him. The older woman yelped. "Oh geez!"

Behind Diana, he saw Mika emerge from the mist as well and stop just shy of bumping into Diana.

"Are we stopping?" Mika said softly.

"Yes," Jace nodded and then pointed to the water's edge. "I think we just hit a lake. We'll have to go around."

"Okay," the two girls said in unison.

Then they all froze as a loud sound pierced the mist. It sounded like the croak of a large frog.

"Froggy," Luna growled softly, her ears back.

Chapter 12

No one in the group moved, other than to swivel their heads around, trying to find the source of the croaking.

"Is that a kroaker?" whispered a wide-eyed Diana. She looked around nervously, her breathing ragged.

Another croak echoed through the mist, this time somewhere to their right. Then another answered from their left.

"I think they know we're here," Mika whispered.

Jace frowned. Could the kroakers see them? Or could they hear them? The mist seemed impenetrable. Unless they had some magical means to see through it, he didn't think they could have been spotted.

He didn't know that the creatures had particularly astute hearing since they were modeled after frogs. But just because something made sense in the real world, didn't mean it would translate into the game world.

Could the kroakers be smelling them? He had no idea whether frogs or kroakers even had a sense of smell. But if they could smell, that might explain it.

"Let's slowly move around the lake," he told them. "Just be ready."

As he said it, Jace saw that both of them already had their weapons out and ready. Motioning to them, he led them to his right around the lake. The croaking continued but there were too many of them to tell exactly where they were coming from.

Keeping himself ready for an attack that might come at any time from any direction started to wear on Jace. He guessed the girls were in a similar situation. Even Luna seemed nervous, her ears twitching and rotating constantly.

Unlike his feline companion, Jace knew the stakes. If any of them died, they'd respawn all the way back in Lasthaven. That was a problem. Not only was it over a day's trip to return, but Damian could be waiting for them there.

Then it struck Jace that he wasn't even sure that the crew would take orders from Diana or Mika. They might be left on the island or worse, killed and thrown overboard. If that happened, they'd lose their corpses and all of their possessions.

As they continued around the lake, it struck Jace that he was hearing croaking and not words. He'd been able to understand every intelligent monster he'd run across with the *Monsterspeak* ability. So, either it didn't work with kroakers, or what they were doing wasn't actually speaking. Maybe it was the kroaker equivalent of whistling.

Or maybe they were kroakers at all, but just very large toads. Until he knew for certain, he had to assume there were kroakers out there. That meant staying ready and staying alert.

Jace watched his compass as they continued around the lake until they once again turned west. Unfortunately, it was almost impossible to determine exactly where they were. He could only hope that they weren't too far off course.

They travelled west around the shore of the lake for an hour and Jace guessed the lake must take up most of the interior of the island. Unless it wasn't a lake. It could have been some sort of bog or swamp. With his visibility so limited, he was only guessing. But a swamp or a bog would make just as good a home as a lake to a kroaker. Or so he imagined.

Finally, the lake to their left disappeared and the croaking sounds faded away. Once again, he gathered up his group.

"It sounds like we're past them," Diana breathed, her face a mask of relief. "At least, I hope that's what the relative silence means."

The older woman still seemed overly nervous. Her face was pale, and her breath was shallow. "Are you okay?"

Diana forced a smile. "I just really hate… frogs."

"Are you okay now?" Jace asked again. "Do we need to rest for a bit?"

Mika put her hand on Diana's shoulder and the older woman smiled. This time it was genuine. "No, I'll be okay. The further we get from them, the better."

"Okay," Jace said. "Let's get moving. The sooner we find the treasure, the sooner we can get off the island."

"Treasure?" Came a low deep voice that reverberated from the mist. "They're after treasure? What a bunch of idiots."

He and the two women were instantly alert, as was Luna. Diana's eyes were wide again. "I just heard someone speak, right? I'm not imagining it?"

"No," Jace hissed. "There's someone out there in the mist and he heard us."

"You can... understand me?" came the voice. The voice was deep and resonating but not threatening.

"We can," Jace replied. "Who are you?"

"Interesting. Very interesting," the voice said. "How is it you understand me, human?"

"Are you a monster?" Jace asked.

"Monster?!" the voice replied with a tone of indignation. "What is a monster? What makes one a monster? Is it the outward appearance? Or is it what is inside that really makes the monster?"

The group exchanged glances. Jace was sure this was a monster player, but he hadn't sensed it like he had with the others. When he came near a player who had been affected by the code which Damian had written, he could "sense" them. Sometimes, it could be for miles. This time there was nothing.

"Were you once a human?" Jace asked. "But now you're something else?"

There was a long moment of silence before the voice answered. "I dreamed I was human, once upon a time. Then I was many things. But no longer."

"You're a kroaker now?" Jace guessed.

"And you're a human," the voice said.

"I was a monster too once," Jace told him. "All of us were. I know how to turn you back to being human."

More silence. This time, it lasted longer and Jace started to believe the person had left.

"Interesting," the voice said, its tone neutral. "You were a monster?"

"I was," Jace told him. "A goblin, an ogre, a kobold and a few other things."

"I was a yeti," Mika offered.

"And you turned into a human at some point?" the voice inquired.

"I used to work for WorldCog," Jace told the voice. "I was a programmer. I managed to 'hack' the game and turn myself human."

"Hmm," the voice responded, the sound vibrating the mist around them. It seemed to come from everywhere around them. Having never spoken to a kroaker, he wondered if this was the way they sounded all the time. "So, you learned how to change yourself from a monster to a human? And now you offer this same ability to me? Why?"

"Why?" Jace asked, confused. "So you can turn back into a human. So you don't have to keep hopping from body to body. So you can talk to other people. Don't you want that?"

"Stop hopping?" the voice said. "I haven't hopped for a very long time. I have to die to hop to another body and I haven't died in a very long time."

"Don't you want to be human again?" Mika asked.

"I don't think he does," whispered Diana.

"What is there for me as a human?" the voice said with a sad inflection. "There is nothing for me. There is no one waiting. No one looking. No one even checking up on me to make sure I got into the game."

"Some malicious code did this," Jace explained. "No one knew except for the person who created the code. It was taking the money from people who died and funneling it to him while trapping the person in a monster body so they couldn't tell anyone."

"Interesting," the voice said. "So, a human creates a program that makes humans into monsters, all so he can steal their money. Tell me. Who is the real monster?"

Jace was starting to get a bad feeling about this person. Once before, he'd met a goblin who had been a human. He had called himself "Big Cheese" and he had gone mad. He'd ended up killing Jace and then disappearing before Jace could deal with him. Now, Jace wondered if this person had gone crazy too.

Maybe that happened. Maybe jumping bodies too many times eventually drove a person crazy. If that were the case, he doubted just turning them human would "fix" them. They'd probably need years of therapy, and there was a lack of therapists in VEIL Online.

"Damian is the monster," Mika responded before Jace could reply. "He is evil."

"Damian," the voice repeated. "Is that his name? Yes, condemning people to torture and stealing their money would make him the monster. Not you or I. So does it really matter what we are or what we look like? Is it really what is on the outside that makes us the monster?"

"No," Jace admitted. "It's what kind a person you are on the inside that makes you a monster."

"And what kind of person are you on the inside?" the voice asked.

Jace opened his mouth to speak but Mika beat him to it. "Jace is a good person! He is helping people!

He helped me and Diana and others. He is a good person."

"Is he now? Or are those just the words of someone in love? People can still love a monster, you know. A drug lord's wife might still love him. A mobster's wife. A dictator's wife. They may even see the monster but their love for them blinds them," the voice replied.

"I am not blinded," Mika said defiantly. "And Jace is no monster!"

"Hmm," the voice said. "Are you… Jace? Are you no monster?"

"I try not to be," Jace said hoarsely. He remembered his parents and sister dying in the car accident on the day of his graduation. He'd wanted to go out with his friend instead of them. Because of that, they'd gone home instead of to the restaurant. They'd died on the way home. All because of his decision. Maybe he was a monster. But he'd tried to be a good person since then. The person his parents would have wanted him to be.

"I guess that's as honest an answer as any of us can give," the voice said. The voice paused and then said. "You are looking for treasure on the island?"

"Yes," Jace replied. "Buried treasure from a pirate captain."

"And then you will leave the island?" the voice asked.

"Yes," Jace said cautiously. The person had still not asked him about how to become human. Were they crazy like Big Cheese?

"Then, I will lead you to the treasure and then you will leave me," the voice said.

"Don't you want to know how to be human again?" Diana asked.

"I was human for almost sixty years," the voice said. "I had a wife who cheated on me and left me for my brother. I had children who ignored me except when they wanted more money. And my dog, Rocky, died two months before I did. What's really so good about being human?"

"I've already contacted support," Jace told him. "They'll find the bug and fix it and then set everyone back to the way they were. You'll become whatever you originally asked."

The voice sighed. "Then, I'll cross that bridge when I get to it." There was silence for a moment. "Let's get you to your treasure before the natives wake up."

With those words, the mist began to clear. Over the course of a minute, the mist evaporated entirely. When it had dissipated, the three of them found themselves staring at the enormous head of a turtle the size of a jet airliner. And not just any type of giant turtle, this was a dragon turtle. One of the powerful creatures in the seas.

Chapter 13

The three of them followed the massive dragon turtle to the west. With the mist gone, it was easy to see.

"You created the mist?" Jace asked.

"Yes, one of my many special abilities," the turtle answered, bobbing its gigantic head. As it opened and closed its mouth, Jace realized the thing could swallow him with one bite. Curious, he looked at the dragon turtle in his HUD.

> *Tieghosdirth (Fabled)*
> *Race: Dragon Turtle*
> *Class: Warlock*
> *Level: 100*

Jace almost stumbled as he read the description. This turtle was an epic raid monster. And not just any epic raid monster, a Fabled monster. They were the most powerful creatures in the game. It was probably on par with the Black Dragon that had threatened Whitecliff. And Jace was walking next to it.

"Geez!" Jace breathed. "You're a Fabled monster."

"Am I?" the turtles murmured. "I'm not even sure what that means."

"It means you're probably one of the most powerful monsters in the game," he told the turtle. He suddenly felt awkward referring to the person as a dragon turtle, even in his mind. "Do you have a name we can call you?"

"Bob." The turtle smiled. At least, Jace hoped it was a smile.

"Are you… serious?" Jace asked hesitantly.

"Well, my name is Robert," Bob replied. "But everyone called me Bob."

"It is very nice to meet you Mr. Bob." Mika smiled up at the dragon turtle. "I am Mika! He is Jace and this is Diana."

The turtle chuckled, a low rumbling sound that seemed to vibrate every cell in Jace's body. "Just Bob little one. Not Mr. Bob. Just Bob."

"Okay, Bob." Mika beamed.

They followed the turtle for almost half an hour and despite turtles having a reputation for being slow, they found themselves struggling to keep up with him. His long, even gait kept them moving at a brisk pace the entire time.

The entire time they have been traveling, they'd been getting closer and closer to the volcanoes. When Bob finally came to a halt, they were between the two volcanoes on a raised area of what appeared to have been a lava flowed that cooled long ago.

Bob tilted his head and brought one of his great eyes to a hole that looked barely large enough for a human to pass through. He blinked a few times and then raised his head. "Down there is where my treasure is. I add to it as I find more and now there is so much."

"Lair?" Diana asked with a raised eyebrow.

"Yes, I found a very large underground cave that I like to rest in when I'm not floating around the ocean. It is warm from the volcanos and the hot water feels good," he grinned, as if imaging being in the warm water.

"There is much treasure down there and you may take what you wish," Bob told them. "I find it on the bottom of the ocean. In the hulls of sunken ships. I bring it back here and put it in my cave. But maybe if there is less treasure here, there will be less visitors."

"Visitors?" Jace asked.

"Raiders," the giant turtle replied, a sad expression on his face. "For almost a year, they would not leave me alone. They came, always forty of them."

"You killed them?" Mika asked curiously.

"Yes, little Mika," the dragon turtle bobbed its head. "I killed them. They came ready to slaughter me, but I was not ready to give up this body. They could not stand against me. The 'raiders', as they called themselves, tried many times before they gave up. Each time, they hurt me, but each time I prevailed."

Jace realized raiders had probably found out his locations and came here to kill him. But because an AI wasn't controlling him, he had no limitations on when or how he used whatever special attacks were at his disposal. Just like the black dragon that had almost destroyed Whitecliff.

"No more questions," the turtle said, looking to the sun in the west. "You are almost out of time."

"Out of time?" Diana asked.

"The kroakers are nocturnal," he told them, glancing back the way they came. "They sleep now in the lake you passed, but they will wake soon and they will smell you. Then they will come for you."

"Oh dear," Diana replied and glanced nervously behind them. "We should get going."

"Hurry little ones," he said. "I return to my cave. Please do not tell others of me. I only wish to enjoy the sun, the ocean and the heat of my cave. I do not wish to fight."

"We won't," they said, nearly in unison.

"Farewell little humans," he said. "Be safe… and hurry."

The giant dragon turtle ambled off down the slope, walking straight into the ocean. He walked out a good hundred yards before the ocean dropped off and he disappeared under the water.

"Jace?!" Diana nudged him with her elbow. She seemed almost frantic again. "Let's get the treasure and get out of here."

"Right," Jace nodded, tearing his eyes away from the spot where the thing had disappeared.

Taking his rope back out of his inventory, he tied it onto a nearby palm tree and climbed down into the darkness. Once he got to the bottom, he pulled out the magical longsword, Ardmore's Bane, they'd found in the sewers of Whitecliff. It was too low level for him to use in combat, but it did shed light and allowed him to see more with his *Cat-Vision*.

What he saw was an enormous watery cavern. The cave stretched out towards the ocean and although the center of the gigantic passage was underwater, there were twenty feet of stone on either side where Bob had stacked up treasure.

The air was hot and humid and stank of brimstone. Down the giant passage, he could see the yellow-orange light of lava pools. The close proximity of the lava must heat up the air and the water around them, which is why it felt like a sauna.

He looked around his side of the passage. It was heaping with gold, treasure chests and items. Jace found a number of big chests. He grinned. Everyone loves big chests. Taking two of the chests of gold, he dumped them into his inventory.

You are mildly encumbered.
Movement reduced by 10%.
Stamina usage increased by 20%.

You are encumbered.
Movement reduced by 20%.
Stamina usage increased by 40%.

You are heavily encumbered.
Movement reduced by 30%.
Stamina usage increased by 60%.

He didn't just see the system messages. Jace felt the change. It was as if he was suddenly Atlas, bearing the weight of the world on his shoulders. With his sensory input stuck at maximum, he literally felt like he was about to be crushed under some unseen burden. He pulled one of the chests out of inventory and set it on the ground.

You are no longer heavily encumbered.

You are no longer encumbered.

You are mildly encumbered.
Movement reduced by 10%.
Stamina usage increased by 10%.

Dropping the second chest greatly reduced the strain he felt and also reduced the movement penalty. If he wanted to take two or more chests back to the ship, he was going to need help.

"Mika," he called up. "Can you come down here?"

The lithe girl answered by shimming down the rope and then dropping dexterously next to him. When she stood up, she glanced around the cavern with wide eyes. "This is a lot of treasure."

"Yes," he told her. "But, carrying just one chest encumbers me. Two chests severely over encumber me."

"It's hot down here," she observed.

"Yeah," Jace agreed. "This must be part of the cave that Bob likes."

The Japanese girl looked around at all of the treasure that lined the walls and floor. "How did Bob get this much treasure?"

"Raiders," Jace told her. "This place is out in the middle of nowhere. Chances are, their bodies expired before they made it back or, they made it back and Bob killed them. Most raiders carry a decent amount of gold on them, potions and other stuff for the raid. The only reason this place isn't filled to the brim with gear is that at raider level, most items are soulbound, so they'd reappear with the player."

"Oh," Mika nodded, still looking at the treasure. Suddenly her eyes went wide and she rushed over to a pile of gold and grabbed a small pouch. As Jace looked closer, he could see it had been partially open and had spilled out gems of all shapes, sizes and colors. "Can I keep these?"

Jace shrugged. "Sure. I don't see why not. I promised to bring back the treasure and that they could have what I brought back. I never said anything about giving them whatever you and Diana brought back."

She clapped her hands excitedly and gathered up the gems. Then she made the pouch disappear into her inventory.

"I want to look around a bit," he said. "Can you do me a favor and climb back up, give this chest to Diana to carry and then come back and get another one?"

"Sure," she flashed him a grin. Then she made a chest disappear and started up the rope.

While she was gone, Jace took a long look around. He had no idea how much gold was down here but he knew it had to be millions of gold. If he had some way to get it out of here, they would never have to want for gold any longer.

His foot stubbed itself on something and he looked down to see a flawless green emerald in a silver setting. He reached down to pick it up and found it was a ring. Then he received a message.

Ring of Arcane Storage is a Soulbound item.
Do you wish to permanently bind this item to your character? (Yes or No)
Warning: This action cannot be undone.

Excitedly, Jace examined the ring.

Ring of Arcane Storage
Type: Ring
Level: 1
Wt: .1 lb
Special: Wearer can store a single non-damaging spell of any level.

Description: These rare rings are crafted by the arch mages of the mage's guild. Their construction is a heavily guarded secret because of the power these rings can give the wielder. Because of the possibility of abuse, they are only given to the most loyal of allies.
Current Spell: Teleportation

Jace looked at the description more closely and his eyes went wide as he read the current spell. It was a teleportation spell! With that, he could teleport himself and his entire group to any city he'd been to!

He quickly chose Yes, to bind it to him.

Ring of Arcane Storage has been bound.
You received Ring of Arcane Storage.

The ring was incredibly powerful since it could store a spell of any level. Unfortunately, if he remembered correctly, once the spell was used, it was gone until you cast a new spell into the ring. So if Jace used the teleportation spell, he'd have to find a high level wizard to recast the spell into his ring and they'd charge him the going rate: 10,000 gold. And that was if he could even find a wizard who would do it.

He sighed as he slipped the ring on his finger. For now, they'd need to be extremely judicious about using the spell. For all he knew, they'd only ever get to use it once. After it was gone, they may or may not ever get it recharged.

Mika scrambled down the rope and grabbed the other chest. A moment later, it disappeared into her inventory. She turned to him and smiled. "All set!"

"Great." He smiled. "I just found a powerful magic ring! Maybe we should look around and see if there are any other…"

"Um," Diana's nervous voice called from the entrance. "It's kind of getting dark up here. I really think we should go!"

Jace looked around the huge treasure chamber and swore. If only he had more time - and more carrying capacity! He wanted to stay but he knew if they didn't leave, they risked the chance of running into the kroakers and if they died, then they'd lose more than just the treasure.

"Okay," Jace said reluctantly, casting one more glance at the treasure. "We'd better go."

Chapter 14

Jace climbed up after Mika. As he cleared the entrance, he understood Diana's concern. The sun was already dipping. Into the western horizon. Bob had said the kroakers were nocturnal. But he didn't know if that meant they woke up once it was fully dark or if they were already awake at dark.

"You have a chest?" Jace asked Diana.

She thrust out her ample bosom and smiled. "So nice of you to notice."

Rolling his eyes, Jace turned to gather up the rope. "You know what I meant."

"I did, dear one," Diana said and her brief playful voice disappeared, replaced by the nervousness he'd heard before. "And I am carrying a chest. I got a message about mild encumbrance."

"Yes," he confirmed. "We all have it. It will slow us a little but we should be okay."

"All the more reason for us to get the heck out of dodge," Diana said, once again glancing back towards the lake they had passed. Even though she hadn't been down in the sauna-like cave, he could see beads of sweat on her forehead.

Luna seemed to share Diana's concern. Her tail was puffed out and it swished back and forth, while her ears were twitching and rotating, as if trying to home in on some unseen sound.

Jace nodded and brought out his compass. He pointed north. "Ok, let's head north to the shore and then follow it back east to ship."

Without any more talk, they followed Jace as he circled north around the volcano. Because of their encumbrance, the going was slower than he had hoped. By the time the jungle opened up into the beach, the last rays of the sun were disappearing into the west.

At the beach, they turned right and began to circle to the east towards the ship. They hadn't taken more than a dozen steps when they heard a loud croaking coming from the jungle. It was answered by a croaking from a different location. And then another. Soon, it was an unnaturally loud chorus of croaks that filled the night air.

Diana went pale and Jace wondered if her dislike of frogs was more like a phobia. She seemed terrified. Or, perhaps just the thought of facing giant, bipedal frogs on the beach at night was terrifying.

Within a few seconds, as if they had coordinated it, they all had their weapons out. Jace looked at the girls. "If any of us die, remember, we'll respawn in Lasthaven. Stay out of sight until the others can come for you."

"That's encouraging," Diana quipped.

"Come on," he said and they hurried along. He wanted to run, but with the mild encumbrance, their stamina usage would be 20% greater. That meant if they got into a fight, especially a long fight, they could easily run out of stamina. Running out of stamina during a fight was tantamount to death. At zero stamina, they'd collapse and be killed by the enemy.

They raced along the beach as the croaking seemed to move throughout the jungle next to them. It had taken them hours to navigate through the thick mist Bob had created. Jace hoped it wouldn't take nearly as long on a clear, open beach. They didn't have that sort of time.

Just then, two kroakers burst out of the jungle and launched themselves towards his group. Jace reacted out of instinct, born from years of playing the game, he immediately popped his *Evade*.

He realized the second one was aimed at Diana but couldn't do anything in time. The older woman just wanted, wide-eyed, as the olive skinned kroaker flew at her, spear first. Then an orange blur collided with the kroaker and they both went tumbling into the sand.

Moonlake Kroaker Warrior uses Springing Attack on Diana Knightly but is interrupted.
Luna uses Pounce Attack on Moonlake Kroaker Warrior for 23 damage.

Luna had leaped at and intercepted the kroaker in midair, knocking the thing into the ground and saving Diana was what would have been a painful charge attack. As the kroaker who had launched itself at Jace approached, he blurred to the side and the kroaker soared past him.

Moonlake Kroaker Warrior uses Springing Attack on YOU but you Evade.

"Come get some!" Jace shouted out his *Taunt* and both frogmen spun to face him. As they hopped over to attack, he cast his *Air Armor* spell. "*Aeris Armatura!*"

Jace spun around so the kroakers were both facing him, using a Feint and then attacking the one that Luna had already damaged.

You critically hit Moonlake Kroaker Warrior for 42 damage plus 18 acid damage.
You critically hit Moonlake Kroaker Warrior for 6 damage.

Mika disappeared briefly as she used her *Vanish* and then reappeared as she skewered the kroaker with her katana.

Mika Knightly critically hit Moonlake Kroaker Warrior for 15 damage.
Moonlake Kroaker Warrior is Bleeding.

Luna bounded after the kroaker she had attacked and clawed and bit at its back.

Luna bites Moonlake Kroaker Warrior for 3 damage.

Luna claws Moonlake Kroaker Warrior for 0 damage.
Luna claws Moonlake Kroaker Warrior for 4 damage.

Unlike her pounce attack, Luna's normal attacks didn't do much damage. He made a mental note to talk to her later about what attacks she had and how they worked. But in the present moment, there were two angry kroakers who wanted to kill him.

Moonlake Kroaker Warrior pierces YOU for 0 points of damage.
Moonlake Kroaker Warrior pierces YOU for 6 points of damage.
Mild Kroaker Toxin hits you for 10 points of poison damage.

The first frogman's spear had glanced off his buckler, but the second one's spear found the spot under his breastplate and stabbed him near the groin. The piercing pain exploded in his brain and Jace sucked in a breath.

Just like the other kroakers he'd encountered as Mordred, these also tipped their weapons with their own poison. Jace felt the intense burning in his veins as the kroaker's poison penetrated his system. It was an instant poison and did immediate damage, versus the damage over time poison that acted more like a bleed effect. But unfortunately, the damage bypassed his *Defense* completely.

Gritted his teeth against the pain, he *Feinted* again and jabbed both his sabers at the wounded kroaker.

__You critically hit Moonlake Kroaker Warrior for 35 damage plus 18 acid damage.__
__Moonlake Kroaker Warrior dies.__
__You gain 150 experience.__

His blow from Kraken's Claw took down the damaged frogman and the thing let out a gurgling sigh as it fell dead. Jace adjusted the aim of his second saber to hit the uninjured kroaker but it skidded off the creature's slimy skin.

__You critically hit Moonlake Kroaker Warrior for 0 damage.__

Mika used her *Vanish* skill to get a critical hit on the kroaker as well.

__Mika Knightly critically hit Moonlake Kroaker Warrior for 20 damage.__
__Moonlake Kroaker Warrior is Bleeding.__

Luna attacked the frogman's back as well but Jace didn't see Diana attacking.

__Luna bites Moonlake Kroaker Warrior for 5 damage.__
__Luna claws Moonlake Kroaker Warrior for 0 damage.__
__Luna claws Moonlake Kroaker Warrior for 2 damage.__

Jace could see Diana behind Mika, her face ashen and her body trembling. He called out to her. "Diana, are you okay?"

The raven haired woman said nothing. She just stared, wide-eyed at the kroakers, her eyes going from the live on to the dead one on the ground. Her mouth was open, but no sound came out.

Jace swore just as the remaining kroaker tried to skewer him with its spear. Luckily, his *Air Armor* diverted the blow.

Moonlake Kroaker Warrior pierces YOU for 0 points of damage.

Worried about Diana, Jace wanted to end this as soon as possible. Using his Feint on the remaining creature, he stabbed at its torso with a double saber attack. Followed by Mika's and Luna's attacks.

You critically hit Moonlake Kroaker Warrior for 54 damage plus 18 acid damage.
You critically hit Moonlake Kroaker Warrior for 10 damage.

Worried about Diana, Jace wanted to end the fight as soon as possible. Using his *Feint* on the remaining creature, he stabbed at its torso with a double saber attack.

Moonlake Kroaker Warrior for 3 damage.

Mika Knightly critically hit Moonlake Kroaker Warrior for 10 damage.
Moonlake Kroaker Warrior is Bleeding.

Luna bites Moonlake Kroaker Warrior for 1 damage.

Luna claws Moonlake Kroaker Warrior for 3 damage.
Luna claws Moonlake Kroaker Warrior for 0 damage.

The kroaker looked the worse for wear and seemed to realize it wasn't going to win the fight. Jace thought it might try to run but instead, it opened its mouth and a long, pink tongue lashed out of its mouth, right at Jace's saber.

Moonlake Kroaker Warrior uses Sticky Tongue Disarm but is interrupted.
Kraken's Claw hits Moonlake Kroaker Warrior for 18 acid damage.

The frogman's tongue had shot out and wrapped around Kraken's Claw. It looked as if the creature was about to yank the weapon out of Jace's hand. That was when the acid of the blade had burned the creature's tongue and it had retracted it.

Jace hated creature's with the *Disarm* ability. It was an attack against a weapon, rather than a player and bypassed any armor or evasion skills. In this case, the only thing that had prevented Jace from losing Kraken's Claw was the fact that the blade did acid damage. By voluntarily touching the blade, the creature had subjected itself to the damage and that had interrupted its attack.

Taking advantage of the surprised kroaker, whose tongue now hung out slightly from it's mouth, Jace *Feinted* and stabbed again, bringing the kroaker's life to an end.

You critically hit Moonlake Kroaker Warrior for 40 damage plus 18 acid damage.
Moonlake Kroaker Warrior dies.
You gain 150 experience.

The kroaker staggered back and then collapsed onto the bloody sand. Jace stepped over the body and strode quickly over to Diana, who still hadn't moved.

Sheathing his weapons, he glanced around her body to see if any darts had hit her. Natives sometimes used paralyzation poison on darts that would render a player immoble. He saw none. "Are you hurt? Are you injured?"

Diana blinked several times, then slowly swiveled her head from the kroakers to Jace. She tried to speak but nothing came out. Jace repeated his question. "Are you okay?"

"Ran…" she said but the sound was little more than a whisper.

"Run?" he asked. Did she want them to run back to the ship?

"Ran…" she repeated and then swallowed. "Ranidaphobia."

"Ran-i-what?" Mika asked, her face a mask of concern.

"Ranidaphobia," the older woman repeated and then took a deep breath. "Extreme Fear of frogs."

Jace looked from Diana down to the kroaker and then back to raven haired beauty. He saw it now. The cold sweat. The shaking body. The look of pure terror. Their poor Diana had an extreme phobia of frogs. And apparently, that applied to kroakers too.

Jace swore.

Chapter 15

"You are afraid of frogs?" Mika asked, concerned etched on her beautiful face.

Diana swallowed and nodded. "Deathly. I don't even know why."

"Why didn't you tell us?" Jace demanded, shaking his head. "You could have stayed on the ship."

"I didn't know if I would still be afraid," Diana replied in a small voice and Jace suddenly felt bad for raising his voice. "And I didn't know if it would apply to frogmen. But it does. Oh my, it does!"

Reaching over to her, Jace put a hand on her shoulder. "I'm sorry. But I wish you would have said something so we would have at least been aware."

"I know, I know," Diana sniffed and seemed to be about to break out in tears.

Not knowing what else to do, Jace pulled her into an embrace and held her for almost a minute before she pushed him gently away.

"Thanks." She smiled. "I needed that." Diana stepped back from Jace and pointedly turned her back on the dead kroakers. "I'm okay now. At least, for the moment."

Jace walked around so he could face her and smiled. "Good. Why don't you walk down closer to the water. If we get attacked again, turn away. You can still target us for healing using the group list in your HUD. Just throw us some heals if you can."

The older woman appeared relieved and looked down at where the waves were washing ashore. "Yes… I can… I can do that."

"Froggies coming," Luna's voice said in his head.

"More kroakers are on their way," Jace told them. "We need to get going but keep an eye open. Mika, I mean. Diana, you just keep your eyes on the beach and the water. Don't look at the kroakers."

Diana shivered. "Right. Don't look!"

"Let's go!" Motioning them to follow, Jace started off down the beach with the girls following behind him and Luna padded along next to him.

The kroakers attacked them four more times, in groups of twos and threes. During the third attack, they had killed two of the three kroakers when two more joined in the fight. They were only level 15, but their poison guaranteed extra damage on any strike that penetrated his *Defense*. And since every kroaker they encountered seemed to use a 2-handed spear, they were damaging him more than he wanted.

The only positive side to the fighting was that they were earning experience. Diana even hit 10th level, allowing her skills to progress. Unfortunately, the other benefits would need to wait since she couldn't learn new priest spells until she went to a temple, and the kroakers weren't dropping anything but spears.

When they reached the section of beach where they had left their rowboat, they found half a dozen kroakers waiting for them. It was a nasty fight. With that many kroakers attacking, too many blows were making it through his *Defense* for him to just shrug off.

With so many kroakers around, Diana was a mess. She was so terrified that she actually started to swim back to the ship, leaving Jace, Mika and Luna to fight them on their own.

Thankfully, Mika had levels in priest and could heal Jace. Not only that halfway through the fight, she hit level 10 in rogue and received Critical Eye II. Doing 3x damage on her critical strikes instead of 2x damage helped them to burn down the remaining kroakers much more quickly.

As the last kroaker dropped dead, Jace looked out to the water and spotted Diana. She was only a little over a quarter of the distance between the beach and the ship.

"More coming," Luna growled as the cat looked into the jungle canopy. The cat was crouched low with her ears back. "Many."

Luna had spoken the words aloud instead of sending them mentally and Mika looked to Jace. She looked from the jungle to the water and then sheathed her katana. "We must go."

Jace couldn't agree with her more and the two of them ran over to the boat and pushed it back into the water. Jace was about to take the oars but Mika put a hand on his chest. "No! You see in the dark. You watch, I row."

Her argument made sense so Jace stowed his sense of chivalry and moved to the back of the boat. Luna moved deftly to the front but cast occasional glances back towards the beach. The cat seemed nervous and that worried Jace.

They'd nearly caught up with Diana when movement from the shore caught his eye. At least twenty kroakers came hopping out of the jungle. The creatures seem to spot their little boat almost immediately. The group began croaking loudly to each other for almost a full minute before they suddenly charged down the beach and then hopped into the water.

Mika was pulling Diana into the boat, causing it to tilt precariously, as Jace watched the kroakers closing the distance with unbelievable speed. Because of the crystal clear water, he could just make out the forms as they torpedoed towards their rowboat.

"Incoming!" he yelled and pulled out his weapons.

Watching the aquatic forms coming towards them, he realized how terrible their predicament was. The kroakers were amphibians. They didn't even need to surface. They could just attack the bottom of the boat with their spears and cause it to sink. Or, they just capsize the boat and attack his group as they tried to stay afloat. Or once they were in the water, they could pull them down and drown them.

In other words, there were no scenarios where they won this fight. Jace swore. They'd been so close too. He didn't see any way they could get to the ship before the kroakers reached them.

The closest kroaker was almost to the boat when a shadow seemed to grow in the water. The next thing he saw was the kroakers darting out in all directions, apparently no longer interested in his group's boat.

He finally recognized the shadow and the two kroakers suddenly disappeared from in front of it, a large turtle head moving quicker than he would have thought possible to snatch up the fleeing kroakers in its huge beak. It was Bob the dragon turtle.

The enormous head broke the surface for only a moment. "I thought you might need some help. Plus, I was a bit peckish."

"Thanks Bob!" he yelled and waved to the dragon turtle as it went back to chasing the fleeing kroakers. He noticed that the creature's legs were now large fins, making him resemble a sea turtle instead of a land-based turtle like before. Must be some dragon turtle magic or perhaps they were retractable.

They rowed the rest of the way back to the ship and climbed aboard. Colette was there, as were the entire crew. They only paid the barest attention to Jace and the group as they climbed back aboard. Instead, their terrified gazes were fixed on the dragon turtle that swam between them and the island.

"Captain," Colette said, her eyes wide. "It's… it's… Tieghosdirth!"

Jace looked back over his shoulder at the dragon turtle as it swam almost lazily after the kroakers. "Yes, he helped us out with the kroakers."

The first mate's mouth fell open. "Helped you?"

Jace nodded nonchalantly. "Yes, he thought we might need some help, so he swam over to help us. Plus, he was hungry."

Colette looked at Jace like he'd grown two heads, and possibly some antennas. "How… it… huh?"

Helping the girls up on deck, Jace continued his nonchalance with the first mate. "Yeah, we talked to him earlier, and he showed us the treasure. I thought he was going back to his hot springs, but I guess he wanted a late-night snack."

Now the entire crew was staring at him and Jace had struggled to maintain a straight face. The fact that Colette had known Bob's in-game name meant that it had some sort of reputation. Jace wanted to capitalize on the fear it generated to both solidify his position as captain and also keep his word to Bob about leaving him alone.

"Tieghosdirth and I talked, and he was fine with you having the captain's treasure," he told the crew. "But, he likes his privacy. So he told me to tell you that if any of you breathe a word of having seen him - to anyone - he will find you and swallow you whole. In his belly, you'll slowly digest for a thousand years."

He looked around at the crew. They all looked terrified. "I assume I can count on each of you to keep their mouths shut?"

Jace had barely asked the question when the crew was practically falling over themselves to answer him. Everyone agreed. No one would say a word. He hoped they were telling the truth. Bob deserved to be left alone if that was what he wanted.

He knew that once WorldCog unraveled Damian's code and figured out what he'd done, they'd return everyone to their normal form. Bob would be back in whatever type of character he was originally supposed to be in. Then he'd have to figure out a new way to be alone.

"Colette," he told the first mate, "I think we should be on our way now."

"Aye, captain," Colette nodded vigorously and began barking orders to the crew.

As the crew did their jobs and made the ship ready to get under way, Jace and the girls watched the dragon turtle as it circled back around. The enormous head broke the water and looked their way. Then Bob raised his right front fin in a wave or salute.

The three of them raised their hands and waved back before the dragon turtle disappeared under the water again and swam out of sight.

"He was a nice dragon turtle," Mika commented. "It's a shame he has to be alone."

Jace chuckled. "Good for us he was nice. That could have gone very, very bad had he not been as talkative."

"I'm sorry I was such a wreck out there," Diana said, breaking down into tears. "I didn't mean to run away. I just… I just… "The woman put her head into her hands and started crying.

Mika put her arms around the taller woman. "It's okay Diana. We are all afraid of something."

"I… I…" Diana sobbed. "I tried... to make... myself stay, but… I couldn't."

"It's fine," Jace said. "Everything worked out."

Colette cleared her throat. "Sorry captain, we're ready to set sail. What's our heading?"

"Nynymmost," he muttered.

"Aye, captain," she said and left to look at their charts.

It was a risk to go to the gnomish capital. Damian could be waiting for them. If he had interrogated any of the servants or intercepted the raven message to Charlena, he would know where they were headed.

Still, he really had no choice. He had told Charlena he could meet her there, and he needed to keep that promise. He hoped to talk to her, even if it were one last time, so he could explain what had happened. Let her know that he hadn't lied or tried to deceive her.

As the wind caught the sales and the ship lurched into motion, Jace just hoped Charlena would listen.

Chapter 16

Jace waited until the ship was well under way before bringing out the large treasure chest and popping it open. Given how heavy the chest was, he guessed there were thousands of gold inside.

"This isn't just the late captain's treasure," he called out to the crew. They were all staring at the chest and practically salivating over it. "It's partially the dragon turtle's treasure. I wouldn't expect this much loot from future endeavors, unless we hit a rich enemy merchant ship."

The crew muttered, but their attention was fixed on the chest. Calling over a wide-eyed Colette, Jace told her to divy up the gold between the crew. She nodded as she stared down at the treasure. "And make sure you take a double portion for yourself. If anyone objects, send them down to me. It won't take long for us to go back to the island and clear up any confusion with the dragon turtle."

"Aye, captain," she grinned and then began to shout out names of crewmen to come forward and get their share.

"While they're doing that, let's go down to our quarters," he told the girls.

Just as he was walking down the steps to go below deck, a black feathered bird landed on the railing. It looked at Jace and squawked. "Message delivered! Message delivered!"

Then the raven jumped into the sky and flew off. Jace looked to Diana and Mika and motioned them to follow him. Once they were all inside the captain's quarters, he shut the door and turned to face them.

By his calculations, it was Sunday in the real world. Assuming it took the bird a day to fly to them, that means she might have logged on yesterday, Saturday. Did that mean she hadn't logged in for a full week?

He was hurt that she had reacted the way she did. He was attracted to her and had thought they'd had some sort of relationship, but her anger and sudden disappearance had really thrown into question whether they had anything at all.

Part of him understood her reasoning for getting mad. She had thought he'd lied to her. But he would have thought she could at least have given him a chance to explain. He just didn't know what to think of her now.

"Does that mean what I think it means?" Diana asked as Jace bolted the door. He didn't really think any of the pirates would mess with them, but he wasn't taking a chance. The crew had their gold now. If ever there was a time for a mutiny, it was now.

"That was the raven returning, right?" Mika asked excitedly.

Jace nodded. "Yes, that was the raven returning and that means the message was delivered to Charlena. At least, I assume it was. I don't know if Damian has a way to intercept messages. Let's hope not, though the only thing it would have told him is where we're headed."

"That's a significant piece of information, wouldn't you say?" Diana raised an eyebrow.

"Yes," he agreed. "But I assume he's going to find that out. He knows where we were, Lasthaven, and if he asked around, I'm sure he'll find out the Sea Tyrant was headed to Nynymmost. And if not from Lasthaven, the servants will be back and he knows I'm a Baronet. If he questions them, they could tell him as well."

"Wonderful," Diana pouted. "So he's going to be waiting for us at Nynmmost?"

"I was always assuming he'd figure it out," Jace admitted. "But now, he may not know what ship we're arriving on. And even if he did, I wasn't planning to sail into the harbor with the rest of the ships. I plan to take a rowboat to shore a few miles from the city."

"So, we'll come by land instead of sea?" Diana asked.

Mika grinned. "He won't expect that!"

"Maybe not," Jace wasn't convinced. He knew Damian was devious. Jace had listened to him relay his exploits in and out of the game. The older programmer was certainly more devious than Jace. He had to assume that anything he thought of, Damian would think of as well. And that gave him an idea.

He looked at the two ladies across from him. "Let me ask you two this: If you needed to sneak into a city and you knew someone was going to try and catch you, how would you avoid being caught?"

That seemed to catch them off guard for a moment and they both looked thoughtful. Mika was the first one to offer a suggestion. "Sneak in the sewers!"

"Possible, but let's assume he has the thieves guild and assassin guild looking for us," he replied.

Mika frowned and scratched her head.

"We can't just disguise ourselves, right?" Diana asked. "The non-players will see through the disguises and the players will see our character names, right?"

"Sort of," Jace replied. "NPCs who have never met you will only see your appearance, except I think assassins or anyone following a bounty on you. NPCs who have met you before, will recognize you, even when disguised. Once they've met you, their recognition is based off of that unique player identifier instead of just appearance. But you are right about players. When they examine us in their HUD, we'll show up as ourselves."

"Hmm," Diana returned to looking thoughtful, tapping her finger against the side of her forehead.

The group thought about it through the night and into the next morning. When the sun would normally have broken over the eastern horizon, they still didn't have a good solution for remaining anonymous in the city. But that wasn't the worst of their problems.

The voyage had begun to get a little rough and Jace had been about to go check on what was happening on deck. Just as he unbarred the door, a sailor knocked. Opening the door, he saw the man swallow and start to stutter. "Uh, captain, Colette wants you up top. We got a storm coming."

Jace and the girls went topside, only to be soaked the moment they stepped out as a huge wave washed over the deck. The sky was dark with clouds and off in the distance, Jace saw lightning strike.

The boat was dipping and rising as they hit the waves or the waves hit them and Jace was forced to grab onto the railing to keep from being tossed around. Luna, upon getting hit by the first wave, scrambled back down the stairs and didn't return.

"Captain," Colette yelled from the helm. "We can't outrun the storm! I'm turning us into the waves!"

That seemed counterintuitive to Jace but since he didn't know anything about seamanship, let alone surviving a storm at sea, he trusted the woman to make the right decision.

"Aye," he called out. "Keep it turned into the waves!"

Jace wanted to go below deck, but he figured a captain's place was on the deck during a storm. He told the girls to go below deck. Diana quickly retreated back down the stairs, but Mika refused to leave his side.

"I stay with you!" she yelled over the storm.

He flashed her a smile just before another wave washed over him, drenching him in cold sea water. He pointed to the wheel where Colette was struggling to keep the ship turned into the storm.

The two of them kept a firm grasp on the slick rail as they climbed the stairs. The rocking of the boat and the waves threatened to throw them around the ship, if not completely overboard. If they did go over, he knew they'd be lost. The ship would never find them in this storm.

At the top of the stairs, Jace took Mika's hand and they staggered across the poop deck, towards the wheel.

"Go below!" yelled the first mate as she fought with the wheel.

"We're staying up here with you," he told her.

The woman looked like she was about to argue but the wheel bucked in her hands and she was forced to wrestle it back into position. "Tie yourselves down!"

Nodding, Jace saw that there were several lines dangling loose from grates in the deck. He grabbed two of the ropes and he and Mika tied themselves off. Then the two of them held onto the rails for dear life while the ship was tossed by the storm.

Three hours later, they were being tossed about by the storm when suddenly the ship dropped unexpectedly, knocking Jace, Mika and Colette to their backs. Slamming against the deck, Jace hit his head hard enough to see stars briefly but, thankfully, not hard enough to do actual damage.

Jace blinked his eyes. Then he blinked them again. He thought he must have hit his head harder than he thought because he was staring up at a clear blue sky. He slowly climbed to his feet and looked around.

Behind them was a wall of clouds or mist or something. Jace could barely make out churning waters only a few dozen yards away. Mika got to her feet too and looked around in wonder.

"We are safe?" she asked, looking at Jace.

"We're in the eye," growled the first mate, as she staggered to her feet. Then she raised her voice to a yell. "We're in the eye! We're in the eye! To the deck men! To the deck!"

Confused, Jace watched as sailors burst from below decks with weapons in hands while other sailors, who had tied themselves off to the masts and other parts of the ship began untying themselves.

He briefly wondered if they meant to perform a mutiny right here and now and dump their bodies overboard before sailing back into the storm. Then he saw the worried looks and the glances they were casting all about the ship. No, something else was going on.

He looked around the calm area they were in. It was a huge circular area devoid of any storm activity and it was huge. It had to be miles in diameter. And, he noticed, there was no wind at all. It was eerily quiet and still. Too quiet.

"Colette," he called out to her. "What's going on?"

"We're in the eye!" she yelled, working on the knot that held her to the wheel. "They always attack in the eye!"

"Attack?" Jace repeated scanning the area. "Who's going to attack?"

"Ninjen," Colette replied, her face ashen.

"The ninjen?" Jace asked. He'd never heard of anything called the ninjen. He wasn't even sure if it was a single creature or a race of creatures. He looked over and saw that Mika had gone pale.

"Do you know what ninjen are?" he asked her.

She nodded slowly. "In Japan, there are stories of the ninjen. They are white sea creatures shaped like a man. They come up and drown sailors and sink their ships. But… but they live in cold climates!"

"Close sister," Colette said, finally pulling out her dagger and cutting the rope. "They're white on the bottom, gray on the top. They're sharks with arms and legs."

Jace cast the first mate a dubious look. "Land sharks?"

"They don't actually look like sharks," the first mate rolled her eyes. "But they have two arms, two legs and bodies like men. Their head is roughly like a man's, but with black eyes and a huge mouth, lined with rows of teeth - like a shark. They can also use weapons like tridents and..."

The first mate broke off as an odd sound filled the air. It almost sounded like something boiling. Jace walked over to the railing and looked over. The ocean immediately around the ship was swirling and bubbling, almost like it was boiling.

"The water's boiling," Jace commented.

"No," Colette grimaced. "That's what the ninjen do. They work themselves into a frenzy - right before they attack!"

Chapter 17

A few minutes later, Jace realized what was happening. The water wasn't boiling, instead it was the movement of dozens of ninjen as they pushed the boat. At first, the boat only lurched slightly, but soon it was moving slowly towards the center of the peaceful part of the storm.

"Why are they…" Jace started to ask.

"Keeping us in the eye! So we can't escape!" Colette growled. Belatedly, she added. "Captain!"

The first mate was barking orders to the crew. Several of them disappeared below deck and returned with crates of weapons and pieces of armor. With practiced familiarity, the crew armed themselves. Once they had weapons, shields and a few armor pieces, they formed into small groups and positioned themselves around the ship.

Looking around at the various groups, Jace scanned them with his HUD. Nearly all were level 20, with some being a level or two higher or lower. Most of them had the pirate class. Yet, scattered here and there were crew members with the pirate tough class. He guessed pirate class was similar to rogue and pirate tough class was the fighter equivalent.

He scanned the formations and found that each three man group had one pirate tough and two pirates. That was one tank and two damage dealers. It wasn't a bad setup but Jace noticed they had no magical or healing support. In a prolonged fight, they wouldn't last long.

"Can you target the pirates as friendlies?" Jace asked, turning to Hiromi and Mika.

Both girls looked at him blankly.

He sighed. "Try casting a healing spell, but don't actually cast it, just see if you can target one of the pirates with it."

They nodded their understanding and then turned their attention to the groups of pirates. In a few moments they looked back. "Yes."

"Good." He smiled. "I want you two to keep the pirates up with your healing."

The two women looked confused. Mika looked between him and the pirates. "We will not be fighting as a group?"

He cast another glance down at the churning waters around the ship. They were almost to the center of the eye. "No, we need to keep the pirates up."

The girls looked at each other and then back at Jace but he held up a hand and motioned them to the back of the ship, away from the pirates.

"What are you going to be doing?" Mika demanded. Jace guessed she already knew his answer.

"If these things are level 20 or lower, I can solo them." He smiled. "If they're 30 or higher, we probably don't stand a chance anyway."

"We should be fighting as a team!" Mika pressed. He could see that she was worried for him.

"True," he agreed, but gestured towards the pirates and lowered his voice. "I agree with you but look around. We only have about 20 crew. I don't know how many we can afford to lose before we can't sail the ship. If we lose too many, we could end up stranded out here."

The girls looked around at the small groups of pirates and then back to Jace. Mika seemed about to object but Diana put a hand on her shoulder.

"We can heal the pirates and keep an eye on Jace," the older woman said. "Nothing says we can't do both."

Mika cocked her head and seemed to consider that before nodding. "Okay, we will do that. But if Jace needs healing, we heal him first."

"No objections from me," Diana replied and the two women gave Jace defiant looks, daring him to disagree.

He chuckled. "Alright! Alright! But focus on pirates unless I look like I'm in trouble. Remember, I still have some potions you got for me."

Mika grinned. "See! I knew they would be helpful!"

"Very," Jace replied.

Jace glanced over at Luna. She had gone to the edge of the railing and was looking down into the churning waters around the ship. She turned to look at Jace. "Fishes?!"

He considered her question. "Mean fishes! Big fishes!"

A predatory look came over her face but her voice was excited. "Big fishes?!"

"Very big," he told her, ignoring the chuckles from the girls.

"I think Jace will have all the help he needs," Diana said, laughing at the huge cat. "As long as Luna waits until the end of the fight to start eating them."

"Big fishes!" Luna agreed. "Eat big fishes!"

The ship reached the center of the eye. He could see by the clouds far above, that they were still moving, but the ninjen were keeping them in the dead center. He wondered how many there had to be in the water to keep the boat centered within the storm's eye.

"If we die," he said. "We'll meet back in Lasthaven. Don't go into the city. There was a road to the south, just outside the graveyard. Go about a mile down it and wait."

The girls nodded grimly. They already knew the stakes. They carried all their money on them, including the recently acquired gold from Bob's hoard. If they all died, they'd lose it all.

"If one or two of us die," he told them. "Don't forget to give loot rights to your body to the survivor."

"Morbid," Diana said but the older woman nodded.

Jace didn't hold out much hope that they would make it through this. There had to be at least a hundred of them down in the water if they were able to move a ship of this size. Looking around at the gathered pirates, he couldn't imagine them being able to hold off against so many.

"Prepare to repel boarders!" Colette yelled out as the churning slowed. "No mercy!"

"No mercy!" came the pirate's answering cry.

The first mate pulled out her own saber and a buckler and joined one of the groups near the center deck.

"Let's take our places," Jace told them. "You two stay at the main mast where your healing can reach everyone, and Luna and I will guard you."

Without another word, his group turned and hurried down the stairs and over to the main mast. There was an eerie, unnatural silence in the eye. It was a surreal contrast. Jace could see the raging storms all around them, but there was that strange quiet, and almost peace, that permeated the area around them. Only the sounds of the churning water and the creak of the ship broke that silence.

The silence lingered for a long moment. The calm before the proverbial storm. Then, without any warning, a dozen ninjen leaped out of the water and landed on the deck, tridents in hand. It was an impressive move and took the crew by surprise.

On the wall of his living room, with his retro items and old vidstream collection, Jace had a replica poster of an ancient vidstream called the Creature from the Dark Lagoon. It featured an green, aquatic humanoid who was able to come out of the water and attack people. He wondered if that creature had served as the inspiration for ninjen.

In shape, the things looked very much like that old vidstream character, but their mouths were much larger and filled with rows of sharp teeth. Not only that, but the creatures had lifeless eyes, all black, like a doll's eyes.

The ninjen were taller and more muscular than the humans who they now faced. Their skin was rough, like that of a shark and, like sharks, it was a darker gray color on their backs and their front were white. The creatures had humanoid looking hands but webbed and with only three fingers and a thumb.

In their webbed hands, each on of them held a long trident, which he guessed was the equivalent of the

Quickly, Jace examined them in his HUD.

Trench Dweller Warrior
Race: Ninjen
Class: Warrior Caste
Level: 25

Jace frowned at their level. It could have been much worse, but it was bad enough. Level 25 was higher than the average level of the crew. And there had to be dozens more of the ninjen still in the water. This wasn't a fight he thought they could win. But he wouldn't go down without a fight.

The shark-men bellowed a war cry and, with his *Monsterspeak* skill, Jace understood it. "Kill the land dwellers!"

Even as the ninjen moved forward to attack, Jace heard the crew calling out their *Taunts*, peeling one or two of them from the main group. There were seven groups of pirates, including the group Colette had joined. Each of the groups, except the first mate's group, had two ninjen on them.

Colette's group moved behind the ninjen at the nearest group and began to lay in on them with their cutlasses. Jace took the hint and did the same. He moved behind the closest one and struck it from the rear with both his weapons.

You Backstab Trench Dweller Warrior for 37 damage plus 18 acid damage.
You Backstab Trench Dweller Warrior for 7 damage.

As usual, the Kraken's Blade did more damage than the saber. Guessing by how little damage it did, he

169

guessed their shark skin must be tough enough that it provided natural armor and *Defense*. This was confirmed when Luna's attacks barely scratched them.

The ninjen was caught in the pirate tough's *Taunt* and didn't turn on Jace, which he found familiar. From years of playing Mordred, he was used to being the backstabbing damage dealer. It was nice to revisit that role.

While the two other pirates in the group focused on one of the creatures, Jace kept his focus on the one he'd attacked. Despite the fact that there were two pirates and both were higher level than him, Jace's ninjen fell first.

You have killed an ocean dwelling creature. You have unlocked Kraken's Claw's special ability: Slay Ocean Dwellers.
Kraken's Claw now does double damage against normal ocean dwelling creatures.
Kraken's Claw now does triple damage against stronger ocean dwelling creatures.

Jace read the new message and almost laughed aloud. Kraken's Claw had a special ability, on top of all its other abilities.

It was a slayer blade. A magical weapon that was created to fight a specific type of creature. There were dragon slayer blades, demon slayer blades and a host of other types of slaying weapons.

If he read it correctly, it would double his damage against regular ocean enemies and triple the damage against boss enemies. He'd never owned a slayer before and finding that he had one gave him a fresh boost of energy.

The sword began to thrum in his hand and he could now feel its need for the blood of these ocean creatures. He felt the saber almost pull him towards them, hungry for their lives. It wanted to be fed - like Luna, he thought. In this case, he was all too happy to oblige it.

Grinning evilly, Jace turned to the next ninjen. It was time to see what this slayer blade could do. With the thrumming sword in his hand, he showed the shark-men no mercy.

Chapter 18

Jace decided slayer blades were awesome! With the double damage, he was able to kill a level 25 ninjen with only two or three backstabs. Moving from group to group, he helped to quickly eliminate the remaining shark-men, earning himself level 11 in rogue.

When the last ninjen collapsed on the deck, the pirates let out a cheer. Jace could see several pirates were down. He guessed the girls' healing hadn't been able to keep up with the damage the shark-men had done with their tridents. While they were cheering, Jace checked out his new level.

Level 11 gave him 8 more health and 4 more mana, which were both welcome. It also gave him the opportunity to switch to the Swashbuckler prestige class he'd unlocked. Jace wished he would have been able to do some research on what it did before switching but in the end, it was a prestige class. It was more, theoretically at least, more powerful than any of the base classes and even more powerful than the premium classes. He crossed his fingers and brought up his HUD.

Class changed. New class Swashbuckler.
Adaptable: No experience penalty for fourth class.
You have gained a new skill: Fencing
You have gained a new skill: Parry

Ability gained: Disarm
Ability gained: Panache

Jace frowned. Somehow, he'd expected more abilities or more skills. Of course, he already had dozens of skills from his other classes and he couldn't receive the same skill twice. But at the same time, classes rarely award two abilities at once.

He was surprised by the *Disarm* ability. He knew certain monsters, like kroakers, could disarm players, but he didn't know any player classes that gave the ability. It was both a great and a limited ability. Some monsters didn't use weapons and therefore couldn't be disarmed. But he could see if being very helpful against any players. Plus, they wouldn't be expecting it.

The *Fencing* skill was a complete mystery. He knew what fencing was in the real world but wasn't sure what the skill did in-game. Would he learn Bonetti's *Defense*, so he could use it on rocky ground. Or may he'd learn how to attack with Capo Ferro or cancel it with Thibault. He grinned. Who knew, maybe he'd need to study some Agrippa.

The *Parry* skill was another skill like *Block* or *Dodge* and would prevent damage, but like *Block*, which required a shield, *Parry* required a weapon in your hand to work. Once he ranked it up, the *Parry* skill would be a third way for him to avoid getting hit.

Then he remembered the *Panache* ability. Given the name, it sounded like something unique to the Swashbuckler class. But that didn't tell him what it did. He brought it up in his HUD.

Panache
Swashbuckler Ability
***Description: Your flamboyant style and confidence
in your own skill allows you to strike a second time
with a single, one-handed weapon.***
***Note: This ability cannot function when holding a
weapon in your secondary hand and therefore cannot
stack with Two-weapon Fighting.***

Jace whistled and slipped his second saber into
its scabbard. It appeared he no longer needed it to get
two attacks. He could now attack twice with his main
weapon. He grinned broadly. That meant Kraken's Claw
would get two strikes instead of one.

A dozen more ninjen leaped onto the deck.
Sailors swore as they quickly got back into their
positions and began shouting out their *Taunts* at the
new wave of enemies. The groups who had lost one of
their members combined themselves with one of the
other groups. This left them only four groups.

Jace moved back to the girls, who were still
around the mast. "How's your mana?"

Mika gave him a pained expression. "I am
almost out of mana. I can't keep up with the damage
they're doing."

Diana nodded after completing a healing spell
aimed at one of the pirate toughs. "Same here."

"Do the best you can," he told them. "I think I
just got a major power boost by switching to
Swashbuckler."

"Cool!" Mika said and Diana gave him a smile.

"Come on, Luna," he told the giant cat. "Let's kill some fish people!"

"Yes," she agreed.

The two of them jumped into the fray and Jace's new *Panache* ability helped to bring down the new wave of more quickly that he would have thought possible. When the last of the new wave was down, the crew once again cheered. But this time, they were cheering for him.

"Captain! Captain!" they chanted and Jace wanted to feel good, but he saw that they'd lost another tank. He hadn't been fast enough.

He checked his log and saw that he was already level 3 in Swashbuckler and rank 9 in *Fencing*. Was it fighting with one weapon that raised the skill? Or perhaps fighting with a piercing weapon? He didn't know but, in one more rank, hopefully he'd get an ability from hitting rank 10.

Then a third wave came leaping on board. The ninjen attacking in waves didn't make any sense from a tactical standpoint when they could have all just rushed onboard and overwhelmed the pirates easily. It was the game AI doing its job and giving them a fighting chance.

Having played the game for years, he knew how the game AI influenced things in specific ways to make certain aspects - especially combat - more game-like than realistic. If his past experiences were a guide, then they'd fight this last wave and then a boss would appear.

At least, that's what would happen in a normal group encounter. There would be waves of lower level "trash" monsters, followed by a boss of some sort. Even raids worked the same way, just at a much more difficult level.

Pushing his thoughts away, he joined in the combat and began hewing down the attacking shark-men as quickly as possible. He was trying to alternate between the last three groups, but he saw another of the pirate toughs go down. He swore. He hoped this was the last wave or there wouldn't be any of their tanks left.

Finally, the last of the third wave fell dead. Jace looked around at what remained of his crew. They'd lost eight pirates. Almost half. Did they have enough to make it to port? Or for that matter, make it out of the storm?

Checking his log quickly, he saw that he had earned a new ability called Lunge at *Fencing* rank 10. He hurriedly glanced at the description.

Lunge
Fencing: 10
Cost: 4 mana
Description: You lunge forward up to 10 feet, inflicting a stabbing wound with your weapon which does double damage.
Note: Can only be used when wielding a single weapon.

He wondered if it stacked with other damaging abilities, like Critical Eye. But he had no time to ponder those questions as he heard a huge splash and a thud behind him.

Turning, he came face to face with a giant ninjen. It looked like the others, but about a foot taller and had been taking steroids. Not only that, but it wore some sort of shell armor. With all the shells, the creature looked silly but Jace didn't feel like laughing. He examined the new monster.

Trench Dweller Frenzy Leader (Legendary)
Race: Ninjen
Class: Warrior Caste
Level: 30

He swore loudly. The thing was a boss alright. And not even a mini-boss, but a full-fledged legendary boss. And it was level 30. Jace swore and cast his *Air Armor*. This was going to be painful, even with his new abilities and Kraken's Blade. Level 30 armor would be impossible for his normal weapon to pierce. Even Kraken's Claw was going to have a tough time since it was only level 10.

Then there was it's weapon. The huge trident it held had to be level 30 as well. A level 30 spear was going to do a ton of damage since it was a two-handed weapon. Of course, Jace suddenly had a way to take the trident out of the picture.

"Any mana left?" he called out to the girls.

"A little," they both said.

"Try to keep me up!" he said and then shouted his *Taunt*. "Get over here!"

The Frenzy Leader rushed him, trident leading the way. Jace waited until it got close and then burned 4 mana to do a *Disarm* attempt.

His arm suddenly went through a series of circular movements and the leader's trident went flying. The surprised leader stared after its trident as the thing went flying up in the air.

Jace didn't hesitate but used the opportunity to *Feint* and then thrust at the enormous shark-man.

You critically hit Trench Dweller Frenzy Leader for 44 damage plus 54 acid damage.
Your Fencing skill has increased by 1.
You critically hit Trench Dweller Frenzy Leader for 45 damage plus 54 acid damage.
Your Fencing skill has increased by 1.

The blows hurt the creature, especially the acid. But even with the slayer ability, the shell armor took most of the force out of his strikes. Luckily, fighting a boss almost guaranteed skill ups and he gained a few more ranks in *Fencing*.

Diana saved her mana for healing and Mika's katana couldn't puncture the creature's armor. Unfortunately, neither of them were going to do much against this thing. Neither could Luna. Her teeth and claws were no match for such a high level monster.

"Stay back," he told them. "And use your mana to heal me!"

Diana nodded but Mika pouted and looked down at her katana. Meanwhile, the boss recovered quickly and slashed at Jace with two claws and then lurched forward and bit him.

Trench Dweller Frenzy Leader claws at YOU for 0 damage.
Trench Dweller Frenzy Leader claws at YOU for 0 damage.
Trench Dweller Frenzy Leader bites at YOU for 0 damage.

The claws didn't appear to have the power to penetrate his *Defense,* but the bite was another matter. Jace's armor had deflected the blow but those rows of teeth would do some serious damage if they locked down on him.

Feinting, Jace performed his own attack.

You critically hit Trench Dweller Frenzy Leader for 47 damage plus 54 acid damage.
Your Fencing skill has increased by 1.
You critically hit Trench Dweller Frenzy Leader for 32 damage plus 54 acid damage.
Your Fencing skill has increased by 1.

Kraken's Claw was doing decent damage but despite it's odd appearance, the shell armor was incredibly resilient and blocked much of his damage. The Frenzy Leader reared back and struck again.

Trench Dweller Frenzy Leader claws at YOU for 0 damage.
Trench Dweller Frenzy Leader claws at YOU for 0 damage.
Trench Dweller Frenzy Leader bites at YOU for 0 damage.

As before, it's blows bounced off his *Defense*, but he knew it was only a matter of time before those teeth sank into him. He attacked again, *Feinting* and following up with two lightning fast thrusts to the thing's torso.

You critically hit Trench Dweller Frenzy Leader for 41 damage plus 54 acid damage.
Your Fencing skill has increased by 1.
You critically hit Trench Dweller Frenzy Leader for 47 damage plus 54 acid damage.
Your Fencing skill has increased by 1.

Ability gained: Precision Strike

Trench Dweller Frenzy Leader goes into a Blood Frenzy.

Jace's *Fencing* skill had hit the maximum of rank 20 for his level and he'd received the *Precision Strike* ability. While the ability seemed intriguing, Jace had no time to look at the actual verbiage at the moment. The boss had just activated its special ability.

Trench Dweller Frenzy Leader bites at YOU for 4 damage.
You are Bleeding.
Trench Dweller Frenzy Leader bites at YOU for 0 damage.
Trench Dweller Frenzy Leader bites at YOU for 5 damage.
You are Bleeding.
Trench Dweller Frenzy Leader bites at YOU but you Dodge.

Trench Dweller Frenzy Leader bites at YOU for 8 damage.
You are Bleeding.
Trench Dweller Frenzy Leader bites at YOU for 6 damage.
You are Bleeding.

The creature went berserk and began biting at Jace over and over again. A couple of the bites didn't penetrate but the others did, ripping into his arm and shoulder. He felt the teeth penetrating his skin and wanted to cry out.

This was the boss' special ability. And it was a nasty one. He looked to the girls for some healing even as he bit down on his lip to stop himself from crying out in pain.

Determined to end this fight as quickly as he could, Jace *Feinted* and prepared to attack. That's when he saw a message he'd never seen before.

Trench Dweller Frenzy Leader is immune to Feint while in Blood Frenzy.

It was immune to *Feint*?! Jace swore. He'd used *Feint* as his vampyre assassin, and he couldn't remember a creature being immune to it. This fight just got a lot more interesting - and deadly.

Chapter 19

Surprised by the turn in events, Jace attacked the ninjen using his normal attack. At least *Panache* still worked!

YOU Bleed for 9 damage.
You pierce Trench Dweller Frenzy Leader for 17 damage plus 18 acid damage.
You pierce Trench Dweller Frenzy Leader for 15 damage plus 18 acid damage.

Trench Dweller Frenzy Leader goes into a Blood Frenzy.

The creature's earlier attacks had taken a good chunk of his health. Too many more of those and he'd be done for.

Then, just before the ninjen hit him with another series of attacks, two healing spells washed over him.

Diana Knightly heals YOU for 7 health.
Mika Knightly heals YOU for 5 health.

Trench Dweller Frenzy Leader bites at YOU but you Parry.
Your Parry skill has increased by 1.
Trench Dweller Frenzy Leader bites at YOU but you Dodge.

Trench Dweller Frenzy Leader bites at YOU but you Block.
You are Bleeding.
Trench Dweller Frenzy Leader bites at YOU for 6 damage.
You are Bleeding.
Trench Dweller Frenzy Leader bites at YOU for 0 damage.
Trench Dweller Frenzy Leader bites at YOU for 0 damage.

Once again, the flurry of bites penetrated his *Defense*, and he felt them shredding his body as the thing attacked over and over again. He noticed that he *Dodged* and *Blocked* several blows but also deflected one of the blows with his sword using *Parry*. He'd take whatever help he could get.

This time, he didn't bother with *Feint*. Instead, he used *Vanish* and rolled behind the creature. Apparently, *Backstab* worked just fine on the frenzied creature.

YOU Bleed for 9 damage.
You Backstab Trench Dweller Frenzy Leader for 34 damage plus 54 acid damage.
You Backstab Trench Dweller Frenzy Leader for 36 damage plus 54 acid damage.

The ninjen boss hissed and spun around, jaws snapping at him. This time its teeth found purchase and it rend his flesh multiple times, dropping him well under half his health.

Diana Knightly heals YOU for 9 health.
Mika Knightly heals YOU for 7 health.

Trench Dweller Frenzy Leader bites at YOU for 8 damage.
You are Bleeding.
Trench Dweller Frenzy Leader bites at YOU for 5 damage.
You are Bleeding.
Trench Dweller Frenzy Leader bites at YOU for 4 damage.
You are Bleeding.
Trench Dweller Frenzy Leader bites at YOU for 0 damage.
Trench Dweller Frenzy Leader bites at YOU for 7 damage.
You are Bleeding.
Trench Dweller Frenzy Leader bites at YOU but you Parry.
Your Parry skill has increased by 1.

Jace pushed down the pain and used his *Vanish* again. Rolling behind the creature once more, he thrust out twice with the Kraken's Claw at the ninjen's back.

YOU Bleed for 9 damage.
You Backstab Trench Dweller Frenzy Leader for 49 damage plus 54 acid damage.
You Backstab Trench Dweller Frenzy Leader for 33 damage plus 54 acid damage.

Trench Dweller Frenzy Leader goes into a Blood Frenzy.

As the creature spun at him, he produced a healing potion from his inventory in his free hand and drank it down.

You use Mild Crimson Potion.
Mild Crimson Potion restores 15 health.

He thought the creature might be down to 25% because of the Blood Frenzy message but he wasn't sure. Not that it mattered, since the creature was still using its special attack.

Diana Knightly heals YOU for 10 health.

Trench Dweller Frenzy Leader bites at YOU for 0 damage.
Trench Dweller Frenzy Leader bites at YOU for 7 damage.
You are Bleeding.
Trench Dweller Frenzy Leader bites at YOU for 6 damage.
You are Bleeding.
Trench Dweller Frenzy Leader bites at YOU for 0 damage.
Trench Dweller Frenzy Leader bites at YOU for 0 damage.
Trench Dweller Frenzy Leader bites at YOU but you Dodge.

The bites hurt but Jace stayed focused and used his *Vanish/Backstab* combination. The potion and healing had helped his health, but he needed to hurry and finish this boss off.

YOU Bleed for 9 damage.
You Backstab Trench Dweller Frenzy Leader for 37 damage plus 54 acid damage.
You Backstab Trench Dweller Frenzy Leader for 41 damage plus 54 acid damage.

The Frenzy Leader suddenly began frothing at the mouth and Jace wasn't sure what he should do, so he used his *Evade*. The ability had upgraded to *Evade II* once he hit rank 20 in *Dodge*. It would now protect him against directed magical or special attacks, but if the thing exploded, it wouldn't help.

Without warning, the thing launched itself at him with inhuman speed with its mouth wide open, aiming for his head. Jace blurred to his left a moment before the jaws snapped shut on where his head and neck had just been.

Trench Dweller Frenzy Leader uses Decapitating Bite but you Evade.

Both angry and relieved that he had almost been decapitated, he used his *Vanish* to slip behind the creature and stab his blades into the ninjen's back. He wasn't sure if the special attack would have decapitated him, but it would most likely have done a ton of damage. Probably enough to kill him.

YOU Bleed for 9 damage.
You Backstab Trench Dweller Frenzy Leader for 39 damage plus 54 acid damage.
You Backstab Trench Dweller Frenzy Leader for 44 damage plus 54 acid damage.

The thing staggered and turned around towards him, so Jace used his new *Lunge* ability.

You Lunge at Trench Dweller Frenzy Leader for 97 damage plus 72 acid damage.
Trench Dweller Frenzy Leader dies.

You gain 1200 experience.

Kraken's Claw had pierced through the armor and into the center of the thing's chest. The ninjen leader looked down at its chest and then its eyes rolled back into its head revealing white. The thing collapsed to his knees and as Jace slid his blade from it, fell face forward onto the deck.

A mighty cheer went up from the pirates who came over and hoisted him onto their shoulders and began carrying him around the deck. He wasn't sure what else to do, so he let them take him around several times before they ended up in front of Colette.

"Well done, captain." She smiled. But then the ship lurched, and she slid her cutlass into its sheath. "They've let the boat go! To your stations! To your stations!"

She was right. Jace could feel the ship drifting now and he hurried over to the railing. Looking down, there was no sign of the ninjen. With the death of the leader, they'd retreated into the depths. For now, at least.

The eye was moving west with the storm, so they headed east and back into the storm. Jace ran around and looted all the corpses, getting a handful of small pearls from the regular ninjen. He guessed they were worth a few hundred gold and every little bit helped.

The leader yielded a large black pearl that was probably worth several thousand gold. He found the trident he'd disarmed from the boss and was about to give up when he remembered that sharks, and perhaps ninjen, ate almost anything. Taking Kraken's Claw, he split open the creature's belly and hoped he wasn't dirtying the deck for nothing.

Trident of the Trench
Type: Spear
Level: 30
Damage: 42 + 9 (Sharp)
Wt: 6 lb
Special: When held, granted the holder the ability to breathe underwater. When used underwater, this trident can summon a school of fish to confuse your opponent.
Description: Created in the depths of the ocean through dark ninjen rituals, these tridents are given to the Frenzy Leaders of the Leader Cast.

Sabatons of the Dire Boar
Type: Foot Armor
Level: 30
Armor: 12 + 9 (Masterwork) + 9 (Sturdy)
Wt: 6 lb
Special: Grants the ability Charge Attack for 4 mana. If the wearer already has the Charge Attack ability, these boots reduce the cost by 2 mana.
Description: Worn by Lord Fardsquon, a necromancer who loved the hunt, on his last hunting expedition, these boots were created accidentally when Fardsquon was gored just as he cast a spell. The spell pulled the soul of the dire boar into the boots but the tusks still gored the necromancer through the neck.

Helpful Haversack of Holding
Type: Miscellaneous
Level: 1
Wt: 5 lbs

Special: The haversack doubles your carrying capacity and retains all items inside itself, rather than in your actual inventory.
Description: Created by the gnomish wizard Helybeck Berrypitch for her many travels, it was lost at sea when a dragon mistook her airship for a mate. Hellybeck and the Haversack were never seen again.
Note: Cannot be used to hold living creatures.

Helpful Haversack of Holding is a Soulbound item.
Do you wish to permanently bind this item to your character? (Yes or No)
Warning: This action cannot be undone.

Jace grinned like an idiot as he picked up the Haversack. It was a magical bag, capable of holding his inventory inside itself! Because it was soulbound, it would reappear with him. They no longer had to worry about losing their money. They could just put it in the haversack and if he died, it would appear with him.

Unfortunately, it wouldn't do anything for the items the girls normally carried with them, like their armor and weapons, but at least their money would be safe. Not to mention his own inventory. If he carried as much as possible, they wouldn't have to worry about losing things as much.

The ship was only a few minutes from re-entering the storm, so he quickly answered in the affirmative and the haversack was his.

Helpful Haversack of Holding has been bound.
You received Helpful Haversack of Holding.

There didn't appear to be anything else in the creature's stomach and he turned his attention to the sabatons and the trident. Both were interesting items. Unfortunately, both items were also level 30. None of them could use them for some time.

He placed them both into the Haversack, along with the other items he'd collected. He looked back at the body and saw that Luna had the leader's body by the arm and was trying to drag it down below deck.

"What are you doing?" he asked the cat.

Luna glanced up at him but didn't release her hold on the ninjen. Her voice came through in his mind. "Fish!"

He raised an eyebrow. "You're going to eat that thing?"

"Big fish!" Her excited voice answered.

He looked towards the front of the ship and saw that they were about to re-enter the storm and he wasn't tied down. He started towards Colette and Mika up at the wheel and just shook his head at Luna as she resumed pulling the dead body of the leader down below deck.

"Go ahead," he sent to her. "You earned it."

He ran up the stairs and grabbed a rope that Mika tossed to him. She smiled at him. "Find good stuff?"

He was about to answer when the ship was suddenly tossed around as the storm closed around them. The fury of the returning storm drowned out his reply.

Chapter 20

It took them nearly two hours for the ship to leave the storm. The girls had retreated down to the captain's quarters, leaving Jace up top to ride out the storm's fury. Tied to the mast, it was actually sort of fun. Like a long amusement park ride.

When they finally had calmer seas, Colette checked some charts and told him they were almost a half day off-course. She also informed him that with over a third of the crew dead, it was going to take even longer.

"But that's not the worst of it, captain," she said. He noticed that since the fight, all the crew responded to him as captain. Apparently, he'd earned their respect. "The storm's done us some damage, as well as those blasted ninjen."

That got his attention. Jace suddenly had visions of the ship sinking and he and the crew floating in the ocean until one by one they were pulled under by ninjen. He shuddered. "How bad is it?"

"The main mast is damaged and I won't risk full sails until we have it properly looked at," she said. "That'll make us even slower and we won't be able to outrun anything if we catch its fancy. The ship was sluggish in the storm and we could have some damage to the keel. But that would take a dry docks to check. There might be some hull damage too from those ninjen. I don't think they were just pushing. I think some of them might have been chopping. I can't be sure and no one is willing to jump into the water and take a look underneath after those ninjen."

"Will we make it to Nynymmost?" Jace asked, trying to hide his concern.

The first mate looked around at the ship and then leveled her gaze back at Jace. "Maybe. Probably. But it will be slow going. Very slow."

Jace frowned. He felt like she was working up to something and he was getting impatient. "Do you have a recommendation number one?"

"As a matter of fact, I do." Colette smiled broadly. "We could make port at Haddare Reef. It's a day or a day and a half's journey with our current speed."

"Haddare Reef?" Jace raised an eyebrow. He guessed it was an island, but other than that, he'd never heard of the place.

The first mate pointed north west. "It's the largest of a small chain of islands to the northwest. It's a pirate city. We can dock there and make repairs, resupply and possibly recruit some new crew members."

"A pirate city?" he asked. He wasn't sure about the logic of going into a town of cutthroats when he was a wanted man. Assuming Damian had put out another contract on him, he'd be cut down as soon as he set foot off the ship.

"Yes," she said. "Old Blackmane runs it. Calls it neutral ground. Pirates who make port operate under a white flag."

"A white flag? So, what does that mean?" Jace asked.

"It means no piracy or other illicit activities on the island," she replied. "It's a safe haven for pirates." She smirked at him. "And privateers."

Jace wondered if that included assassinations. Even if it did, would the assassin's guild abide by it? If not, and an assassin was waiting for him, he might be giving his location away to Damian. And on an island, with a damaged ship, he wouldn't be fleeing in a hurry.

The alternative wasn't pleasant either. If the Wyvern's Tail was as badly damaged as Colette said, then they're voyage would take longer. That meant they could run into another storm, other pirates or even some sort of sea monster and they'd be in no shape to outrun them or outfight them.

"Fine," he relented. "Let's set course for Haddare Reef."

"Aye-aye, captain," she said and began barking orders.

Knowing he was no longer needed, Jace stepped back against the railing and finally took a moment to relax. He knew he'd leveled up several times throughout the fight, but he hadn't had the time to review what that meant. Bringing up his HUD, he looked at his new level.

Swashbuckler: 6

Not bad. But the first few levels were easy, especially when you were killing level 25 monsters and level 30 bosses. Next, he looked through his log to see if he had received any class abilities.

Scrolling through the messages, he finally found what he was looking for. He had gained a new ability at level 5.

Ability gained: Bladed Defense I

Bladed Defense I
Swashbuckler Ability
Description: Swashbucklers are masters of a one handed blade. When using a single weapon, they gain an Armor bonus of their Swashbuckler level.

Jace read over the ability again and smiled. One more way for him to gain *Defense*. At the moment, at level 6 in Swashbuckler, it was 6 points of armor. That equated to a single point of *Defense*, but every little bit helped.

He looked at his character sheet. He'd come a long way since starting off in Sinking Springs. Of course, none of his stats had changed and none of the armor he wore now were boosting them.

Brawn: 10
Agility: 10
Hardiness: 10

Intellect: 10
Piety: 10
Personality: 10

He knew that stats were the hardest thing in the game to boost and purposefully so. It gave the racial bonuses more impact over the longer term. He looked at his class list next.

Swashbuckler: 6 (Current)
Fighter: 4
Rogue: 11
Mage: 10

He chuckled to himself as he looked at all of the classes. Jace wasn't used to seeing so many classes. Because the other races received a 25% experience penalty for each class past the first, few people had more than one premium class and one prestige class. He knew of some people who had an extra prestige class, but it was extremely rare. The sheer amount of experience needed at the higher levels became prohibitive.

Next, he checked his new Swashbuckler skills.

Fencing: 20
Parry: 2

Fencing seemed to increase as long as he was using a single weapon, which he found interesting. And the skill had given him two new abilities, one at rank 10 and another when he'd hit rank 20.

Lunge

Precision Strike

He brought up the description for *Precision Strike*.

Precision Strike
Fencing: 20
Cost: 8 mana
Duration: 1 minute
Description: You can enter a state of focused concentration where your strikes are so precise, they bypass a creature's Defense for a short time.
Note: Can only be used when wielding a single weapon.

He wished he would have had time to read the skill description during the fight. Precision Strike would have been great against the frenzy leader. The cost was high for a rank 20 ability, but considering that it bypassed all *Defense*, it could prove very useful.

Next, Jace reviewed the abilities he'd received from Swashbuckler so far.

Disarm
Panache
Bladed Defense I

The abilities were much better than his normal class abilities, which was to be expected. But the class really seemed to want him to fight with one weapon. That was the limitation of the prestige class. With great power, came great limitations. Having already seen the other abilities, he examined *Disarm*.

Disarm

Swashbuckler Ability
Description: A special attack against an opponent's weapon that causes it to go flying.
Note: This ability cannot function when holding a weapon in your secondary hand and therefore cannot stack with Two-weapon Fighting.

It was like his assassin prestige class. It gave him extra abilities and skills, but he had to only use daggers. At first it had been a hindrance, since normally, a rogue class would be using sabers, since they did the most damage of any one-handed piercing weapon. Gradually, the class abilities allowed him to do more and more damage with daggers to the point where he could out damage most rogues using sabers.

He closed his character sheet and looked at his inventory. He had the haversack now and he needed to take advantage of it. He moved all of his gold and the items he didn't use all the time to the haversack. When he'd done that, Jace felt a sense of relief that his money and items were safe if something were to happen to him.

With the sailors bustling to get the ship ready to sail, he decided to go below deck to check on the girls. When he arrived, he found Luna sprawled out on the bed and the girls sitting in the two chairs.

"She ate the whole thing!" Mika grinned as he came in.

"The what?" he asked, confused.

"The ninjen," she replied. "Luna ate it all!"

Jace remembered the ninjen leader the cat had dragged down below deck and looked around. There was no sign of it and luckily no remains of it either. He looked over his familiar, sleeping on the bed and nodded. He was impressed she had been able to eat the entire thing. It made no logical sense how she could do that, but it was a game after all.

Then he noticed the two large chests on either side of the bed.

"They were starting to chafe," Diana complained.

"Having those in our inventory caused our stamina to go down very quickly during the fight," Mika nodded. "If we had been fighting instead of just casting spells, we would have run out."

Jace grinned. "I think I have a solution for that!" He pulled the haversack out and showed it to them.

They stared uncomprehendingly at the small leather backpack. Diana furrowed her brows. "It's… a backpack."

"It's a magical haversack!" He smiled. "It can hold the chests and still only weighs 5 lbs. And… it's soulbound. Which…"

"Oh," beamed Mika. "That means we won't lose it if we all die!"

"Wait," Diana looked confused. "You're saying you can put all of this stuff in your haversack and if something happens to you, the haversack appears with you?"

"Like his sword." Mika nodded.

"His sword?" Diana raised an eyebrow.

"It's soulbound too," he said. "Just like your signet rings. They appear with you when you die."

"Oh…" Diana smacked her head lightly. "Is that what that means? That makes a lot of sense now."

Mika and Jace chuckled and Diana rolled her eyes. "It's not like I played this game before, you know."

"Good point," Jace said. He indicated himself and Mika. "If there's things you don't understand, feel free to ask either of us."

"I will remember that," the older woman said and then looked around the cabin. "We're moving again. Are we back on course for the gnome capital?"

Jace shook his head. "No. The ship was damaged, and we have to stop at a pirate haven called Haddare Reef and do some repairs and take on some more crew."

"A pirate haven?" Diana asked.

"It's some special pirate place where no one's allowed to do any thievery or piracy." He shrugged. "At least, that's what Colette says."

"A pirate haven where pirates can't be pirates?" Diana questioned skeptically. "Seems fishy."

At the mention of fish, Luna lifted her head and looked around. Seeing no fish in sight, she sniffed the air. After a moment, she settled back down and closed her eyes.

"I'm not sure if we have a choice," he replied, remembering Colette's words. "From what she tells me, we're limping along out here. Easy pickings for anything that comes along - pirates, sea monsters or even another attack from the ninjen."

Diana held up her hands in a gesture of surrender. "Fine! Fine! You had me at sea monsters."

"Tell us about Swashbuckler!" Mika said. "You said you switched. What can it do?"

Both girls looked at him expectantly. He smiled and sat down on the bed next to Luna. The cat opened one eye and, seeing it was him, closed it again. Jace stroked the cat's fur as he explained the various abilities and limitations of his new prestige class.

Chapter 21

They limped into the Haddare Reef just before sunset on Midweek, which was Wednesday in the real world. Thoughts of the real world made Jace think of Charlena and he wondered if she was okay. She'd gotten his raven message. But would she meet him in Nynymmost?

He wanted to explain things to her. Jace didn't like the way they'd left things when she told him about his body in the real world. He'd been too shocked at learning that he wasn't in a medical pod to say anything before she had logged out. Now, he thought he knew what was going on and he just wanted the chance to tell her.

A shouted command from Colette snapped him back to the present and he looked out at town they were approaching. He'd asked the first mate if the town had a name, but she had only shrugged and told him everyone just called it Haddare Reef, since it was the only town on the island.

It was a town unlike any he had seen. What he considered the main part of town was flush against the slope of the large volcano which seemed to take up most of the island. The buildings were of all styles, from something that looked like a stone house of the dwarves to a collection of Tudor type buildings.

Whoever had settled on the island had kept their unique racial or regional flavor when designing their homes or businesses. Because of this, the town was a jumbled collection of every culture Jace could remember seeing in-game, as well as some he hadn't.

Then there was the secondary part of the town, or as Jace was calling it to himself, the water town. At some point, the town must have run out of space and the residents began building on the docks. When those docks became full of houses, inns and taverns, they built more docks and started the cycle all over.

Now, there were hundreds of yards of these water homes and businesses, some of which were several stories tall. And the town hadn't stopped growing. He saw docks and buildings that were currently under construction.

"Nothing like it," Colette said as she smiled out at the town.

Jace nodded. "You can say that again."

"It's a special place," she said. "Every type of people, every type of food, every type of everything!"

Looking out at the huge diversity of architecture, Jace couldn't help but agree with her. Already, his nose was picking up on some interesting, and even familiar, smells. Even though he didn't need to eat to survive, after eating the pickled or dried fish, he couldn't wait to taste something else.

The first mate barked out more orders and the ship pulled alongside a large dock. Feeling the ship being tied down, Diana, Mika and Luna came up on deck. He watched their faces as they caught their first glimpse of the strange town.

"This is wonderful," Mika said, her eyes darting around all the different buildings. "So much to explore!"

Diana shrugged, a look of disdain on her face... "Looks like a good place to get your throat cut."

"If you're not careful." Colette laughed. "But it's not as bad as you think."

The crew and the men on the dock quickly secured the ship to the dock and then the gangplank was lowered. In the past, the crew had rushed off the ship as soon as possible. Yet instead of rushing down the plank, everyone waited.

Confused, Jace looked to the first mate. "Are we waiting for something?"

"Oh yes, the boys are anxious to go spend their share of the treasure." Colette nodded grimly. "But no one enters the city without Blackmane's permission. It's like asking permission to come aboard."

Jace looked around the dock for any sort of welcoming committee or official looking person but saw nothing but the dockworkers. "Shouldn't there be an official here?"

Colette rolled her eyes. "This isn't Whitecliff. There are no officials. Blackmane himself greets every ship."

"One man?" Jace gave her a dubious look. "Greets every single ship that comes in?"

"Just the ones that dock," she said pointing to the dozens of ships moored in the cove. As he watched, he could see one of the ships lowering a boat full of men.

"So," Diane cut in, "if you actually put in at the dock, you have to wait for Blackmane to clear you. But if you stay out there and boat people onto shore, you don't need to be cleared."

"Aye," she confirmed.

Jace, Diana and Mika all exchanged puzzled glances but then Jace just shrugged. It was a pirate town with pirate rules. He wasn't going to look for logic where there was none.

"So, we just wait here until Mr. Blackmane shows up?" Mika asked.

"Just Blackmane," Colette corrected. "And yes. If we went ashore before getting permission, no one will service us. No one crosses Blackmane."

"Who is this mysterious Blackmane?" Diana wondered aloud.

The first mate turned around to face them. "He's the oldest and richest pirate in these waters. After he retired from piracy, he built a mansion here on the island and entertained guests. Some of the guests stayed and soon, the entire place sprung up around him."

A thought suddenly struck Jace. "Is there black market here?"

"Of course." The first mate looked at him as if he were a child. "That was the first and only market here for years. But over the years, more and more people have called this home. Now there is a real market here as well."

Jace smiled and turned to the girls. "We need to get you both some upgraded gear."

"Oh." Diana purred. "Shopping. That's my idea of a good time."

"Fish?" Luna looked up at them hopefully.

"Didn't you have enough fish after eating that frenzy leader?" he asked her.

Luna just continued to stare at him without saying a word. He understood that must be a negative reply.

"We'll see what we can do," he told his familiar. He looked around. "Once we can finally get off this ship."

Two hours later, Blackmane finally appeared on the deck. The first thing Jace noticed was that he was a werelion. He was at least seven-feet-tall and dressed in a long jacket, shirt and wearing a large tricorn hat. And, of course, the werelion had a thick, black mane.

The huge creature stalked up onto the ship and stopped just before stepping onto the ship. "Permission to come aboard."

Colette and the crew looked to Jace and he realized that, as captain, it was his right to grant people access to the ship. "Permission granted. Welcome aboard."

Blackmane smiled a tooth grin and stepped aboard. He looked around at the crew and then up and down the masts before seeing Colette. "Colette! With another captain I see!"

"Aye, Blackmane," she said. "He is my new captain."

"Good," the werelion threw back its head and laughed. "I didn't care much for that other one."

Blackmane walked over and towered over Jace, looking down at him. "Is this the new captain?"

"I am," Jace answered before Colette could reply. He'd had plenty of experience with bullies in his life, especially once he'd worked with Damian. He knew he needed to stand up the person right away, so he stared back at the huge werelion. "I am Captain Jynx Knightly."

"Jynx Knightly." The werelion chuckled. "Seems I might have heard of you. Or, at least, heard of the bounty on your head."

Jace tensed, moving his hand nearer to Kraken's Claw. Unconsciously, he scanned the werelion in his HUD.

Blackmane
Race: Werelion
Class: Pirate
Level: 100

He swallowed hard and let his hand relax as he saw Blackmane's level. Jace wasn't sure what he'd been expecting, but level 100 was not it. The old pirate wasn't a legendary or epic boss, but he was still at maximum level - well, maximum level for players. He'd need to tread lightly with this werelion since the thing could probably tear him apart with it's bare hands - or did it have claws?

Jace tried to imagine what a real pirate captain would do in this situation. He crossed his arms over his chest and put on the best cocky grin he could muster. "That sounds about right. It seems I always have a price on my head lately."

The werelion smirked. "Don't we all. Don't we all. There will be no collecting bounties on my island. And no thieving or piracy on the island. Those are my rules. Take them or leave, but I wager you won't get far with your ship in this sort of condition."

Blackmane gestured around to the city. "Abide by the rules and the entire island and its services are yours - at a price, of course. Break the rules and…

well… I wouldn't advise it. I deal with rule breakers personally. Will you abide?"

Eying the huge werelion, Jace believed him. At level 100, he doubted there were many, if any, on the island who could stand against him. Certainly not Jace and his friends. No, Jace and his friends needed the services on the island right now and they would abide by his rules.

"We accept." Jace nodded and held out his hand. The werelion looked at it for a moment and then gave him a wicked grin before engulfing Jace's hand with his own huge paw. He held the pirate's grasp for a moment before they both released.

"Well then," the werelion said. "Welcome to Haddare Reef."

"Thank you," Jace replied.

The werelion winked at Colette, then turned and stalked away. When he had left the ship, the first mate walked over to him. "I'll talk to one of the work crews about repairs. But don't think they'll come cheap. Can we afford it?"

By we, Jace knew she met him. He was the captain and he'd be expected to pay for any repairs. He nodded to the woman. "Any idea how much?"

"Probably ten or twenty thousand," Colette said nonchalantly. "Depends on whether or not there's serious keel damage."

He sighed. "Do you need the money up front?"

The first mate shook her head. "No, they'll hold the ship as collateral until we pay."

"Fine," he said. "Just let me know how much."

Jace turned to the girls and Luna, who were all giving him excited looks. He gave them a come-hither gesture. "Come on, let's go check out the town."

Chapter 22

Navigating the strange town proved to be a challenge. In some instances, the only way around a cluster of buildings was through them. In each instance, they found an inn, tavern or shop they could walk through to get to the next area of dock.

As Jace passed through the various establishments, he did notice that people were staring at them. He assumed it was because they were outsiders until Diana stopped them as they left one of the building clusters.

"You know they're all looking at you, dear one," she told Jace.

"What?" he asked, confused.

"The pirates here," she told him. "They're all looking at you. Normally, I get a fair share of looks, as does Mika, but not here. The pirates we are passing are looking at you."

He frowned. Jace wasn't a social person so he wasn't used to really paying attention to people, even in-game. At least, he didn't pay attention to people in-game unless there was a potential for combat. Normally, towns were safe zones but he wondered if the same were true for Haddare Reef. Was it even part of any faction?

Jace remembered Blackmane's comment about his bounty. Was that what these pirates were seeing when they looked at him, a bounty. He wondered how much it was and whether it would be enough to tempt some of these pirates into crossing Blackmane.

Remembering that his spawn point was all the way back in Lasthaven, Jace suddenly felt very vulnerable. He wouldn't lose much if he died here, but Damian might be watching for him there. His former "friend" might even have someone watching the graveyard. Not only that, but he'd lose access to the ship and crew since they'd have no idea where he'd end up.

"I'm guessing it's the bounty," Jace replied. "And the fact that most people here are probably pirates or outlaws."

"That makes sense," Diana said, running her hands down her voluptuous body. "For a moment, I thought I was losing my touch."

Mika's hand was on the hilt of her katana. "Do you think they will try to kill you for the bounty?"

"I don't know," he shook his head. "Blackmane doesn't really seem like the kind of person you cross. But everyone has a price. And if they think the price is worth the risk and they think they can get out of here before Blackmane finds them… maybe."

"What about your hat?" Mika asked. "What if you change your appearance?"

Jace had already thought of using the hat but he wasn't sure if it would work now that he had a bounty.

Having a bounty seemed to allow NPCs to zero in on you, even through a name change. Then again, he wouldn't know unless he tried.

Taking out his hat, he placed it on his head and, with a thought, altered his appearance to look similar to most of the other pirates he'd seen. "What do you think?"

Mika nodded approvingly. "You do not look like you at all."

"Good," he chuckled. "Let's see if we can find the black market and use some of our money to get you too some upgraded gear."

"Fish?" asked Luna.

"And some fish for Luna," he added.

As they made their way through the various buildings, Jace continued getting a lot of stares. Like the assassins, these NPCs were keying in on his unique game ID, rather than his appearance.

Jace quickened their pace through the next few clusters until they were finally stepped onto the actual island part of the town. He let the illusion slip and reverted back to his own appearance.

"I just noticed something," Mika said, glancing around. "There are no guards anywhere."

Jace and Diana both looked around as well. Thinking back, he realized she was right. He hadn't seen anyone resembling a guard since they arrived. "You're right. I had noticed that there were no other players that I saw either."

"Why do you think that is?" Mika asked.

He looked around. "I'm not sure. Maybe it's just not interesting enough. Or maybe there are no quests or things to fight."

"So, speaking of fighting and the lack of guards. How do they keep the peace around here?" Diana asked.

"Maybe they are all afraid of Blackmane," Mika suggested.

Just then, a man came flying out of a nearby tavern, followed by an angry dwarf. The dwarf walked over to the man and kicked him with heavy looking boots. "Cheat me again and I'll do more than just throw you a beating!"

Men and women had rushed out of the tavern to see the conclusion of the fight and seeing that the dwarf was not going to inflict further damage on his opponent, appeared disappointed. As the dwarf walked away, the crowd went back into the tavern without so much as a second glance at the man lying on the ground.

"Should we help him?" Mika asked.

Jace was about to tell her no when Diana shook her head. "Best to leave private matters alone. We don't know if he did something to deserve that beating or if he'd welcome our help if he didn't."

Mika looked back at the man getting up from the ground and gave a slight nod. Then Jace lead them away from the scene of the fight a bit.

"So, I guess this place isn't as peaceful as it first appeared," Jace chuckled. "This town might be like a wild west town and Blackmane's the sheriff. He probably lets the little stuff go, but anyone who breaks his rules, he comes down hard on."

"Apt analogy," Diana gave him an impressed smile. "I didn't realize you youngsters even knew what the wild west was."

Jace gave her a look of mock indignation. "I've seen westerns on the old vidstreams."

"Really?" Diana raised an eyebrow. "I thought those were on the censored list."

Jace felt his checks grow warm but gave her a toothy grin and a wink. "I must have seen them at a friend's house."

The older woman gave him a knowing look. "A friend's house, huh?"

"Oh, yeah."

"I have seen westerns," Mika blurted out with a smile. "We can watch them in Japan. With Japanese subtitles. They are very popular. Especially Clint Eastwood."

Exchanging looks with Diana, they both gave her an impressed look. "Who knew our little Mika would know about westerns."

"They do not ban as much of the old vidstreams in Japan," she told them. "We can still watch many of the things English speaking countries cannot."

"So, you get to watch the stuff the censors won't let us watch anymore," Diana noted. Then she smirked at Jace. "Except for Jace's friend."

Jace felt embarrassed but he knew there was no reason to. He was no longer a part of the real world. Did it really matter that he pirated old vidstreams or that he liked the pre-censorship era? He'd never get to watch another old vidstream. Now, all he had were his memories.

He thought about it. Actually, memories were all he had. In fact, that was all he was now. He was all of the real Jace's memories up until the point when the brain backup had been made and inserted into the game.

Not for the first time, Jace felt a strange sense of disconnection and loss. Knowing he could never go back into the real world again made him feel hollow. Like he wasn't real anymore. Of course, he wasn't real, but sometimes it hit him harder than others. He wondered if those people who had been inserted when they died felt the same way.

"Jace?" Mika said and he started. "You okay?"

Forcing a smile, he nodded. "I'm fine. Just thinking about everything we need to do."

Happy to change the topic, he went down a mental list he'd been keeping. "One, we need to repair the ship. Two, we need to get you both level 10 gear. Three, we need to see if there is a mages guild or some place I can buy the level 10 spells and also see if we can find a prayer book for Diana."

"Oh," Diana cooed. "That's right. I should be able to cast new spells… or prayers… or whatever they're called."

"They're called spells for mages," he told her. "And prayers for priests. But they're all basically the same thing - just a different name."

"What about changing our names again?" Mika asked. "Won't that help prevent Damian from finding us?"

"It would." Jace shrugged. "But I don't really think there will be a place around here to do that, but we can ask around."

He remembered their bind point in Lasthaven. "Actually, our first business should be to find out if there is a graveyard and then change our bind point."

"Are we sure we want to be bound here?" Diana asked, casting a dubious glance around the strange town. "Is this where we really want to respawn?"

"If Blackmane's prohibition on things includes assassination, this might be a good spot to regroup," he said. "Plus, the lack of players may be in our favor."

"That much might be true," Diana conceded. "But then what? We hitch a ride on one of the pirate ships? Could we trust them to deliver us safely?"

"Maybe," he frowned. "Or maybe we just pick on where the sailors are all the same level as us and if they try anything, we take them out."

"And then what? It's not like any of us can sail a ship. Certainly not alone."

"Good point," Jace nodded.

"What about your ring?" Mika asked.

He'd told them about the ring earlier and its ability to teleport them. "We could use the ring to get back to one of the cities but once we use the spell, we'd need to approach another player to refill the ring."

"Is that risky?" Mika asked.

"I don't know," he said. "It would be risky for Damian to place a player bounty on us, because that can be traced back to him. If support is looking into him - and hopefully they are - then I doubt he would want anything that leads back to him."

"But we wouldn't know for certain," Diana reasoned. "Until it was too late."

"Right," Jace said. "And I'd rather not take that risk unless we absolutely have to."

"Fine, fine," Diana said. "But that means trusting pirates."

"Maybe," he said. "Or maybe other ships dock here as well. If it comes to that, we can go ask around."

"So, we are binding here?" Mika asked.

"It looks like it," Diana sighed.

"Unless either of you have any other objections," he said.

When neither of them voiced any objections, he looked around. "I wonder where the graveyard would be on this island?"

Chapter 23

It took them an hour to find the graveyard. He'd considered asking for directions, but he was from Philadelphia. Jace knew the dangers of asking shady characters for directions at night. They were just as likely to be given directions to an ambush and get mugged as they were to get actual directions. And since all the characters on this island were shady, he didn't risk it.

They finally found the graveyard northwest of the town, in a cleared out patch of jungle. All three of them set their bind point to the island and then went back into the city. In their efforts to find the graveyard, they discovered that there was no regular market, or player auction.

Jace assumed this was because the island was not actually part of any faction. In a normal city, the player auction market contained items for sale from that faction. Without a home faction, the player market had nothing to display. Instead, all items were in the black market. Which made them more expensive, of course.

Luckily, level 10 gear was relatively inexpensive. Even with the markup, it was still reasonable. At least, for normal gear. Unfortunately, it seemed like most of the regular gear they could purchase all came in pirate fashion. He guessed because players hunted pirates in the area, so there was an excess of it in the local market.

Mika bought a set of leather armor that looked more like a pirate wench's outfit than a suit of armor, yet it afforded the same protection. She seemed to like the look, and he had to admit that the outfit did look better on her than the bulky armor she had been wearing. She also found a magical serrated katana, which was more than the entire set of armor, but which she had to have.

"I am a pirate ninja now!" she said, holding up her katana. Jace examined it and had to admit it was a nice upgrade. She no longer had a bleed effect but the extra damage from the serrated ability would help her penetrate more armor.

Serrated Katana
Type: Two-Handed Sword
Level: 10
Damage: 21 + 3 (Sharp) + 3 (Serrated)
Wt: 4 lbs
Special: Penetrates 3 armor
Description: Originally created by the gnomish blacksmith Glesi Wrenchsprocket as part of a steam-powered weapon, the serrated katana blade was later adopted as a standalone weapon by other smiths.

Diana, meanwhile, found armor that looked to Jace to be of gnomish design and had a very steampunk vibe to it. Despite the short shirt and low cut blouse that came with it, the armor value granted by it was the same as normal leather armor for level 10.

She pouted when she couldn't find a wand in her price range, but did find a staff.

Gnarled Mage Staff
Type: Staff
Level: 10
Damage: 6 + 3 (Arcane)
Wt: 7 lbs
Special: Reduces cost of all spells by 1 mana.
Description: Warog Mekok, a feared ogre magi from the badlands, subdued a village of goblins during the Ogre wars and took this staff from their tribal shaman. He lost it at the same time he lost his hand to a troll's axe.

"Nice staff!" Jace complimented as she showed it to him. "It will help with mana, as well."

"Yes, do you think it will reduce the cost of the priest spells?"

"Good question," Jace said, trying to remember anything he'd read about mage and priest items interacting. "Only one way to know for certain and that's to try it out in a fight and see."

"Or you could cut yourself and I could cast a healing spell," she said.

"Maybe later," he rolled his eyes. "Did you find any prayer books with level 10 prayers?"

"I did," she sighed. "I found one for the level 10 healing spell. But it's 5,000 gold."

Jace whistled. That seemed high for a level 10 book of prayers but higher level healing spells could make the difference between life and death if they ran into something else like the ninjen. "I'd get it. It cures twice as much as the level 1 heal and if we run into anything like that ninjen boss, we might need it."

"Okay," she told him. "I'll get it. I can't get higher mage spells yet, right?"

"No," Jace shook his head. "You have to be level 10 in that class."

"Should I switch back to mage?" she asked with a raised eyebrow.

He considered her question. Healing was important and it didn't appear that Mika would be changing back anytime soon. She seemed to enjoy being a melee fighter too much. That only left Diana. "No, I'd stay a priest for now - if you don't mind. I think we could use a healer more than a mage."

"That's fine with me." Diana smiled. "As long as I'm not getting pummeled, I don't really care what I am."

He chuckled at the older woman. Apparently, she would do whatever it took to avoid pain. Not that Jace liked pain, but he knew he had to deal with it. Diana wouldn't even summon her own familiar, because it was painful. But to each their own. He wasn't about to judge her.

With the two girls taken care of, they began to look for items for Jace. One item jumped out at him immediately. He found a more powerful armored ring. Considering his recent encounter with the level 30 ninjen, he thought extra *Defense* was a good investment.

> ***Armored Ring of Drarx***
> ***Type: Ring***
> ***Level: 10***
> ***Wt: .1 lb***
> ***Special: Provides +3 Defense***
> ***Description: Forged by the goblin jewelcrafter, Zruitzeakz, as a gift for the young prince Drarx, it was lost when the prince's hand was bitten off by a rabid dire wolf.***

"Jace!" Mika called out enthusiastically. "What about this?"

Hurrying over to the stand she was in front of, he looked at the item she was pointing at.

"It's a buckler. It says fencer. Didn't you say you got the *Fencing* skill as part of the Swashbuckler class?"

Reaching her, Jace saw she was pointing to a buckler. Surprisingly, it was only a 1,000 gold and he checked out the description.

> ***Fencer's Buckler***
> ***Type: Shield***
> ***Level: 10***
> ***Armor: 6 + 3 (Masterwork) + 3 (Sturdy)***
> ***Wt: 3 lb***
> ***Special: Fencing abilities which use mana have their cost reduced by 1 mana.***
> ***Description: This enchanted buckler was crafted for the dwarven great fencer, Muhrdamdorm***

Sternbrew. Renowned for his fencing, he was equally renowned for his gambling and lost the buckler in a game of knucklebones.

He was surprised it was so cheap until he remembered he had never heard of the *Fencing* skill before he'd switched to Swashbuckler. It was possible the Swashbuckler class was the only one which had the skill. If that were the case, there wouldn't be any demand for something that reduced *Fencing* abilities. Feeling lucky for a change, he purchased it and replaced his existing buckler.

Next, he looked for better armor. Jace already had level 10 armor, so there wasn't much to improve it without buying magical gear. He didn't find anything that justified spending the money.

"What about this?" Diana asked. Jace examined the armor she indicated.

Sea Captain's Coat
Type: Chest Armor
Level: 10
Armor: 4 + 3 (Masterwork) + 3 (Sturdy)
Wt: 3 lb
Special: Protects the wearer from extreme heat and cold. Keeps the wearer afloat if they are in water deeper than 10 feet.
Description: Originally commissioned for the Whitecliff naval officers, these magical electric eel-skin coats became so popular that sea captain's everywhere began ordering them.

"It's better than what I have now, but I'm not sure the abilities are that useful," he replied.

"But it will look good on you," Diana insisted. "Very dashing."

"Dashing, huh?" Jace asked and eyed the captain's coat. "Fine. It is a little better than what I have now."

The jacket was leather armor instead of plate mail, so he bought a pair of plate reinforced boots to replace his leather boots. That put him back at three pieces of plate armor and three pieces of leather armor, so he got the bonuses from his abilities. After that, they left the black market and found their way back to the ship. Colette was waiting impatiently for them near the gangplank.

"About time you came back!" she huffed. "They want 38,000 gold for repairs!"

Jace frowned. He had no idea how much a ship cost, but 38,000 gold seemed like a steep price. "Why so much?"

"Because they're thieves!" she said. "Filthy little parasites!"

"Can the repairs wait until we get to gnomish territory?"

"Maybe. There was damage to the keel from the ninjen. We might make it. Or we might not."

"And by 'not make it' you mean sink?"

"Aye captain." She smiled. "I mean sink."

"So, we can't really afford to not get them done," he told her.

She eyed him but relented. "No, not really. But it's still robbery!"

"Is there another shipwright we can go to on the island?"

"It won't matter. They all have the same rates."

"What? No capitalism?" Jace smirked.

"No. The rates are set by Blackmane."

"Let me guess, he gets a percentage of the rates."

"Of course, it's his island."

Jace shrugged. "If we have to get it done, then we have to get it done. Who do I pay?"

Colette blinked. "You're going to pay it without getting money from the crew?"

"It's my ship, right?" he asked her. The game had said it was his, but he wasn't sure if that carried over into the minds of the crew.

"Aye, she's your ship," she said warily.

"Then I pay the bills," he said. "Isn't that why the captain's supposed to get an extra share or something?"

She gave a slight nod. "That's the prevailing theory, but not too many captains put that into practice."

"If we get into a fight to take loot and the damage happens during that fight, then the cost of repairs should come out of the loot before we divvy it up," he told her. "This incident happened when we were on the high seas. That makes it my responsibility."

"Aye," she agreed. "I think the crew wouldn't argue with that, especially since I think most of them may have spent their share by now."

"Really?"

"Aye," she said. "The ale is cheap, but the brothels aren't. But they are clean."

"Brothels, eh?" Jace asked. It did make sense, even in a real world sense. Sailors who were cooped up on a ship would want to take care of all of their needs once they hit land. And apparently, that little bit was built into the game AI as well.

"Thinking of using their services?" The first mate grinned.

Jace tried to stop himself from blushing in front of his first mate, but felt his cheeks grow warm. The first mate looked behind him at the two girls and gave him an apologetic look. "Sorry captain, I forgot you already have two wives. I guess you won't be using their services after all."

Jace cleared his throat. "No."

He looked back to see Mika with her arms crossed over her chest and Diana staring at him with a smile and a raised eyebrow. He cleared his throat again, anxious to change the subject. "Who did you say I need to pay again?"

Chapter 24

The shipwright was easy to find but was closed by the time Jace and the girls arrived. Jace glanced at his gnomish timepiece and was surprised to see how late it was. "Geez, it's 10pm already."

"Really?" Mika asked. It was nighttime, but the entire town was lit up with torches, usually on multiple levels. The effect was a warm illumination that seemed to permeate the area. Added to the various noises of merrymaking, Jace guessed it must truly be a town that never slept. Like a college town back in the real world.

"Yeah," Jace confirmed. "We'll need to come back tomorrow."

Diana looked around. "So, what do we do until then? Other than bar hop."

Mika fingered her new katana. "Is there something we can do to get more experience?"

Jace scratched his chin. "Good question. There should be something here to kill. Every location generally has some monsters to kill. There are probably even some quests here. We just have to find them."

"That alone could take all night," Diana complained.

"Maybe not," Jace said. "I have an idea."

After leading them to several bars and inns to check with the innkeepers and bartenders, they found out there were monsters to kill on the island. On the outskirts of the town, near the water, there were some sort of crab people who regularly attacked the buildings on the fringe of town.

The group retraced their steps back to the graveyard and then down to the water. As they got close, they could see the crab people coming out of the water and form groups of two or three and then heading off towards the town.

"They look pretty big," Diana whispered. While Jace had no issues seeing them with his *Cat-Vision*, he was surprised that Diana could. But the moon was out and with the reflection on the white sand must enable her to make out their shapes.

The creatures were about seven feet tall, with the build of football linebackers. They weren't quite bipedal, since their lower body looked like that of a lobster, with multiple short legs. Their "arms" were almost human-like but they were oversized, like gorillas, and ended in huge pincers. Jace could just make out their reddish hue that made them resemble crabs.

"And armored," Mika said softly. "Those shells must make them very armored."

"What level are they?" Diana asked.

Jace squinted at the small groups that were coming out of the water. They were too far away from him to examine in his HUD. "Stay here while I *Stealth* over to them and find out."

Slipping into the shadows, Jace entered *Stealth*. He circled around the girls and stepped out of the foliage onto the sandy beach. Slowly, he crept closer to the creatures, who seemed to be coming out of the ocean endlessly in small groups. Given the number he'd seen so far, he was surprised the town hadn't made a bigger deal out of them.

He moved to the edge of a dune that partially obscured him from the area where they were gathering. He pulled up his HUD to see if he was close enough to examine them.

Cobalt Lagoon Claw-Warrior
Race: Krustacian
Class: Warrior
Level: 25

The creatures were something called krustacians and they were level 25. That was higher than a normal group should be able to handle, but they'd held their own against the ninjen of the same level. They should be able to do the same against these creatures.

That was provided they could penetrate their armor. Kraken's claw should be able to get through some of it. And luckily, Mika had just bought that new katana, so it's higher damage range would at least give her a better chance. He looked at the hard exoskeleton and doubted Luna's claws would do much.

Ducking back down, Jace circled back around to the girls and informed them of the creature's levels

"And you're sure we can take them?" Diana asked.

"If not." Mika smiled and pointed north. "We're only a short distance away from the graveyard."

"That's reassuring," Diana pouted. "I'm really not into the whole pain thing. I've had enough of that in my life and the stuff I feel here is much more intense."

"That's because we're at 100% sensory input," Jace reminded her. "Which is actually 110% of human normal. They upped the sensory feedback because so many people play on lower settings."

"Remind me to thank them," Diana said dryly.

"So, we attack them?" Mika asked brightly, her katana already in her hand.

"Yes," he told her. "Now that you're level 10, you should both see your skills going up again until they hit rank 20. Once they do, you'll get another skill ability. At least, if that skill offers one."

He pointed out the dune he'd been ducking behind. "Let's see if we can get to that dune and then I can pull them there. We want something far enough away that we don't get adds while we're fighting."

Luna looked up from where she was lying down. "Fish?"

"Crabs," he told the big cat. "They taste like fish. But they have a hard shell."

"Fish?" the cat asked again, more excitedly this time.

"Yeah, basically," he told the cat. He wasn't sure if she could help them, but every little bit helped. Plus, she'd eaten an entire ninjen. Maybe the krustacian would taste about the same. "Come on, let's go."

Luna and the girls followed him back to the dune without any reaction from the crab people. Once there, Jace told them to wait while he pulled the monsters over to them. It didn't take long.

He was only a few feet from the dune, when one of the krustacians noticed him. It clattered something with its claws, almost akin to morse code and then the two crap people with it both turned towards Jace. Not knowing what else to do, he waved to them.

The crab like creatures rushed towards him faster that he would have thought possible on their multiple legs. Two of them even skittered sideways like a crap. Jace cast his *Air Armor* spell as he quickly retreated and by time he got back behind the dune, they were on him.

"Fight me!" he used his *Taunt* and the creatures attacked him obediently.

Cobalt Lagoon Claw-Warrior pinches YOU for 0 damage.
Cobalt Lagoon Claw-Warrior pinches YOU for 0 damage.

Cobalt Lagoon Claw-Warrior pinches YOU for 0 damage.

Cobalt Lagoon Claw-Warrior pinches YOU for 0 damage.

Cobalt Lagoon Claw-Warrior pinches YOU for 0 damage.
Cobalt Lagoon Claw-Warrior pinches YOU but you Dodge.

With his new gear, his *Defense* was now a whooping 24, more than most level 30 tanks. The huge claws of the claw-warriors couldn't quite penetrate his defenses. And considering the size of those claws, he was glad.

He *Feinted* and attacked the center crab man, trying to drive his saber through the creature's armor or find a weak spot.

You critically hit Cobalt Lagoon Claw-Warrior for 19 damage plus 0 acid damage.
You critically hit Cobalt Lagoon Claw-Warrior for 39 damage plus 0 acid damage.

His first strike scraped along the krustacian's thick chest shell but managed to score some minor damage. The second strike caught the thing at its neck joint, causing much more damage. The creature didn't react to either strike and Jace wondered if the thing felt pain or simply lacked any ability to vocalize it.

He noticed that his saber was pulsating again and appeared to be doing double damage against the crab man. They must be considered ocean dwelling creatures. Unfortunately, the blade's acid did no damage against these things. The shell must provide them resistances to acid.

Mika had disappeared briefly and then reappeared as she sliced her katana across the things armored back.

Mika Knightly critically hit Cobalt Lagoon Claw-Warrior for 10 damage.

She let out a groan of frustration as her slice mostly slid off the krustacian's slick shell. Then Diana used her wand to shoot the crab man while Luna clawed and bit at it.

Diana Knightly shoots Cobalt Lagoon Claw-Warrior for 0 magic damage.

Luna bites Cobalt Lagoon Claw-Warrior for 3 damage.
Luna claws Cobalt Lagoon Claw-Warrior for 0 damage.
Luna claws Cobalt Lagoon Claw-Warrior for 0 damage.

Like his acid damage, the magical damage from her new staff did nothing against the creature and Jace guessed it must have high resistances to elemental and magical damage due to its shell. Just great.

"They've got resistances," he yelled to them. "Spells and acid aren't going to affect them. Diana, save your mana for healing, if I need it."

The crab men attacked again, snapping their giant claws at his arms and legs.

Cobalt Lagoon Claw-Warrior pinches YOU for 0 damage.

Cobalt Lagoon Claw-Warrior pinches YOU but you Parry.

Cobalt Lagoon Claw-Warrior pinches YOU for 3 damage.
Cobalt Lagoon Claw-Warrior pinches YOU for 4 damage.

Cobalt Lagoon Claw-Warrior pinches YOU for 2 damage.
Cobalt Lagoon Claw-Warrior pinches YOU for 0 damage.

Even though their pincer claws only did a small amount of damage against him, it was the worst pinching sensation he'd ever felt and he jerked his arms away from the seeking pincers even as he cursed. *Feinting* again, he tried to aim at the more vulnerable joints this time.

You critically hit Cobalt Lagoon Claw-Warrior for 36 damage plus 0 acid damage.
You critically hit Cobalt Lagoon Claw-Warrior for 44 damage plus 0 acid damage.

His attacks managed to penetrate the inner joints of its arms but still the acid damage didn't seem to affect it. Then Mika and Luna hit the krustacian from behind.

Mika Knightly critically hit Cobalt Lagoon Claw-Warrior for 9 damage.

Luna bites Cobalt Lagoon Claw-Warrior for 0 damage.

Luna claws Cobalt Lagoon Claw-Warrior for 0 damage.
Luna claws Cobalt Lagoon Claw-Warrior for 0 damage.

Mika's katana couldn't seem to cut deeply enough in the shell to do any real damage and this time neither Luna's claws nor her teeth found a soft spot on the creature's body.

The krustacians didn't waste any time and came in with their pincer claws, trying to snap at him.

Cobalt Lagoon Claw-Warrior pinches YOU for 0 damage.
Cobalt Lagoon Claw-Warrior pinches YOU for 0 damage.

Cobalt Lagoon Claw-Warrior pinches YOU for 0 damage.
Cobalt Lagoon Claw-Warrior pinches YOU for 0 damage.

Cobalt Lagoon Claw-Warrior pinches YOU for 0 damage.
Cobalt Lagoon Claw-Warrior pinches YOU for 0 damage.

Jace managed to avoid the claws and then struck back with his normal *Feint*/Stab combo, while Mika and Luna attacked its back again...

You critically hit Cobalt Lagoon Claw-Warrior for 28 damage plus 0 acid damage.
You critically hit Cobalt Lagoon Claw-Warrior for 34 damage plus 0 acid damage.

Mika Knightly critically hit Cobalt Lagoon Claw-Warrior for 23 damage.

Luna bites Cobalt Lagoon Claw-Warrior for 4 damage.
Luna claws Cobalt Lagoon Claw-Warrior for 1 damage.
Cobalt Lagoon Claw-Warrior dies.
You gain 250 experience.

They moved onto the next claw-warrior and, after Jace suffered a few more pinches from the crab people's claws, they finished the remaining two off. Once the things were dead, they searched the bodies only to be disappointed at finding nothing at all.

"Really?" Diana said with an exasperated tone. "These things don't drop anything at all?"

Jace shrugged. "Some monsters don't. Or some only drop rare loot. We might still find something interesting."

"Do we still want to farm…" Mika had begun to ask but a loud crunching sound caused them all to look at it's source. Luna had managed to use her paws to hold one of the arms until she had bitten it open with her teeth. She was now happily ripping the stringy white meat out of the thing's arms and chewing.

She looked up with what Jace could only assume was a feline grin. "Fish!"

Chapter 25

The fight had pushed both of the girls to level 11 and Jace was almost to level 7 in Swashbuckler. They continued to pull groups of two to three of the krustacians until morning. Unfortunately, no boss appeared and none of them dropped any loot. It was disappointing, but it happened sometimes.

Sometimes, in VEIL Online, you could camp monsters for days and get no loot and no boss spawn. They'd been lucky at lower levels, but at the higher levels, the game became more of a grind. There was less reward for the work. And still people played, slowly building up their "retirement" plan.

When morning finally came, Jace had something even better than a little extra loot, he had reached level 12 in Swashbuckler and both girls were at level 14. Best of all, when he had hit level 10, he had unlocked a new Swashbuckler ability. The description had been very confusing and he hadn't taken the time to look at it until they called it quits.

Once daylight hit, they stopped their farming and decided to return to the town. The three of them began walking back to the town with Luna trailing behind. Mika was so happy about her new level, she was practically skipping.

"So," Diana said as they walked, "what's this new ability you were frowning so hard about earlier?"

Jace laughed mirthlessly and called up his HUD. He brought up the ability in his character sheet and read it off to the two of them.

Lucky
Swashbuckler Ability
Special: You are lucky. This manifests in many ways at unusual times.
Description: Your daring exploits and near misses with death have made you lucky.

"You are lucky!" Mika said brightly.

Jace shrugged. "Yes, but what does that mean. I looked through the logs after each fight and I didn't see anything that indicates that the ability was used. I even tried activating it but there doesn't seem to be any way to do that directly. There's no cost. No duration. No information at all really."

Mika looked thoughtful but Diana grinned wickedly.

"Maybe it means you'll get lucky," Diana said seductively and flicked her eyes from Mika to Jace and then back.

The two of them got her meaning and they both blushed, although Jace entertained the thought a little longer than he probably should have. He really liked Mika, maybe more so than Charlena at this point, but she hadn't really shown him that she liked him the same way.

And they'd been so busy with trying to get to the *Help Desk* and then fleeing the city and Damian, he really didn't have time to think about a relationship or what that would mean. He was also not sure he could do anything intimate in the game.

In-game sex was definitely a thing, both with players and non-players, but it required a consent from all parties when they were players, or just the player when it was with a NPC. Unfortunately, the part of the HUD that allowed you to give consent was the same part that controlled sensory input. Since he didn't have one, he assumed he didn't have the other.

He glanced at Mika walking next to him. She'd never really hinted that she wanted to take their relationship to the next level. Well, she had kissed him. Several times. But there was a world of difference between kissing and more intimate encounters.

"Thinking naughty thoughts," Diana said from his other side.

"What? Huh?" he stuttered, as he realized something must have been showing on his face. "I mean... No."

Diana gave him a knowing smile and he turned his head to look straight ahead, trying to ignore the heat in his cheeks.

They made it back in town and stopped a tavern that had not appeared to ever have closed, judging by the passed out sailors in front and at some of the tables. They grabbed a table and each of them ordered breakfast.

They didn't serve waffles, so Mika ordered french toast. Diana ordered an omelet and Jace ordered a full halfling breakfast. Luna looked at him expectantly until he ordered a salmon fillet for her.

"I can't believe you can still eat," Jace said, looking at his familiar. She'd eaten several of the huge crab men carcasses. Maybe not the whole thing, but enough that Jace would have been sick for days. And that was if he could have eaten that much at all.

"Fish good," was her only reply.

Just as the barmaid walked away, there was a squawking from the door. Someone had just entered and a large black bird came flying in the open door. The bird circled the inside of the tavern and then landed on their table. The thing turned towards Jace and began speaking. "Jynx Knightly. Got your message. We will meet you there. At the place we told the others about in Whitecliff. Charlena."

"Repeat?" the bird squawked.

"Yes," he said, and the bird repeated the message.

"Repeat?" the bird squawked.

"No," he told the bird and the thing jumped into the air and flew out the still open door.

"You heard that too, right?" he asked. It'd been a long time since he was on the receiving end of a message raven. He couldn't recall whether the magic of the message was for his ears only or if anyone in hearing distance could hear it.

Mika and Diana nodded. Diana looked at him with a questioning look. "Did I hear that right? Did she say 'we' will meet you?"

Mika looked at Diana and nodded and Jace followed suit. "That's what I heard too. But I'm not sure who the 'we' is?"

The barmaid returned with their food and the group immediately stopped talking. The NPC barmaid wouldn't care what they were talking about, but Jace didn't want anyone that Damian might be able to interrogate or bribe later.

Waiting until their food was in front of them and the barmaid was gone, they each took a bite of their food. Jace sighed with contentment as he bit into the delicious sausages. After days of pickled fish, the tavern food was pure bliss.

"You don't think Charlena's bringing the servants do you?" Diana asked, washing down a bite of her omelet with some mead. "I mean, we only brought them because we thought the city was going to be destroyed."

An uncharacteristic worried look crossed Mika's face. "Do you think she means Damian?"

"What?" Jace was shocked to hear her say that. "You don't really think she would work with Damian, do you?"

"No," Mika shook her head. "I mean, do you think she knows that Damian might be following her or know where she's going?"

"Oh," Jace muttered. That was a possibility. She may have run into Damian or he might have actually approached her to get information. Jace slammed his fist on the table as he swore, causing a few people to look over and Mika and Diana to start. "I forgot to tell her Damian's character name. He could have come right up to her and she would never even have known."

Both Mika and Diana's expressions changed from surprise to alarm. Diana pursed her lips. "So, she could be leading Damian right to us."

"Yes," Jace growled. "How could I have been so stupid? Of course, she wouldn't have known what he looked like."

"Is there anything he can do to her?" Mika asked, her voice full of concern. There hadn't been any love lost between the two girls and Jace suspected he was the reason. But Mika was a gentle soul and he knew she didn't wish the other girl any harm.

"I'm still not sure on how he can really harm any of us," Diana said. "I mean, we're in the game, right? What can he really do?"

Jace let out a frustrated breath. "I'm not sure. But he's a really good programmer and hacker. He created that insertion hack and it went unfound for years. Who knows what else he might have put into the game. He could have some item that changes our spawn point to the middle of a volcano for all I know. We'd endless respawn in molten lava."

Both of the women gave looks of horror. With their sensory levels at maximum, such a thing would be an endless torment of pain until it eventually drove them mad like Big Cheese. Either that, or force them to stay in spirit mode forever.

"How could a person do that to another person?" Mika asked.

"The same way he could rob people of their life savings and stick them in bodies of monsters to be killed over and over," Jace responded. He thought back to Damian's words in the castle. He'd actually enjoyed the prospect of causing Jace trouble and watching him squirm.

"Fine," Diana conceded. "I believe you. Best not to risk it. What about support?"

Jace sighed. "I gave them the information and they said they'd contact me but now I don't know. I've changed my name since then. They may not be able to reach me. Or, they may still be investigating."

"Still?" Mika asked. "Why so long?"

"Because," he told her. "I accused an employee of doing something that should be impossible. They're going to want to verify it before they do anything. He obfuscated the code, so it might take them a week just or more to figure out what's going on."

Mika's face fell. "It's been almost two weeks."

"I know," he said. "I've been thinking about that. We may need to contact them again, in Nynymmost."

"Are you serious?" Diana looked at him like he was crazy. "After everything we went to before? Now we have to do that again? And how will we afford a title to look around the Nymmy Moist place?"

Mika chuckled at her mispronunciation. "Nymmy moist!"

"It won't be easy," he told them. "The gnomes don't have a monarchy, if I remember correctly. They have a parliamentary form of government, where the prime minister is elected. And I don't think players can be members of parliament."

Mika looked confused. "So, does that mean no titles?"

"There's still some sort of titles," he said. "But I think they're union or guild based."

"Oh dear," Diana rolled her eyes. "Unions! Guilds?! What are they? The freemasons?"

"So, if we join a union, we can get into the parliament building and look around?" Mika asked.

"I'm not sure," he confessed. "I never really did much with the good faction. I only remember bits of what I read on the forums."

"Union? Does that mean the titles are cheaper?" Mika asked hopefully.

Jace shook his head. "No, the name of the title may be different, but its standard across all of the countries and all of the factions. If they weren't, people would just go to the cheapest faction and buy their title there."

"I would," Diana admitted. "Why pay more for the same thing."

"So, what do we do?" Mika asked.

"If we want to get into parliament, we have to buy a title," he replied and looked at each of them. "Which means we need to go after the rest of the treasure."

Chapter 26

After their breakfast, they found the shipwright and paid him the money for the repairs. He said it would be done by the end of the day. Considering how much he was paying for the repairs, he thought the repairs would be so extensive that they might take days or even a week. Not for the first time, he wondered if many of the costs were manipulated by the developers to keep players from accumulating gold.

He checked in with Colette and let her know the bill was paid and that he would return to the ship at dusk. Then he led them back to the krustacian area.

"Are we sure we want to spend all day killing crab people?" Diana asked, clearly not happy with the prospect. He wasn't surprised. Other than healing there was very little she could do against them with their resistances. This was one case where magic was at a severe disadvantage.

"You know," he told the older woman. "We could buy you a flail. You could at least do some damage with it in between healing spells."

Diana looked aghast. "No thank you! I'd really prefer to be as far away as possible from them."

Jace considered her options. They hadn't been able to find a more powerful wand, and even if they had the krustacian's shell would simply allow it to shrug off the magical damage. A melee weapon didn't seem to be her style.

"You could switch to fighter," he suggested.

"You can get a katana like me!" Mika added.

"Tempting dear one, but I thought I just said I didn't want to get close to them," she said to both of them.

"I know. But fighter's get all weapon skills, except for wands and staffs. You could use a crossbow and stay nice and far away."

"A crossbow?" Diana looked thoughtful. "That might work."

"Plus," he told her. "You get access to plate armor, which would give you more protection."

"Plate armor?" she looked at him dubiously.

"It's got the highest armor rating," he grinned.

"Like the knights of the roundtable? I have a perfect body and you want me to hide it inside a suit of armor?" she asked incredulously.

Jace smirked. "It's a fantasy game. They have more...ah.. Feminine versions."

"Oh really?" Diana raised an eyebrow. "And what about me leveling up priest?"

"We still need you to do that," he told her. "But these are level 25 monsters and you'll level up fighter quickly. Once you get a level above priest, you can switch back. It's one of the perks of being human."

Diana looked thoughtful. "My staff did nothing before. It would be nice to have a backup weapon. And better armor - as long as it's not too… concealing."

"What do you want to do?" Jace asked her. The last thing he wanted was for her to feel like he was telling her what to do.

"I think," she said wistfully, "that I'll change classes. Using a crossbow sounds more interesting than just waiting around for you to need a heal."

Mika clapped and Jace smiled. "That sounds good."

"Of course," the older woman said, "you know this means more shopping."

Diana switched to classes and dropped back down to level 1 fighter. Then they marched back to the black market and Diana spent nearly an hour looking through then items until she found the skimpiest plate mail top he remembered seeing. It was really nothing more than a chain bikini and plate cups over the breasts. In the real world, the only defensive properties it might have would be to distract her opponent.

She also found a bow that seemed to be made to hunt krustacians.

Penetrating Bow of Penelope

Type: Two-Handed Sword
Level: 10
Damage: 15 + 3 (Sharp)
Wt: 4 lbs
Special: Penetrates 5 Defense
Description: Crafted by a master bowyer for his
daughter who wished to be an adventurer, the bow was
sold by a thief and sole survivor of her group's
excursion into the Deeping Dark.

"Do I need to buy arrows?" she asked.

"No," Jace shook his head. "They changed that really early in the game, when so many people complained about having to carry around so many arrows. Whatever quiver comes with the bow will have an unlimited supply."

"That's handy," she commented, as she tried the bow. "I'm like Isolde."

Jace and Mika gave her puzzled looks.

"I weep for today's youth," she said dramatically. "Isolde was a Irish princess and legend has it, a bit of a warrior princess. She had an affair with a English knight named Tristan. It's what the Arthurian legends were probably modeled after. Isolde and Tristan were Guinevere and Lancelot."

"You learn something new every day." Jace smiled at her and the older woman rolled her eyes.

"How do I look?" she asked, when she had her new plate armor on.

"Less like a princess and more like a Valkyrie," he told her.

She nodded appreciatively. "I can accept that. If only I had a flying horse."

"There are Pegasus in the world," he told her. "You can even buy one as a mount, but they're insanely expensive. They're like the top end Italian sports cars of the game."

"Maybe I'll get me one, one day," she mused.

Jace shot her a disbelieving look.

"What?!" she said. "Did you forget? We have an eternity to save up for it."

He considered her words. Jace hadn't really thought of it like that. For the longest time, he thought he was still alive. Alive but in a coma. He'd wake up, live out the rest of his life and then die and be inserted into the game. He was used to measuring things in human years.

Now, he was in the game permanently. A rogue brain backup. Assuming that he wasn't deleted by WorldCog, he would have all eternity to save up money. It might take him a hundred years, but he could eventually become rich enough to be a Duke or Count and maybe even buy a Pegasus or Griffin mount. But that was a long way off.

They returned to the crab people and began pulling again. This time, with her new bow, Diana was able to do as much damage as Mika. The older woman seemed to enjoy herself much more as a warrior-priest.

They fought the krustacians all morning, gaining experience at a fantastic rate. When they finally took a break and went back to town to eat some lunch, Diana had already earned level 7 in fighter.

"I think I need to switch back to priest when I hit level 17," Mika said as they waited for their lunch to be delivered. "I don't want to hit level 18 before Diana catches up. If I do, she will not gain experience when I am in the group."

"Wow," Jace said. "I didn't realize you were gaining so quickly."

Mika nodded. "I think we would have been okay, but now with Diana leveling up fighter, I fear I will outpace her soon."

"I'm sorry," Diana said in a pained voice. "I realize you'd have to switch classes again."

"It's okay." Mika smiled and patted Diana's hand. "We are a team. I do not mind. Plus, it will be good if I can get better healing spells too. Last time we fought a big boss, it took both of us to keep Jace up!"

"That is the bad thing about switching classes," he said to no one in particular. "We'll need to be cognizant of our levels going forward. It's getting to a point where switching will cause these sorts of problems. One of us will end up getting three levels above the other, then we won't be able to group and get experience."

"Too bad we're not in a big city," Diana said. "I could do quests to get caught up."

Jace nodded. "True. Maybe once we get Nynymmost, you can do some quests to make up for lost experience."

"If we don't find Damian waiting for us," Diana said wryly.

"If we don't find Damian waiting for us," Jace sighed. "Or Charlena is somehow bringing him to us."

"Do you really think so?" Mika asked.

"Damian's a snake," he told them. "I wouldn't put it past him to introduce himself as someone who can help or an old friend of mine or something just to have her lead him to us."

"He sounds very slimy," Diana observed.

"Oh, he is," Jace said. "In hindsight, I should have seen it, but he was a coworker and…"

"And you're the type of person who tries to see the best in people," Diana finished.

Jace blushed. "Damian used to call me naive, but I really do want to believe that people are basically good."

Diane looked him over. "I think I was called cynical by more than one of my husbands, but I've met a lot of unsavory characters in my days. And the more success you have, the more unsavory characters you meet. But I did meet some good people too. And those are the people you have to cherish."

"What you say is very true," Mika agreed. "I have met many people who have tried to take advantage of me. But I have also met many kind people. There are both. It is yinyang."

"I guess so," Jace agreed. "But someone like Damian. Someone who would steal from people and condemn them to an eternity of pain inside a monster. People like him really skew the results."

The girls nodded and the barmaid returned with their food. Luna had fish, of course. Mika had ordered pancakes and french toast, while Diana ordered some type of fruit tart. Jace went with his old standby, fish and chips.

Afterwards, they returned to the crab people and farmed them until sunset. Throughout the entire day, they never got a single piece of loot. Nor did any sort of boss spawn. When they finally made their way back to the ship, Diana had just made level 10 in fighter. Mika was level 17 in rogue and just shy of level 10 in priest. Jace was level 14 in Swashbuckler.

Climbing aboard the ship, which looked ready to sail, he heard Colette yell down to him from behind the wheel. "Just in time captain. Repairs are done and we can sail with the tide."

"Lay in a course for Nynymmost and engage!" he said. When, when he saw the blank looks on everyone's faces, he tried, "Make it so, number one." The sailors and even his companions just looked around

at each other and at him. Jace sighed and yelled out.
"Aye! Set sail!"

Chapter 27

Colette informed them that the voyage to Nynymmost was supposed to take two days, provided the weather held and they had no unexpected visitors. Jace agreed wholeheartedly. To the first mate, and unexpected visitors, might be the ninjen, pirates or some other sea menace. For him, the only real unexpected visitor he was worried about was Damian.

He still wasn't sure exactly what Damian might be able to do, but he wouldn't put anything past him. The man had obviously been adding things to the game for years. If he could modify the insertion routine, who knew what else he could have modified. He hoped WorldCog would get off their collective butts and figure out what was going on and who was behind it. All without deleting him, of course.

"We also picked up some more crew," Colette told him, after they had finished talking about the voyage to the gnomish capital.

Jace suddenly had visions of Damian sneaking onboard as one of the crew. Or the fact that the last captain had died at the hands of one of his crew. He ordered the first mate to assemble the new crew after they were out of the harbor so he could inspect them.

"And captain," Colette winked at him. "Part of the repairs was fixing up the captain's cabin. It's all yours."

"Oh really?" Diana chimed in. "No more living below deck?"

"Aye." The first mate smiled at the older woman. "They fixed it up with new furnishings and everything."

"Thanks," he told Colette and then looked at the girls. "Shall we go check it out?"

"Absolutely," Diana replied, and Mika nodded excitedly. The three of them, and Luna, went down to the door that led to the original captain's cabin and opened it.

The room inside now looked much like the cabin Jace had broken into to steal the tiara from Drakkar. The furnishings looked almost identical and Jace guessed this must be the default state of the room. When they'd repaired the ship, the crew, using game logic, had restored it back to its default state.

The window he'd smashed had been repaired, and the desk replaced with what appeared to be an exact, if much cleaner, replica of the one he'd seen before. To the side of the room were the bookcases he'd remembered seeing. They were again stocked with books, though he doubted there were any valuable books among them.

To the opposite side was the captain's bed. It wasn't as large as the bed had been downstairs. If he had to guess, Jace would guess that the one downstairs had been a king size bed and this was a queen size. It could probably fit three people, but it would be cramped. Not that any of them needed sleep. And virtual sex seemed off the table. At least, he thought it was.

Luna padded over to the bed and sniffed. Seeming satisfied, the huge cat hopped up onto it and began kneading it.

"Size!" he reminded her.

His familiar glared at him for a long moment. Then, the big cat shrunk back down to her normal size and continued kneading the bed. After a few moments, his familiar walked around in a circle before settling down on the bed and putting her head on her paws.

"Luna likes the new room," Mika said, giggling at the cat.

"I can't say I blame her," Diana whistled. "It's smaller, but cozier. Much nicer than that one below deck."

"There are chairs too!" Mika pointed out the leather bound chairs. The one behind the desk, the captain's chair, looked especially comfortable. Mika walked over to the nearest chair, turned it around and fell back into it. She smiled contentedly. "I like this chair."

Mika turned the chair so she was facing Jace. "You told Colette to go to Nynymmost. I thought we were getting more treasure."

The luxurious room forgotten, Jace walked over and sat down on the bed and began stroking Luna. The cat opened one eye to look at him and then closed her eyes and allowed him to stroke her and give her chin scratches.

"That's still the plan," he told them. "But we need to go meet Charlena."

Jace saw a brief shadow cross Mika's face, but it was gone almost immediately. She crossed her arms over her chest. "Why? Why not get the treasure first?"

"Because," he replied, "we need to get there and find her before Damian does. And if somehow she's gotten mixed up with him, we need to extricate her from the situation."

"And how are we supposed to do that, dear one?" Diana asked. She walked over to the chair next to Mika and collapsed into it. She wiggled around for a few seconds and then looked at Mika. "You're right. These are comfy."

Mika beamed.

Diana turned back to Jace. "I mean, you make this guy out to be the boogeyman, baba yaga, some unstoppable force. If that's true, how can we get her away from him?"

"I don't know," Jace frowned as he thought about her question. "We'll have to play it by ear. Follow them around and look for opportunities."

"If we can even find them," Diana retorted.

"We can find her," he replied. "She'll meet us at the first tavern inside the main entrance of the city, just like we told everyone to do to meet us."

"Too bad that groll hunk couldn't meet us," Diana said wistfully. They'd freed another player named Yosyp, who had looked like some sort of eastern European male model. Jace still remembered the way the girls practically drooled over his body when he had morphed.

"But Damian can't do anything permanent to her," Mika protested. "Not like us."

"True," Jace admitted. Mika was right, of course. Anything Damian did to Charlena could be nullified if she just deleted her character. She was still in the real world after all. Then he remembered what Damian had done to him with the car accident. "Except, we don't know if he might do something to her in the real world."

"The real world?" Diana asked. "Can he find out that information about her?"

"I'm not sure if he can look that up in the company database," Jace told him. "Player demographic information is well protected because of government regulation. But nothing's to stop him finding some other way to weasel it out of her. He can be charming when he wants to."

"So, she could be in real danger?" Mika said in a quiet voice.

"Possibly," he said. "I'd rather not take that chance."

"But she abandoned you," Mika protested. "When you needed her."

"Maybe," he nodded. "But are we going to do the same to her? Knowing what happened to me in the real world? I don't know about you, but I couldn't live with myself if I let something happen to any of you."

Diana sighed. "There's another possibility too." She paused dramatically while Mika and Jace both turned to her. "He could recruit her. If he's as manipulative as you say, he could come up with some story about you that might turn her against you and us."

Jace frowned. He hadn't even considered that possibility but Diana was right. Damian used to boast about always being three steps ahead of everyone else. Could he come up with some plausible story that might make Charlena turn on Jace? Would it even take much? She had turned her back on them right before they went into the castle to find the support center.

Since he'd met Charlena, he'd been attracted to her and it seemed like she had been attracted to him. But then something had changed when she first found out he was dead - or thought he was dead. And then, it changed again when she thought he was alive. They'd kissed and he thought that she actually cared for him.

Had he not paid her enough attention? Had he been too focused on his goal of getting to the *Help Desk* and contacting support? At the time, he'd thought it was critical. He'd thought he might be trapped inside a medical pod with no way to logout.

But then she'd told him about his real body, back in the real world. He was in a coma, but not in a medical pod - not hooked up to the game at all. That was when she'd left. When she'd thought he was a liar or pretender.

Was it really so difficult to believe that she could be swayed by Damian into believing that he was a rogue program or some sort of experiment gone wrong? His ex-coworker was good at finding people's weaknesses.

He looked to Diana. "You might be right. We have to at least consider the possibility."

Mika looked torn. "Do you really think she would turn against us? She was our friend."

"We have no way of knowing. He could be feeding her lies about us right now," he told Mika. "As I look back at it, I can see he did that with the other team members. Turning them against each other, creating strife. I think he's the kind of person who thrives on that."

"He sounds lonely," Mika said in a quiet voice. "Then what do we do?"

Both the girls looked to Jace and he realized once again that he'd become the defacto leader. He didn't mind it so much when the stakes were just whether or not his group would wipe and get death penalties. He was starting to realize that being the leader wasn't a glamorous job

"We'll have to play it safe," he told them. "Until we know what's going on with her. Until we know for certain she hasn't been compromised, we have to treat her like she has the plague."

"Are we still going to meet her?" Mika asked.

"Yes," he told them. "But we'll need to come up with some plan. Some way to observe her and the area without being seen. Damian seems to have nearly unlimited money. He'll be able to afford any magical item he needs to obscure himself from us."

"Sounds very cloak and dagger," Diana approved. "I like it."

"Yeah, " he replied. "But the stakes are high. If she betrays us to him, it could mean that all of us end up in some eternal torment."

"Do you really believe he can do something like that?" Diana asked him.

"I think he caused the accident that put the real me in a coma," he replied. "I think he was aiming to kill me. Or... him, the real Jace. If he could do that, kill someone in the real world. Not to mention trapping people inside monster bodies to be killed over and over, I don't think he'll have any qualms about causing us eternal suffering."

"And you have a plan?" Diana asked dubiously.

"I'm working on it," he said. "Hopefully, we can think of something before we get there."

"We'd better," the older woman, "because I have no desire to spend an eternity in a literal hell."

Chapter 28

They arrived in the Nynymmost harbor in the early evening of Weeksend, or Saturday in the real world. Being from the evil faction, Jace had never seen the gnomish capital before as Mordred. But he had heard stories of it.

The gnomes were tinkerers and delighted in building things, then improving on them and then improving on them some more, well past the point where any sane human would have stopped. As he looked upon the gnome city, he realized the stories didn't do it justice.

From his vantage point on the deck, Jace could see the oddly-shaped buildings rising from the main city. They were far taller than any human building, save the castle towers. They were also strangely positioned all around the city, as if someone had just randomly selected spots to build up.

To make the spectacle even more bizarre, Jace could see plumes of colored smoke coming from most of the buildings. The plumes stretched high into the sky where they blended together in a strange cacophony of colors that made the sky above the city look like some sort of mad painter's canvas.

Jace held his hand up to shade his eyes as he caught sight of the most famous gnomish building, the High Altitude Docking Station, or H.A.D.S. The HADS looked like some sort of misshapen, mechanical tree that jutted out of the center of the city. He guessed it had to be three hundred feet tall, easily the tallest building he'd ever seen in the game, except possibly in old ruins left over from the Veteribus, or Ancient Ones.

While the building itself was both a wonder and an eyesore, it was what was attached to the building that captivated their attention. Attached to the main structure at odd intervals were long, branch-like appendages that were wide enough and tall enough for an ogre to walk through. At the end of most of those appendages were gnomish airships.

The gnomish were famous for their flying airships that looked like small normal ships attached to one or two giant balloons. Jace knew there had to be some magic involved as well since as large as the balloons were, there was no way they should be able to hold up a ship that size. It had to be magic. Or, the devs had made an exception to the physics laws regarding airships.

No matter how the gnomes had accomplished it, the flying ships were a sight to see. And he wasn't only one to think so.

"And people actually go in those flying deathtraps?" Diana asked, looking at the HADS with morbid fascination. "How many of them actually stay in the air?"

"All of them," Jace replied, "as far as I know. They don't actually build regular ships like the other races. Only air ships."

"Can we ride in one?!" Mika asked with wide eyes. She seemed to remember their predicament and her face fell. "I mean, after we meet Charlena and defeat Damian."

Jace chuckled at her characterization of defeating Damian, as if he were just some game boss who needed to be vanquished. He really loved her enthusiasm and zest for life. It reminded him of himself before his family had been killed. It was only seven years ago, but it seemed a lifetime ago now.

He still blamed himself, of course. They'd wanted to take him out to eat after his high school graduation. Instead, he'd insisted on going out with his friend. They'd died when a truck jumped lanes and hit them head-on. And it was his fault. If he'd just said yes and gone out with them, they'd still be alive.

"Are you okay, Jace?" Mika asked and he started.

"What?" he looked over at her. He wasn't sure how long he'd been lost in his own thoughts, but they seemed closer to the city than they had been.

"Are you okay?" Mika asked again, her face a mask of concern.

Jace forced a smile, trying to bury his dark thoughts and the emotions came with them. "I'm fine."

Diana looked at him and gave him a dubious look. "You don't really expect us to believe that?"

"I'm fine," he told them, more forcefully this time. "Just a bad memory."

Mika put her small hand on his shoulder. "Do you want to talk about it?"

"No." He smiled, genuinely this time. "Maybe some other time."

Both girls eyed him but, thankfully, neither pushed the issue. They looked back to the city, as they drew closer to it and Jace did the same.

As he watched, one of the airships disengaged from the tower and began to slowly move off to the east. The ship moved slowly at first but then quickly picked up speed. It circled around the city and then accelerated out of the city to the west.

"I really want to ride one!" Mika said excitedly as she watched the airship growing smaller.

Jace chuckled as he watched the craft shrinking in the distance. "That would be fun."

"You two can have all the fun you want," Diana said. "I'll pass."

"Pass?" Jace asked.

"The thing looks like it could fall from the sky at any moment," the older woman replied. "No, thank you."

"You wouldn't really die," Mika said. "You'd just respawn."

"No thanks," Diana shook her head. "I'm just not interested."

"Are you afraid of heights?" Mika tilted her head at Diana.

Diana gave the younger girl a hard look but it quickly softened. "Yes, if you must know. I really don't care for heights. Flying was always so ghastly! And my coping mechanisms usually involved enough alcohol that I didn't wake up until we got to our destination." She chuckled. "I ended up at some strange airports because I didn't wake up and change connections."

Mika listened and then looked away wistfully. "I never drank much. I never had enough money to spend on drinks."

"You wouldn't be paying for any drinks in an American bar," Jace told her. She was an extremely attractive girl and if she looked anything like her avatar, she'd have guys lining up to buy her drinks at any bar. He also remembered Mika had died in an airplane crash before being inserted into the game. He was surprised she didn't have a fear of heights.

Mika blushed and cast a sidelong glance at Diana. She gave him a slight smile. "I don't believe American men would be lining up to buy me drinks."

Jace waited for her to elaborate or make it into a joke but she just turned away. Diana flashed him a look that told him not to pry and he listened to the older woman.

He didn't understand it though. Avatars were usually very similar to the original person since they were based on the person's DNA. Sure, they were the perfect version of the players's DNA in the best shape, but it was still the person. Most people were recognizable as long as they took a human-like form. Once you applied some of the more exotic player race templates, the person could get lost in the racial alterations.

He glanced at Mika. Jace tried to figure out what she could possibly mean by her statement about not getting bought drinks. He just couldn't imagine her as anything except an attractive Japanese girl with a great personality.

"We're coming up on the dock! Make ready!" yelled Colette from behind them.

The sailors began to leap into action around them, tying and untying things, unfurling sails and all the mundane actions that needed to be done to bring the ship into the dock. He only half noticed all of the action.

Jace and the girls heard a heavy cranking sound and then watched as the dock in front of them began to move towards them. Looking around, he saw a small section where a gnome sat at some sort of control panel that was attached to several large gearboxes that whirred and whistled. Occasionally a burst of steam would emerge from one of the many pipes that stuck out of the contraption.

Finally, the ship and the dock were close enough that the pirates tossed down mooring lines to the gnomes below, who quickly fastened them to some sort of elaborate looking mechanism built into the dock.

As the little gnomes went scurry around, tying up the boat, Jace couldn't help but be reminded of an ancient vidstream he'd pirated. He couldn't remember the exact name now, but it was about a boy and a candy factory. Under his breath he began singing "Oomba...oomba..."

"Lower than gangplank!" yelled the first mate, once the boat was secure. The men did so but rather than immediately head down onto solid land, they stood back. Jace saw something zooming along down the dock towards them. It raced down their section of the dock and then made a sudden turn and shot up the gangplank.

As it reached the top, Jace got a better look at it. The thing appeared to be a steam powered unicycle. And sitting atop of the thing was a gnome with wispy white hair sticking out of a leather cap and wearing goggles.

The gnome didn't move his head, but instead manipulated a control on the unicycle and the seat rotated until he was looking at Colette. "Are you the captain?"

"No me," the first mate pointed at Jace. "Him."

The little gnome pulled another lever and he spun around so fast that Jace thought he would fly off.

Amazingly, the gnome stayed on the steam unicycle. "You are the captain?"

"Aye," Jace said, keeping in character. "Captain Jynx Knightly, Baronet of Whitecliff."

"Oh, sir," the gnome blinked. He inclined his head. "I am Gluthec Oversprocket, Chief Berthing Collection Accumulator. It is my great pleasure to ask you for your berthing fee of 500 gold."

The gnome's words were punctuated by a sudden expulsion of steam that came out sounding like a train whistle. It was loud enough that Diana and a few of the crew members covered their ears. Reaching into his inventory, Jace pulled a small pouch of 500 gold and handed it over to Gluthec.

The gnome took the money and then pulled out a pad of paper and began scribbling on it furiously with a large writing contraption that looked like someone took a thick ballpoint pin and glued a bunch of random objects to it.

Nearly a minute later, the scribbling stopped and the Chief Berthing Collection Accumulator ripped off the piece of parchment he'd been writing on and handed it to Jace. "This is your receipt and berthing license. Keep it with the ship at all times and must present it when asked to by any officer of the Docking Guild. Got it? Okay. Good. Welcome to Nynymmost, sir."

The gnome had spoken the entire sentence without taking a pause or a breath. Once Jace took the parchment from his outstretched hand, he threw a few levers on the unicycle and zoomed back down the gangplank with several pops, bangs and a trail of steam.

"What an odd little man," commented Diana, and Jace could only nod in agreement.

Chapter 29

They left the ship after giving Colette orders to sail back to Haddare Reef if they didn't return in two days. Their respawn point was on the pirate island and if they were killed before they could reach the bind point for Nynymmost, they'd need to be picked up.

Before leaving the ship, he altered his appearance with his hat and made himself look like a tall gnome. It was an interesting change, as his vantage point was now two feet lower than it was when he was a human. Both girls had a good laugh at him, but he wasn't taking any chances.

"Do you really think that's necessary?" Diana chuckled as they left the ship. It was clear she was still amused by his gnomish appearance.

"The last time we were in a normal city, Mika and I were assassinated," he replied, recalling the incident in Lasthaven.

"Yeah," Mika said and drew her finger across her throat, "and the assassin killed the messenger guy too."

"Better safe than sorry, I guess," she said and looked down at him. "My husband, the little person. Who would have thought."

Jace smirked. "When in Rome, do as the Romans… or gnomes, in this case."

"You're so small, you could ride Luna!" Mika exclaimed, her eyes flicking from his small form to his giant familiar.

Luna, who had been eyeing a bucket of fish next to a wary gnomish fisherman, suddenly perked up. She looked at Jace, sniffed, and then pointedly turned around and looked forward.

"I think that was a no on being my mount." Jace chuckled. Too bad. For a moment, he imagined himself atop Luna with his sword raised high yelling "I have the power!"

They wandered around the strange, moving docks until they finally reached dry land. There Jace asked a passing female gnome for directions to the graveyard. The female looked him up and down and then glanced at the two human women with him. She made a face and then rattled off a bunch of street names before turning and continuing on her way.

The three of them exchanged glances. Jace scratched his head. "Did either of you catch that?"

Both girls shook their heads. Mika rubbed her chin. "I think she said something about front street."

"I think it was font street," Diane corrected. "At least, that's what I heard."

Just then, a gnome-sized clockwork golem came walking around the corner. The thing was made of metal but had gears and pipes showing and as they watched, it let loose a huge puff of steam through a whistle on its head.

Thing carried a crate in its little metal arms and seemed to be in a hurry to get to the docks. It nearly ran into them but stopped suddenly just before colliding with them. Luna hissed at the thing and its head tilted towards her. It looked back at the rest of the group.

"Excuse me," the thing said in a mechanical voice. "Please move aside."

The group moved aside, and the strange golem continued on with its task. They watched it go and then resumed their own journey.

"That was odd," Diana said, casting a glance over her shoulder. She shivered, even though it was warm out. "That reminds me a little too much of the spider golem creature I was when you met me. I can't say those are pleasant memories."

Jace nodded, remembering when he first met her in the Crystalburrow. She'd been a Veteribus construct in the ancient underground city. Jace had been sure she was going to kill them until he realized she was a player. Now, she was part of his group and he liked to think, a friend.

"At least you're human now," Mika smiled. "I was a yeti when he found me. I was very hideous."

The two girls continued to chat about their experiences as monsters as they walked. Jace managed to stop another gnome and get real directions to the graveyard by telling the gnome he wished to pay his respects to his departed uncle.

The city seemed to have no pattern to the streets and they became lost several times before finding the east gate. From there, it was easy to find the graveyard but Jace held them back as they came within a hundred yards of the cemetery.

"What is it?" Mika asked.

"If Damian found out we were coming here," he told her, glancing around the entrance to the graveyard, "he could be waiting for us. Most players know the first thing you do when you get to a new place is to set your bind point. It would make a great ambush spot."

They each looked around but none of them spotted anything out of the ordinary. They saw players, mostly gnomes, spawning and running naked out into the forest or back into the city.

Jace frowned. Damian was high-level and rich enough that he could afford an actual invisibility item. They were very rare since they took away a vital function of rogues, namely their scouting ability. But with the money Damian had, he could afford it. And that was if he didn't just create some item with code and insert it into the game where his character could find it.

"I don't see anything," Mika said.

"Me either," Diana said. "Except for naked gnomes, which honestly, I could do without that sight."

"Okay," Jace motioned them into a huddle. "You stay here. I'm going to sneak over there and see if I notice anything."

He brought out his magical cloak and started to put it on but paused. "If anything happens, don't try and help. If it's Damian, there's nothing any of us can do. He's too high-level."

Mika opened her mouth to object but he held up a hand. "There's nothing you can do. You can't hurt him and he would just catch more of us."

She looked hurt but bit her lip and nodded. Then she rushed at him and threw her arms around and kissed him hard. He wrapped his own arms around her and kissed her back. After a moment they broke away, breathless.

"Don't let anything happen to you," she breathed.

Jace nodded mutely, not quite sure what to say. He smiled and then threw his cloak on and disappeared. He started creeping across the space between them and the graveyard, keeping out of the way of passing players. While he might be in *Stealth* but if someone ran into him, they'd know he was there. And he didn't want the attention.

He approached slowly, throwing glances all around him. He half expected Damian to suddenly pop-up in front of him. Yet, as he made his way to the entrance of the graveyard, his old co-worker didn't materialize.

Of course, it was possible that he was here and just watching. Jace didn't have any delusions that his level 10 cloak would be infallible against a level 90+ warlock. There were spells that allowed the caster to see invisible creatures and Damian would undoubtedly remember that Jace was a rogue from their last meeting.

Nervously, Jace entered the graveyard and stopped off to one side. Gnomes continued to appear as players respawned but otherwise, Jace saw no one. If Damian was here, he was hidden too well.

Knowing there was only one way to know for certain, Jace prepared to come out of *Stealth*. Then he remembered his ring. He had a teleport. If he could use it before Damian did anything, he just might have a chance. He touched the ring and a prompt appeared.

Do you wish to activate the stored spell? (Yes or No)

Jace left the prompt up so he could hit yes with a thought. Taking a deep breath, he left *Stealth* and hurriedly looked around him, trying to see if Damian or anyone else appeared. He jerked his head around for a full minute before finally accepting that no one was going to appear.

He quickly reset his bind point and then sent a mental note to Luna to tell the girls it was safe. A few minutes later, Nynymmost was now their new spawn point.

"Okay," he said. "Let's go check out the first tavern inside the gate and see who's waiting for us."

"What if it is Damian?" Mika asked.

"We use the same plan," Jace told her. "I go in first, alone. No, it's okay. I forgot about the teleportation spell in the ring. If I'm fast enough, I can activate it and get away. If so, I'll port back to the pirate island and if that's not an option, then back to Lasthaven. You two can catch up with me there."

"Can't you teleport all of us?" Mika asked. "Doesn't it work on the whole group?"

"Yes but…"

"Then why does it matter if we're with you or not? You can teleport us all out. Right?" she demanded.

"I… uh..."

Diana suddenly chimed in. "She's got a point. If you can teleport us all, then there's no reason to leave us behind."

Jace looked from Diana to Mika. Both girl's expressions were adamant, and he knew he wasn't going to win this argument. He had unwittingly given them the ammo they needed to overcome his objects. Plus, they had a point. He could teleport the group.

"Fine! Fine!" he conceded, throwing his hands up in surrender. "We go in together. But stick close to me. The range is only about ten or fifteen feet."

Mika moved in real close. "I can stay very close to you."

Diana rolled her eyes, but he saw the corners of her mouth turn up. As for Jace, he found her sudden affection very pleasant. The feel of her body pressing against his was starting to make him react physically and he gently disengaged from her.

They reentered the city and walked down the main street. It was lined with shops of all sorts and they had to go almost two blocks before they found a tavern on their right. Above the door hung a sign with a large gear. Underneath the gear were the words "The Squeaky Wheel".

"I hope they serve actual food inside and not an oil change for those little mechanical gnomes," Diana said.

Mika nodded. "Hopefully they have waffles!"

"There's only one way to find out," Jace said and opened the door. At the same time, he pulled up the ring again and left the activation message on his HUD. One thought and they'd be gone. He hoped.

They entered the bar and looked around. Against the far wall, Jace caught the flash of familiar red hair and the long tapered ears. It was Charlena. She was sitting with her back to them, but it had to be her. He hadn't met many other elves with red hair. And what were the chances that a red-headed elf would be in the same bar they were meeting Charlena in?

Then Jace caught sight of the person sitting opposite and his eyes opened wide. He recognized the person immediately. But it wasn't Damian with her. It wasn't the dark elf he'd met in Whitecliff. "Holy -"

"What?!" Mika asked. She'd seen his eyes go open wide and was looking around frantically. "Is it Damian?"

"No," Jace managed to say and released the magic of the hat, allowing his appearance to go back to his normal self. "It's…. Mordred. It's… me."

Chapter 30

Mordred stood up as he caught sight of Jace. In his mind, Jace referred to him as Mordred since referring to him as himself was just confusing. He knew this had to be the real him, the real Jace Burton, alive and in the real world.

Did this mean he, er the real Jace, was out of the coma? Or had he been put into a medical pod? And how was it that he was with Charlena? They didn't even know each other in the real world. He suddenly felt unreasonably jealous of… well, himself.

Charlena saw Mordred stand up and she spun in her chair to see what he was looking at. She saw Jace and the girls but didn't smile. If anything, he thought her eyes narrowed slightly. Jace sighed inwardly. What was up with this girl? One minute she likes him, then she runs off, then she comes back, then she runs off again. It was enough to drive him nuts.

The patrons gave Mordred wary glances and none of them reacted friendly to him. This told Jace he must have been working on his faction for the gnomes and probably had just gotten enough that he was tolerated inside the city. Had he not, the guards would have attacked him on sight since he was in the evil faction.

His alter ego, or perhaps original ego, looked him up and down. He also saw the two girls beside him and raised an eyebrow. The vampyre walked towards Jace and for a moment he considered using the teleport ring. Considering Charlena's reaction to him, he had no idea what she might have told his real persona. Would the real him attack? Kill him? Or worse, report him and have him deleted?

Stopping a few feet from Jace, Mordred eyed him again, moving his head slightly to the right and left to get a better look at him. He didn't mind. Jace knew he looked like a better version of his real body. The resemblance would be impossible to miss.

"So," Mordred said. "You're supposed to be me."

Jace smiled. "I am you. At least, I was you up until the brain backup before the accident."

Mordred didn't react except to narrow his eyes. "Charlena told me that she told you about the accident, so that doesn't prove anything. They don't put backups in the game unless a person actually dies."

"Normally, that's true," Jace admitted to himself. "But did she tell you that you, er we, or whatever, you were declared dead at the scene. My guess is, they called it in and that got the ball rolling. Then, they must have revived you on the way to the hospital or at the hospital or something but somehow you became a John Doe, so they never rescinded the death to WorldCog."

Mordred's brow creased as he considered Jace's words. "That seems a bit far-fetched."

"And yet here I am," Jace retorted.

"But how do I know you're really my backup?" Mordred asked. "And not just some elaborate hoax to get to me about the code I found?"

"You remember the code?" Jace asked.

Mordred looked pained. "Mostly. Things from the last few hours before the accident are a bit hazy."

"I'm not a hoax," Jace told him. "I'm you. At least, you as of when you left work that day. Since then, I guess we've diverged."

"Prove to me that you're really me," Mordred said. "Tell me something only I would know."

"Our family was killed in a car accident," Jace told him.

Mordred snickered. "Anyone could have looked that up."

"...and..." Jace continued. "The reason they died is because we didn't go out with them to eat. We wanted to go with Lou and his family."

"Also, something that could be looked up. I'm sure there's an article on it somewhere on the internet," Mordred frowned.

Jace sighed. The memory of his family's death and the day or so surrounding it was burned into his memory. Both of their memories. And he knew details no one could know. "What no article will tell you is that while we were at the restaurant, Lou went to the bathroom and I, er you, us, whatever… we pretended we ate the rest of his fries but we were holding them under the table. But he got upset and punched us in the arm and caused us to drop the plate and spill them."

Mordred was quiet. Jace could see he was trying to figure out any way someone else could know what he had just said. Jace added, "Dad loved the old vidstreams but his favorite one was the Princess Bride. But Luna hated it because when she was little, the giant guy scared her."

He saw the corners of Mordred's mouth curl up into the beginnings of a smile but he wiped it away and then shot back at Jace. "What's my favorite old vidstream?"

Jace answered and then his alter ego fired back with other questions that he was able to easily answer. This went on for several minutes. Mordred would ask a question about a hobby or his life and Jace would answer it. Finally, he seemed to be satisfied and turned to Charlena. "I think he really is me. I mean, you know, a backup of me."

Jace rolled his eyes. "I'm right here."

Mordred cast a sidelong glance at him and smirked. "Sorry. This is really weird. Especially after waking up and finding out I was dead. Literally and figuratively."

Charlena got up and walked over to stand next to Jace. She took Mordred's hand in her own and Jace got the sense that this wasn't something new. What was going on? They didn't even know each other.

"So, you were telling the truth," Charlena said, looking at Jace. He let his eyes drop to their intertwined hands and the back to her face. She blushed and looked sheepish. "We've been spending a bit of time together."

Jace looked between his alter ego and Charlena. "What? When? How?"

Mordred chuckled. "I guess from your perspective this must seem pretty weird. Let's sit down and we can fill each other in."

The five of them cautiously went over to the table Mordred and Charlena had been sharing. Jace introduced Diana and Mika to his alter ego and they all sat down. Luna was already shrunk down to her normal size and she began to sniff at the two newcomers.

"It's your familiar, right?" Mordred said as he slid into the chair next to Charlena. "You named it after Luna."

Jace nodded, reached down and picked up Luna. He set her on his lap and began to stroke her. "I always wanted a cat."

Mordred chuckled. "But mom was allergic."

"Yup, so now I finally have one," he said.

"And Charlena tells me you can talk to it?" Mordred asked, giving the cat a curious look.

"Not just Luna," Jace replied. "Any monster. I have some left over skill from being a monster that allows me to talk to and understand any monster I've run across."

"That's fascinating," Mordred nodded. "I wonder why the developers…"

Mordred trailed off as Charlena nudged him with her shoulder. He looked over at her sheepishly and smiled. "Sorry, tell me about what's going on with Damian and you all being monsters."

Jace smiled and looked over to the girls. "From what I can tell, that code we found is some modification to the insertion routine. It strips people's money away and gives it to him and then puts the person inside of a monster, flagging them as some sort of AI.

"AI? How is that possible?" Mordred asked.

"No idea." He shrugged. "Damian's been at WorldCog a long time. Who knows how long he was working on this."

"And you're sure it's Damian?" Mordred asked, his brow furrowed. "I mean, he's a jerk…"

"I saw him," Jace said. "He's a Duke and an Ambassador. You know how much that costs…"

Mordred stared off into the distance for a long moment and then slowly nodded. "That's millions of dollars."

"And if he had that kind of money, you know he'd be flaunting it at work," Jace pointed out.

Mordred chuckled. "Oh yeah, he wouldn't be able to help himself." Mordred's face grew concerned. "But then how did you uh we get put into a monster body? We don't have any money."

"To shut us up and keep us quiet," Jace replied. "When you're a monster, you can't communicate with players. Whatever you say comes out as *Monsterspeak*. My guess is when he thought I... I mean, you… died, he hard coded it to insert you into a monster body."

"Weird," Mordred said.

"I know," he replied. "I managed to use a code injection attack to change my entity type to human."

Mordred nodded grimly. "About that. Charlena told me you all have changed classes several different times, without any penalty. Is that true?"

"Yeah, we're human, we don't get a penalty on experience when switching classes," Jace replied.

"Actually," Mordred countered, "that's not true. I looked it up on the wiki to be sure. Humans don't have penalties for the first class change, but after that, they incur the normal 25% experience penalty."

"No," Jace shook his head. "That can't be right. We've all changed classes two or three times. Heck, I have four classes now. No experience penalty."

Jace and Mordred both looked thoughtful and the girls all remained silent.

"What if…" Jace started.

"… you made yourself a beta character," Mordred finished. The two Jace's looked at each other and then burst out laughing.

"We're like twins," Jace said.

"Finishing each other's sentences," Mordred agreed.

"So, you think we're really some sort of beta race that never got deleted from the game?" Jace asked.

"Makes sense," Mordred told him. "You've seen their code and the database. How much left over junk is there?"

Suddenly an idea flashed into his mind and he wondered if his alter ego was thinking the same thing. "So maybe the AI entity is left over from beta as well, and Damian just repurposed it to hide his victims."

Mordred thought and then nodded. "That makes sense. It's much easier to re-use something without being noticed than to create something brand new without being noticed."

"Did you ever contact support?" Charlena interrupted and then flushed when Jace and Mordred both looked at her. "Sorry."

Jace watched as Mordred put his hand over hers and wondered exactly how close the two had become and what that meant for him, if anything. "We did. That's where I ran into Damian and found out he was a Duke. He pretty much admitted that he had done this."

"And you told all of this to support?" Mordred asked.

"As much as I could. After I met Damian, he logged off and then rushed back into work to change the position of the *Help Desk*," he explained.

"Then what happened?" Mordred asked.

Jace shook his head and nodded towards Mordred and Charlena. "First, what's going on with you two?"

Chapter 31

Mordred and Charlena both blushed and looked at each other. Mordred cleared his throat. "We've gotten to know each other over the past couple of weeks."

Raising an eyebrow, Jace motioned for him to continue.

"I woke up in the hospital and Charlena was there," Mordred looked over at Charlena. "She told me a little about what was going on and came to visit me in the evenings all week until they released me. She also let me know I was dead."

"Dead?" Jace echoed.

"Officially, I mean," Mordred clarified. "You're right that I was declared dead at the scene. But then they must have lost my id and when I got to the hospital, I was a John Doe. From what I can tell, I lost my job, lost my apartment and everything else."

"The apartment?!" Jace exclaimed. He saw other patrons of the tavern look over and he lowered his voice. "And all of our stuff?"

"Gone," Mordred said sadly. "The retro posters, the pirated vidstreams, our pod, everything."

On an intellectual level, Jace knew the stuff wasn't his. It couldn't be since he could never enter the real world again. But on an emotional level, he felt the loss of all of his stuff deeply. The pod had been the only thing he'd really inherited from his family, after paying for college. And his retro collection was priceless to him. It had taken him years of collecting, trading and searching underground forums to find some of that. Now, it was just gone.

He knew his real self must be feeling it even more acutely. He actually was in the real world. Plus, he lost his job. Could he get it back? Well, maybe get it back after the company fired or arrested Damian.

He looked up at Mordred. "Wow. I'm sorry. I mean, that stuff meant a lot to me, but I could never see it again anyway. You must really be taking it hard. Wait! Where are you living now?"

Charlena and Mordred glanced at each other. "I'm staying at her place. At least for now. Until her roommate comes back when classes start. That's how I was able to login. I'm using one of the college pods."

Jace gave his real self a sly smile and raised an eyebrow. "Staying with Charlena, huh?"

Both Charlena and Mordred blushed, and he guessed something else was going on, other than just a place to stay. He wasn't sure how he felt about that. Part of him was glad that his real self actually might be having a relationship, or whatever it was. Another part of him felt betrayed. Like Charlena had traded up for the other him. It was so confusing. He really didn't know what to think or feel.

He looked over at Charlena. She lowered her eyes with a guilty expression but then looked at him. "Listen Jace, I know we kind of kissed and stuff, but that was when I thought you were alive. I mean, that's what I wanted. Something real. Not just a virtual boyfriend." She looked over at his real life alter ego. "He's just like you, or you're like him, but he's real. And that's what I want."

From the corner of his eye, he saw Mika grinning broadly. He knew she had feelings for him too. Had she been holding back because of Charlena? Jace knew he had. After all, they'd started some sort of relationship before he'd met Mika. It wouldn't have been fair to just dump her or expect her to be happy that he was showing affection to another girl.

He laughed inwardly. Who would have guessed he'd have two girls interested in him at the same time, let alone that they'd both be gorgeous? Of course, he only knew them in their optimal DNA form, but still. He had to admit, it sounded like the subplot of some cheap novel.

Charlena must have seen Mika's grin because she turned to the Japanese girl. "I guess this one's mine and that one's yours."

Mika intertwined her arm in his and nodded curtly. "Yes, he is mine."

"This is like some weird episode of the twilight zone," Diana said, breaking into the conversation. "So, there's two Jaces now. And Charlena seems to be shacking up with one while the other is a backup like us and stuck in the game. And now it's like Charlena passed off the virtual Jace to Mika." She let out an exasperated breath. "I take it back. It's like an episode of the Jerry Springer show!"

Everyone looked at her in confusion. Jace, and his other self he assumed, knew what the Twilight Zone was but what was the Jerry Springer show? He kept forgetting that Diana had actually lived in the 20th century. She had a first-hand knowledge of the retro stuff he liked so much.

"Nevermind," Diana said, waving them away. "Go back to your story. Ignore the old woman in the corner."

Jace and his counterpart both had red faces, as did Charlena. Jace cleared his throat. "So, uh… about getting your life back."

Mordred nodded, obviously happy to change the subject. Jace wondered if the real him felt guilty at all that Charlena had gone for him first and then switched over to his real world version without so much as a breakup message. Jace thought he'd feel guilty if the situation were reversed. He'd still keep the girl, but he'd have some guilt.

"I'm not sure what we do from here," Mordred replied, looking over to Charlena. "Since Charlena got your message, we've been lying low. Your message mentioned Damian and implied that he might harm us. For now, we thought it would be better off if I stayed dead to the world."

"I've been making some discrete inquiries," Charlena cut in. Her face had finally resumed its normal color. "I pretended to be a bill collector who is looking for him. That's how I found out about the apartment. The job, I just called and asked for Jace Burton and they said there was no person with that name working for them."

Jace snickered. "A bill collector. Not bad. Hopefully that will keep Damian from figuring out someone's checking up on me...uh… him. You know what I mean."

Mordred nodded. "Trust me. It's confusing for us too."

"How long are you going to lie low?" Jace asked.

"It sounds like Damian could come after me, and by extension, Charlena," Mordred replied. "So we have to wait until he's arrested."

"Assuming WorldCog moves their butt and actually investigates him."

"But you told everything to support. Why wouldn't they investigate it?" Mika asked.

"Remember I said I met Damian right before I got to the *Help Desk*. He logged out and I assume he went into work to move it. Who's to say that he didn't revert the code? He'd made millions of dollars already. He might just cut his losses," Jace suggested.

"In which case," Mordred nodded. "They won't find any traces of the code. I doubt they'll look through the code archives if they don't see anything suspicious in the current code."

"No, not if he rolls back all of his changes," Jace agreed. "If he does, means, they'll never know what's going on, unless they dig deeper."

"Are two even speaking English?" Charlena asked, glancing between the two Jaces. They both shrugged at the same time.

"Then they won't be able to set me straight," Diana complained. "Right? If he erases all traces of what he did, they won't know about people like us and those still trapped in the monster bodies."

"I don't mind so much." Mika smiled.

"That's because you got the guy," Diana rolled her eyes. "I'm supposed to be living on an estate with servants catering to my every need. Not that our little adventures haven't been fun, but I would like to relax for at least the first twenty or thirty years of my afterlife."

"Yes, I got the guy." Mika beamed. The small Asian girl looked defiantly at Charlena, as if daring her to contradict her.

Charlena held up her hands. "That one's all yours. I have my own."

"I suddenly feel like a piece of meat," Jace said to his alter ego.

"Or a toy," Mordred grinned. "Or a piece of candy."

"Don't get a big head," Charlena told them. "Either one of you."

"Right," Mordred said. "So what do we do about Damian then?"

"The first thing we need to do," Jace told him, "is neutralize the in-game version of Damian."

Mordred gave him a dubious look. "Why the in-game version first?"

"Because," Jace replied and gestured to Mika and Diana, "we are stuck in full sensory feedback. If Damian comes for us, he can literally torture us to death. Only he could do it over and over."

"Ow," Mordred made a pained face. "I didn't think about that. And there's no way to turn down your sensory level?"

Jace shook his head. "The menu option isn't even there. I assume that's because we're not in a pod and I'm guessing the real inserted people have a similar menu. Which means we're stuck at full sensory."

"That sucks," Mordred sympathized.

"Dear one," Diana said. "You have no idea. I've felt every little blow since I woke up here. It's no picnic."

"But wouldn't getting Damian arrested in the real world have the same effect?" Charlena asked. "If he's in jail, he can't log in."

"Do you have any ideas how to get him arrested?" Jace asked. "Because at the moment, it's basically our theory versus his word. And I don't think we can even really give any evidence to support our theory."

"What about us?" Mika said. "We are proof."

"Maybe, maybe not," Mordred said before Jace could answer. "No one would disagree that you're bugged. But trying to pin that on Damian might be difficult without proof."

"What about all the money he has?" Diana asked. "That's what cued off Jace."

"Yes," Jace agreed. "But nothing would stop him from saying he earned it in-game."

Mordred nodded. "Right, technically, he doesn't have to declare it as income unless he moves it outside of the game, into the real world."

"So what are you saying?" Charlena interrupted. "That he's going to get away with it?"

Jace and Mordred both looked at each other. Jace guessed the real him knew it would be an uphill battle for them to prove anything. It would have to be WorldCog. They'd need to look at the logs, the old code, everything to figure what he did and when.

"You know what they need to do," Mordred said, as if reading his mind.

"I know," Jace nodded. "And that means getting to the *Help Desk* here. But first, we'd need to neutralize Damian in-game, so he can't stop us."

"Wait," Diana said. "How will getting to the *Help Desk* again help anything?"

"We can tell them where to look," Mordred and Jace said at the same time. They looked at each other and grinned.

"Yes, yes," Diana said. "You two are adorable."

"But won't they erase you?" Mika said, her brows furrowed.

"Hopefully not," Jace said. "Last time I told them I was your twin brother."

Mordred chuckled. "Nice. We would have the same DNA. But what happens when they don't find any trace of you?"

Jace didn't say anything. That was his fear too. That WorldCog would try to find information on him and, finding none, would discover that he was actually a brain backup of someone still alive. Then they'd be forced to delete him.

"We can't let them delete you!" Mika pleaded.

Neither Jace nor Mordred could think of anything to say. It was a very real possibility and there was very little either of them could do about it. A movie line popped in his head unbidden. "In the end, there could be only one."

Chapter 32

"So, we need to go to the *Help Desk*," Diana said after an uncomfortable silence. "How are we supposed to do that? It was hard enough to get into the palace in Whitecliff. And that's with Jace, er.. Um… our Jace, becoming a Baronet. How are we supposed to manage it here?"

"Especially if Damian is looking out for us," Mika added.

"Are we even sure Damian can really hurt you?" Charlena asked.

Jace exchanged a glance with Mordred. His alter ego shrugged. "You seem to have more experience with him than I do at this point."

"You know how cruel he could be at the office," Jace reminded his real self. "And that was more or less just for his amusement. We're actually threatening his livelihood."

"Can't you guys just wait until support does its investigation?" Charlena asked. She gave Mordred a concerned look. "You know you shouldn't be in the game much."

Jace raised an eyebrow at his real life counterpart.

Mordred waved away their concern. "I'm still weak. I sleep a lot. Apparently being in a coma does that."

"I'm surprised they released you," Diana murmured. "I mean, shouldn't they be keeping an eye on you or something?"

"Apparently," Mordred sneered, "when you're dead, you don't have insurance. And when you don't have insurance, they are all too happy to give you the most minimal treatment and send you out the door."

"We haven't started the process of trying to have him declared alive," Charlena told them, "because of your concerns about Damian. But it will be a long process for him to prove he's alive."

"So what you're saying is," Diana interrupted, "that it's going to all be on us."

Mordred shook his head. "No, I can help out where I can, but I can only be on for a few hours a day. Had you guys shown up a half hour later, we would already have logged out."

"Can you help us out with money to buy a title?" Jace asked. He remembered he had quite well over 200,000 gold on Mordred. Or, his real self did.

"No, sorry," Mordred apologized. "I want to help you that way but that is all I've got. I'm going to have to cash that gold out for real money. It won't be enough but it will help until I can find another job."

Everyone at the table was quiet. Jace realized his real self was right. If he had lost everything in the real world because he was declared legally dead, then he'd need every dime he had to buy even the basics, like food and clothing. He was staying with Charlena for now, but her roommate would be back in a couple of months and he'd be out on the street if he didn't find a job.

Jace nodded and looked at the girls. "We have to go after the rest of the treasure."

"Treasure?" Charlena and Mordred said at the same time.

"Oh," Jace said nonchalantly. "We have some treasure maps to some buried pirate treasure."

"How'd you get those?" Mordred asked.

"I decoded a pirate journal." Jace smiled.

"An encoded journal?" Mordred asked enthusiastically. "Which cipher?"

"Caesar shift cipher," he replied. "And not just a normal one, he used the day of the week as the number cipher, so every page was different until the day of the week repeated."

"Nice." Mordred smiled. "How much treasure is it?"

Jace shrugged. "We don't know. He doesn't say anywhere how much each stash is."

"But the first one was Bob," Mika announced.

"Bob?" Charlena and Mordred said together, confused looks playing across their faces.

"He's a giant dragon turtle," Jace replied. "We met him on the first island and he let us take some of his treasure. He just wanted to be left alone."

"You spoke to a dragon turtle?" Mordred asked incredulously. "And it didn't eat you?"

"It was a player," Mika supplied. "He was very nice. He was sad though."

"I don't think that one had a very good life, especially at the end," Diana said bitterly. "I understand that. At the end everyone's like a flock of circling vultures."

"He didn't want to be human again," Mika said solemnly.

Diana shrugged. "That part, at least, I don't understand. Though maybe being an enormous turtle is very zen."

Jace cleared his throat. "So, long story short, we don't know how much treasure is in each location since the first place we went had an epic dragon turtle's loot as well. We'll just have to start going out and collecting them to find out."

"Assuming it's enough, what then?" Charlena asked.

"Then we get into the parliament building and search for the *Help Desk*," Jace told her.

Charlena crossed her arms. "And what about Damian?"

They went quiet again for a good minute before Jace spoke up. "We have to neutralize him somehow."

"How?" Mordred shot him a dubious glance. "I'm sure I could kill him with my assassinate ability, but he'd just respawn. He's high enough level that all his gear is probably soulbound. At most it would annoy him and let him know that I'm alive."

"No," Jace shook his head. "We need to keep you under wraps as long as possible. We don't need him finding you or Charlena in the real world. He already tried to kill us, I mean you, with a car. Who knows what else he'd try."

Charlena gave them a defiant look. "Can't we just go to the police? I mean, he's stealing money and trying to kill people!"

Jace was about to answer her but Mordred beat him to the punch. "We'd sound like crazy people. We have no proof and the police won't do anything against WorldCog without major proof. They probably own the police, at least in Philadelphia."

"Why don't you go kill him, or seriously mess him up?" Diana said matter-of-factly. "Consider it self-defense. He's already tried to kill you once."

Everyone turned to look at the older woman. She merely shrugged. "It would be better than waiting for him to come for you."

"I'm not killing anyone," Charlena said adamantly. "I can't believe you would even say that."

Diana shrugged again. "I'm just saying. If it's him or us, I go with team us."

"Even if we wanted to do it," Jace said and then caught Charlena's angry glare. "Which we don't. But even if we wanted to, it's very risky. It would have to be you and the, um, other me, and if you miss or get caught, you could go to prison. And if you do manage it, that's something we'd… I mean you'd have to live with."

They all got silent again until Jace had a sudden flash of insight. He looked at Mordred. "What about a scroll of imprisonment!"

Mordred grinned. "That would work. He'd be bound until someone released him with a dispel scroll."

"What's an imprisonment scroll?" Mika asked.

"It's a special scroll that used to drop as monster loot," Mordred answered. "It casts a bubble of pure energy around a target that is completely impenetrable from the inside. You can't even teleport through it."

"It was really good at separating bosses, especially in epic raids. If you ran into a double mini boss situation and had an imprisonment scroll, you could cast it one of the bosses to isolate them until you dealt with the other boss. Once the first one's dead, you release the second and kill it. Made things much better."

"But like everything else," Mordred continued. "It got abused. People began to use them in PvP. A thing used for capturing epic monsters, used on a player. Needless to say, it caused a lot of trouble, since the person was permanently trapped if no one let them out."

"So they took it out of the drop table," Jace chimed in. He and Mordred seemed to be completing each other's thoughts, which was kind of cool. He wondered if that was how real twins were. "But some still exist. They're worth a lot of money. Millions of gold."

Mordred frowned. "Do you think you'll get enough gold from the treasure to buy one?"

"I don't know," Jace responded. "But even if we did get one, he could potentially just get someone to free him. Then he'd be free in a day or two."

"Unless we take him somewhere where no one will find him," Diana offered. "Like one of the islands. Maybe even Bob's island. No one would find him there."

"And how would we get him there?" Charlena asked.

Diana rolled her eyes. "Don't you people ever read books? Or watch movies? Once again, I weep for the youth. We lure him there and then we trap him."

"And how do we lure him there?" Mika asked, curious now.

"By offering what he wants," Diana replied. She looked pointedly at Jace. "You."

"No!" Mika said and grabbed his hand again.

"Relax," Diana said soothingly. "I didn't say we give him Jace. I said we offer him Jace. Then when he shows up, you use the scroll thingy on him and he's trapped in the middle of the ocean with no one to free him."

They glanced around at each other and either nodded or shrugged. Jace looked at Diana. "I like it. But he'll probably be expecting a trap."

"Maybe," she admitted. "But we have two things in our favor. One, we have the element of surprise. He expects you and Mika at the bare minimum because of that nasty business with the ear cutting. He might expect me, perhaps even Charlena. But he won't be expecting the real Jace, I mean, Mordred, right?"

Mordred nodded. "Mordred's fine. Two Jace's is confusing, even for me."

"So we're the bait," Diana explained. "And he's the trap. We'll distract him with some offer and Mordred will use the scroll and that will be that. Or do one of you have a better plan?"

Everyone looked around the table and each of this shrugged. Finally, Jace turned to her. "Fine. We'll go with that plan. But first, we'll need to get the treasure. If it's not enough, then our plan won't work. If it is, we'll take it from there. In the meantime, as we get the treasure from the various islands, we'll see if we find one with some out of the way cave or something, he can lure him to."

They all nodded in agreement.

"Okay," Mordred said. "Now that we have that settled, I really need to log. Sorry, I just don't have the strength right now to stay in-game."

"We understand," Jace told his other self. "Take care of you, or us, or whatever."

Mordred grinned. "We'll try to log in here once a day around this time. Just meet us here or send a raven message. We'll get that the next time we log in."

With that he and Charlena faded away. They all watched them go and then Mika spoke up brightly. "You are mine Jace Burton!"

Chapter 33

After Charlena and his alter ego logged out, Jace and the girls ordered some food. They would be heading back out to sea and it would be nothing but dried or pickled fish for some time. Mika, who moved her seat closer to his, ordered waffles, while Diana ordered a bread and cheese plate. Jace ordered the fish and chips and a large tuna fillet for Luna.

The group ate slowly, knowing it would be the last good meal they had for sometime, then they left the tavern. Jace had barely taken two steps when he felt a pain in his back. And then he was dead.

Alarine Palerest uses Surprise Attack on YOU for 863 damage.
You have died.
Do you wish to respawn at your last spawn point? (Yes or No)

As Jace suddenly found the world gray as he emerged into spirit form, he saw a female assassin clad in black had already killed Mika and stabbed Diana through the heart even as he watched.

Around their bodies, NPCs were running. The assassin didn't seem phased. She calmly bent over their bodies and cut off one of each of their ears. Jace couldn't help but flinch when she cut his ear off, despite the fact he couldn't feel pain in spirit form.

Having collected her trophies, the assassin ducked into a nearby alley and disappeared into the shadows. Jace cursed soundlessly as he watched the alley a moment longer. Unable to do anything else, he clicked Yes and respawned.

You have died recently.
Your experience gain has been decreased by 14% for 14 hours.
Your skills have been decreased by 14% for 14 hours.
Your maximum health has been decreased by 14% for 14 hours.
Your maximum mana has been decreased by 14% for 14 hours.

He had appeared in the graveyard next to Mika and Diana. Jace blinked and read the message in his HUD. He groaned. Once again, he had a death penalty. He would need to avoid fighting for a while or he'd be at a disadvantage. Mika and Diana were over level 10, so they'd have penalties as well.

Kraken's Claw and his haversack were on him and he equipped his saber, just in case. That was when he noticed Diana was clutching her chest and her ear. "Diana, are you okay?"

"I hate that!" the older woman spat. "I FELT that knife in my chest. It was like having a… heart attack. And my ear! That assassin cut off my ear!"

"At least you have it back!" Mika pointed out. The older woman glared daggers as she stood up.

"I take it I just joined the assassinated club?" Diana asked, brushing the dirt off her mostly naked body. Jace hadn't really seen her in just a loin cloth and bra before and he had to admit, she had an incredibly voluptuous body. Once again, he had to remind himself that she was old enough to be his grandma and looked away.

"Let's get our bodies and then get out of here," he told the two girls and jogged off towards the gate.

"What about Luna?" Mika called from behind him.

"I'll summon her when we get back to the ship," he yelled back and kept jogging.

Luckily, the tavern was just inside the gate, so they didn't have far to go. With the assassin gone, the NPCs had gone about their business and resumed their normal routines, stepping over their dead corpses.

"That's disturbing," Diana said, looking at where their bodies lie. "Our bodies are just lying there and people are just walking over them like we weren't even there."

"In their minds, we don't," Jace reminded her. "It's part of the AI. They purposefully don't notice certain things that players do, like dying. Otherwise, someone would probably come, collect our bodies and bury them. Then we'd spend the entire day hunting down where they took them and digging them up.

"I guess that makes sense," Diana conceded. "But it's still disturbing."

Jace bent down and quickly looted all of his items. He equipped his items and then waited for Diana and Mika to do the same. Once they were all ready, the group headed back to the ship.

"Does this mean Damian knows where we are?" Mika asked as they jogged back.

Still running, Jace shook his head. "Not yet. If he's still in Whitecliff or even Lasthaven, then it will take a day or so to get back to him. But once he gets it, he'll know we were here."

"Does this mean changing our names again?" Diana asked.

"No," he replied. "By time he gets the ears and realizes where we are, we'll be gone."

"What about the other Jace?" Mika asked.

Jace skidded to a halt and the two girls following him slammed into him. All three of them went down in a tangle.

"Ow," Diana said pointedly. "You could have warned us you were stopping."

"Sorry," he apologized. "But Mika's right. We need to warn Jace and Charlena that Damian might be here."

"How?" Diana asked.

"Raven messenger," he replied.

After asking several gnomes for directions, they found a raven messenger. Jace sent the message to his counterpart, letting him know that an assassin had killed them and Damian would most likely be coming to the town. He recommended they change the meet time to noon on weekdays, when Damian would be at work.

He sent it and then they went back to the Wyvern's Tail. They climbed up the gangplank and found Colette on the deck, ordering sailors around as the loaded provisions aboard the ship.

"How soon can we leave?" Jace asked.

"Trouble?" the woman asked and then she turned to bark some orders as two sailors nearly dropped a crate.

"You could say that," Jace replied. "Let's just say I'd like to leave the gnomish capital as soon as possible."

Colette looked to the sky and then out to the ocean. "Storm's coming. We should weather it in harbor and then sail with the tide tomorrow morning, assuming it's let up."

"Make it so…" Jace started but then simply said, "Aye. Make sure we have extra guards posted."

"Serious, is it?" Colette asked.

"Let's just say there may be a dark elf who wants to kill us and destroy this ship," he replied. He wasn't quite sure the last part was true, but he knew Damian wouldn't hesitate to destroy the ship if it meant putting an end to Jace, or even just greatly inconveniencing him.

"Aye," the first mate nodded. "They won't like it, not with the storm, but I'll double the guard tonight."

"Thank you," Jace told her and then he, Diana and Mika retired to the captain's quarters. Once inside, Jace took the time to summon Luna back. As he grimaced through the pain of the summoning, he saw Diana watching him.

"Summoner die?" the cat asked as she appeared.

"Yes," he told her. "Assassin killed me."

"Assassin bad," the cat replied.

"Yes," Jace chuckled. "Assassin bad."

Luna hopped up on the bed and after rubbing herself against Jace, found a spot on the bed to knead and then laid down.

"I can't believe you can do that," Diana said. "How do you tolerate the pain?"

Jace shrugged. "It's not that bad once you get used to it. And she was my only companion for a long time. I can't really imagine not summoning her back."

Diana looked thoughtful but didn't reply. Mika went over to the bed and began stroking Luna's fur. As she did, she looked over at Jace. "We have to hide out here until it's time to leave?"

Jace shrugged. "I'm not 100% sure. He may still be after me. But the assassin in Lasthaven got both of our ears. So he may have put a contract out on you too."

"But not me?" Diana asked. "Am I free to roam about?"

"Probably," Jace admitted. "For now. But the assassin got all of our ears this time. Damian must still be paying to kill me and everyone around me so he can see who my friends are. Now that he has your ear, the next time he puts out contracts, he'll include you too."

"Isn't that just wonderful," Diana said bitterly. "He's a real jerk."

"Yes," Jace and Mika said at the same time and then looked at each other. They both smiled.

"Well then," Diana said. "I'm going to run out. Do you want me to bring you back anything?" Mika opened her mouth but Diana held up a hand. "Other than waffles, which I will bring you."

Mika smiled broadly and shook her head. "Just waffles!"

"I don't need anything, " Jace leaned back in the captain's chair and frowned. "Unless you happen to come upon a scroll of imprisonment lying around."

"Somehow, I doubt it, dear one," Diana told him. "Things that like that are never easy in the stories. And even more difficult to come by in real life."

"But Jace is the hero," Mika protested. "Good things should happen to him. He's been helping others. It is karma."

"Mika, dear," Diana said. "I hope you never lose that innocence. And no, that's not really true. Not in books and not in real life."

"That's not fair," Mika crossed her arms over her chest and pouted, which Jace found incredibly adorable. Now that Charlena had made her feelings clear and seemed to like the real him, he was less conflicted about being attracted to her.

Diana shook her head and reached for the door handle. Before she did, Jace remembered that they might need to communicate with her. "Luna, can you go with Diana so we can communicate?"

His familiar opened one eye and glared at him. Apparently, his interruption didn't even qualify as important enough for her to open both eyes.

"She'll buy you a fish," he bribed her.

Bribe or no, it was enough to get her attention. The orange tabby got to her feet, stretched and then hopped off the bed. She padded over to Diana and rubbed up against her leg.

"Come on little Luna," Diana said in baby-talk. "I'll buy you a nice big fish. How's that?"

His familiar's tail began to shake and she began to purr as she rubbed herself against Diana's leg again. "Fish!"

Jace chuckled. He wondered how life would be if his biggest worry was finding a place to nap and waiting to be given food. It must be nice to be a cat.

"Ta Ta," Diana waved. Then, opening the door, then she and Luna left the cabin and headed back into the city.

That left Jace and Mika alone in the room. And although he'd been alone with her before, now there seemed to be a certain tension in the room. He glanced over to see that she was looking at him.

She got from the bed, where she had been petting Luna, and walked over to him. Stopping in front of him, she looked him in the eye. "Charlena wants the other you now, so now you are free to care for someone else."

Jace was about to reply when she climbed into his lap and before he knew what was happening, she was kissing him hard. It only took him a moment to realize that he was kissing her back just as passionately.

Chapter 34

Jace quickly learned Mika was a fantastic kisser. Whether she had a lot of experience or was just a natural, he didn't know and wasn't about to ask. This time, he felt no hesitation or guilt because of Charlena. Before, he had been torn between his conflicting feelings for the two girls, but Charlena had wiped that away now that she had chosen his alter ego.

As their kissing session continued, their hands had naturally roamed each other's body only to be abruptly stopped by an invisible force. A mood breaking red message appeared in his HUD.

You have initiated intimate contact with player Mika Knightly.
Mika Knightly has declined intimate contact.

Note: Repeated attempts at declined intimate contact will result in expulsion from the game.

Jace looked at Mika in confusion as to why she would decline but then he immediately received another red message.

Player Mika Knightly has initiated
You have automatically declined intimate contact.

Note: You are currently set to automatically decline intimate contact. This setting can be changed in your HUD menu.

Both of them looked at each other, their passion quickly fizzling away at the unexpected pop-ups. Jace quickly looked for the menu option but he knew what he would find. Like the sensory control, the menu option to change his intimate contact setting was missing. In that moment, he was sure of it: God hated him. Or maybe just WorldCog.

"What is all of this about declined intimate contact?" Mika demanded.

Jace growled in frustration. "Have you ever tried doing anything intimate with someone in-game?"

Despite being already flushed, Mika's cheeks colored slightly, and she shook her head. "No. You are the first."

He gave her a reassuring smile. "To keep people safe in-game, they implemented a consent system. As soon as contact becomes... sexual in nature... the game registers it and the consent pop-up appears. Once you consent, it lasts for an hour or until you revoke it."

"Only an hour?" Mika asked.

Jace raised an eyebrow at her and her cheeks reddened again, but she didn't look away. "That's what they decided on, but you can renew it when you start a new...uh...session."

"What about the declining," she pressed, and he saw the hurt expression she was trying to hide.

"Bear with me for just a minute longer." Jace smiled again, feeling a bit frustrated himself - and he understood what was going on. "By default, you auto-decline any sexual content. This prevents people from trying to do things like cop a feel or slap a player's butt and constantly creating pop-ups asking for permission."

"Oh." Mika let out a frustrated breath. "Where do we change it?"

It was Jace's turn to let out a frustrated sigh. "We can't."

"What?!" Mika's tone turned angry.

"We can't change it," he repeated, taking her hand. "I'm sorry. It's like the sensory input setting. It just isn't there for us. Even though we both wish it were."

That seemed to placate her slightly then a look of confusion crossed her face and her brow furrowed. "Why is kissing allowed?"

"I think you can turn that off too, but it's on by default," he told her. Then he winked and added, "thank God!"

She giggled at that and bobbed her head. "Yes, thank God."

They resumed their kissing, but it seemed to be confined to the face area. If Jace or Mika ventured to the neck or lower, they received the prompt and quickly had to abandon any further attempts for fear of expulsion warning.

Jace wasn't completely sure what would happen to them if they were "expelled" from the game. Theoretically, those people who had been inserted couldn't be permanently expelled. Instead, from what he understood, they were moved to a special "pocket dimension" by themselves. Basically, they went to solitary confinement.

Since disciplinary actions were never made public, it was hard to know how an inserted person's expulsion worked but Jace was sure he didn't want to find out. If his real life self was right, they might be some sort of beta entity, so they could experience something entirely different.

But those thoughts were soon gone as he focused on Mika. Before he knew it, the door was thrown open and Diana came striding in. When she saw the two of them in the middle of a makeout session, she stopped her tracks. She chuckled. "It's about time."

The older woman looked them up and down. "Honestly, I'm surprised you're both still wearing clothes."

They both blushed and Mika leaned away from him and pouted. "We can't! The game won't let us!"

Diana frowned. "What do you mean, the game won't let you?"

"The game is set to auto decline any intimate contact," Mika shot back. Then she smiled. "Except kissing."

"Auto decline?" Diana looked confused.

Jace started to reply but suddenly remembered that back to when he and Charlena had first met up with Diana and Mika in Whitecliff. When they talked about making some money, Diana had wanted to go out and "use her new body" instead of doing quests. But if she were in the same boat as them, with auto decline stuck on, how had she done that?

"What a minute," he said. "Didn't you already have intimate encounters back in Whitecliff?"

Mika looked from Diana to Jace and back to Diana. "That's right! How did you get it to work?!"

Diana's face went white and she walked over to the table and slumped into a chair. She buried her head in her hands for almost a minute before sitting up. "I lied. I wanted to be like one of my heroines in my book. I wanted to be confident in my sexuality and be a bold, independent woman who knew what she wanted and wasn't afraid to ask for it." She sighed deeply. "But I'm not. I couldn't go through with it. I'm not even Diana Stewart, daring romance writer. In my heart, I'm still just plain old Anika Holden."

Jace was stunned by her admission and her use of her real name, Anita, instead of her pen name, Diana. He'd always seen her as a strong, independent woman. He would never have guessed it was just an act.

Mika's face fell. "You didn't get it to work?"

"I'm sorry, dear one," Diana said, a pained expression on her face. "I didn't even try. I just couldn't muster up the courage."

Mika got up and walked over and gave the woman a hug. Watching, Jace thought it was curious that they allowed hugs, but he guessed if he tried grabbing Mika's butt while they hugged, it would trigger an intimate contact alert. Too bad.

"It's okay," Mika said.

The two girls embraced for several minutes before Mika let go and walked back over to Jace. She reached over and took his hand in hers. Jace could see that Diana's eyes were puffy and she wiped them with the back of her hand.

"I'm sorry I lied to you," Diana told them, her voice chagrined. "But I'm not really brave. I'm the same scared writer I've always been, hiding behind the characters from my books."

Jace gave her a reassuring smile. "You are brave. Look what you've been thrown into. Any sane person would be going nuts." He thought back to Big Cheese and how the player trapped in a goblin had gone insane. "Trust me. I've met some of them. And I freed others too. You and Mika are only ones who made it to Whitecliff. That takes some courage. You could have just stayed in whatever starter town you spawned in."

"Jace is right! You are brave!" Mika declared with a grin.

"You're kind," Diana replied with what Jace thought was a forced smile. "But I can't even summon my familiar. I'm not brave."

"Not liking pain isn't the same as not being brave," Jace retorted.

"I don't like pain," Mika agreed. "But I am brave!"

Diana chuckled and nodded her head. "Yes, dear, you are." She straightened up. "Okay, I'm done feeling sorry for myself. At least for now. Besides, I come bearing gifts."

With that, the older woman brought out a platter of waffles from her inventory, a plate of fish and chips and another plate with two raw fish fillets. Luna's head shot up as her nose sniffed the air. Diana also produces several mugs of mead. They all gathered at the table, except for Luna whose plate they sat on the floor, and dug into their food.

"I love waffles!" Mika announced, as she finished wolfing down her plate. "Waffles are the best! Especially with the maple syrup!"

"You know," Jace said. "They actually hired the best cooks to create versions of the food and then digitize the sensations of eating it. That's why the food in the game tastes so good."

"Whoever made these waffles is a great chef," Mika said.

Diana looked at him dubiously. "Really? Some of the food we've had was good, but it tasted like it was from a greasy spoon."

"A what?" Jace asked.

"Uh," Diana thought. "A cheap diner."

"Oh," Jace nodded. "They digitized all sorts of cuisine and they matched it with in-game establishments. We've been mostly going to taverns, so the food there is basically like bar food or diner food. There are inns where they serve the equivalent of world class cuisine. And of course, you pay for it too."

"Just like in real life," Mika said.

"Yes," Jace replied. "But it would be cool to try. Many famous chiefs contributed some of their best creations to the game. Well, by contributed, I mean, they were paid handsomely for them."

"Of course," Mika nodded.

"I don't suppose there's a burger place," Diana said wistfully. "I'd die for a good burger."

"Yeah, me too," Jace replied sadly. "But unfortunately not. They keep it mostly period, though some of the more exotic races have some more modern cuisine."

"Maybe once I get my fortune back," Diana mused, "we can go visit some of those higher class places."

"That would be nice," Mika agreed.

They finished up their food and spent the rest of the night talking about what the girls would do once WorldCog restored their money. Jace sat back and listened, interested at what they had in mind.

While he listened, he kept wondering what would happen to him. Would he get deleted? He thought he would be happy that part of him was living on, the real part of him. Yet, he realized he was still scared of being deleted. Of ceasing to exist. Of dying.

Thoughts of dying brought up memories of his family and their death. The memories caused his mood to quickly sour. But the girls seemed to be enjoying their conversation, so he forced a smile and pretended to be enjoying things. He didn't need to bring them down. He let them enjoy their fun.

That was especially true when shouting from outside interrupted them and they all ran on deck to see what the excitement was about.

"Storm horizon!" a sailor yelled down from the crow's nest. "It's a big one captain!"

Colette looked over to him. "Looks like we won't be leaving anytime soon! You can weather it in the ship or weather it on shore."

Knowing the dangers he and the girls faced each time they stepped onto the shore, the decision was easy. "Aye, we'll stay aboard."

Chapter 35

They weathered the storm in the harbor that night. Because of the strange moving docks, the gnomes were able to manipulate them to form a sort of artificial reef between the ocean and the inner docks. Because of this, the ship was spared from the worst of the waves. Once the storm broke, Colette took them out of the harbor and back onto the open sea.

Since he didn't know what treasure waited at each location, Jace picked the nearest one. The treasure marker was along the coast, north of the gnomish capital. When he gave Colette the coordinates, she whistled.

"That will take us a day and a half into raider territory," the first mate told him. "We won't get there and back without a scuffle."

"Raider?" Diana asked.

"Raiders are this world's equivalent of Vikings, only much more prolific," Jace explained. "They inhabit the northern reaches and raid the towns and vessels of all three factions. In that way, they were both neutral and hostile towards everyone."

"Oh, aye!" Colette confirmed. "They are hostile to everyone, even themselves. They're divided into tribes, or clans, and they raid each other too."

"And we're going into their territory?" Diana questioned. "Willingly? Weren't Vikings the master of the oceans in their time?"

Jace shrugged. "Perhaps. But I doubt they are any more difficult than the ninjen. They have to be around level 20 or 30, the same as them. If they were higher, they'd probably wipe out the smaller towns."

He looked at Colette. "Can we take a longship? How many raiders would that be?"

Colette looked thoughtful before answering. "I might be saying no, except I saw you with the ninjen. The ninjen be tougher than any raider I have ever come across. If we can take on the ninjen, we can take on a longship. But, there will be casualties."

"Is there anything we can do to push the odds in our favor?" Jace asked. "Longships are lower in the water, right? What about dumping oil on them and lighting it?"

"Aye," the Colette nodded. "You could do that - if you don't care about the loot. No one will be getting loot from a burning ship."

"That makes sense," Jace conceded. They'd have to defeat all of the raiders on the ship and then they'd be able to loot the ship of any valuables. Too bad.

Diana looked between Jace and Colette. "You two actually want to go up against a ship full of Vikings?"

"He's the Captain," Colette responded to Diana's look. "Where he says to go, I go. Captain, I take it we are planning to raid the raiders?"

He hadn't told Colette or the crew about the treasure. While normally he wouldn't mind sharing some with the crew, at the moment they needed every bit to buy a scroll of imprisonment. He hadn't given them any reason for their northern excursion, nor did he have to as the captain. But they would expect some plunder.

"I want to scout it out," Jace told the first mate, knowing she'd relay his reasoning to the crew. "We might be able to find a few of their bases and see if it's profitable."

Colette nodded. "I would hope it is, after how much raiding they do. But we don't have the manpower to go after one of their clan bases."

Jace thought about it briefly. "You're right. The key would be to hit one of the ships AFTER they raid someone but before they get back to their base. Then they'd be loaded with loot and none of the blame would be on us."

The first mate grinned broadly. "And that means we get to keep making port in the major cities."

"Exactly." Jace smiled. "Who knows, there might even be a reward for destroying raider ships in some of the coastal towns."

"We can skirt the coastline and look for outbound longships," Colette suggested. She looked thoughtful. "Might add a half day to the journey but we might get lucky. And the crew are itching for some plunder."

"I agree," Jace said. "Set course and take us up along the coast. Set someone in the crow's nest as a lookout. If I remember correctly, longships have no crow's nest, so that might give us an edge on spotting them before they spot us."

"You are correct, captain," the first mate looked pleased. "I will do as you order."

"We'll be in my quarters," he told her. "Have someone inform me the minute we spot something. Remember, we're privateers now. No alliance ships. Just raiders."

Colette smirked and gave him a wink. "Right. Privateers."

He and the girls retreated into the captain's quarters as his first mate began barking orders to the crew.

"I know we want treasure," Diana started as soon as they were in the captain's quarters. "But are we really going to look for trouble on the open seas?"

"We killed the ninjen," Mika pointed out.

"Yes and it was terrifying!" Diana retorted. "The storm, the things in the ocean. I know I put on a brave front, but that whole episode was terrifying."

"Diana," Jace said, trying to make his voice as soothing as possible. "You did great then and you'll do great if we're in another fight. And don't forget, we're higher level now. You heard Colette. The raiders aren't as tough as the ninjen. We won't have a problem. Trust me."

"Trust you," sighed the older woman. "I do trust you Jace. That's the only reason I'm on this crazy adventure. You seem like you know what you're doing in this game and I'm trusting you to see us through this. I just don't understand why we are throwing ourselves into danger that we don't need to."

Jace and Mika exchanged knowing looks. Unlike Diana, they'd both played the game before. They knew that the game was all about putting yourself in danger and coming out ahead. Or if you didn't, you went somewhere else, gained levels and then came back. That was the nature of VEIL Online.

But that wasn't Diana's reality. She had been in her nineties when she died. Likely the most activity and adventure she'd had in the last twenty years was a game of golf. He tried to see it from her perspective. Maybe he did seem a bit rash but he'd always just leaped in first and figured out how to swim as he went along.

Of course, now the stakes were higher. They were going up against Damian, not some game-controlled monster. Just like they had come up with a plan to neutralize Damian, he likely had plans to do the same - or likely, much worse - to them. And he had infinitely more resources than they had.

Diana was still standing there with her arms crossed over her large chest. He gave her the most genuine smile he could. "I promise that if it looks like they are too much for us, I'll tell Colette to turn the ship around. I won't throw us into needless danger. Is that good enough?"

"I just don't know why you want to do it in the first place?" she asked. "Can't we just get the treasure, imprison Damian and get on with our lives?"

"I wish it were that easy," he said. "But I don't know how many of these treasure sites we'll need to visit to get enough gold for the scroll. And we don't know what will be there waiting for us. If we can gain a few levels on the way and get a little more loot, that will help us in the long run."

"Jace is right," Mika agreed. "We must be ready to face Damian. The more levels we earn the more prepared we will be!"

Diana looked between the pair of them and then threw her hands up. "Fine! Fine! Let's go kill some Vikings!"

She stomped over to the bed and collapsed on it, waking Luna from a nap. The cat glared at the woman with one sleepy eye and then closed it and resumed her nap.

Jace walked over and sat down next to her. "I know you said you had never played before. Maybe things would be easier if I gave you a crash course in the game. I know you've learned a lot but between Mika and I, maybe we can give you some tidbits that will make you more confident."

Diana looked at him and exhaled sharply. "I guess that wouldn't hurt." She looked sheepish. "I actually do have some questions about the way some things work."

Mika furrowed her brow. "Why didn't you ask us?"

Diana rolled her eyes and sat up. "Pride, I guess. I figured out enough to get by, especially when we were fighting simple things. I wanted to…"

"… appear to be a strong, confident woman like the characters in your book," Jace finished and flashed her a grin.

The older woman slapped him playfully. "Respect your elders young man!"

"We are a team," Mika said. "A family. We will stick together and beat Damian and get our lives back!"

Something in his brain bristled at being called a family, after what had happened to his own family. He forced himself to push it to the back of his mind and smiled. "She's right. We're all in this together. And if we stick together, we'll make it."

"Ah." Diana smiled wistfully. "The optimism of youth. How I miss it. Fine, give me that crash course and let's see if an old dog can learn new tricks."

Jace and Mika took turns explaining different aspects of the game, the classes, spells, combat and a host of other game related topics. Jace let Mika cover the broad areas and then he filled in the details and the reasons why certain aspects of the game worked the way they did.

As they did, Diana listened with interest and asked questions about various topics that they were able to answer. They would take breaks occasionally to walk up on the deck and stretch their legs and when they came back, Diana always seemed to have more questions.

He was just glad she wasn't complaining any longer. And she did seem to feel better about things once certain game mechanics and reasoning was explained. Jace just hoped it was enough to ease her fears and give her more confidence.

That was especially true the next morning, when shouting from outside interrupted them and they all ran on deck to see what the excitement was about.

"Ship on the horizon!" a sailor yelled down from the crow's nest. "Raider!"

Colette looked over at him excitedly. "It looks like you'll get your wish. It's a raider and it's heading away from land. Time for us to plunder the plunderers!"

"Aye," Jace replied and looked off to the horizon. It was time to see if they really were a match for the raiders.

Chapter 36

Despite their spotter announcing the solitary raider longship on the horizon, none of them were able to see it yet from the deck. They were within eyeshot of the coast, and they could see large plumes of dark smoke rising from a spot to the north. Most likely it was the town or village the raiders had come from.

At his direction, Colette adjusted course to intercept the longship and the distance between them narrowed over the next hour to where they finally spotted it. Unfortunately, that meant the raiders spotted them too.

Instead of turning away and trying to outrun them, the ship turned towards them. That's when Jace and the other crew members were in for a surprise. It wasn't a raider longship the lookout had spotted. It was three.

"Three ships, captain!" Colette yelled out, her voice shaky. "We can't fight off that many!"

Jace wasn't so sure. Depending on what level they were, he and the girls might be able to fight them off. He had a *Defense* score well above his tier and combined with his new *Disarm* ability, he could probably take them on. But that was assuming he could somehow get them to all fight him. And it also counted on all of the grunts being around the same level as the ninjen. That was a lot of if's.

Perhaps this was one of those times with discretion was the greater part of valor. He turned to his first mate. "Can we outrun them?"

A pained expression crossed her face. "No captain. They are lighter and have a shallow draft. They can more than match our speed."

Jace frowned. Suddenly, they had gone from being the hunter, to being the hunted. He looked around and saw that the sailors were all looking at him, waiting for his decision. Great. No pressure.

He used Colette's spyglass to look out at the raider ships. They definitely looked like the quintessential Viking longship, at least, the pictures of Viking ships he'd seen. They were sleek, narrow ships with a single, rectangular sail. It was too far for him to see, but he knew there would be rowers as well, helping to speed the ship along.

They were like a pack of agile lions, nipping at the heels of an elephant or rhinoceros. Of course, these leopards had ships full of men who could board his ship. His scowl deepened. Even if there were only 20 or 25 men on each ship, he couldn't hope to *Taunt* them all to him. A lot of his crew would die. Maybe all of his crew.

And if Jace and the girls died, they'd respawn back in Nynymmost, which is where Damian would be headed. Of course, he could use his one charge of teleport to take them elsewhere, but that would just be putting off the inevitable. Even now, Damian had probably received their ears and placed a new contract on them.

He brought the spyglass down and glanced at Mika and Diana. Mika looked concerned or possibly just anxious for a fight. Diana, no longer putting up a brave front, looked very worried. Then he realized it wasn't just them. The whole crew looked worried. Even Colette.

Jace remembered the raiders had a reputation for being fearsome fighters in addition to great seamen. They really were like lions. Only, they were in the ocean. Sea lions? No, that didn't really fit. It seemed the lions were going to feast well tonight.

Suddenly something he had thought popped back in his head. Lions going after a rhinoceros. A rhino. Rhinos weren't exactly helpless. What did a rhino do when it was being attacked? It charged.

Bringing the spyglass back to his eye, he took another look at the raiders. Those ships couldn't be more than eight or nine feet wide. The Wyvern's Tail was almost three times that width. It made them faster, and her slower. It also made her heavier. Much heavier.

Still looking at the ships, he grinned. "Colette, what would happen if we rammed one of those raider ships?"

"Rammed, captain?" the first mate repeated.

He handed the spyglass back to Colette and grinned wider. "Yes. What would happen if a great big ship like the Wyvern's Tail hit one of those raider ships?"

Colette glanced towards the dots on the horizon. When she turned back around, she was smiling too. "We split them in half, like gutting a fish."

"And if we take one out of the fight," he asked, "can we take two ships?"

The first mate rubbed her chin but nodded cautiously. "I think that would be a much fairer fight than three against one. With you fighting, we could take them but we'll take some casualties."

Jace nodded. "Full speed ahead."

"Aye, captain!" Colette smiled broadly and began shouting orders. The sailors, who appeared to get confidence from the fact that their captain and first mate were both smiling, leaped into action.

"We're going to ram them?" Diana asked, now looking slightly less worried than before.

"We have mass, they have speed," he replied. "If we can hit one of them, we'll take it out of commission."

"Just one?" Mika asked.

"My guess is, they're more maneuverable than we are," he told them. "Once they see what we're up to, they won't let us catch them like that again."

"At least we can take one of them out," Mika said.

Jace nodded but he was already formulating a plan to take out and possibly cripple the other two ships. He just needed to work out the fine points. He turned to Colette. "How long before we intercept them?"

"It be hard to say from here," she replied. "They probably have a few knots on us when it comes to speed and once all the sails are up, we'll hit about eight knots. Given that we're headed straight towards each other, maybe a half hour or so."

"Stay on course," he told the first mate. "I'm going to see if I can figure out a way to take out another ship."

"If you manage that," the first mate laughed, "they'll be talkin' about this fight all over Haddare Reef!"

Jace chuckled and turned to the girls. "Find what we have that's flammable. I'm thinking of Molotov cocktails. We'll need rags, bottles and something flammable."

Mika looked confused. "What are Molotov cocktails?"

Jace was about to answer when Diana spoke up. "It's a bottle filled with flammable liquid. You stick a flaming rag into it and throw it. When it hits something, the bottle breaks, the liquid scatters and the flame ignites it."

"Oh, kaebin," Mika nodded. "Fire bottles."

Jace and Diana looked at each other and shrugged. Diana smiled. "Fire bottles."

"I don't think lamp oil will work," he told them. "At least, not by itself. We need something very flammable."

"Spirits?" Diana raised an eyebrow.

"Do we have some?"

"Didn't you notice the liquor cabinet in the cabin?"

Jace looked sheepish. He hadn't noticed it. Or he'd forgotten about it. "I didn't. Check it. The higher the proof the better. Test it somewhere safe to make sure it burns."

"Aye, aye, captain," Diana said and Mika giggled and then saluted him before the two girls went back into their cabin.

With the girls gone, Jace was left alone to wander the ship. He wasn't sure what he was looking for but he hoped he'd get some additional ideas.

At the moment, he thought he might be able to cripple at least one of the ships with a combination of *Flame Bolt* spells to the sail and Molotov cocktails into the deck of the ships. If he remembered correctly, there were just a bunch of niches for rowing on the deck. Nothing they could really use to hide from the flames if they rained down a dozen or so cocktails on them.

If he could ram one, take out the sails and the rowers on another, that might cripple the longship long enough for them to finish fighting the sailors of the remaining ship before the second ship joined in.

They could also put archers on the fore and aft decks, he thought he remembered hearing them called the forecastle and the quarterdeck. Given how much more above the sealine they were, they towered over the smaller ships. That meant they had the high ground.

He just needed one or two more tricks up his sleeve, but he was out of ideas. He walked around the deck, looking at the various equipment, sails and layout. He was almost tempted to have his sailors barricade themselves below deck while he and the girls fought the raiders.

Jace doubted the sailors would agree. And if they did, they'd likely resent him. Pirates liked a good fight almost as much as they liked the plunder. Depriving them of either wouldn't win him any points.

Then he came across the anchor. He guessed they were too deep to use an anchor given that the thick rope that it was tied to looked to be at most a hundred or so feet long. Would that really help them anyway? Staying in one place didn't seem like such a great idea.

He looked at the anchor again, then tilted his head and looked at it from another angle. An idea was forming in his head but he needed more information to formulate it. If it worked, he just might be able to take out or disable the third ship as well.

He spun and hurried back to Colette. The woman was at the wheel again, still barking orders for the sailors to adjust the sails.

"Colette," he said when he got close enough. "If we were to drop anchor, what would happen?"

She looked at him like he was crazy. "Here? Nothing. It's too deep. We'd just be dragging it behind us."

He nodded. "But what if we got to more shallow water?"

She scrunched up her forehead in confusion. "It would be doing what it was meant to do. Slowing us down in a hurry."

"How quickly?" he asked.

"Quickly enough," she told him, her face a mix between confusion and annoyance.

"How much would our speed decrease?" he asked, this time putting some steel in his voice.

The first mate sighed. "We'd drop from say, 8 knots to about 4 knots in a few minutes."

He grinned. "And what would happen if we had grappling lines tied to another ship when we suddenly slowed down like that?"

"They would be…" she stopped as she suddenly realized what he was planning. When she continued, she shared his grin. "If the grappling lines were fixed to something like our main mast, they would pull the other ship around very quickly. Probably capsizing it."

"That's what I was thinking too," he said. "I can almost hear those pirates in Haddare Reef talking now."

Chapter 37

Under Jace and Colette's direction, the sailors worked to put Jace's plan into action. They tied longer grappling lines to the main mast, ready to be thrown at the enemy longship. The sailors also located every bow on the ship and took them to the fore and aft decks, ready to pelt arrows down on the ships as they passed them.

Diana and Mika had returned with several bottles of rum that was high enough proof to burn quickly. After having the crew retrieve empty bottles - of which there were many - they were able to create 12 Molotov cocktails, mixing the high alcohol rum with some lamp oil. Unfortunately, Jace didn't know of any way to test the concoctions without setting the deck on fire. They'd just have to pray that they worked.

"Diana," he called out to the older woman. "You and I will take the places among the archers and cast as many *Flame Bolts* as possible at the enemy sails. Our goal is to destroy the sails and force them to use rowers only. That should give us an edge if we need to flee."

Although she appeared frightened, Diana nodded. "I can do that."

"Just save some mana for healing me," he smiled.

"What about me?" Mika asked.

"You've got levels in fighter," he told her. "So, grab a bow and see how many arrows you can put into the enemy before the board."

She gave him a smile and a little salute. "Aye, aye captain!"

"Just remember to meet me on the main deck once we get bordered," he reminded them. "We'll try to take the brunt of the enemies to save as many crew members as possible." He lowered his voice. "And if it comes down to going down with the ship or escaping, I'll use the ring."

Both girls nodded solemnly.

Jace walked to the forecastle and looked out at the quickly approaching longships. Now that he was closer, he could see the various raiders sitting at their oar stations, helping to propel their ships towards them.

"It won't be long now," Jace muttered.

And he was right, five minutes later, the ships were only yards away. Now on the forecastle, Jace could tell by the shouting and movement on the enemy ships that they weren't quite sure what to make of the Wyvern's Tail. Most likely, they were used to their prey trying to escape, rather than coming straight towards them.

From his position at the front of the ship, he could hear the approaching staccato beat of drums that set the rowing pace for the raiders. It was strangely reminiscent of a scene from an old vidstream his dad had enjoyed about a roman slave galleon.

Beating of the drums aside, the raider captains began to realize that they would pass each other too quickly to use grappling lines and the longships began to turn to give chase. The move was exactly what Jace was hoping for.

One of the raiders broke to the left side, while the other two broke to the right. He looked back to Colette and grinned. "Ramming speed! Hard to the right… er… starboard!"

"Aye, captain!" she grinned back and turned the wheel towards the nearest ship.

The captain of the closest ship to their starboard side, realized his mistake too late. He screamed commands to his men, but they had only enough time to look at the incoming ship in horror before the collision rattled the Wyvern's Tail and the sounds of snapping timbers and crunching wood filled the air.

Running to the port side, Jace looked down to see the remains of the longship quickly sinking below the waves. The men who hadn't been crushed in the collision were in the water, kicking and sputtering as they tried to find pieces of the wreckage to hold onto.

"Ship to starboard!" the first mate yelled and Jace ran back over to see them narrowly miss the second ship. It would have been nice to have taken two of them out with that maneuver but he'd take what he could get!

"Archers ready! Grenades ready!" Jace yelled and prepared his own *Flame Bolt* spell. As they passed the second ship he gave the command. "Unleash hell!"

Jace cast two *Flame Bolts* at the sails while arrows and Molotov cocktails rained down on the deck of the second ship. Not all of the Molotov cocktails hit the deck and of the ones that did, not all exploded. But enough did that the deck was soon a burning inferno.

While men screamed and tried to extinguish the flames, others jumped overboard to extinguish their burning bodies. No one was bothering to put out the flames Jace and Diana's *Flame Bolts* had caused on the sail. By time they even noticed, the sail was useless.

"Ship coming up on our port!" Colette's voice echoed shouts from the sailors at the stern. "They're coming after us!"

"Good," Jace grinned. There was one ship left and he had one more trick up his sleeve. He just needed them to get into range.

Colette kept the Wyvern's Tail on a straight course, forcing the raiders to struggle to catch up with them. Surprisingly, they began gaining ground more quickly that Jace would have expected. Even with the rush of the wind and the sound of the ocean, Jace could hear the drumbeat of the ship behind them, a quick, almost musical beat, that urged the raiders to row faster.

Moving to the stern, Jace looked over the aftcastle railing to the approaching ship. With their sail and the rowing, they were quickly catching up to them. No doubt, this was exactly the maneuver they were used to performing. Catch up to a fleeing ship, pull alongside and then board them. Only this time, their prey was ready for them.

It took the ship ten minutes to pull alongside the Wyvern's Tail. As they did, the raiders closest to them stood up and grabbed grappling lines. Even as they worked to throw lines at his ship, Jace signalled his own men to cast out their own lines.

Lines from both ships crisscrossed in midair, landing all about the decks of both ships. Once he saw his crew's lines hit the enemy ship, he gave the command. "Clear the deck! Prepare to drop anchor!"

Crewmen scrambled off the main deck, eager to be away from the lines. Once he saw the last man clear the area, he yelled "Drop anchor! Hold fast to something!"

Jace and the girls grabbed onto the railing as the clanging of the metal anchor chain could be heard reverberating around the ship. The raiders, who were about to swing across to begin boarding, looking around to see what the noise was.

Then the anchor must have hit the seafloor and the *Wyvern's Tail* began to slow dramatically. It wasn't like slamming on the brakes, but it was enough that the raider ship quickly outpaced them. Then, as it started to pass them, the grappling lines caught on railings, benches and alcoves in the enemy ship and suddenly the raider ship was spinning around.

Raiders were thrown overboard at the sudden jolt and then side of the raider ship was pulled to into the water. It wasn't enough to capsize the longship, but Jace could see water pouring over the side and into rowing compartments and other areas of the ship.

The captain of the ship reacted quickly and ordered his men to cut the lines, but not before the longship took on even more water, causing it to list unnaturally to the side. But the ship was still afloat.

It had almost worked. And even though it hadn't capsized the ship, it was still damaged and had taken on water. Unlike modern ships, he doubted they had an easy way to pump the water out of the ship.

Looking further behind them, he saw that thick black smoke was billowing from the burning ship in the distance. For the moment, it seemed out of the fight. There was no sign at all of the ship they had rammed.

Walking over to Colette, he lowered his voice. "Suggestion? Do we fight or leave?"

She looked around at the crew and then turned back to him. "A fight will be good for morale. And if we get some plunder, even better!"

He stepped back a little and pointed back to listing raider ship. "Cut the lines and alter course to intercept the raider! Battle stations!" Under his breath, he said "Shields at maximum. Lock phasers."

"What was that captain?" Colette asked.

"Nothing," he grinned. The crew gave a quick cheer and then scrambled to cut the lines still attaching them to the raiders. Then they gathered up their weapons and prepared for a fight.

Jace and the girls made their own way to the main deck and took up their positions. He was down to half his mana, but he still had plenty for his *Taunts* and a few *Feints*.

"So now we fight?" Mika asked.

"Now we fight," he answered. "I'm not sure how many went overboard or if they're back on the ship, but I counted about 25 on each side, plus two more. The captain and whoever bangs the drums."

"The coxswain," Diana supplied. "At least, that's what they were called on old galleys."

Jace nodded. "So including the captain and the coxswain, that's 52 men."

"Less than all the ninjen we faced." Mika smiled.

"Was it?" Jace asked. "I lost track after a while."

Mika shrugged. "Me too. But I was being optimistic."

The crew had cranked the anchor back up and the ship had turned to approach the raider. While it was clear they were struggling to keep the ship afloat, the raiders cheered and yelled challenges as the Wyvern's Tail approached. Clearly, they were not out of the fight.

It took a few minutes and some fancy navigating by Colette, but their ship pulled alongside the injured raider longship and they allowed the raiders to throw their grapples. This time, there weren't as many since the first wave of grapple lines had been ripped from their hands.

This was good. Less grappling lines meant less raiders at one time. He yelled for his men to take their places and prepare for battle. The sailors did just that. They broke into their groups of three and four and waited for the raiders to climb aboard.

They didn't have to wait long.

Chapter 38

The raiders were in a hurry to abandon their listing longship and began to throw up their grappling lines. As the first of the raiders pulled himself onto the deck, Jace got a better look at them.

Like the Vikings of the real world, they were bearded with long, unkempt hair that flowed out from underneath metal helmets. Some of the helmets had horns, but the vast majority were just metal skull caps. Nearly all of the raiders were clad in quilted jerkins and furs bound around them with leather cords. Each carried an axe or sword and a round wooden shield.

Jace didn't waste any time and immediately called up their stats in his HUD. As he looked at them, he was almost disappointed.

Bear Tribe Raider
Race: Human
Class: Warrior
Level: 18

Jace had expected them to be higher level, similar to the ninjen. These were only a few levels above them and about the same level as the sailors. They should make quick work of them.

Jace *Taunted* several of them over to his group and they began to make short work of them. None of their axes could penetrate his *Defense*. It did take slightly longer to bring them down, since he was low on mana, but the raiders did go down.

As more raiders boarded his ship, he pulled them over with *Taunts* as well, killing them as quickly as possible before moving on to another group. Between each, he'd glance around the ship to see how the other groups were doing. He was happy to see that there were only a few deaths among the crew.

Then a larger raider dressed in a chainmail shirt and wearing a horned metal helmet pulled himself aboard. Unlike the others, this one carried a large warhammer instead of a sword or axe. Given his larger size, better armor, and different weapon, Jace guessed this was the leader. He checked his HUD to make sure.

Bear Tribe Warleader (Legendary)
Race: Human
Class: Warrior
Level: 25

Sure enough, it was the leader, and a legendary boss to boot. Jace shouted his *Taunt* and the warleader spun in his direction. The raider's face was a mask of anger and fury and he let loose a primal battle cry before rushing in their direction.

Although he was low on mana, he'd counted on having to fight a boss and had saved enough for a few abilities. Plus, he had Luna's mana to draw on. Jace waited until the large warrior was about to strike him and used his *Disarm* ability.

His sword flourished and the man's hammer went flying, landing several feet away on the deck. The big man, suddenly off balance and unable to swing, slid to a halt in front of Jace. As he did, his companions rushed in to attack.

Mika Knightly slashes at Bear Tribe Warleader for 0 damage.

Diana Knightly shoots Bear Tribe Warleader for 13 damage.

Luna bites Bear Tribe Warleader for 0 damage.
Luna claws Bear Tribe Warleader for 0 damage.
Luna claws Bear Tribe Warleader for 0 damage.

Mika's blow slid off the raider's chainmail tunic and Luna's claws and bite couldn't penetrate the tough rings of steel. The arrow from Diana's bow had no problems penetrating the raider's armor and an arrow now stuck out of the man's shoulder. Jace *Feinted* and did two lightning fast thrusts at the warleader's chest.

You critically hit Bear Tribe Warleader for 44 damage plus 24 acid damage.
You critically hit Bear Tribe Warleader for 50 damage plus 24 acid damage.

Like the ninjen leader he had disarmed, Jace expected the raider to attack with his fist. Thus, he was surprised when the man's shield suddenly smashed him in the face.

Bear Tribe Warleader hits YOU with Shield Bash for 0 damage.
You are Stunned.

Jace staggered and his weapon dipped as he saw stars. He imagined he was one of those animated characters from the cartoons where birds were going around his head. He was dimly aware of the warleader striding over and retrieving his hammer before coming back over to him, grinning broadly.

Before the warleader could attack, Luna and the two girls got their own attacks in, slicing, shooting and clawing at the big man. This time, he managed to catch Mika using her *Vanish* ability before reappearing and slashing at the warleader.

Mika Knightly critically hit Bear Tribe Warleader for 21 damage.

Diana Knightly shoots Bear Tribe Warleader for 9 damage.

Luna bites Bear Tribe Warleader for 2 damage.
Luna claws Bear Tribe Warleader for 0 damage.
Luna claws Bear Tribe Warleader for 1 damage.

This time, each of them connected to some extent, doing some damage but Jace was still stunned and couldn't perform his own attacks. The big raider continued to smile broadly and brought his hammer down at Jace's head.

Bear Tribe Warleader crushes YOU for 0 damage.

Bear Tribe Warleader hits YOU with Shield Bash for 0 damage.
You are Stunned.

Whether the rocking of the ship threw off the man's aim or his *Air Armor* deflected the blow, the warleader's hammer skidded off him without doing any harm but the man's other arm smashed the shield into him again, staggering him.

Jace wanted to scream in frustration as once again unable to do anything. He was effectively helpless while he was stunned. Or, at least, he couldn't use any abilities or attack. He still maintained his *Defense* but other abilities were useless. He could only watch as his companions attacked the warleader's back.

Mika Knightly critically hit Bear Tribe Warleader for 26 damage.

Diana Knightly shoots Bear Tribe Warleader for 3 damage.

Luna bites Bear Tribe Warleader for 0 damage.
Luna claws Bear Tribe Warleader for 0 damage.
Luna claws Bear Tribe Warleader for 1 damage.

Their attacks did some damage, but if the big raider even noticed, he gave no indication. Instead he swung his hammer at Jace again.

Bear Tribe Warleader crushes you for 0 damage.
Bear Tribe Warleader hits YOU with Shield Bash but you Dodge.

Despite being stunned, Jace's body moved of its own accord, dodging the shield bash. Cheering inwardly, Jace tried to attack but realized he was still stunned from the warleader's last blow. He cursed inwardly at his own impotence as he watched his party pressing their attacks.

Mika Knightly critically hit Bear Tribe Warleader for 25 damage.

Diana Knightly shoots Bear Tribe Warleader for 10 damage.

Luna bites Bear Tribe Warleader for 5 damage.
Luna claws Bear Tribe Warleader for 0 damage.
Luna claws Bear Tribe Warleader for 2 damage.

Jace could do nothing but watch his companions attack the boss while he just stood there, swaying and unable to do the least bit to help.

The warleader shrugged off their blows and continued to focus on Jace.

Bear Tribe Warleader crushes you for 6 damage and 9 lightning damage.
Bear Tribe Warleader hits YOU with Shield Bash but you Block.

Somehow, his body moving once again on its own accord, his left arm moved up and deflected the warleader's shield bash with his own buckler, effectively cancelling the bash. Then Jace saw the message he was waiting for on his HUD.

You are no longer Stunned.

Wasting no time, he *Feinted* and attacked, driving Kraken's Claw at the raider's chest.

You critically hit Bear Tribe Warleader for 39 damage plus 24 acid damage.
You critically hit Bear Tribe Warleader for 30 damage plus 18 acid damage.

Mika Knightly critically hit Bear Tribe Warleader for 29 damage.

Diana Knightly shoots Bear Tribe Warleader for 14 damage.

Luna bites Bear Tribe Warleader for 1 damage.
Luna claws Bear Tribe Warleader for 1 damage.
Luna claws Bear Tribe Warleader for 0 damage.

The warleader grunted with Jace's blows but he continued to grin as he prepared to attack. Jace knew what to expect and he timed his own counter to match the man's strikes. As predicted, the raider struck out with his hammer. It was a glancing blow but he shuddered as the hammer discharged electricity in him.

Bear Tribe Warleader crushes you for 2 damage and 9 lightning damage.

Then the raider swung his body forward, intending to bash Jace again but this time, he was ready. He pulled mana from Luna and popped his *Evade.*

Bear Tribe Warleader hits YOU with Shield Bash but you Evade.

Jace watched with satisfaction as the raider's grin slipped at his missed attack and then *Feinted* and counterattacked with his saber, while his companions made their own attacks

You critically hit Bear Tribe Warleader for 20 damage plus 24 acid damage.
You critically hit Bear Tribe Warleader for 43 damage plus 18 acid damage.

Mika Knightly critically hit Bear Tribe Warleader for 21 damage.

Diana Knightly shoots Bear Tribe Warleader for 10 damage.

Luna bites Bear Tribe Warleader for 0 damage.
Luna claws Bear Tribe Warleader for 0 damage.
Luna claws Bear Tribe Warleader for 0 damage.

Bear Tribe Warleader goes Berserk.

Jace swore as he saw the new message. The bosses special ability had kicked in and Jace knew what Berserk would do. The boss would now randomly attack someone in range, ignoring all *Taunts.* By his mental tally, the boss was at half health. That meant the Berserk ability could last the remainder of combat. That wasn't good.

The warleader's face grew red and his eyes seemed to bulge out before he let loose a blood curdling scream. The raider spun around and slashed out at Diana.

Bear Tribe Warleader crushes Diana Knightly for 12 damage and 9 lightning damage.
Bear Tribe Warleader hits Diana Knightly with Shield Bash for 12 damage.
Diana Knightly is Stunned.

Diana let loose a scream of pain but it was cut short as she was staggered backwards by the shield bash to her face. She swayed on her feet, unable to focus or do anything.

Growling in anger, Jace rushed the warleader's back. There was no need to Feint. It was Backstab time.

You backstab Bear Tribe Warleader for 55 damage plus 24 acid damage.
You backstab Bear Tribe Warleader for 53 damage plus 24 acid damage.

Mika Knightly critically hit Bear Tribe Warleader for 37 damage.

Luna bites Bear Tribe Warleader for 0 damage.
Luna claws Bear Tribe Warleader for 2 damage.
Luna claws Bear Tribe Warleader for 1 damage.

Both he and Mika got good hits on the boss, but in his berserking state, the raider didn't so much as flinch from any of the blows. Jace expected the warleader to attack someone else, but he stayed focused on Diana.

Bear Tribe Warleader crushes Diana Knightly for 11 damage and 9 lightning damage.
Bear Tribe Warleader hits Diana Knightly with Shield Bash for 9 damage.
Diana Knightly is Stunned.

He flinched as he saw the looks of pain in Diana's eyes but her stunned debuff prevented her from crying out or doing anything but swaying on her feet.

Poor Diana didn't have the armor or *Defense* he had so she was soaking up a lot of damage. He turned to Mika. "Save mana to heal her."

Mika nodded and didn't use her *Vanish*, opting for normal attacks. Not for the first time, he wished he could convince her to use a piercing weapon so she'd get backstabs. Gritting his teeth, he attacked again.

You backstab Bear Tribe Warleader for 51 damage plus 24 acid damage.
You backstab Bear Tribe Warleader for 47 damage plus 24 acid damage.

Mika Knightly critically hit Bear Tribe Warleader for 31 damage.

Luna bites Bear Tribe Warleader for 5 damage.
Luna claws Bear Tribe Warleader for 1 damage.
Luna claws Bear Tribe Warleader for 2 damage.

He and his companions attacked and the wild-eyed warleader spun at him. The raider was foaming at the mouth and his eyes were wide and bloodshot. He attacked so quickly, Jace wasn't able to use his *Evade*.

Bear Tribe Warleader crushes you for 2 damage and 9 lightning damage.
Bear Tribe Warleader hits YOU with Shield Bash for 0 damage.
You are Stunned.

Cursing inwardly, Jace could do nothing again but stand there and sway. He could see that Diana still swayed as well, which only left Mika and Luna to attack.

Mika Knightly critically hit Bear Tribe Warleader for 27 damage.

Luna bites Bear Tribe Warleader for 2 damage.
Luna claws Bear Tribe Warleader for 0 damage.
Luna claws Bear Tribe Warleader for 0 damage.

The crazed berserker didn't waver from Jace but attacked him again. Despite the pain and the helplessness, he was at least happy that the warleader was no longer attacking Diana. He did see that his health was getting low and he was going to need healing if they couldn't finish off the raider boss.

Bear Tribe Warleader crushes you for 2 damage and 9 lightning damage.

Bear Tribe Warleader hits YOU with Shield Bash for 0 damage.
You are Stunned.

Mika Knightly critically hit Bear Tribe Warleader for 35 damage.

Luna bites Bear Tribe Warleader for 4 damage.
Luna claws Bear Tribe Warleader for 0 damage.
Luna claws Bear Tribe Warleader for 1 damage.

Mika and Luna got their attacks off and the maddened warleader spun again. It seemed like he would go after Luna, but at that moment, Diana started to move again and seemed to attract the warrior's attention.

Seeing him bearing down on her, she screamed and turned to run away. Unfortunately, he reached her before she got two steps and his hammer rose and fell and Jace heard that sound of his wooden shield slamming into her body.

Bear Tribe Warleader crushes Diana Knightly for 9 damage and 9 lightning damage.
Bear Tribe Warleader hits Diana Knightly with Shield Bash for 7 damage.
Diana Knightly is Stunned.

Seeing Diana being pummeled, Jace tried desperately to will his body to move. It was useless. He was unable to do anything at all, not even scream in frustration.

Mika Knightly critically hit Bear Tribe Warleader for 33 damage.

Luna bites Bear Tribe Warleader for 0 damage.
Luna claws Bear Tribe Warleader for 0 damage.
Luna claws Bear Tribe Warleader for 0 damage.

Then, as if sensing Jace's mental pleading for the warleader to focus his attacks on him, the berserker spun and charged at Jace. As he ran past, Mika sliced her katana along his side.

Mika Knightly critically hit Bear Tribe Warleader for 18 damage.
Bear Tribe Warleader dies.
You gain 1000 experience.
You have gained a level.
You are now level 15 in Swashbuckler.

Ability gained: Bladed Defense II

Bladed Defense II
Swashbuckler Ability
Description: Swashbucklers are masters of a one handed blade. When using a single weapon, they gain an Armor bonus of their Swashbuckler level times 2.

Not realizing he was dead yet, the warleader continued several more steps before falling lifeless on the deck in front of Jace. From the corner of his eye, he saw that he had gained a level and an upgraded Swashbuckler ability but that wasn't his primary concern at the moment.

As soon as the stun wore off on Jace, he and Mika rushed over to Diana. Her stun wore off too and the older woman immediately began sobbing. Jace put a hand on her shoulder while Mika embraced her.

He looked around at the crew, who had started cheering when the warleader had died. Jace motioned for silence and then ordered the crew to search the longboat for plunder. The crew let loose another cheer and leaped to their task while Jace and Mika helped Diana to the captain's quarters.

It had been a tough fight and Jace just hoped Diana could recover from it. She'd taken a bad beating and knowing her aversion to pain, he was worried that she might give up on them entirely and asked to be dropped off at the next port.

Chapter 39

The pirates made short work of searching the listing raider longship. In the hold, they found two chests of coins and small valuables, along with various trade goods like furs, cloth and, of course, several crates of alcohol. The cheer that went up when they found the alcohol was nearly as loud as when they won the fight.

Mika was in the captain's quarters with Diana, but Jace needed to remain outside. He and Colette kept a wary eye on the remaining ship. The raiders had managed to get the fire under control but they appeared to be picking up raiders from longship the Wyvern's Tail had rammed.

"Do you think they'll attack us?" he asked Colette.

Colette looked out at the scorched ship and shook her head. "The mast is burned and the sail is gone. It looks like some of the oars are missing and some of the oar stations are burned. They're taking on men from the other ship, so they'll be heavy. Even if they come after us, we can outrun them."

Jace cast a glance at the pirates still loading their goods from the longship. "Let's have the crew hurry and then get on our way. I'd rather not test our luck."

She nodded, obviously sharing his caution. "Aye, captain."

Colette walked away and began shouting orders to the crew. Jace took the opportunity to return back to the body of the warleader and loot it. From the body, he received two items and a pouch containing some gold and gems.

Warhammer of Lightning
Type: Crushing
Level: 25
Damage: 18 + 6 (Heavy)
Wt: 4 lbs
Special: Enemies struck with this hammer take an additional 9 points of electric damage.
Description: Warleaders are often granted weapons from their chieftain for particularly profitable or brutal raids. This one bears the mark of the Bear Clan.

Skald's Chainmail
Type: Chest Armor
Level: 25
Armor: 15 + 6 (Hardened)
Wt: 10 lbs
Description: A gift from a mighty chieftain to the skald who sang at his wedding, the chainmail was subsequently taken from the skald after the chieftain found him with his wife a month later.

Jace frowned as he read the descriptions of the items. While the chainmail might be nice for Diana or himself, it was level 25. He'd need 10 more levels before he could wear it. The hammer seemed nice, but none of them used hammers. Too bad.

Throwing the items into his inventory, he checked the other bodies his group had put down and received a handful of coins. He also found a silver ring inset with a blue sapphire. The ring did not look like a raider crafted item and Jace guessed the raider had taken it from one of his victims.

By the time he was done looting, the sailors had loaded all of the plunder on the ship and had raised the anchor. It was time for them to leave. Walking up to the wheel, he looked back at the remaining raider ship.

"I don't think we've seen the last of them," Colette said over her shoulder, reading his mind.

He turned to face her. "You think they'll want revenge?"

"Wouldn't you?" she asked. "And they're a proud people. I think the Wyvern's Tail is about to be the most famous ship in the Bear Clan."

"How many did we lose?" he asked, changing the subject.

"Three," she said. "Two of them were new, Hendrick and Whitley. The other was one of the dog-kin, Rakktor. He'd been on the ship for a couple years."

"Was it worth it?" Jace frowned.

"Oh yeah," Colette slapped him on the shoulder. "We all know the life. We chose to be here. It's a dangerous life. If they wanted something safe, they would have stayed on dry land, tending a field or something."

He forced a smile and looked back at the ship, growing smaller behind them. "How long before they come back with more ships?"

"No idea." The first mate shrugged. "I'd guess that it would take them a day or two to get home, maybe more with no sail. If they have more ships, and they decide to come after us, it will be another day or so before they return."

"So, we have three or four days."

"If I'm right. We should be long gone by then."

Jace nodded and started towards the captain's quarters to check on Diana. "You've got the helm, number one.

"Captain," Colette said tentatively from behind him and he turned back around to face her. "The men are curious about the plunder."

"Oh?" he raised an eyebrow.

"They want to know the shares," she asked.

Jace thought for a moment. "I want to go through the chests and see if there is any magical plunder, but then then you can split among them. Keep a double share out for a ship fund, so we can cover port fees and repairs. When we get to a port, we'll sell the trade goods and throw that into the ship fund too."

"What about you, Captain?" Colette insisted. "You should be taking your share."

"I took some items from the warleader," he replied. "That will be my share."

Colette considered his words but then nodded. "Aye, captain."

He left her and went back to the captain's quarters, pausing just outside the door. He paused there, debating whether he should go in now or find something else to do for a while longer. Diana had been crying when she went inside and he didn't do well with crying women.

Thinking back, Jace realized that was most likely because he really hadn't dealt with a crying woman or girl since his sister. Sure, he'd had some girlfriends, but he had never done anything to make them cry. In fact, he'd actually never broken up with any of them. They'd always broken up with him.

He wondered why that was but guessed his simple existence wasn't very exciting. He just wasn't a partier like others his age. The only club he ever went to was Club 20/20, a retro club that played the old pirated vidstreams on multiple screens while blasting the music from the last 20th century.

He thought about his life now. It had been anything but boring. Since he arrived in the game, it had been one thing after another. There had barely been any downtime or time just to really sit back and consider everything that had happened.

In fact, he had purposefully been keeping himself busy lately to avoid thinking about the real elephant in the room - his impending death. Technically, it wouldn't be "death" but it would be the end of his existence when they deleted him.

The thought scared him. No. It terrified him. Jace knew he was just a series of 1's and 0's in the computer, but everything felt real. HE felt real. He accepted that he wasn't the real Jace and that even if he was deleted, the real Jace would go on. But he was more than the old Jace now. He had experiences and memories the real Jace didn't have. He was unique now. Didn't he have a right to keep existing?

The answer was no, of course. The real Jace might have rights and if the real Jace was actually dead, then he might have some protections under the law. As it was, he doubted he had any legal protection. In fact, by law, WorldCog would be legally bound to remove him as soon as they realized the mistake.

He shuddered, feeling suddenly cold. He'd probably have no warning. One moment he'd be a living digital person. The next moment: nothing.

Would they save him off somewhere or just delete him outright? Not that it would really matter. The moment they removed his program from the server, he would lose all awareness. For all intents and purposes he'd be dead. Or was it more like being in a coma. A coma just like his real self had been.

He smirked at the irony. First, his real self was in an accident and left in a coma. When that happened, he - Jace - was inserted into the game. He'd been living and experiencing things while the real Jace was in the coma. Then the real Jace woke up and now he, the digital Jace, was going to be either saved off, meaning he'd be in the digital equivalent of a coma, or killed outright.

Jace took a deep breath. There was nothing he could do about it. It would happen when it happened. He guessed that was just like real life. You never knew when your time was up. His real self had almost been killed in a car accident. He hadn't been expecting it or even seen it coming.

He smiled bitterly. At least it should be painless. There were certainly worse ways to die than simply ceasing to exist. Or worse, if Damian caught him and figured out how to make him experience a painful death over and over again. Jace would settle for oblivion rather than an eternity of torture. He certainly didn't want to end up like Big Cheese, the strange insane player inside the goblin chief he'd met.

Nodding his head in acceptance of his fate, Jace reached for the door handle. Once more he hesitated but he knew he needed to check on Diana. He owed it to her. Taking the handle, he opened the door.

And was met with peals of laughter. He saw Diana and Mika sitting at the table and they were laughing. He blinked. Was he seeing things or hearing things? He had expected the older woman to be crying but she and Mika were laughing.

He glanced between Mika and Diana, trying to figure out what was going on. The girls looked at him, at the stupid expression on his face and burst into more laughter.

Jace looked down at himself to see if suddenly he'd grown a shark tail or something. He looked back up at the pair of laughing girls. "What?"

Chapter 40

Jace looked from the laughing girls to Luna, who lay on the bed in her smaller form, and then back to the girls. He felt like there was some joke that he wasn't in on. An irrational fear seized him and he quickly looked down to make sure he was wearing pants. He was.

He looked back to the girls. "What?"

The girls looked at each other and then laughed again. Jace was confused and it must have shown on his face.

"We are not laughing at you Jace," Mika told him, still grinning.

"It's a girl thing," Diana told him, "you wouldn't understand."

Jace opened his mouth and then closed it. From where he stood, he could see the wet lines down Diana's face, from her earlier tears. But now she seemed fine. More than fine. She was laughing.

"You can leave," Diana said, making a dismissive gesture.

Opening his mouth again to ask what was going on, he snapped it shut and shook his head. Then he spun on his heels and left the cabin. He didn't appreciate being dismissed like that, but at the same time, it was much better than dealing with a crying woman.

He didn't understand it, but he was glad that Diana seemed to be okay now. He had been worried about her taking the damage she did. Jace had no idea what pain she might have endured throughout her life, but she seemed to shy away from it here in the game.

Then again, the pain they felt in-game was 10-20% more intense than it would be in real life, so he couldn't really blame her. He wasn't a fan of pain either, but he forced himself to push through it. Remembering the mental pain he'd gone through when his family died, the physical pain was easier to deal with.

Climbing back up to the aft deck, he saw Colette near the wheel while another sailor held it steady. The first mate was staring at a map and compass. She looked up as he approached and gave him a knowing look. "Women kick you out?"

Jace glanced back at the door to the captain's cabin and shrugged. He hadn't exactly been kicked out but he had definitely been dismissed. He had no idea what was going on with the girls, but he knew better than to stay when he was asked to leave.

The first mate flashed him a smile and glanced back to the map. "We should reach your destination around midday tomorrow."

"I don't suppose you're going to tell me what's there?" she asked and then cast a look at the sailor behind the wheel. "Later."

"Honestly, I don't know. Something that will help me against the dark elf that's trying to kill me and destroy the ship," he replied. It was mostly the truth. He wasn't sure what was there. And he wasn't sure what might be guarding it.

At the last treasure map location, they'd found the kroakers. By themselves, the frog people might not have been too difficult. But then there was Bob, the ancient dragon turtle. Bob was a raid level monster. Had he not been friendly, they wouldn't have had a chance.

What if they ran into another epic monster and this time it wasn't friendly? His thoughts turned to the dragon that was currently terrorizing the area around Whitecliff. The dragon was a player like Bob. Unlike Bob, the dragon player didn't want to be left alone. It looked more like he wanted to destroy everything.

"Well," said the first mate, folding up her map. "I hope you find what you need to dispatch this troublemaker, so we can get back to piracy…" She smirked. "I mean, privateering."

She took the helm from the sailor who had been manning it and stared off in the horizon in front of them. Jace snorted as he realized that another woman had dismissed him. He was three for three apparently.

Walking to the back railing, he leaned over and looked out to the ocean behind them. It was easy to forget that he was inside a game when there was endless water all around him. Glancing to the east, he couldn't quite see the land even with his *Cat-Vision*. The coast was there, but just out of sight.

He wasn't sure how long he stared out over the water, but he felt a light touch on his shoulder and turned to see Mika there. He smiled without thinking, happy to see her. "Girl stuff over?"

She returned his smile and moved up to stand next to him, placing her hand atop his. "She is okay now."

Jace raised an eyebrow. "She wasn't before?"

Mika shook her head. "No, she was crying because of all the pain but she cried so hard she started laughing and then I laughed, and then we both laughed and kept laughing until you walked in."

Jace had no idea what she was talking about. He rarely cried. In fact, he didn't remember crying since his parents died. Even then, he hadn't cried much. His sorrow and anger had quickly turned to numbness. The therapists he'd seen while he was in foster care had tried to help him to "feel" again but he'd never fully managed to break out of that hole in his center.

"How is she dealing with things now?" he asked, worried that the older woman would swear off adventuring and fights.

"She's okay with things now," Mika replied. "I think the pain was intense, but now she sees that it is short lived and that she is fine."

"So, she doesn't want to be let off at the first port we come to?"

"I don't think so," Mika chuckled. "I just think she really likes you and didn't want you to see her breaking down or is it cracking up?"

"Maybe both," Jace said, his brow furrowed. "She… likes me?"

"Not that way," she elbowed him playfully. "I think she thinks of you like a son, or maybe a good friend. You have helped her, and me, and you treat us both with respect. I think maybe she was not treated very well by people in her life."

"Like Bob," Jace remembered. The dragon turtle had mentioned some bad experiences with his children or something like that. Maybe in a way, they were all loners - or just, alone.

Suddenly, a thought struck him, and he looked to Mika. "Were you alone in the real world?"

Mika's brow creased as if remembering something painful and she made a small nod. She bit her lip before finally speaking. "I was in a car accident as a little girl. I was in the front seat, and not wearing a seat belt. I went through the window and skidded down the road. I survived, but I had scars on my face since I was six."

He moved his hand atop hers and squeezed. "I'm sorry, I didn't know."

"In Japan," she took a deep breath, "beautiful things are appreciated. Ugly things are not. I did not have many friends and no boyfriends."

Jace didn't know how to respond to that. He had thought maybe she was just a hermit or lived in the middle of nowhere. Now he realized why she had said she didn't have any guys falling over her. She had been scarred. He couldn't imagine her flawless face with scars, but he knew it must have been terrible growing up with that sort of stigma.

But it did add to his theory. Bob had been alone, estranged from his family because they were after his money. Jace had been alone. He had no family and no friends. Mika had been alone as well. And Jace guessed that while Diana was well known by her pen name, she probably didn't have a huge social presence as her real name.

Was that their common thread? Had Damian built some sort of algorithm to target loners? It must look at social media presence for friends and then living relatives. If they fit that criteria and had over a certain amount of money, then they would be inserted into a monster when they died and their money somehow siphoned off to Damian.

But Jace didn't have money. Except, Jace had information about the code he had found and if he were inserted into the game and talked to other players enough, word would eventually make its way back to WorldCog and there might be an investigation.

He cursed. Asking Damian about that code had been signing his own death warrant. There was no way his ex-coworker would risk losing all of his money and his lucrative money maker. So he'd tried to kill Jace over it. "Bastard!"

Startled, Mika looked over. "Who?"

"Damian," he replied, trying to suppress the anger so he didn't take it out on her. "I think I just figured out how he chose us, well you and the others, to be inserted into monsters."

"Really?" she asked.

"He's targeting loners and people with no family," he retorted. "It makes sense. If someone has no friends or family, there will be no one looking for them online. Less chance of them creating a ruckus."

Mika thought for a moment. "But Diana is famous, right?"

Jace smiled bitterly. "Her pen name is famous. My guess is, her real name probably has no social presence and she had been old enough that the rest of her family were dead. At least, she never mentioned any kids or grandkids."

Mika's face contorted into an angry mask. "He is a despicable person! Preying on lonely people! He is a monster!"

"Graverobber," Jace muttered. He'd heard right from Damian what he thought of the people he robbed. To him they were dead. They had no rights and no right to the money they meant to transfer into the game.

Mika growled and pounded her fist on the railing. "We must make him pay!"

"I agree," he told her. "But the best we can hope for is that WorldCog investigates him and that he gets arrested."

"Bah," she spat. "That is not bad enough for him!"

"Maybe," Jace grimaced. He agreed with her but he was realistic. There was nothing they could do to him in the game that would affect him. Even if Mordred assassinated him, he'd just respawn. Other than imprisoning him, they couldn't do anything that would affect him in any meaningful way.

They two of them drifted in silence, each lost in their own thoughts. Tomorrow was a new day and they'd be able to find the next treasure cache. And whatever dangers protected it.

Chapter 41

They arrived at a large peninsula just before midday. According to the coordinates on his map, the treasure was somewhere to the east of the peninsula's tip. Based on the map's scale, it appeared the treasure was a day's journey inland.

Jace gave instructions to Colette to sail back to Nynymmost if they didn't return in a week. He explained that he had a teleportation ring and if they got into dire trouble, he would use it to return to them. He thought that was a better explanation than: If we don't come back, we died and respawned.

Several sailors rowed Jace, Luna and the girls to the shore in one of the longboats. Diana hadn't said much since the laughing incident and he didn't press matters. Mika seemed to think she was okay, and that was good enough for him.

Once his companions were on the beach, Luna immediately resumed her larger form. The sailors pushed the small boat back into the water and began rowing back to the ship. Jace looked at the Wyvern's Tail, anchored several hundred yards away. He hoped it would be there when they returned. He still didn't quite trust the pirates, but considering they'd just gotten some more plunder, he hoped he'd bought some good will.

Turning from the ship, he brought their map and his compass. He tried to compare where he thought they were with where they needed to go.

"Were there any notes on the location?" Diana asked, speaking for the first time today.

"No," he shook his head. "But judging from this map, it's somewhere in the middle of this peninsula."

Diana frowned. "That could be ten or twenty square miles."

"That's a lot of distance to cover," Mika agreed. "In a week?"

"I figured if we haven't found it in a few days," he replied, "then we won't find it. We'll just head on back and go to the next one."

"There's also the chance that he came back for it," Diana offered.

"True," Jace agreed. "But we had to start somewhere, and this was the closest spot."

"We'd better get moving then," Mika said, looking at the sky. The sun was just starting to reach its zenith. That meant they had about eight hours of light left.

"Alight, let's go," he told them and motioned them to follow him into the forest.

The forest reminded him of the area around Sinking Springs, with large oaks and pines forming a canopy that nearly blocked out the sun. He kept his eyes open, but other than normal forest animals, he saw nothing that indicated any monsters.

They walked for several hours before taking a break and eating a salted fish they'd taken from the mess hall. They each had several of the fillets, in case they couldn't find anything edible. Thus far, they'd seen nothing but birds high in the trees above them and tiny rodents that scoured through the foliage before they could get a good glance. What he wouldn't give for a nice deer.

When they resumed their trek eastward, Jace continued to stop periodically to adjust their course. The hike was oddly peaceful but that just made him more and more anxious. No part of VEIL Online was uninhabited. He kept expecting something to jump out at them at any moment.

Just as the sun was beginning to disappear behind them, they reached a huge ravine. The ravine cut directly through their path like some great giant had sliced through the earth with an enormous axe. The jagged drop off was at least twenty feet wide and extended north and south as far as the eye could see.

Walking to the edge, Jace carefully peeked over. The sides of the ravine were sheer stone, worn bare by years of exposure to the elements. They dropped off at least a hundred feet and disappeared into the shadowed darkness.

Mika and Diana had come up next to him and looked down as well. Mika looked at him. "That looks like a very long drop."

"Please tell me you have some sort of plan," Diana said, still looking down.

Jace frowned and looked left and right again. To the north, far in the distance, he saw something. He pulled out one of the spyglasses he'd brought with him from the ship and looked towards the area that had attracted his attention.

A mile or so to the north, a large tree had fallen across the ravine. Even with the spyglass, he couldn't make out much detail, but it could be a way across. "I see a tree lying across the ravine, up north."

"A tree?" Mika asked, her eyes brightening. "Can we walk across it?"

"Walk across that ravine on a tree?" Diana grumbled in disbelief. "What do you think we are? Poor lost circus performers?"

"Let's at least check it out," Jace said and began walking north. Casting glances down the ravine, he couldn't say he much liked the idea of walking across it on a narrow tree either. It was a long way down and even if he hit water, it would most certainly do enough damage to kill him.

According to his gnomish timepiece, it took them ten minutes to reach the tree he'd seen. Once they reached it, he realized how much larger it was up close. The tree was easily eight feet in diameter on their end and tapered down to six or seven feet on the far end.

There were no branches on the tree, just stubs where large branches had once been. The tree had sunk into the ground on both sides, either from time and elements or the regular foot traffic of creatures.

Jace stared at the smoothed trunk and then looked around near the base of the tree. He looked around the whole area and then walked towards the forest.

"Okay," Diana said, looking at the tree. "This isn't quite as bad as I envisioned. It's actually the size of some small bridges."

Mika, who had been looking at a tree trunk, turned her head to follow Jace. "Are you looking for something?"

Jace didn't answer right away but looked all over the tree line before turning around. "Where's the stump?"

"What?" Mika asked, clearly confused.

"There's no stump that I can see," he said and gestured around the area near the base of the tree.

"No stump?" Mika wrinkled her forehead and followed his gaze around the area. "What does that mean?"

Diana turned around, her lips a thin line. "It means, dear one, that this tree didn't just fall here. It was put here."

Mika turned around and looked at the gigantic tree. "Someone put here? But how? It must weigh more than a car, maybe more than several cars."

"Probably," Jace nodded. "Given how thick it is, it probably weights several tons. And I don't see any stumps around here."

"Could it have fallen from the side?" Mika asked.

"No, see the tapering?" he pointed out. "It's thicker on this side, so the bottom would have been on this side."

All three of them looked around, trying to find a stump, but there was nothing. Mika's brow was still furrowed. "What does this mean?"

"I think it means," Diana answered for Jace. "That someone or something brought this from somewhere and put it here… on purpose."

"What could carry that?" Mika said, her eyes wide.

Jace took a deep breath and searched his memories for creatures that could move a tree trunk that large. "A dragon could do it. But I think we'd see more devastation. A couple of lesser giants could do it or a greater giant. Maybe a cyclops."

"Many people or monsters," Diana cut in, "working together could have done it too."

"True," Jace conceded. He'd been thinking of monsters that do it by themselves or in small groups but a dozen ogres might be able to lift it as well.

"So there's something out here with us?" Mika asked.

Jace felt the hairs on the back of his neck stand up. "Very possibly. The tree didn't put itself here."

As he was imagining what could be in the forest with them, he had a thought. Jace realized he could be both right and wrong. While the tree obviously couldn't have gotten there on its own. There was another possibility.

It was possible this area had been tweaked by a developer and they had placed the log here specifically to allow players to access both sides of the area. But why would they have given special treatment to this area? This was really off the beaten path and for all he knew, they were the first players to ever see the area.

He pulled out his map and looked over the area they were in. There were no settlements for a half day's journey by ship. So why would a developer take the time to put a giant log bridge across a ravine.

"What are you thinking, dear one," Diana asked. "I know that look. You're figured something out."

Jace grinned despite himself. He wasn't used to anyone spending so much time with him, let alone enough time to know his "looks." He rubbed his chin. "It's possible that this was put here by the developers."

"They put a log here?" Mika asked. "Why?"

"That's the question I was just asking myself," he said aloud and looked over the tree again. Looking more closely, he could see that all of the bark had been worn off by age. He didn't know how long that would take, but he guessed it would be more years than the game had been out. He pointed to the barkless tree. "See how old this tree looks. I think this was placed here when this area was designed."

"But why?" Mika asked again.

"That's the question," he retorted, looking around again. Nothing else in the area looked disturbed or significant. Jace looked to Luna. "Do you smell anything weird?"

The cat sniffed the air and looked at him. "Nothing."

"Luna doesn't smell anything. What does that mean?" Diana asked.

"It means there was probably nothing here in a while," he replied, "possibly ever. At least, nothing that was here within a few days. If it had been, Luna would be able to pick up its scent."

"So, there's nothing to worry about?" Mika asked brightly.

Shaking his head, Jace looked across the log bridge to the forest on the other side of the ravine. "Quite to the contrary. The developers spent the time to put this bridge here. Why? Because they wanted people coming from the shore to be able to get across."

"Why? Mika asked again. She was scratching her head and looking across the ravine too.

"Because," Diana answered for them. "They made something they're proud of and they want us to find it."

Jace chuckled. "Bingo."

"What do they want us to see?" Mika asked, her eyes growing wide.

"Probably nothing good," Jace told her, looking across the ravine. "Probably nothing good."

Chapter 42

Jace wasn't completely confident in the bridge, despite its size and sturdiness. He envisioned it collapsing while they were in the middle and they'd all plummet to their deaths. Knowing he could resummon her, he sent Luna across first. The surefooted cat bounded across and then back again without an issue.

In her larger form, she probably weighed as much as either Mika or Diana, but Jace wasn't taking any chances. He brought out his rope and tied it across Mika's waist while wrapping the other end around his own waist to support her if she fell.

Mika walked cautiously over the log bridge with the rope tied onto her. Apparently, she had no fear of heights and practically skipped across the log. When she reached the far end, Mika turned and waved. She untied the rope and Jace pulled it back across the ravine.

"Your turn," he told Diana and started to tie the rope around her shapely waist.

"Is this really necessary?" Diana asked, holding her arms up.

"Do you really want to be without it if the tree collapses?" he asked.

Diana cast a sidewards glance at the ravine and shuddered. "I guess not."

Once he was finished tying the rope, she started across the bridge. In contrast to Mika's almost cavalier approach to going across, Diana was slow and methodical. She was careful to stay as close to the middle of the fallen tree as possible. Finally, she was across and turned to started untying the rope.

"Keep it on you while I cross!" he yelled and started across.

He went across as quickly as possible, much less gracefully than Mika. As he did, he could feel the bridge move slightly beneath him. He could see small sprays of dirt from where the tree bridge met the sides of the ravine and felt glad he had a rope attached to him. As soon as he got within a few feet of the edge, he jumped the rest of the way.

"That doesn't seem very stable," he said. Diana looked pale but Mika just shrugged.

"Will it hold on the way back?" Diana asked worriedly.

"Let's hope so," he said. "And let's hope we have time to use the rope on the way back."

Diana swallowed, glancing back at the dark ravine but Mika stratched her head. "Why wouldn't we have time?"

"I think he believes we might be chased," Diana supplied.

Mika looked wide eyed at Jace. "Really?"

"Who knows," Jace said. "I'm just thinking about the kroakers and how they chased us back to the ship."

"Oh," Mika pursed her lips. Then she brightened again. "Now what?"

Jace glanced back to catch a fleeting glance at the last rays of sunshine as it sank below the western horizon, illuminating it in sky shades of red and orange. It would be dark soon, very dark. And while he could see fine, thanks to the *Cat-Vision* ability he gained from Luna, neither of the girls could see in the dark.

He brought out Ardmore's Bane, the longsword they'd acquired on a quest in Whitecliff and blinked against the bright light that burst forth from the magical weapon's blade. He held out the blade to Mika.

"Can you carry this, so you and Diana have light?" he asked Mika. "Luna and I can scout ahead about 30 or 40 feet, just outside of the sword's light.

Mika nodded and took the sword from Jace, giving him a dazzling smile. He smiled back but then turned and moved just outside of the sphere of light the magical sword created. "Follow me."

The group walked on for another hour without incident. Jace stopped and walked back into the light every 10 minutes or so to look at the map and his compass. With the tree canopy, there was almost no light from the two moons or the stars. The only real illumination came from Ardmore's Bane.

"I think we're in the general area," he said, looking at the map again. "It's a little hard to guess how far we've travelled, but by my estimates, it should be around here somewhere - possibly to the north or south."

"Do we know what we're looking for?" Diana asked. "Is it a mound? Packed earth? A big X?"

Jace shrugged. "I have no idea. The journal didn't mention anything of note. But the last treasure was in a cave, so let's keep an eye out for a cave."

"Preferably one without a dragon turtle," Mika added.

"Yes, preferably one without a dragon turtle," Jace agreed. "Unless it's friendly."

"I hope Bob is okay," Mika said wistfully. "He was nice."

"Poor man just wanted to be alone," Diana said. "I can sympathize with that."

Mika and Jace both looked at her and even in the pale light of the sword, they saw the older woman blush. "I didn't mean it like that. But when I was sold this 'adventure' I was told I could live alone on a nice chateau somewhere with green meadows and a nice brook running through my estate. I had planned to live alone for some time and eventually start inviting people over."

"You wanted to be alone like Bob?" Mika asked, her eyes sad.

Diana shook her head and put her hand over Mika's. "I did. But then I met you two wonderful people. Once I get my chateau, you two will be welcome any time."

Mika brightened at that and looked back at Jace. "We can visit Diana any time!"

Jace nodded but part of him noticed how Mika just assumed that they'd be together, and that he would still exist. Either she was in denial over the possibility that he would be erased from the system, or she was being her normal optimistic self.

Either way, he didn't mind. Jace wished he could go visit Diana with her too. He just didn't know how realistic it was. And he was a realist.

"Which way do we go?" Diana asked, and Jace was glad to change the subject.

"Let's go north," Mika said, looking to her left.

"Why north?" he asked, following her gaze. Had she seen something he'd missed.

"Why not?" she asked with her unwavering grin.

He chuckled and shrugged. "Why not."

They turned to their left and headed north, Jace and Luna once again taking a spot ahead of the light. The procession moved through the forest without encountering any creatures or monsters.

In a game that was all about killing monsters and doing quests, Jace found it very odd and worrisome that they hadn't run into anything bigger than a forest creature yet. They hadn't even seen any large game. Why were there no large creatures or monsters in this area?

Had the developers simply never stocked the area? Or was there something here that had hunted all of the other animals? He'd kept an eye out for any sign of a large creature but there was nothing. No knocked over trees. No scratch marks on the bark. And Luna hadn't smelled anything, which meant nothing was roaming around marking its territory. So where were all the animals?

They walked on for fifteen minutes before the trees suddenly disappeared and gave way to a large clearing. Jace held up a fist, signally his group to stop. The clearing was two or three hundred yards wide and equally as long. The strange thing was, from what he could see, the clearing seemed to be a perfect circle. But that wasn't what caught his attention.

In the middle of the clearing was the ruins of a large, stone structure that was overgrown with plants and vines. It resembled some sort of temple or possibly a small keep of some sort. The structure looked ancient and had long ago fallen into disrepair.

"How did the captain ever find this place?" Diana asked.

"I don't know," Jace replied and looked around. They weren't anywhere near the water. What would have possessed the captain to stop at this particular peninsula and then search around it for days until they came across this structure - just to hide some treasure.

"Are we sure that those entries are places where he buried his treasure?" Diana asked, looking thoughtful in the glow of the sword's magical illumination. "Or is it just a list of places where he thought treasure was?"

Jace looked at the ancient ruins. They appeared not to have been disturbed for years, decades, maybe even a century. Was it possible that someone else found this place and told the captain about it? Or maybe he read about it. He remembered all of the books that had been in the captain's cabin when he'd stolen the tiara.

"This just seems an awfully strange place to bury a pirate's treasure," Diana told him. "And how would he have gotten it here alone?"

"Maybe he had help," Mika said.

"And risk other sailors knowing?" Diana asked.

Mika looked thoughtful and then pulled her finger across her throat. "Maybe he killed them afterwards."

"Possibly," Jace agreed and looked back at the structure. "So this may not be the captain's treasure. Or any treasure at all. It could just be a strange place the captain read about or heard about and decided to keep in his journal.

"But what about Bob's island," Mika protested. "It had treasure!"

"Bob's treasure," Jace replied, remembering back. "And he said that he found it on the bottom of the ocean and brought it back to his lair. He never said anything about a captain."

Mika made a face. "Maybe Bob ate the captain."

"Maybe," Jace said. "But I'm wondering if the captain had ever even been there. Maybe he heard about the dragon turtle's treasure from another ship or a survivor from a ship that Bob scuttled."

"So, there may be no treasure here?" Mika pouted.

Diana let out an exasperated breath. "Please don't tell me we came all this way for nothing!"

Jace gestured at the crumbling structure. "I didn't say that. I'm just wondering if, like Bob's treasure, there's some guardian inside this structure, guarding the treasure. That might explain why there are no large animals in the woods."

"Something has eating them?" Mika asked, eyes wide.

"It could be," Jace said and gestured towards the ruins. "There's only one way to find out."

Chapter 43

Leaving Diana and Mika huddling around the sword's magical light, Jace and Luna entered *Stealth* and began slowly making their way towards the structure. The closer they got to the ruins, the more it looked like some sort of ancient temple.

It appeared that at one time, the main temple had a wall which, judging by the tallest part still standing, had been about twelve or fifteen feet high. Time, disrepair, some sort of fighting or even a natural disaster, had caused large gaps in the wall now.

The two of them approached the edge of the wall, near a spot where the outer wall had collapsed. The spot looked like it might have one time been an entranceway. Possibly it had once held doors, but those had long since rotted away. Motioning Luna to the other side, he moved so that his back was against the wall and he peered into the inner courtyard.

Like the outer wall, the inner courtyard and buildings were overgrown and crumbling. The area of the outer wall appeared to surround an area 200 or 250 feet long and about 70 feet wide. Forty feet from the entrance he now stood at, were stone steps that lead up to the temple.

The closer he got, the more and more he thought it looked like pictures of older Indian temples that had been abandoned in the jungles. Only this was no jungle and the architecture, while it reminded him of India in real life, didn't look familiar to any game races he was familiar with.

"Do you smell anything?" he whispered to Luna.

Luna raised her head and sniffed the air. After a moment, she looked back at him. "No."

If there was a raid boss like Bob here, it might not be a creature. It could be a construct, like a golem. He fought bosses made of stone, and some made of ice, in some of his quests when he had played as Mordred. And technically, Diana had been a construct when they first met her.

If there was a construct, or more than one construct, they wouldn't have a scent for Luna to pick up. He looked around the courtyard again but saw nothing that looked like a construct or even parts of a construct. The area between him and the main structure contained only plants and overgrown rocks and stones.

He turned his gaze to the main structure. From this vantage point, it definitely looked like an old Indian temple. The front part of the structure was fifty feet tall, supported by six stone pillars. At least, it once had six pillars. The second pillar from the left end appeared to have crumbled and fallen inward.

The roof of the structure was made of the same pale stone as the rest of the structure but appeared to have once held carved images. Time, rain and erosion had marred what had once been intricate carvings. Now, only vague deformations in the stone gave any hint that there had once been carvings.

The foundation of the temple was about fifteen feet off the ground and a wide set of stone stairs lead up to the main level of the temple. Jace strained to see the blocks of stone that made up the foundation but from where he stood, it appeared that it was carved out of a single piece of stone.

Giving Luna a mental command, the two of them entered the courtyard and paused. He glanced around, alert to any movement. There was none. Not even the creatures of the night seemed to care about Jace's intrusion into the temple courtyard. Their night song and noises continued all around him.

Creeping through the courtyard, Jace paused on a mound of dirt at the base of the steps that led up to the temple. He looked around the courtyard, making sure nothing was moving up behind him. Something didn't feel right about this place. He couldn't quite put his finger on it, but there were questions which nagged at him.

What was this place? What was its purpose? How long had it been abandoned? How had the late captain learned of it, so far from the coast? Was there some guardian that would appear and kill them all? It was the last question that really occupied his mind.

Having done many quests in his time playing VEIL Online, he knew that some bosses were completely dormant until triggered. Oftentimes, that trigger came in the form of entering a certain place. Was that what he was about to do? Trigger a boss fight with a high-level raid boss?

He shifted his weight, and something crunched under his boot. Looking down, he saw that it was a partially buried skull. Had it been one of the priests who had cared for the temple? Had they died defending it? Who or what had attacked them?

Realizing that he would get no answers from the skull he had stepped on, he looked up at the stone stairs. Maybe there would be answers in the temple.

"Here goes nothing," Jace said and raised his foot to begin climbing up the stairs. Just before he was about to set it down on the first step, a glow appeared on the step. A trap!

Your Find Trap skill has increased by 1.

Seeing the glow and the skill increase, he immediately stopped. Jerking his foot away from the step, he set it back down on the ground. He bent down and examined the step. It was covered in leaves and other foliage and it was hard to see the actual step.

Jace frowned as he looked at the step. Now that he knew what to look for, he saw that the entire top of the step glowed, though the foliage hid most of it from him. As he concentrated on the second step, he saw that it glowed as well. Perhaps all the steps were trapped.

A terrible thought struck Jace and he stepped off the mound of dirt in front of the steps. Taking out his sword, he began to poke around at the dirt mound. As he did, he uncovered not one, but six different skulls and their accompanying skeletons. These hadn't been priests. They'd been adventurers or looters who had been killed by the spikes.

He swallowed as he realized he could have been one of them. As he started to resheath his sword, his eye caught the glint of moonlight reflecting off something shiny in the pile. Bending down, he dug around the piles for several minutes and found almost 100 gold that must have spilled from rotted coin pouches. But that wasn't his big find.

Brushing away the dirt, Jace revealed a completely unblemished set of leather gloves. As he began to pull them off the skeletal hands that still wore them, Jace received a prompt.

Gloves of the Duelist is a Soulbound item.
Do you wish to permanently bind this item to your character? (Yes or No)
Warning: This action cannot be undone.

Jace grinned. Another soulbound item. He wasn't sure if he wanted them, or whether one of the girls might benefit more. He quickly examined them in his HUD.

Gloves of the Duelist
Type: Hand Armor
Level: (14)
Armor: 6 + 3 (Legendary) + 3 (Hardened) + 3 (Supple)
Wt: 2 lbs

Special: This item is Legendary and scales to the wielder's level. In addition to normal protection, the wearer can make one additional attack with a one-handed or thrown weapon whenever he makes a normal attack. They also provide immunity to poison and poison effects.

Description: Created by the master leathersmith Solomon from the hide of an ancient Green Dragon, these gloves were given the Duke of Ardor for service to the crown. They were lost at sea when the Duke's ship disappeared in the north.

Soulbound: This item has been soulbound. It cannot be sold or traded and appears in the wielder's inventory when they respawn.

Eyes wide as he read the description. Another legendary item. And it was like they were made for him. Of course, a fighter with a shield and one-handed weapon would benefit just as much, but since he could only use a single weapon for his Swashbuckler skills, they worked out perfectly. Plus, the immunity to poison was incredible. Items that granted blanket immunity to poison were extremely rare and highly sought after.

Gloves of the Duelist have been bound.
You received Gloves of the Duelist.

Unable to stop grinning like an idiot, he quickly bound the gloves to himself and slipped them off the skeleton's bony hands. As he did, he saw something fall out of the gloves and he looked on the ground to see what it was.

It was a ring. A golden ring. He picked it up and held it up to get a better look. It was a signet ring, similar to his own ring. Looking closely, he could see that the ring held the seal of Whitecliff and the crest of the royal line. Had this been the Duke's ring? Was one of the bodies he'd just found the body of an ancient Duke of Ardor?

He wondered if there was any reward for its return. Or perhaps word of the duke's final fate. Slipping the ring into his inventory, he dug around the mound for several more minutes to see if he could find any other magical items but there were none. He finally gave up and turned his attention to the steps.

Obviously, the steps were trapped in some way. But how and what did they do? Looking around, Jace grabbed a nearby stone the size of his forearm. Moving to the side of the steps and telling Luna to do the same, he tossed the stone onto the first step. The piece of stone hit the top of the step with a muted clatter. There was a sound, and the stone was displaced as rows of four foot tall, thin, barbed spikes shot up on all of the steps. The spikes stayed exposed for only a moment, then disappeared back into the steps.

Your Find Trap skill has increased by 1.

"That would have hurt," he said to Luna. The cat just looked at him, saying nothing. The spikes had been wickedly barbed and would have created painful, bleeding wounds. They were tightly packed together, and he didn't want to know how much damage each one would do.

He grabbed another stone and again threw it onto the second step. The same thing happened. The spikes shot out on all of the steps for a few seconds, and then quickly retracted back into them.

He tried it again with the third step, expecting the same thing. Nothing happened. He waited. No spikes came out. He made a mental note. The third step didn't have a trigger. He tried it with the next step and the step after. He began to see the pattern. Every third step was safe to step on. Every third step still glowed because they contained spikes that shot out if someone stepped on the other steps, but they themselves weren't the triggers.

The process took fifteen minutes to complete and he managed to max out his *Find Trap* skill, getting a new ability when it hit rank 20.

Ability gained: Eye For Details

Eye For Details
Find Traps Ability
Description: You have become more proficient at discovering traps and this has given you an eye for details, allowing you to find secret doors and passages.

Jace smiled when he saw the new ability. There were many hidden things in the game that only someone with magic, like the glasses they'd bought, or someone with the *Eye For Details* ability could discover. It had come in useful many times when he'd been playing Mordred. It was good to have it back.

He looked to Luna. "Can you hop on every third step in your big form?"

His familiar, who had watched the spikes popping in and out with some degree of fascination, stared at him for a long moment. Then, reluctantly, shrunk down to her normal cat size. She hopped up to the third step, stopped and looked back at him as if to tell him to get moving.

Following the little tabby cat, he carefully stepped only on every third step, climbing to the top. Luna kept ahead of him and when he realized she was about to hop off the steps onto the main floor of the temple, he sent her a mental command to stop. Luckily, she did.

Catching up to Luna, Jace saw that the floor of the temple was tiled, some light, some dark. He tilted his head. It was almost like a chess board. Each tile was two feet by two feet, and they alternated as darker stone and lighter stone. But that wasn't the disturbing part.

The disturbing part were the dozen or so skeletons scattered throughout the tiled floor. The tiles had to be trapped and looking at the number of skeletons and their positions around the chessboard like floor, there might not be a safe passage across it.

Chapter 44

Looking around at the tiled floor, Jace frowned. After looking closely at the tiles in front of him, Jace wasn't able to see any holes in them. The holes on the steps weren't obvious, being hidden by the pattern carved into the stone. Once he knew what to look for however, they became easy to pick out.

This wasn't the case with the tiles. The two-feet by two-feet square tiles looked completely smooth. He looked out at the dozen or so skeletons that littered the tiled area. Something had killed them. But what?

Frustrated, Jace carefully made his way back down the steps. He made sure to stick only to every third step so his feet wouldn't be impaled. When he reached the bottom, he gathered as many pieces of stone as he could easily carry in his inventory and then returned to the top of the stairs.

He tossed on onto the white tile directly in front of him. Nothing happened. He bent down and got closer to the tile. There was no glow. Were white tiles safe to step on? Jace repeated the procedure with the darker tile to the right. The stone hit the tile and bounced, but nothing happened.

"Maybe they lure you in with a false sense of security," he told Luna. The cat stared back wordlessly.

Was that the way the trap was laid out? Were the first few rows of tiles fine and then afterward they were randomly trapped? Or was there some other pattern? And what had actually killed the other people who had tried to cross the floor? The tiles all looked uniform, other than the alternating colors.

Whether due to his newly acquired *Eye for Details* skill, or just a play of the moonlight, something about the many pillars in the area caught his eye. The pillars that held up the stone ceiling were spaced every ten feet, judging by the number of tiles between them. They took up the same space as tile, meaning they were roughly two feet by two feet. They started three tiles, or roughly six feet from the steps. But that wasn't what had caught his attention. It was the carvings on them. Or more precisely, a glint of something on the carvings.

Jace strained to see the carvings on the pillars but erosion and the vines that covered them made it impossible to see if they had actually contained writing or runes. But something had caught his eye and he continued to stare at them until he caught the glint of something shiny. Was that a gem?

He wanted to walk over to the pillar and take a closer look, but he didn't trust the floor. Looking at the skeletons, he had over a dozen reasons not to trust it. He bent down and examined the tiles again. Why weren't they glowing? If they were trapped, why weren't they glowing like the steps?

"I've got a bad feeling about this," he told Luna.

"Yes," Luna replied as she looked up from cleaning herself. Jace just shook his head and went back to examining the pillars and floor. A flash of inspiration struck him and he pulled out the spyglass he'd been using on the ship. Bringing it up to his eye, he focused on the pillar to the right.

He used the magnified view to zoom in on the part of the pillar where he'd seen the gem. It took him a minute to focus. The spyglass was meant for longer distances and was slightly out of focus with something so close. But even though it was blurry, he could definitely make out a green emerald like gem embedded in the pillar. Nice!

Moving the spyglass up and down the pillar, Jace was pleased to find more of the green gems. He wondered how much they were worth. He turned and looked at the pillar on his left. Just like the previous pillar, it had gems embedded in it as well.

Then he caught sight of something he almost missed. The gems were space about six inches apart and in between them, barely visible, were round holes. He brought the spyglass down and strained his eyes again. Now that he knew what to look for, he could pick them out.

Gems and holes. What did the two have to do with each other? And why were the gems still there? Why hadn't they been pried out and taken long ago? There were skeletons near some of the pillars, but there were also skeletons four or five feet from pillars. The pillars were strewn over different tiles, so it was impossible to know the last tile they had been standing on.

Jace brought the spyglass down and looked from pillar to pillar. The gems lined up exactly on the pillars to his left and right, each gem having a twin on the opposite pillar. Two gems that lined up exactly on each pillar. Each gem with an associated hole below the gem.

On a hunch, he pulled his sword from its scabbard. Leaning forward, he swiped the sword between the two pillars, breaking the invisible lines between the green gems.

As soon as the invisible plane was broken, he heard a clicking sound and felt the impact of something against his sword. Even as he sliced his sword down, he felt the small impacts along his sword until it had completed its arch through the pillars.

He brought Kraken's Claw back quickly and examined it but saw no damage. He squinted at the ground where he'd sliced the sword. They were hard to see, but he spotted tiny, thorn-like darts lying on the ground. Even from where he was at, he could make out the dark liquid that stained their tips. Poison.

The pillars shot poison darts as soon as someone interrupted the line between the gems. They were like magical, invisible tripwires. Which meant there was no way to disable them like a normal tripwire. He was surprised he'd never run into them before, especially with Mordred at higher level.

Poison shouldn't affect him with his new magical gloves but even if those darts only did a single point of damage, he could be hit by dozens, even hundreds of them. He looked down at all the skeletons. He wasn't willing to risk it. Not yet, at least.

He stared up and down at the pillars, trying to figure out what to do. Maybe he could pry them out from the side? Or would that just cause a nonstop barrage of the tiny thorn-like projectiles? Was that even possible?

Now that he knew how they worked, he stepped up onto the first square. Nothing happened. He had guessed that it wouldn't since the pillars began on the third row of tiles. That left a two tile wide walkway that he could transverse.

Thinking he might be able to just walk around the trapped pillars, Jace walked left, all the way to the end. He found that the pillars at the far left actually flush against the foundation. There was no way to just walk around them without breaking the magical tripwire.

Next, he walked right, past the steps. He had intended to go all the way to the end, to see if it was the same on both sides but stopped in his tracks. The second to last and last pillars did not have green gems set in them. These two pillars had red gems.

"These gems are different," he said absently to Luna, who was walking next to him. She was still in her smaller form and glanced up at him.

Taking his sword out again, he passed it between the two pillars. Nothing happened. He didn't feel any impacts of tiny darts. Jace looked down on the ground where the sword had passed. He didn't see any darts. Just to make sure, he sliced Kraken's Claw between the two pillars again. Nothing.

Jace put his sword away. Steeling himself for pain and ready to snatch his hand back, he broke the invisible plane with his hand. Nothing. No darts came shooting out from the pillars. Was that the key? Red gemmed pillars were safe to pass through but green ones weren't?

He pushed his arm through the invisible tripwire, further this time and still nothing happened. Satisfied, he looked down at Luna who was watching him with some interest. "Follow me exactly. Okay?"

Luna looked up at him and tilted her head. "Yes."

Taking a deep breath and hoping he was right, Jace leaped past the pillars. Nothing happened. So far, so good. Luna trotted after him and stopped next to him, looking up expectantly.

Now that he knew what to look for, Jace was able to find a twisting path that snakes between the pillars. He followed it forward, then turned, then came backwards, then turned again, then went all the way to the left end before looping back and finally depositing him on the other side of the tiled area, in front of the two metal doors that lead into a new area.

Jace glanced down at Luna. "Think the door is trapped too?"

Luna just stared back at him.

"Me too," Jace nodded and started examining the door. For some reason, the magical, invisible tripwires hadn't registered as traps for him. Was that because his skill was too low? Or was it because they were, by their nature, invisible. And could he trust his *Find Trap* skill to find other traps?

Realizing he had no choice, Jace poured over every inch of the door, looking for any sort of trap. He also looked at the area to either side of the door. There were no hinges, they must be on the other side of the door. That meant the door opened inward into the room beyond.

He checked the floor as well, looking for any indications that there might be a pit that opened below him if the doors were open, but he saw no signs of any traps. He spent several more minutes going over everything a second and third time before finally giving up.

"If there's a trap," he told Luna. "It's hidden well. What do you say? Do we just open it?"

Luna stared at him for a long minute. "Yes."

"Fine," he smiled. "If I die, it's your fault."

He pushed on the door and, despite their obvious age, the double metal doors swung open silently. As they opened, they revealed a large inner room. It was at least as large as the tiled area he'd just navigated, but was an enclosed room.

As the doors opened, magical torches bolted to the walls on either side of the room burst into light, illuminating the room in a pale golden-orange light. It was impressive but his attention was immediately drawn to something at the far end of the room.

Against the wall, or perhaps carved from the wall, was a stone idol. The idol was of a humanoid, sitting cross legged on the floor. It's arms were on it's lap and in the statue's hands held a large stone bowl. Magical fire burst from the bowl, further illuminating the large room.

With the light, Jace could see that the idol was not of a human. The nose was broad and flat and the eyes were too big. The thing's mouth was open and its teeth were pointed. From the sides of its head sprouted horns. Was it supposed to be some sort of demon? Or some ancient god?

But even that didn't capture Jace's attention. The things that captivated him were two enormous gems that served as pupils for the creature. They had to be as large as his fist. Maybe larger. Just one the gems might be worth enough to get the scroll of imprisonment they needed to trap Damian.

Then Jace looked at the forty or so feet of tiled floor between him and the idol and wondered what sort of final traps there might be to protect something so valuable. In his experience, he'd learned that the developers always saved the most diabolical and deadly traps for the final room.

Chapter 45

Letting out a frustrated breath, Jace squatted down at the entrance to the idol room. He'd spent the last fifteen minutes searching, prodding and throwing things on the floor tiles without any result. At this point, it looked like there were no traps. But he couldn't accept that.

In his experience playing 90+ levels as Mordred the assassin, the final room was always the most difficult. The traps were more carefully hidden and more deadly. So where were the traps?

Was he not high enough level to find them? Or, like the invisible trip wires in the previous room, did these not show up on his *Find Traps* skill? There was no way to know for certain and nothing he'd done so far had triggered any sort of effect. He was starting to get frustrated.

Luna meowed and looked up at him. She was still in her smaller form and had been cleaning herself. Now, she was done grooming and giving him a bored look.

"I can't find any traps," he told her.

"Traps?" she meowed.

"Like the spikes or the little darts," he replied. "There's got to be something between us and that idol. Some other trap."

Luna sniffed and stood up. She walked back and forth across the doorway and Jace thought maybe she was smelling something. Perhaps it was some sort of acid or gas trap and she was getting a whiff of it.

Then, as he was watching her, she turned and trotted off into the room before he could do anything. Reaching out and trying to grab her, he yelled out for her. "Luna!"

Ignoring him, the cat trotted across the forty feet to the base of the idol. When she got there, she turned around. Still facing him, his familiar sat back on her haunches and stared at him. "No trap."

Recovering from his panic that Luna was about to be impaled, shot full of darts or dropped into acid, Jace let his outstretched hand drop to his side and stared open mouthed at the orange tabby in front of the idol.

Had Luna known there were no traps? If so, how had she known? Or was it just sheer dumb luck?

Jace looked at the floor, glancing from tile to tile. Maybe she was too light to set off any pressure plates? He looked back at her. "Grow big and come back."

He hated himself for asking her to do that. If he was right and it took a certain weight to set off the trap, then she'd probably be killed. On the other hand, if he walked out onto the tiles and died, she'd be banished anyway. At least, that's how he tried to justify it.

Giving Jace the equivalent of a cat shrug, Luna grew to her giant size. Now the size of a tiger, she had to weigh nearly the same as him. No traps went off. She trotted across the room and stopped in front of him. "No trap."

Jace had nearly covered his eye, afraid to see what would happen to Luna. When she stopped in front of him, he bent down and scratched her under the chin and behind the ears. "You're a good cat!"

"Yes," she replied, purring from the scratching.

Jace stood up and took a deep breath. If Luna could make it, then so should he. Theoretically. He put a foot out onto the first tile and slowly put weight on it, ready to move it back at a moment's notice.

Nothing happened. He put more weight on the foot and still nothing happened. Cautiously, he moved his other foot to the tile next to it. He waited to be killed in some gross and painful way, but nothing happened.

While Luna watched him curiously, Jace slowly took a step. Then another. When nothing happened, he continued slowly stepping across the room, ready to dive to the side or roll out of the way. Finally, he was in front of the idol and Luna padded up next to him. She looked up. "No trap."

"Yeah, yeah, smarty pants," he teased and scratched her behind the ears.

He looked up at the strange idol at the huge gems embedded in the eyes. He reached out and carefully put a hand on the idol and then quickly withdrew it. Jace hadn't really expected anything to happen but one never knew.

"Time to get some loot," he told Luna and climbed up onto the huge statue. He first climbed onto the legs, then reaching up, pulled himself onto the right shoulder. Squeezing the statue's neck with his legs, he withdrew a knife. Jace leaned over the face and, after a little effort, pried the gem out of the eye socket.

Jace caught the eye and then quickly glanced around the room, expecting something to happen. But nothing happened. The only thing moving was Luna's tail as it swished back and forth while she watched him.

Jace placed the gem in his haversack. If he died because of some trap, at least he'd take the gem with him. He then carefully made his way to the other side and repeated the process with the left eye. With a little work, the second gem popped out and fell into his hand. That's when things began shaking.

"INFIDEL!" a voice bellowed with the grating of stone. Jace realized the voice had come from the idol and in the momentary confusion and shock, he lost his grip and slipped from the idol. He fell to the side and came down hard on his side.

YOU take 0 falling damage.

As Jace grunted as he hit the floor but his *Safefall* ability had spared him any falling damage. He looked to see Luna moving away from the idol, her ears back. Then movement caught his eye and he looked up to see the huge stone head of the idol turning to look down at him.

"INFIDEL! RETURN WHAT YOU HAVE STOLEN!" it bellowed and it's left arm began to slowly move, reaching out to him. It was a golem! A giant stone golem. And he had just triggered it.

Scrambling away, Jace tucked the gem into the haversack and backpedaled away from golem. The thing was leaning forward now, both arms reaching for him. It was starting to move faster and Jace barely had time to examine it in his HUD before he turned and ran.

Lost Temple Guardian (Legendary)
Level: 50

The golem was level 50! He and the girls had no chance against it. Their only hope was to outrun it and lose it in the forest. He ran full speed towards the door with Luna next to him but grabbed her by the collar and skidded to a halt as he exited.

"The darts!" he told Luna and pulled her to the side as he heard a thunderous footstep from the room behind him and then another. It was coming after them.

As fast as he could, he retraced the safe path and was almost through when the golem came barreling out of the temple and crashed into several of the pillars. The thing had had to be almost twenty feet tall and his arms and legs were now moving at full speed. He heard darts pinging off the stone golem but knew they couldn't damage the golem.

"RETURN WHAT YOU HAVE STOLEN!" the creature bellowed and turned towards him.

Leading Luna through the last part of the safe path on the chessboard floor, Jace dived off the foundation and onto the ground.

YOU take 0 falling damage.

At the outer temple wall, he saw Diana and Mika in the globe of the sword's light, their eyes open wide. They must have heard the crashing sounds from the temple and the bellowing of the golem.

"Jace?" Mika said as he ran closer.

"What's going…" Diana started to ask but then a booming sound drowned her out and the earth shuddered as the golem jumped off the temple's foundation, onto the ground.

"RUN!" he yelled to the girls and turned to Luna. "Lead us back to the bridge!"

"Yes," the cat said and easily outpaced him to move to the front of the group.

"Follow Luna back to the bridge and get across it!" he yelled just as heavy, ponderous footsteps began to sound behind him.

Glancing back, he saw a piece of the outer wall explode outward as the golem just ran through it without even pausing.

They made it to the treeline and then plunged into the forest, following Luna. The thing's enormous strides nearly allowed it to catch Jace but the golem's outstretched hand just missed him as he ran between two trees.

The golem slammed into the trees and bounced back. The thing looked uncomprehendingly at the trees, as if not able to understand what they were. Then, it swung both it's huge fists at one of the trees and there was a large crack as the trunk splintered. Another blow from the golem and the tree topped to the side.

The animated creature pursued Jace through the forest as he ran after Luna and the girls. Any trees which got in the golem's way were quickly toppled. But the time it took the thing to knock down a tree allowed Jace and the girls to stay ahead of it.

Suddenly, the trees disappeared and they were back at the ravine. He pointed to the tree bridge. "Get across! Quick!"

Behind him, the golem crashed through trees, closing quickly. Luna reached the bridge first and bounded across. Mika and Diana followed, the bridge visibly shaking as the two ran across at the same time.

Jace pulled up short, just shy of the bridge and waited for the girls to get to the other side before adding his weight to it. Then the golem burst through the trees and turned its head to look down at him. "RETURN WHAT YOU HAVE STOLEN!"

The thing started towards him, but Jace was already running across the bridge. Sprinting as quickly as he could, Jace was about two-thirds of the way across when the enormous golem reached the edge of the ravine and started across the tree bridge, causing it to shake and vibrate.

The girls screamed at him, but he couldn't hear what they were saying through the sound of the thunderous footsteps of the golem. He had almost reached the other side when he heard a loud crack and then lurched as the bridge snapped in half and began to fall.

Jumping for all he was worth, he sailed towards the girls. In mid-flight, Jace watched himself soaring closer and closer to the edge of the ravine. But his arch was wrong. He wasn't going to make it.

Jace hit the side of the ravine and his hands scrambled to find something, anything that he could grab onto. His right hand closed around what felt like a root and he held on as he began to fall.

Behind him, growing distant he still heard the voice of the golem. "Return…. What…. You … Have…."

As his full weight was put on the root, he felt it tearing away from the side of the ravine. Just before it gave way, he felt a slim but strong hand grip his wrist.

"I have you!" Mika yelled and he felt himself being pulled up. As soon as his other hand reached the edge, Diana caught his other hand and together two girls pulled him onto the edge as a huge crash sounded from far below.

Lost Temple Guardian dies.
You gain 2000 experience.

Once on firm ground, he turned over on his back while the girls collapsed to the ground. They were all breathing hard, unable to speak for several minutes while they're heart rates slowly went back to normal.

Finally, their ragged breathing returned to normal and Diana spoke. "Making friends I see."

Chapter 46

"What was that thing?" Mika asked, still panting.

"A stone golem," Jace retorted, trying to get his breath back under control. "It objected to me prying out its eyes."

Both girls looked over at him, confusion and shock written on their faces.

Jace brought out the two large gems and held them up. Both girls gasped in surprise at the sight of the fist sized rubies.

"Those were its eyes?" Mika asked, her own eyes wide as she stared at the gems in the light of the sword. Even Jace noticed that they seemed to sparkle more in the light.

"How'd you get them out?" Diana asked, her brow furrowed and her eyes fixed on the huge gems.

Jace sat up and put them gems back into his inventory. "The golem wasn't moving until I pried out the eyes. Then it came to life and tried to squash me."

"And almost succeed!" Mika said. Her voice was light, but her eyes held concern.

Jace knew she cared about him and he gave her a lopsided grin as he shrugged. "I didn't know it was going to come to life."

"How much do you think those things are worth?" Diana cut in.

Jace thought back to the various gems he'd looted as Mordred. As he sorted through his memories, he scratched his head. "I don't know. I've never found anything this large. The biggest ruby or diamond I found when I played Mordred was maybe a twentieth of this size."

"How much was it worth?" Diana pressed.

"I think I got about 50,000 gold for my share, so I guess around 200,000 gold," he said.

"200,000 gold?" Diana repeated. "And it was a twentieth the size? So, one of those could be worth twenty times as much? That's 4,000,000 gold!"

Grinning, Jace nodded. "One of these is more than enough to pay for the scroll."

"So, we don't have to go after any other treasure?" Mika asked.

Jace shook his head and frowned. "I'm not even sure there IS any other treasure to go after. I don't think these are treasure maps for buried. I think this is a list of places that the late captain found out about that he thought might have treasure."

"And monsters," Mika added.

"And monsters," Jace agreed. "Powerful monsters. Bob could have killed all of us, the entire crew of the Wyvern's Tail and destroyed the ship without even blinking. And that golem was a level 50 boss. One solid hit and it would kill any of us."

He let his words sink in before continuing. "Who knows what could be at the other locations. As far as I can tell, this list of locations is a high level dungeon list, or at least, monster list. I've seen and heard of similar things in the game. Tablets that lead to abandoned ruins. Scrolls with the descriptions of lost fortresses. Usually there's some sort of quest chain involved but not in this case. We probably missed the quest start because Drakkar killed the captain instead of us."

"And that prevents a quest?" Mika asked with some confusion. "That's not fair."

"It happens." Jace shrugged. "I've read a few instances where quest chains have been broken because another group found a dungeon first and cleared it, effectively ending the event that would have led to the next quest."

"So," Diana broke in. "About the huge gems… What do we do now?"

"Back to Nynymmost," he replied. "Avoid Damian. Buy the scroll. Contact Mordred and Charlena. Trap Damian."

"Is that all?" Diana smirked. "You make it sound so simple."

"How do we lure Damian out where we can use the scroll on him?" Mika asked.

Frowning, Jace stood up. "That's the question. We need to get him somewhere other players won't find him and be able to release him easily. Otherwise, the scroll will be a waste if someone dispels it."

"But he can't dispel himself, right?" Mika questioned.

"No," Jace replied. "The sphere is immune to all damage and magic from the outside. Technically, it could be destroyed by enough damage but that would take a full raid an hour or more. Most people just use a Dispel Scroll. They're fairly common and used in many raid boss fights to debuff the boss."

"So even if Damian has one of those dispel thingies," Diana asked, "he can't use it to get out?"

"No," Jace shook his head. "Not from inside. And he can't teleport out of it. Until someone lets him out, he's effectively trapped."

"For how long?" Mika asked.

"The sphere lasts indefinitely," he told them. "But my guess is, Damian will log off and hop on the forums and offer a million gold or some ridiculous amount for someone to come and let him out."

Diana threw her hands up. "Then what's the point?"

"The point is," Jace explained calmly. "That we lure him someplace out of the way, that can only be reached by ship. It needs to be someplace about a week away. That should give us enough time to get to find the *Help Desk* in Nynymmost."

"Which should be easier is we can buy a noble title with the gold from the second gem," Diana said.

"Exactly," Jace agreed. "It should make it so much easier. If we have four million gold, we can buy a decent title. That should allow much better access to the parliament building. I would hope we can find it within a week."

"And then what?" Diana asked. "I mean, we've already talked to them, right?"

Jace shrugged and deflated a bit. "I don't know. I'm hoping they'll have an update for us, a timetable for when they think it will be fixed, something. I don't know what else to do."

"That will be enough," Mika stood and placed a hand on Jace's shoulder, giving it a little squeeze.

Diana rolled her eyes again as she stood too. "How will it be good enough if they don't help us and we have some lunatic in the game assassinating us every time we step into a city?"

"What else can we do?" he asked.

"I don't know," Diana sighed. "Maybe we just sail off somewhere and have them leave us on some tropical island until those idiots fix us."

"Don't forget about Mordred," Jace said and then corrected himself. "I mean, the real me. He's having to play dead in the real world, and he's lost everything he ever had. The longer we prolong this, the longer he has to hide out."

"Fine," Diana let out a breath. "But after we talk to support this time, then can we go to a tropical island?"

"If support doesn't give us good news," he replied. "We may have no choice. We may have to hide out somewhere."

"Let's go," he said, motioning the girls to follow him.

The three of them walked through the night without a word, each of them apparently lost in their own thoughts. As for Jace, he was thinking of places where they could lure Damian. He briefly thought of Bob's island. If they could enlist his help, Bob would make a perfect guardian for a trapped Damian. Bob was a raid level monster, so a single player or even a group would have no chance against the dragon turtle.

Eventually he decided against it. Bob had made it clear that he just wanted to be left alone. If Jace trapped Damian on his island and Damian tried to hire players to free him, Bob would get lots of unexpected visitors. They might not prevail against the dragon turtle, but they would bother him. No, Bob's island just wasn't an option.

Other than the pirate haven, he really didn't know any other islands around the area. He'd need to talk with Colette when he returned to the ship. Hopefully she would know of an isolated island about a week away from any ports.

He frowned, the action hidden from the girls behind him. Jace didn't know if the week would be enough to find the *Help Desk* in the gnomish parliament building. Since they'd been assassinated in the gnomish capital, Damian would know they'd been there. He could already have moved the *Help Desk* to the most obscure area of the building.

Jace hadn't told the girls about the possibility because Diana was already anxious about it. He knew she just wanted this to be over with and move on with her afterlife. Jace couldn't blame her. He was sure he'd feel the same way if he'd lived as long as she had. And now, knowing she'd been unhappy in life, she had probably just wanted to sit back and be pampered for a few hundred years.

But Jace wasn't in such a hurry. He knew it was a very real possibility that this situation would end with him being deleted. And he'd come to realize it really wasn't a comfort to know that his real self would live on.

He was surprised to find that he actually envied his real self. Not only because his real self could go back and forth from the game to the real world. It was because his real self would get to live.

Was that selfish? Was he selfish to want to live? He understood he was a mistake. That he shouldn't have been inserted into the game since his real self hadn't died. But he had been inserted. And he'd lived in the game. Created new memories. Memories that were unique to him.

He thought of Mika and how she would feel if he were deleted. How long would she remember him once he was deleted? A month? A year? Ten years? A hundred? He wanted to be remembered. Maybe he was vain, but he really wanted to be remembered and not just fade into oblivion. Was that so wrong?

With his mood as dark as the night around him, Jace continued in silence through the forest. Luna was leading the way home and he'd learned to trust her nose. She was a good cat. And a good companion. His frown deepened when he realized that when he was erased, so would Luna.

That wasn't fair. Even if they had to delete him, they should at least keep Luna alive. But he knew that was impossible. She was his familiar. She was bound to him. He silently cursed the unfairness of it all. When he went, so would she.

Looking ahead at Luna as the cat led them back to the ship, he felt something on his cheek. He reached up to find it wet. He hadn't cried when he'd found out about his parents and his sister being killed. But now he was shedding virtual tears for a virtual cat. Ironic. Wiping a hand across his eyes, he followed Luna through the forest and back to the beach.

Chapter 47

They made it back to the shore just as day broke. Jace was glad to see the Wyvern's Tail was still moored in the same place they'd left it. He'd been worried that they might weight anchor and leave them stranded. They were pirates after all and it wouldn't be the first mutiny.

He wondered if the fact that he had taken possession of the ship in-game had anything to do with it. Having never owned a vehicle in VEIL Online, he had no way of knowing. But he was glad it was still there.

Jace cast a few *Flame Bolts* straight up into the air to get the attention of the ship. Within a few minutes, the sailors had launched a small boat to come pick them up. Twenty minutes later, they were onboard the Wyvern's Tail.

"Find what you were looking for, Captain?" Colette asked.

"Maybe," Jace replied, purposefully vague in front of the crew. "We'll have to see."

"Good," Colette grinned, flashing Jace white teeth. "I don't want no dark elf chasing us around, threatening to destroy the ship."

"Make ready to cast off!" the first mate yelled, and the crew burst into action. She looked to Jace. "Where to captain?"

"Maybe you can help me with that," he replied.

Colette raised an eyebrow. "How so?"

"I'm looking for an out of the way island," he told her. "At least a week from any major port. Someplace isolated and not well known."

"You planning to become a hermit?" the woman chuckled.

Jace had spent the walk home wondering what he should tell Colette. He had considered keeping the truth from her but he gave up on the idea and just decided to go with the truth. "We're going to trap that dark elf in a magic prison and I need a deserted island to do it on."

"Why does it have to be deserted if it's a magical prison?" she asked, her expression curious.

"The prison can't be broken or dispelled from within," he explained. "But someone from the outside can break it open. We want to make sure no one finds him anytime soon."

The first mate turned her head and barked some more orders before turning back to Jace. Her face was somber. Her lips pursed. She was quiet for a long minute before finally speaking. "I might know of a place. It's out of the way. About a week from here. Very isolated. Not on any map I know."

"Great! That sounds..." Jace started her but the woman's expression made him trail off. "What's wrong?"

Colette's expression was serious and her brow was furrowed. She made a warding sign in the air before speaking. "Bad for ships. Some have gone there and not come back."

Jace raised an eyebrow. "It's dangerous?"

"That's what the stories say," the first mate bit her lip.

"What's there?" he asked. "Some sort of monster?"

"I don't know." She shrugged, her expression haunted. "But anyone who's been there doesn't want to go back."

"Why?" he prodded.

"It's called the Demon's Grin," she said finally, lowering her voice. "It's a cursed island."

"Cursed how?" he asked. He could think of several cursed places he'd run into during his adventuring days as Mordred. In every instance, he'd gotten a solo or group quest to remove the curse. Could this be the same? Some out of the way quest?

"I don't know," she said, throwing up her hands. "That's just what the stories say."

"But you know how to get there?" he asked.

She was quiet for a long moment before nodding slowly. "Aye. An old lover had been there with his crew. He's not one to be afraid of anything. But he was afraid of the island. He told me where it was so I would never go there."

Jace nodded and stayed quiet as a range of emotions played across the first mate's face. After waiting patiently for several minutes, Colette looked up at him. Her face was set in a hard mask. "It's dangerous, aye. But, if this dark elf is as bad as you say, then it's the perfect place to imprison him."

"So, you'll take us there?" he asked.

She sighed. "Aye. I will take you there."

"Good," he grinned and gave her shoulder a reassuring squeeze. "I know you don't want to, but the Demon's Grin sounds like the perfect place to leave him."

"Aye," she said quietly, her eyes distant.

"I need you to give me the coordinates so I can send him a message to meet us there," he said. "And then we need to head back to Nynymmost."

"Back to the gnome city? Why?"

"We're going to pick up some people who are going to help us imprison him."

"If this dark elf is as powerful as you claim, it must be someone even more powerful," the first mate said and raised an eyebrow at him.

"Maybe not quite as powerful," Jace replied. "But very sneaky. Plus, we also need to send a raven message to the dark elf, letting him know where to meet us."

"And you think he's going to just come by himself?"

He remembered Damian relating various adventures he'd been on. His former co-worker always bragged about how much smarter he was than the other players. Plus, Jace knew Damian wouldn't risk him blurting out his secret in front of anyone else. "Oh, he'll come by himself. He's too paranoid and arrogant to bring anyone else."

Colette eyed him before nodding. "I hope you're right."

"Me too," Jace admitted. He was sure Damian would have some surprises for them, but once he was imprisoned, none of those would matter. No magic would operate in the sphere. And with Mordred's *Stealth* skill, sneaking up on him should be no problem.

"So, then we go back to Nynymmost?" the first mate asked.

"Yes," he nodded.

"Fine," she said. "Then let me get us on the way and I'll come bring you the coordinates."

"Sounds good," he told her and spun to walk away.

"And you're sure this plan of yours will work?" she asked.

Jace stopped and looked over his shoulder. "It'd better. Or we're all in a lot of trouble."

He left the first mate to get the ship on its way and returned to his cabin. The girls were sitting at the table chatting and Luna was napping on the bed, her giant form taking up the entire thing. He briefly thought about telling her to shrink down but decided to let the cat sleep.

"What did you talk to Colette about?" Mika asked.

"I think we've found an island to trap Damian on," he told them and both girls perked up. "A place called Demon's Grin. It's some remote island about a week from here."

"Sounds ominous," Diana said.

"Colette says it's cursed," he told them. "She's spooked by it."

"We're going to a cursed island?" Mika excitedly. "What kind of curse?"

Diana rolled her eyes at the enthusiastic girl across from her. She turned to Jace. "Are you sure that's wise? Going to a cursed island for this plan of yours?"

Jace shrugged. "She said it's not on any maps that she knows of and the sailors who do know about it don't want to go there. That works in our favor."

"Unless it really is cursed," Diana said. She stopped and scratched her head. "What does cursed even mean in the game?"

"Something bad happened there," Mika answered. "The ground becomes barren and sometimes the inhabitants become disfigured."

Jace looked at her curiously.

Mika smiled. "I did a quest to lift a curse from a village."

"Same here," Jace smiled. "A few of them."

"So, it's safe?" Diana asked.

Jace and Mika exchanged looks. Her look told him she'd had a similar experience with cursed quests. In his first curse quest, the villagers had burned a gypsy they suspected of being a witch. She had cursed the village with her dying breath.

When he'd come upon the village, it was in shambles. The crops had failed and the game had all run off, so the villagers were starving. Jace had agreed to help, only to find out that night that the villagers themselves were cursed.

When the sun had fallen, the villagers had all become rotting zombies. Jace had killed three of them who attacked him before realizing that killing five or more of them would cause the quest to fail. Unable to fight them, the other zombies had chased him to the outskirts of the village. Luckily, they'd stopped at the edge of the village, unwilling or unable to actually leave.

He'd gone back in the morning and none of the villagers had remembered anything of the previous night. Jace quickly learned that if he wanted to finish the quest and break the curse, he'd need to stay out of the village at night and investigate it during the day.

Of course, since he worked during the day, he ended up having to wait until the weekend to work on the quest and even then, barely survived and barely completed the quest. He'd learned one important lesson from that first curse quest: Cursed villages did not have bind points while they were cursed.

Given how close he'd come to dying throughout the quest and the handicap it put on him by not being able to kill the villager zombies, he would say that no, curses were definitely not safe.

"No, I wouldn't say that," he told the older woman. "But we're not going there to do a quest. We're going to lure Damian there, trap him and then get back to Nynymmost."

Diana looked between Mika and Jace several times before finally letting out an exasperated breath. "Fine! Fine! Let's go to this cursed island and fight flesh eating zombies!"

"In my quest it was there were no flesh eating zombies," Mika offered brightly. "There were carnivorous baboons!"

Diana shook her head as she massaged her temples, under her breath, Jace heard her mutter, "Carnivorous baboons…"

Chapter 48

It was late afternoon on Friendsday, or Friday in the real world, when they arrived back in Nynymmost. Jace spoke to Colette about keeping a low profile. Damian would have received their ears by now and would have known where they were. If he did some digging, he might know the name of Jace's ship and have players or NPCs looking for them.

After speaking with his first mate, Jace learned that the pirate ship knew some seedy thieves guild members in the gnomish capital worked for the harbor authority and would keep their arrival a secret - for a price. Knowing he had no choice, he handed over 1,000 gold to Colette to make the necessary bribes.

Next, he had the first mate pick her most reliable sailor to deliver to act as an errand boy. Since they were going through the trouble of hiding their ship, it didn't make sense for him and the girls to walk into town and expose themselves to assassins. Better to have someone else send a raven message to his real self. At least, he hoped that would work.

After giving specific instructions to the sailor, a dog-kin with a black nose and pointy ears like a Doberman, they sent the crewman on his way to send the message. The crew was anxious to get off the ship and began murmuring when Colette announced no one else was leaving the ship.

Not wanting a mutiny, Jace had the first mate reach out to her thieves guild contacts and had barrels of ale brought to the ship. It was easy enough to get done. All he had to do was offer three times their normal price. Once the ale was brought aboard, the crew's morale increased instantly, and he was toasted many times.

An hour later, his messenger returned to the ship and informed him the message had been sent. Jace thanked him, let him keep the change and sent him off to drink with friends.

"Very cloak and dagger," Colette murmured as the crewmen walked over to the barrels of ale. She had filled her own mug with ale and took a long sip. "Even for a privateer."

"I don't want to take any chances," he replied, glancing around the deck.

The first mate looked him up and down. "I've seen you fight the raiders and the ninjen. You are a skilled warrior. If you are afraid of this dark elf, then so am I."

Colette looked up and down the dock, her dark eyes looking for trouble. She took another sip of her ale. "He must really want you dead to go through all this trouble."

"He already thought he killed me once," Jace told her, thinking back to the car accident.

He couldn't explain all the details to her since she was an NPC. Either her programming would make her ignore his non-game talk or she would think he was mad. He had to keep it in terms she understood. "I know the details of his operations. He can't afford to let me live."

The first mate gave him an understanding nod and took a sip. "What do we do now?"

"We're taking on two people who are going to help with our plan."

"What kind of people?"

"One's an elf," he replied and then turned to face the woman so he could gauge her next reaction. "The other's a vampyre."

Colette had raised her mug to her mouth and had been about to take a sip when she froze. The first mate lowered her mug and stared hard at him. "You are bringing a vampyre onto this ship?"

"Half-vampyre," Jace corrected. "And don't worry. He'd my… half-brother."

That surprised the first mate, and she didn't even try to hide it. "You have a half-brother who is a vampyre?"

"On my dad's side," Jace grinned. He'd already pretended to be his real self's twin. He saw no harm carrying it over into the game. It wasn't like anyone could prove otherwise.

"And your half-brother won't be biting any necks?" she asked with narrowed eyes.

"None," he replied. "I promise."

"You'd better," she retorted. "Or you may have a full scale mutiny on your hands."

Jace nodded. "Don't worry. He'll be on his best behavior."

"This elf you were talking about," she frowned. "Is it a dark elf like the one who is after you?"

"No." He shook his head. "She's a wood elf."

"Good." She smiled. "I don't trust those dark elves. They are always plotting something."

He nodded. "Let me know when they arrive."

"Sure thing, captain," she replied and then stalked off to refill her mug.

Jace returned to the captain's quarters and found Diana sulking in the captain's chair behind the desk. Mika was sitting on the bed, stroking Luna. Shutting the door, he dropped into one of the chairs at the table and looked from Mika to Diana. "What's going on?"

Mika opened her mouth, but Diana answered first. "I don't understand why we can't go out for a little bit. Just to a tavern or inn for some real food."

Jace let out a breath and turned towards the older woman. He checked his watch. It was 5pm in-game and that meant it was 5pm on the east coast in the real world.

Damian would be leaving work soon and would be home in thirty minutes. "None of us can go out right now. Damian will just have gotten off work. He'll be logged in any time. If assassins find any of us, he'll get the ears in a few minutes and know we're here. It's too risky."

"I don't have to go far," she protested. "I can find a tavern on the docks."

Jace shook his head. "It's too dangerous right now. I'm sorry."

He knew how the woman felt. All they ate on the ship were dried fish and they got really old, really quickly. But he was telling the truth. If Damian found out they were in the city, he might be able to track them down in no time. All he had to do was offer a very generous reward and the Colette's thieves guild acquaintances would most likely sell her out.

"What about," he told her as an idea popped into his head, "take out?"

Both women perked up. Diana tilted her head and looked at him. "Is that a thing in the game?"

"Who knows." He shrugged. "But I can have one of the crew go out and get something. They're not on his radar, so they won't pose any risk."

The girls began chatting about what they wanted and soon Jace had an order to give to the dog-kin. Because of the earlier tip, the crewman, whose name was Ravel, was eager to go on another errand.

Just over an hour later, Ravel returned with their food wrapped in cloth napkins. The girls immediately attacked the food and were just finishing up with a knock on the door made them all look up.

"Your guests are here," said Colette's muffled voice.

He exchanged looks with the girls, finished off the fried fish he'd been eating and wiped his hands on the cloth napkin. Walking over to the door, Jace opened it to reveal Colette.

"I see the family resemblance," she winked and moved out of the way, revealing Mordred and Charlena.

They entered, holding hands, and Colette shut the door behind them. Mordred's eyes darted around the captain's quarters and he smiled. "Nice ship."

"Thanks. Have a seat," he replied and motioned for them to sit down at the table.

Mordred and Charlena sat down and Jace was once again struck with the strange sensation of looking at the vampyre character he'd played for so long, only from the outside now. As he looked at Mordred, he realized Colette was right. Their characters did look alike.

Both avatars were based on Jace's DNA, so it made sense they'd look alike. The main difference was the vampyre template that had been applied to Mordred. He was slimmer and had finer features than Jace's human avatar. Mordred was also paler and looked a bit younger because of the vampyre template. Still, they could be brothers.

"What's that about family resemblance?" Mordred asked as he sat down.

Jace smirked. "I told her you were my half-brother and wouldn't be eating any of them."

"You mean…" Mordred smiled. "I'm not allowed to eat these men?"

Jace rolled his eyes. "No eating the crew. They'll probably give you indigestion. Besides, it's time to get down to business."

Mordred and Charlena exchanged incredulous looks. "You have the money for the scroll already?"

"And then some," Jace replied and set the two large gems on the table.

"Holy smokes," Charlena gasped.

Mordred reached out and picked one up, examining it. He looked to Jace. "These things have got to be worth a fortune. How the heck did you get them?"

"From a really mean stone golem who was using them as eyes," he replied.

"Golem? You'll have to tell me that story later," Mordred said, picking up one of the large rubies. "You know, this is way more than we need to buy the scroll."

Jace nodded. "I figured you can sell them both, buy the scroll and then use the rest of the money for living expenses."

Almost comically, both Charlena's and Mordred's mouth jaws dropped at the same time. Jace chuckled.

"But…" Mordred started but Jace held up his hand.

"No objections. You're in the real world. You need money. You can exchange the gold for real currency and use that to pay for your expenses."

"I… I can't," Mordred stuttered.

"Sure you can." Jace smiled. "We're brothers, right? Twins."

Mordred nodded. "About that. I've been doing a bit of hacking."

"Hack?" Jace raised an eyebrow at his other self.

"I've left a few pieces of a trail for you," Mordred replied. "A few social media profiles, some memberships, that sort of thing. It's not much, but it's something. You know, if they look."

Jace didn't know what to say. If he thought about it, he realized he would have done the same thing. He smiled. It was nice to have a brother, even if it was really just a copy of him. Or, rather, he was a copy of Mordred. "Thanks!"

"I don't know how much it will hold up to scrutiny." Mordred shook his head. "But it's something at least."

For the first time since learning he was just a copy of his real self, Jace actually had hope that he might make it out of the situation alive.

"So then, what's the plan?" Mordred asked.

"Go sell the gems, buy the scroll, send Damian a message that we want to talk and to meet us at the island, then come back here and do an auto-follow," Jace told him. "Bring back the remainder of the first gem. We'll need that to buy a title. Transfer the gold from the second gem to your account."

"Transfer the gold?! I can't…" Mordred started to protest.

"Of course, you can…" Jace started but Mordred shook his head.

"No," his real self said and shook his head. "I literally can't. I have no account. Like everything else, it's gone."

Jace swore. He'd forgotten about that.

"You can put it in my account," Charlena offered. She gave Mordred a smile. "If you trust me."

Mordred returned her smile and Jace could tell his real self was smitten with the redhead. "Of course, I trust you."

"Then give the money to me," Charlena said, "and I can transfer it into my account. I can take it out and give you the cash."

"Don't forget to set aside money for taxes," Jace told her.

"What?!" Charlena asked, turning towards him. "What do you mean?"

"Money going into the game doesn't get taxed," Mordred said, facepalming himself.

"But money coming out of the game does," Jace finished.

Charlena screwed up her face. "That's not fair."

Jace and Mordred shrugged at the same time. "That's the government."

Charlena looked at the gems and then from Jace to Mordred. "So how much money are we talking about?"

"We just need two million gold to get a royal title for the gnomish parliament," Jace said. "The scroll's about two million. That should leave you guys about four million gold."

Mordred and Charlena's eyes went wide, their mouths hanging open. "That's…. That's…"

Jace nodded. "Almost a half million in real money."

It took a few minutes for Mordred and Charlena got over their shock. The group talked for a few minutes more before Jace and Charlena went to sell the gems, send the raven message and buy the scroll from the auction house.

By ten o'clock, the two of them had returned and set themselves to auto-follow Jace. They promised to check in once a day but Jace was still recovering and couldn't spend long in the pod. Apparently, he was mostly sleeping nowadays, despite having been in a coma for months.

"You have the scroll?" Jace asked.

Mordred brought out an ivory scroll case and started to hand it to Jace but he held up his hand. "You keep it. You're the only one who can use it."

It was true. The imprisonment scroll was level 95. The only one in their group who could use it was Mordred. His other self-nodded and the scroll disappeared back into his inventory.

"What about the message?" Jace asked.

"I sent the Raven message telling him to meet us next Sunday at the coordinates you gave me," Mordred replied. "And then I got out of there as quickly as possible."

"Good," Jace nodded. The plan was set in motion.

"We're going to log off now," Charlena said. "You want me to auto-follow you like before?"

"Yes," Jace replied. "Both of you."

Auto-follow would keep their avatars in the game even after the two of them logged off. The game would make the avatars follow Jace around, though they couldn't react, attack or defend to anything.

"We'll log in at least once each day," Jace told him. "Oh, I gave the money to Charlena and walked her through transferring to her account. It'll take a couple of days, but we should get it. Thanks again."

"Sure." Jace smiled.

Charlena and Mordred both logged off, leaving behind their avatars in auto-follow mode, just as Colette and the crew got the ship underway.

"That's creepy," Diana said, watching the two vacant eyed avatars following Jace. They didn't move much in the cabin, but wherever he was in the room, they did turn towards him. "Really creepy."

"Yeah," Jace agreed, looking at his old avatar staring blankly at him. He remembered how much fun he'd had as Mordred. How much fun he'd had playing the game. And now, the game was his life. He smirked to himself. Life was strange.

Chapter 49

They reached Demon's Grin on the following Friendsday, or Friday in the real world, around 3pm in the afternoon. Jace had Colette sail around the island so he could look for any signs of Damian, or monsters. Luckily, there were no signs of either. At least, there were no signs he could see.

The island of Demon's Grin was dominated by a volcano in the center. The rest of the tiny island seemed to have been formed by lava from the volcano and as they circumnavigated the island, he understood where the name of the island had come from.

As far as islands went, Demon's Grin was tiny. He guessed it to be roughly a mile or two long and a half mile wide at its widest point. The most notable feature was an active volcano which seemed to be the source of the island.

Even as they circled the island, Jace could see the bright yellow-orange lava rolling down the face of the volcano. It was definitely an active volcano. He could see some of the lava reaching the ocean and sending up plumes of steam as the molten rock hit the cold ocean water. As long as the lava flowed, the island would continue to grow.

"See there," Colette pointed out to the spot close to the island. "That's what I mean by cursed."

Jace looked where the first mate was pointing. At first, he didn't see anything, but then he realized what she was pointing at. It looked like the mast of a ship, sticking up out of the water. "Is that a ship?"

"Aye," she said. "All you can see is its mast."

As they sailed around, Jace saw two more shipwrecks. On the southern tip, part of the hull of a ship had been washed to shore and the remains of the ship lay on its side.

"See, the island is cursed," Colette said grimly.

Jace doubted it was cursed as much as possibly the home of some large monster, like Bob the Dragon Turtle. He remembered the steamy cave Bob enjoyed on his island. Was there a dragon turtle on this island too? Or some other creature who called it home?

"Let's keep our distance for now," he told her, folding up his spyglass. "Keep circling until I talk with the others."

"Aye, captain," she said, casting a wary glance at the island. "The further the better."

Jace went back to the captain's cabin, the vacant eyed avatars of Charlena and Mordred following him. Whether because they were programmed to ignore auto-following player or they didn't say anything out of respect for him as captain, none of the crew commented on the strange behavior from the two auto-followers.

That was fine with Jace. It meant he didn't have to make up a story to explain what would be bizarre behavior in the real world.

"Is it really cursed?" Diana demanded as soon as he had shut the door.

Jace chuckled. "Not that I can tell. As far as I can tell, it's just a volcanic island with some shipwrecks. But there's no telling what caused them to wreck."

"A monster?" Mika asked curiously. Diana flashed her an annoyed look but then she looked to Jace for an answer.

"No idea." Jace shrugged. "But considering it's a volcanic island and Bob liked the steam from his volcanic island, it's a possibility."

"What?" muttered Diana, her brow furrowing in concern. "You think it's another dragon turtle."

Jace shrugged again. "I don't know. Maybe not a dragon turtle but it could be something else. I'd like to keep the ship as far away from the island as possible. So, I'd like to go over in one of the boats."

Diana looked around. "What? Now? It's only Friday."

"Friendsday," Mika corrected but the older woman ignored her.

"We have to assume Damian got the message the same day we sent it," Jace explained. "He could get here anytime. I'd like to get the lay of the land as soon as possible."

"That makes sense," Diana admitted. She frowned. "How do we know he's not already here?"

"He should still be at work," Jace said but there was no conviction in his voice. He wouldn't put it past Damian to take off work to get here ahead of them. But then again, they'd made the meeting for Sunday, so they were days early. Would he really come this early? It wasn't like he could stay on 24 hours a day.

"I take it we're there?" Mordred asked from behind him and Jace jumped. He spun to see Mordred blinking and looking around. "Charlena's not home yet but I thought I'd login and see where we were."

"Yes. We got here an hour and a half ago and did some long distance reconnaissance," Jace replied.

"Cool!" Mordred replied. "I've been resting all day so I could log on and stay on for a few hours in case you need me."

"Good thinking," he told his other self. "I was telling the girls we should head over now and check it out. There's a good chance Damian is still at work, so even if he's on a ship heading this way, he hopefully can't login until around 5:30 or so."

"Sounds like a plan," Mordred agreed. "Let's go."

"What about Charlena?" Diana asked, pointing to the vacant eyes redhead.

"As long as she'll follow me onto the boat," Jace replied, "we should be okay. She followed me on a raft for a couple of days when we were making our way to Whitecliff."

He saw a look pass Mordred's face but it was gone in an instant. Was that jealousy? What did he have to be jealous about? Jace wasn't even real. Or was it the fact that Jace had technically gotten to know her first? Either way, the look was gone.

After taking some of the dried fish to eat for the next few days, the group went out on deck. Colette called down from the wheel. "You heading to the island, captain?"

"Aye," he said. "Once we're gone, I want you to take the ship about a day away and stay there. Avoid any other ships and come back at sundown on Sunday. If you don't see us after an hour, sail back to Nynymmost and wait for there for us."

"For how long, captain?" the first mate asked.

Jace let out a breath. "If we don't find you in Nynymmost after a week, we won't be finding you."

Colette was quiet for a long moment before she gave him a curt nod. "Aye, captain. We'll wait the full week for you."

He returned the nod and then motioned his group into the boat. Colette followed him over to the side of the ship, watching them climb aboard the boat. Just before they started to lower the boat, the first mate called out to him. "Be careful captain."

He gave her a smile and the crew began to lower the boat into the water. Jace looked over the deck of the Wyvern's Tail until it was out of sight. It was a good ship and he hoped he'd see it again.

They were going up against Damian, someone who had nearly unlimited access to the source code of the game. There was no telling what he might be able to do. For all he knew, Damian could have a pouch full of imprisonment scrolls. They were some of the most powerful pieces of magic in the game. It wasn't much of a stretch to think that Damian might think of them too. He certainly had the funds to buy them.

If Damian imprisoned them, it would certainly keep them out of commission. Without the resources that Damian had, Mika, Diana and he would be trapped in the spheres indefinitely. His real self and Charlena would be forced to delete their characters and start over if they couldn't find someone to help them. But at least they wouldn't be trapped forever.

His team would need to make sure they struck first. Even if he imprisoned one of them, if they got Damian, they could always come back later and release the person trapped, after they contacted the helpdesk.

The boat touched down in the water, jarring Jace from his thoughts. He and Mordred disconnected the hooks from the boat and began to row towards the shore. Luna was at the front of the boat, back in her normal size, looking warily at the water.

Jace and Mordred kept up a fast pace, trying to get them to the shore as soon as possible. They were focused on the shore, concentrating on rowing when the boat hit something. Freezing, Jace and his counterpart stopped rowing.

Charlena was still vacant-eyed, obviously not logged in yet but everyone else was looking around nervously. The group waited for another sound or some sort of attack, but nothing happened. They all exchanged worried glances, hands on weapons, and waited. But still there was nothing.

Jace motioned to Mika with his head, signaling her to look over the edge of the boat. They were close enough to shore that the water was clear and hopefully she could see something below them. He silently mouthed the word: carefully.

Mika peered over the side of the boat and moved her head around, looking into the water. Her brow furrowed and she looked at different angles for almost a full minute before pulling her head back. She looked at the two Jace's. "There's something there but I don't know what it is."

He and his counterpart exchanged looks. Each of them took a different side and peered over carefully. Jace put his head over the side of the deck and looked into the water. Mika slid in next to him, their bodies touching and pointing with her finger to something just to the side of the boat.

He could barely make it out, but there was something long and transparent next to the ship, barely touching it. He watched carefully for any signs that the transparent thing was a creature but there was no movement, other than the movement of the water.

"What is that?" Mordred asked.

Jace looked but wasn't sure. "I don't know, but it's transparent or translucent. Hard to tell in rippling water."

"It's glass," Diana said, also peering over the edge. She pointed a few feet away to their left. "There's another one."

"Glass?" Mika looked up confused.

"Sand makes glass when it gets hot enough," Diana said, sitting up. "Probably magma pips underneath us have caused glass pillars by slowly heating up the sand to a point where it forms glass. Over the years, it's formed these pillars."

Both Jaces exchanged looks and then shrugged. It seemed as plausible an explanation as any.

"So, they are all over the island?" Mika asked as her dark eyes searched the area.

"Probably," Diana nodded.

"So, it's not cursed." Jace smirked. "The shipwrecks are probably being caused by ships running into these glass pillars. Like the…"

"Titanic," Mordred finished, and they grinned at each other.

"That makes sense," Diana agreed.

"Mika?" Jace asked her, "Can you go to the front and keep an eye out for the pillars and let us know where they are so we can navigate around them?"

"Aye captain," she saluted and climbed across his lap to the front with Luna. Gently, she lifted the cat, who briefly objected and handed her to Diana, who gave her scratches.

With Mika's help, the Jaces were able to navigate around the pillars and make it to shore. Pulling the boat onto the shore, the group scanned the island for any signs of Damian. There was no sign of him, so they dragged the boat onto store and hid it in a crevice.

Now, it was time to explore the island and find the best place to ambush Damian.

Chapter 50

By the time Charlena had logged in an hour later, they had already explored the small island. It really was small and most of it was featureless, having been created by the lava flows from the volcano. They did find two large lava tubes that lead into the volcano.

The first tube, a long tunnel that led down into the heart of the volcano, grew increasingly warmer the further down it went. When it finally opened up into a large cavern far below sea level, the edge of the tube dropped into a pool of molten lava about twenty feet down.

"Unless we're going to lure him in here and push him into the lava," Diana said, wiping sweat out of her eyes with a handkerchief and then covering her nose and mouth with it. "I don't think this is what we're looking for."

The heat from the lava was suffocating and each of them were covered in sweat. The heat, as well as gases released from the lava, made it difficult to breath, though none of them had taken any damage. It also reeked of rotten eggs, which Jace guessed was sulfur gas.

"I agree with her," Mordred said, wiping his own face. "I don't see any strategic advantage here."

Suddenly Charlena blinked and looked around. She immediately wrinkled her nose. "Geez, where the hell are we? And what is that smell?"

Diana chuckled. "Hell is a good word for it. We're at the bottom of an active volcano."

"Probably sulfur gas of some sort," Mordred said and walked over to her. He took her hand. "Glad to see you're back."

"I got a little worried," she said, looking up at him. "I came back, and you weren't in the apartment."

Mordred gave her a sheepish grin. "Sorry, I should have left a note. I wanted to log in early in case Damian was waiting for them."

"Not that I don't like reunions," Diana blurted out. "But can we take this conversation somewhere else. I think I just went from medium-rare to medium-well."

Mika, who was in the back, didn't need any more prompting. Turning, she began to walk back out the tunnel. Luna, who had followed them in, saw that the group was turning around and bounded past them and disappeared up the tunnel.

"I guess Luna did not like it down here either," Mika said as the cat disappeared up the tunnel.

"Probably the smell," Jace grinned, remembering how sensitive Luna's nose was.

The group left the lava tube and investigated the second tube. This one did not slope down but stayed around ground level. Several times, it widened into a larger chamber, before narrowing back down into a tunnel.

After only a few minutes of walking, the lava tube ended in a large ledge inside the main open area of the volcano. The ledge was at least fifty feet wide and twenty feet long. There were also large pieces of rock that must have broken off the inner wall of the volcano and fallen onto the ledge. While the ledge was warm and stank of sulfur, it was bearable.

"Not bad," Jace and Mordred said at same time. They looked at each other and exchanged grins. Jace got a kick out of seeing how often the two of them thought of the same thing at the same time. Once again, he wondered if this was what having a twin brother would be like.

Thoughts of a twin brother reminded him of what the real Jace had told him. His real life counterpart had planted some evidence that he "existed" in the real world. During the journey to the island over the past week, the other Jace had planted even more.

But would it be enough? There would be no official records anywhere. No birth certificate. No orphanage records. No death certificate. Would the fake profiles and little things the real Jace was doing really make a difference? Or would WorldCog see through it and delete him?

It was something that had been weighing heavily on his mind since his counterpart had told Jace what he was doing. He had all but accepted that he was going to die, that WorldCog would delete him from the system. In a way, he had come to terms with it.

Now, he was daring to hope that maybe they wouldn't. Maybe, just maybe, they wouldn't purge him from the system and he'd get to keep living. And while he had a better chance to live now, the uncertainty was eating away at him. He sighed and turned his attention back to the group.

"Assuming he comes down this tunnel," Mordred said, pointing back to the way they'd come. "I could hide over there."

Mordred was pointing to a large group of rocks just to the left of the entrance. The rocks were large enough that it did make a good hiding spot. Except that Damian was high enough level and rich enough that he would likely have an item to detect invisible and hidden creatures. He shook his head. "Damian will have something to allow him to detect you."

Shaking his head and grinning, Mordred pulled out an amulet from underneath his jerkin. "I might have spent some money on a little something extra."

"Is that an amulet of obscured location?" Jace asked with his own grin. An amulet of obscured location was a high level item that was sought after by those *Stealth* classes who engaged in PvP, player versus player combat. They prevented detection by any means except mundane eyesight and hearing. That meant magical scrying and detection would not reveal

Mordred nodded. "Even if Damian has scrying glasses or some other detection spell or magic, he won't be able to detect me."

"Good job." Charlena smiled and elbowed him playfully. Mordred smiled down at her and Jace knew his real self was smitten with her. Not that he blamed him, she was a cool girl. He smirked inwardly, she just apparently preferred live men.

"How will we get Damian to come down here?" Mika asked, looking around.

"Luna can lead him down," Jace told them and all eyes turned to his familiar.

The big cat paused and looked up from where she had been circling, apparently about to lay down. Luna looked at the faces staring at her. Purposefully, she ignored them, circled two more times and then plopped down.

"I think she was saying how thrilled she'll be to play a part," Diana said dryly. The group chuckled but the mood quickly became somber again.

"When Damian comes down," Jace continued and walked to a spot fifteen feet from where the tunnel opened into the chamber. "Mika, Diana and I will be over here."

"Isn't that a bit close to the edge?" Diana asked with concern.

"Damian is a level 90 warlock," Jace told them. "It won't matter where we are in the room. If he wants to, he'll be able to instantly kill us."

Jace glanced over at his ledge only five feet away. Even from where he stood, he could feel the stream of hot air as it rose past them and out the top of the volcano. "Falling into the lava might be preferable to anything he has planned for us."

Diana crossed her arms over her chest and pouted but didn't say anything else. Jace realized she was scared and let her sulk in silence.

Mordred walked over to the spot where he would be hiding and ducked down. He moved his head back and forth, looking at the area in front of the tunnel. "Charlena, can you walk back up the tunnel and then come into the room. Jace, stay where you are so I have a point of reference."

Jace did so and Charlena hurried out of the chamber before turning around and walking back into the room. She stopped at the entrance and then slowly walked in.

"Keep going," Mordred said. "Keep going. Stop. Right there! That's the point I'll be able to see him and have line of sight."

Jace looked where Charlena was standing. It was about four feet into the chamber and only a little over ten foot from where he and the girls would be. Not much room to maneuver or get around Damian, if things went wrong. Then Jace chuckled mirthlessly. If things went wrong, they didn't have a chance against Damian anyway. "That'll do."

"How quickly do you want me to cast the scroll?" Mordred asked.

"As soon as you can," Jace replied. "He'll have something up his sleeve. I know it."

Mordred grimaced. "Yeah. He's definitely the sort to have some sort of nasty surprise."

Jace looked at Charlena. "If she's here, she'll need to stand with us. Unless you have another one of those amulets."

Mordred swore. "Darnit! No! I didn't even think of that."

"I just thought of it myself," he replied. "She can't hide in here, especially around you. Damian will be able to pick her out and that might give away your position."

Charlena looked from Jace to Mordred. "But I should be with you…."

Mordred looked at Jace and his face grew grim as he turned to the red-headed elf. "He's right. We don't want anything giving away my position or even the hint of my position. We'll only get one shot at this."

She frowned but Charlena nodded her head. "Okay, fine. I just want this to be over."

Mordred raised an eyebrow. "Want me out of your place?"

The red-head blushed. "No! I meant, I want this constant worry that Damian is going to track us down and do something to you, or us."

His other self-nodded. "I know. Me too. I'd kind of like to get back to whatever I can scavenge of a normal life."

Everyone was quiet again for a long minute. Finally, feeling the silence stretch into uncomfortable nervousness, Jace cleared his throat. "I guess that's our plan. We set up the meet for Sunday, but we should expect him at any time."

"What do we do if he shows up while … uh… other Jace isn't logged in?" Diana asked, looking from Jace to Mordred.

Jace's mind raced, going through the various scenarios. There was no way for them to contact anyone outside of the game. If Mordred wasn't on to cast the scroll, they'd be screwed and completely at Damian's mercy.

Mordred must have seen the deer in the headlight look on Jace's face. He glanced over at Charlena and she nodded. "Charlena and I will be taking shifts in the game. As soon as someone spots the ship, whoever is on will log out and get the other person."

Jace felt himself relax and he nodded. "That sounds like a great plan."

"I'd say you owe me one," Charlena joked. "But considering how much money will be in my account in a couple of days, I guess we're more than even."

Jace chuckled. "We definitely appreciate you two taking turns like that. Now, let's hope we see him before he sees us."

The companions looked from one to another and then Jace shrugged. "I guess it's time to set up our watches."

"And wait for the little weasel to show up," Diana muttered and one by one they filed out of the room and returned to the surface.

Chapter 51

It was dark when they reached the surface of the island. Jace quickly assigned each person to a part of the island. Since Charlena and Mordred were splitting their shifts, they were both assigned to the same area.

The plan was simple. Each person would keep an eye open for a ship. If they saw the ship, they would run to the person next to them. Once they told the person next to them, that person would run off and tell the next person and so on until everyone was informed and they all met in the cave. Two issues immediately presented themselves when Jace had finished explaining the plan.

"How do we find our way without killing ourselves?" Diana asked, motioning around the dark landscape of the island.

Mika made a pained face, as if she wanted to ask something but didn't want to spoil Jace's plan. He motioned her talk. "Looks like you have something to say too."

The asian girl gave an apologetic expression. "How do Diana and I see the ship? We cannot see in the dark."

Everyone looked at Jace. He sighed. Why did they always think he had all the answers? He looked around the dark landscape and over the dark waters. The twin moons were climbing into the sky, casting pale light across the island and the ocean. Jace could see just fine with his *Cat-Vision*. Charlena and Mordred both had the ability to see at night as well. That left Diana and Mika.

"This is going to be a problem," Diana frowned. "If half the group can't see in the dark."

Running his hand through his hair, Jace struggled to come up with a solution. He was still thinking when Mordred spoke up. "Sorry Mika and Diana, I don't really know your capabilities. Do any of you have any magical way of making light?"

The two girls looked at Mordred and then each other. Mika's eyes went vacant as she looked at her HUD then quickly came back into focus. "One of the priest spells is a light spell. You have it too, right Diana?"

"We have a magic sword that sheds light too," Jace added. He thought he knew what Mordred was going to say but he let his alter ego finish.

"You can't use the light to find the ship or even while you're looking for it because it will kill your night vision," Mordred explained. "The ship will most likely have running lights so that the crew can work. So, you want to keep your eyes open for a moving light on the horizon. With everything else stationary, it should be hard to spot. Once you spot it, cast your light spells to make it to the next person."

"So, we're supposed to be looking for a moving spec of light on the horizon?" Diana asked.

"Yes," Jace said. "Like Mordred said, it will most likely stand out since it should be the only bit of light moving. This is supposedly a cursed island, avoided by sailors. There shouldn't be anything with lights on the horizon. Anything you see moving will mostly be Damian's ship."

Diana let out a breath but nodded. She didn't seem convinced. "Fine. Look for moving lights. Got it."

Mika smiled, her unwavering optimism a sharp contrast to Diana's more pragmatic and almost pessimistic attitude. Was it her youth that made her more optimistic and trusting? Or was it just their personalities? Jace would probably never know.

"Alright," Jace said after the girls had agreed. He pointed to the southeast part of the island. "Mordred, you and Charlena head to the southwest tip of the island. You should both go over now and one of you log out. That way, when you change shifts, the person will already be ready to take over."

"Okay," said Charlena and took Mordred's hand. The two of them turned and headed to the spot Jace had indicated.

"Diana, you will take the northeast and Mika, you will take the northwest," he told his companions. "I'll take the southwest. I'll walk you both to your spots and then come back here to mine."

"We can make it." Mika smiled and looked at Diana. "Right?"

Diana looked like she was about to object but the other girl's enthusiasm seemed to win out. "Yes, we'll manage."

"You guys can do this," he told them, trying to sound encouraging.

"I just want all this stuff to be over," Diana said, her body sagging. "This may be a young body, but mentally, I'm still the same old woman I was when I died. I can't take all of this stress. It's just too much. This constant running and looking over our shoulders."

"Once we have him trapped," Jace told Diana. "I can use the ring to transport us all back to gnomish capital. At minimum, we'll have a week to explore the parliament building and find the *Help Desk*."

"And that will magically solve our problems?" Diana asked, throwing her hands up in frustration. "I thought they were supposed to be doing something after the first time we contacted them!"

"I know, I know," Jace said in the most soothing voice he could muster. "You're right. I thought they'd be able to do more. If we hadn't been interrupted by Damian moving the *Help Desk*, I think I could have given them more information to go on. This time, hopefully they have a file open already. I can fill in more details and let them know that Damian is after us in the game."

"And that will make a difference?" Diana asked, her voice almost pleading.

"I don't know for certain," Jace admitted. "But it's the only thing I know to do."

"So, we could be in the same situation again?" Diana said. "And have to go to another city and find another *Help Desk*? When does it all end?"

Jace opened his mouth to respond but realized he didn't know what to tell her. His plan was to keep trying until they got a solution - or until Damian caught up to them and did whatever nasty stuff he could to them. The prospect of giving up had never even entered his mind.

Mika looked from Jace to Diana. She bit her lower lip as she seemed to be considering something and then seemed to come to a decision.

"If this doesn't work," Mika walked over and took Diana's hand in her own. She looked to Jace. "Can we just go to a deserted island somewhere and stay there? Some place where Damian won't find us?"

Jace didn't like the idea of running away and letting Damian get away with it, but he realized there was nothing else he could do without putting them in more risk. Knowing how this "adventure" was affecting Diana, he realized he had no choice. He nodded. "Sure. As soon as I talk to the *Help Desk*, we'll take a ship as far away as we can and get lost somewhere."

"See," Mika told Diana. "One way or the other, you won't have to worry about this after we trap Damian. No more running."

The older woman said nothing but nodded to the younger girl. Mika flashed him a smile and then led Diana away towards their part of the island.

Jace watched them go for almost a minute before looking over to where Luna was lying down. "Let's go to our spot."

Luna hopped off the ground and padded next to him as he made his way to the southwest part of the island to begin his watch and think. Think about their next moves and how those moves might affect Diana.

***

Morning came and went, turning into afternoon without any sign of a ship. He hadn't spoken to anyone else in the group since they'd parted but he had checked up on them with his spyglass. He cursed himself several times through the night for not having the foresight to get them all spyglasses, but hindsight was always 20/20.

He'd checked in on Mordred and Charlena several times and was happy to see that they were taking turns in four hour shifts. He knew it had to be hard on them, getting so little sleep, but he didn't see any way around that. Without a way to get an instant message to the outside world, they needed someone in the game at all times.

It was late afternoon, 4:30pm by his gnomish timepiece, when he heard yelling. Looking in the direction of the sound, he saw Diana and Mika running towards him. One of them must have seen a ship!

Jace immediately started running towards them, not wanting to wait the few extra minutes for them to reach him. Luna, who had been playing with a crab near the water, saw him break into a run. The powerful cat bounded after him and quickly caught up to him, running alongside him.

"Boat?" the cat asked in his mind. Jace had explained to her last night that he was looking for a boat on the water and that Luna should tell him if she saw one. He wasn't completely sure she'd understood what he wanted but two sets of eyes were better than one.

"Hopefully," he replied to her and suddenly felt anxious at the upcoming confrontation. So many things could go wrong and they could end up trapped themselves. Or worse. The idea of Damian torturing any of them made him angry but especially Diana, who already seemed near her breaking point.

If things came to it, he promised himself he would either teleport himself away or kill her somehow so she respawned back in Nynymmost. The same with Mika. One way or another, he'd figure out a way to save them.

The three of them nearly collided with each other but slowed down just in time to avoid a collision. They were all breathing heavy and Diana started to speak but then stopped and had to catch her breath. Finally, she looked up. "Ship!"

Jace opened his mouth to ask a question but Diana held up a finger to silence him. He shut his mouth and waited for her to finish.

"Ship," she said again and pointed towards the northeast. "Flying ship!"

Jace's eyes went wide. An airship? Damian had hired an airship! Jace wanted to smack himself. Of course, Damian hired an airship. He had almost unlimited money. He could probably buy an airship. He cursed himself for not considering that as a possibility.

"It'll be here soon," Mika said. "It's really fast!"

Jace nodded. Having never ridden in one, he didn't have first-hand experience, but he'd read on the forums that they were nearly twice as fast as regular ships. Suddenly, their response time was cut in half.

"You two get to the cave," he said, already turning towards where Charlena was on watch. "I'll go tell Charlena so she can get Mordred."

They nodded and ran off towards the cave. Jace raced towards where he knew Charlena was and began yelling. Her elven ears picked up his voice quickly and he saw her lithe form running towards him.

As they came closer, he yelled out again. "Get Mordred! Tell him Damian's coming on an airship. Tell him to *Stealth* as soon as he logs in and come to the cave."

Wide-eyed, she nodded and in the next instant she was fading to blue and then disappeared as she logged out of the game.

Left alone with Luna, he glanced down at the cat, who was looking to the northwest. Even without the spyglass, Jace could see the sleek airship coming at the island. Mika had been right. It was fast.

Jace turned to the cave entrance and ran back. He just hoped Charlena and the real Jace were able to log back in and get to the cave before the ship got close enough to make them out. If Damian saw Mordred, they would lose their element of surprise and the whole plan would be down the drain.

Chapter 52

The airship was still several miles out when Mordred and Charlena logged back in and ran up from the shore and ducked into the cave. His alter ego paused at the entrance and gave Jace a thumbs up before running down the tunnel to get into place.

Jace glanced out at the approaching airship. Even if Damian had been looking out at that exact moment, he doubted the hacker would be able to tell exactly who it had been running. Spyglasses in VEIL Online just weren't that good.

Jace looked down at Luna, who was rubbing against his leg. While they were waiting for Mordred and Charlena to login, Jace had convinced the cat to shrink back down to normal size. It hadn't been easy. The cat sensed the tension and must have guessed a fight was coming. He'd finally explained that he wanted her big size to be a surprise and she had relented and shrunk down.

"You ready for this?" he asked the cat.

Luna looked up at him as she rubbed herself against his leg again. "Yes."

The plan was simple. He just needed to sell it. He needed to make Damian believe they wanted to make a deal. A simple deal. They'd stay silent and not try to contact the *Help Desk* and Damian would leave them alone.

Jason knew his former co-worker would never truly agree to that. He had too much at stake. Damian simply couldn't afford to have anyone who might reveal his plan. The man would have some plan of his own. Some way to neutralize them. The key was to use the scroll of imprisonment on him before he could do anything to them.

Looking up, he saw the airship circling the island. Jace stepped out of the cave and waved at the airship for several minutes before retreating back into the entrance of the cave. The airship was still almost a mile out. He didn't really believe there was anything on the ship that could affect him at this range, but he needed to act like the paranoid player. He needed to bait the trap.

The airship circled two more times before finally dropping to about 100 feet from the ground. It came to a halt and hovered for several minutes before a long rope ladder was dropped down. Did that mean the airship wasn't going to land? Jace frowned as he realized Damian wouldn't need the airship to stay around. He could just teleport back to any town he'd been to after things were done.

Looking up at the hovering airship, Jace waited. He expected to see Damian climb out onto the ladder. Instead, he saw some sort of commotion near the ladder. It was too far up to make out what was being said but it looked like there was an argument going on.

He took the opportunity to look down at Luna. "Remember. Go up to him and then lead him back here. But make sure you stay small until I say so."

She just looked at him for a long minute. "Yes."

Jace knew Damian would recognize the familiar since he had pointed her out last time they had met. He needed the hacker to come to him without exposing himself to whatever Damian might have up his sleeve and Luna was perfect for it. If anything happened to her, Jace could always resummon her.

Luna looked up at them, then over to the airship and the ladder. The little cat trotted over to where the rope ladder was dangling and sat down on her haunches. She stared up, waiting for Damian to climb down the ladder.

Damian didn't climb down the ladder. Instead, as Jace watched the commotion aboard the airship, a figure hopped over the railing of the airship and plummeted to island. As it was falling, Jace could just make out the inky black skin and realized it was Damian.

Part of Jace would have liked to see Damian's character go splat on the ground, but then they would have had to wait until the hacker respawned and made a second trip. But instead of seeming to take any damage at all, Damian landed on the ground a few feet from Luna. Jace heard the crash of Damian hitting the earth but if it caused any damage or discomfort to him, the hacker didn't let it show.

Damian stood up and looked around. He immediately saw Luna and turned his head from side to side, obviously looking for Jace.

"Jace," Damian called out in an almost sickly sweet tone. "Come out! Come out! Wherever you are!"

Jace had a bad feeling about this in the pit of his stomach, but they had gone too far now. The island was tiny and even a cursory search and Damian would find them. No, it was too late to turn back. Damian was here and they would have to face him: one way or the other.

"We're not coming out," Jace yelled back. "Not with your airship around. You could have a small army up there!"

Damian cast a glance at the airship and seemed to chuckle. "You don't really think I'd need an army to deal with you and your...uh… wives, are they? Three wives, right? At least, that's what the nice gnome at the patents office told me. I have to admit, I didn't think you had it in you."

Jace had expected Damian to do some research into him but hearing him say it aloud made that uneasy feeling in the pit of his stomach grow. He bit back the feeling of dread. He needed to play his part. "We want to deal. We just want to be left alone."

The dark elf's face split into a crocodile grin as he held his arms open. His tone was still that sickly sweet, almost condescending tone. "That's why I'm here! To make a deal!"

"Then follow Luna!" Jace said. "And no tricks. I have a teleportation ring. Try anything and we'll disappear!"

"Start leading him to the cave," he told Luna through their mental link.

Luna turned and began slowly walking towards the cave. Damian didn't move at first but then Jace saw him shrug and began following her. "A teleportation ring? That must have cost you most of whatever little inheritance you received with that tiny little estate you were given. What was that title again? Baronet?"

Jace knew Damian was baiting him and he kept quiet. He watched as Damian got closer and began retreating further down the tunnel, towards the main chamber keeping just out of eyeshot of the hacker.

"A tunnel," he heard Damian's voice echo down the lava tube. "I wonder where this goes..."

Damian had to expect some sort of trap, but he was probably too cocky enough to believe that a bunch of lower level characters could do anything to him. And he was right. Without the level 95 Mordred, they wouldn't have a prayer. But now, if they could get the scroll off before Damian could do anything, they'd have him!

Reaching the chamber where they had prepared the ambush, he turned towards the girls. Charlena, Diana and Mika were spread out on the spot they had chosen to make their stand. Jace gave them a meaningful look. "He's coming down the tunnel now."

Walking over, he saw that Mika looked ready for a fight, her hand on her katana. Charlena gripped her bow with white knuckles, obviously nervous. Diana looked terrified. The woman was pale and looked like she might turn and flee at any moment. Not that there was any place to go. Damian now blocked the only exit. Their only way out now was his teleportation ring.

Reaching the girls, he whispered. "Remember, play it cool. And whatever you do, don't look where Mordred is hiding."

He gave a pointed look to Charlena, whose eyes kept flitting over to the pile of rocks where Mordred should be hiding. The elf blushed and looked embarrassed. "Sorry. I won't do it again."

Jace turned around when he heard Damian's booted footfalls getting close to the chamber. Luna, who had been walking in front of the dark elf, sped up and trotted over to Jace. The orange tabby cat crouched down next to him, her tail bushy twitching back and forth.

"Good girl," he sent to her.

Damian stopped just outside the chamber and made a show of producing a pair of glasses. "It's not that I don't trust you Jace, but… well, I don't trust you."

The dark elf put on the glasses, which Jace knew must be some sort of magical scrying glasses to see invisible and hidden players and objects. Damian around, his gaze lingering in the corners of the chamber. When his gazed past the pile of rocks Mordred would be behind, he didn't even pause.

"Isn't double crossing your forte?" Jace asked, unable to help himself. "I mean, you did have me killed."

Damian's head snapped back to look at Jace, and he pulled off the glasses. His eyes narrowed and he took several steps into the room. His gaze traveled across the line of women behind Jace before his face split in a grin. "One of them is a real person, isn't she? That's how you know what happened to you."

"They're all real," Jace countered, growing angry. He remembered how dismissively Damian had talked about the people who had been inserted the last time they'd met in Whitecliff, as if that justified his actions.

His former coworker just chuckled and shook his head. "They're not real. They're not alive. They're just ghosts in the machine. Like you. Just a bunch of 1's and 0's."

"And that justifies stealing their money?" Jace asked angrily. "And making their lives a living hell?"

"You always were melodramatic," Damian rolled his eyes. "How can I steal from dead people. They're dead. The dead can't own property. They can't own money."

"That was money I worked my whole life for!" Diana said from behind him. "You don't have any right to it!"

"And that was my grandmother's inheritance," Mika said. "It does not belong to you!"

Damian smirked and then chuckled. "So those two are inserts. Does that mean the red-head is the real girl?"

Jace swore silently. Had Damian just played them? Had the hacker been goading the girls into revealing themselves? He motioned to the girls with his hand. "Don't say anything else. He's baiting us. Whatever you're up to, it won't work."

Damain threw his head back and laughed. "You always were a slow one."

The hacker took another step towards them, the mirth vanishing from his face. "Did you really think I came here to make some sort of deal? The redhead complicates things, but I can deal with her later. It's time to say goodbye Jace."

"Yes it is," Jace grinned. "Now!"

His shout caught Damian by surprise and the dark elf started, looking from Jace to the girls, obviously expecting an attack. Then he spun as Mordred appeared with the scroll in hand. He had been reading it quietly but he said the last word aloud as the scroll burst into blue light. ".. *Claudo!*"

Blue light from the scroll streaked towards Damian. It looked like Damian might be trying to cast a spell or perhaps he was just getting his hands up defensively. Either way, it didn't matter. The magic shot forward, encircling the dark elf. It spun quickly, and as it did, the blue glow intensified for a brief moment and then dulled into a translucent blue sphere around him.

"It worked?" Diana asked from behind him.

Jace looked at the figure trapped in a translucent sphere and nodded. He felt a grin spreading across his mouth. "It worked! We did it!"

Charlena ran over to Mordred and jumped into his arms, wrapping her legs around his waist and kissing him. Jace smirked. Obviously, they had no problem with the intimate setting in their HUDs.

He was about to turn to Mika when they heard laughter. Turning around, Jace saw that it was Damian laughing from inside the sphere.

Chapter 53

Damian was still laughing. As Jace looked at him, the dark elf brought his hands together in several exaggerated claps. "Very good, Jace! Very good! Honestly, I didn't think you had it in you." The dark elf glanced around at the girls and his tone became condescending. "Or was it one of the girls who came up with this idea?"

The dark elf's eyes moved to Mordred and then widened in surprise, the laughter immediately trailing off. "Mordred?" Damian looked from Jace to Mordred. "But that was your avatar." His eyes went even larger and he shook his head. "That's not possible. You can't be in the game. You're dead. I killed you."

"You tried," Mordred retorted, his face hurt and angry. "I thought you were my friend."

Damian smirked. "You? My friend? You should have figured out by now that I don't have friends. And I don't need friends."

"So, you tried to kill me?" Mordred demanded.

"What else was I supposed to do?" Damian shrugged calmly. "You found out about my modifications to the insertion routine and were going to tell the boss. You left me no choice."

Mordred just shook his head. "This time you won't get away with it."

Damian just smirked calmly. Too calmly. Something was wrong. Damian must have something else up his sleeve. Were there high level players on the airship? Were they waiting for some word from him to come in here and free him? Jace wracked his brain to think of what he might have missed. Was there some other way out of the spheres of imprisonment that he didn't know?

The dark elf yawned from inside the sphere. "Well, this has been fun. But I think it's time to end this."

Jace tensed as Damian moved to the inside of the sphere. The dark elf reached out and pushed on it the side of the sphere with his hands. Jace held his breath and felt his brow furrow as he watched Damian. Did he really think he could just push it? Or was he trying some sort of spell? Had Jace missed something.

"Well…" Damian shrugged and backed up. "That didn't work." A wicked grin crossed the dark elf's features. "But I think I might have something that just might."

Damian produced a glowing sword that seemed to be completely made of pure light. Jace frowned and looked at Mordred who shrugged. Neither of them had seen anything like it. It looked like those laser swords from the old vidstreams.

"Nice, isn't it," Damian said, the evil grin still on his face. "It's a little something I created myself. I had it hidden away and had to go retrieve it before coming here. You see, it's not what I would call… part of the system. But that's how I designed it."

No one moved or said anything. Next to him, he saw the girls tensing, Mika's hand tight on the hilt of her katana. Jace's right hand drifted down to his own weapon. If Damian got loose, he knew they had no chance alone. But Mordred could kill him. His Assassination ability would be ready and could take out Damian in one strike.

Damian held up the sword, looking into its light. "I'm actually quite proud of this. It uses a polymorphic algorithm to stay outside of the normal game mechanics. As far as VEIL Online is concerned, this little baby doesn't exist."

Jace looked over at Mordred and saw he had his daggers in his hands. The vampyre looked over and nodded, silently letting Jace know that he was ready to attack if it came to that. This island wasn't in any faction, so it was a PvP area. That meant, they could attack one another. And it meant Mordred could kill the dark elf, even though they were in the same faction. He returned the nod and turned his attention back to Damian.

"I know, I know," Damian said. "You're all wondering what my little toy does. Well, just think of it as a concentrated virus. Whatever it touches, it injects with a virus that will eat away at the game code in memory that is creating the item or person until there is nothing. Poof! Gone! Like this!"

The dark elf lowered the glowing sword of light until the tip of the sword touched the blue sphere which was imprisoning him. The moment the sword touched it, the sphere burst into the light that momentarily blinded all of them.

Jace blinked several times and when his eyes cleared, the blue sphere was gone. Damian was free. Glancing where Mordred had been, he didn't see his alter ego. He had already *Stealthed* and was going to attack Damian.

Damian looked around and then suddenly flinched as Mordred appeared behind him.

Mordred Blacklock assassinates Alalorn Shadegazer for 0 damage.

The dark elf grinned and slowly turned around. Smirking, his voice dripped with sarcasm. "Oh, did I forget? I'm using the test pod at work right now and I'm logged in as the admin account. Nothing you can do can harm me." Damian looked thoughtful. "I was actually surprised that the sphere of imprisonment worked, but since it wasn't a direct attack against me, I guess the admin account doesn't prevent the spell."

Mordred was still standing there next to Damian, a look of disbelief on his face. Damian pretended to remember the vampyre assassin was there. "Oh, right. You're still here. Let's fix that, shall we?"

Damian lunged out with the sword of light. Jace saw his alter ego raise his daggers to deflect but as the sword touched them, they dissolved into light. The sword continued forward and touched his real self.

When it did, light engulfed Mordred and there was another blinding flash. When it cleared, Mordred was gone.

"Jace! No!" Charlena screamed and lunged at Damian. The dark elf snorted, turning to face her.

"Charlena! Don't! Stop!" Jace called out but the redhead was enraged.

As she rushed into range, Damian causally, almost dismissively, flicked the sword at Charlena. The tip of the sword hit her in the chest and just like the real Jace, she was engulfed in light. When it cleared, she was gone too!

"No!" Diana sobbed from behind them. "You monster!"

"Are they dead?" Mika asked quietly, her voice trembling.

Just then he saw Luna getting ready to pounce. The cat only understood that Damian was an enemy. She didn't understand that he held a weapon that could utterly destroy her. He started to send a mental command but it was too late. He saw her leap at the dark elf's back.

Damian saw the movement and spun, leading with his light sword. Willing himself into his HUD faster than he ever had, he tried to dismiss his familiar before she was destroyed. There was a flash, and Luna was gone.

"Luna!" Mika yelled and drew her katana.

Jace looked on in horror at the space where Luna had been. He had tried to dismiss her but he didn't know if he had gotten to the option in time. Was Luna gone? Forever? Burned out of existence.

Jace drew Kraken's Claw, hate filling his eyes. He wanted to make Damian pay. He wanted to make him suffer. The problem was. He had no idea how.

Damian tsked. "Aw. Was that your little kitty cat?" He laughed and Mika started forward until Jace held out an arm, blocking her way.

"Oh," Damian continued, taking a step towards them. "No, sadly, those two players aren't dead. Their characters are gone. Permanently. If I'm lucky, the feedback to their pods caused brain damage." He held up the sword in front of him. "This little baby even purges the backups. Your cat though, it's gone for good."

Furious, Jace took an involuntary step forward but stopped himself. He had no *Defense* against that sword. And even if he did, Damian was logged in as the admin account. The admin account controlled the entire game. It was basically god-mode. He was completely invulnerable from harm. No blade could pierce him. No magic could directly affect him.

Jace gritted his teeth together, knowing there was nothing they could do. All they could do now was run away and keep running. He went to activate his ring to teleport them away. Best to run and fight another day.

Nothing happened. He tried again. Nothing happened. Damian laughed. "Oh, I brought along a handy little item. I'm sure you're familiar with an anchor bracelet." Damian held up his wrist to show a silver bracelet with runes inscribed.

Jace swore. He hadn't even considered that Damian might think to bring one of those. Truth be told, Jace hadn't even remembered they existed until the dark elf mentioned it. They were mostly used in PvP to prevent enemy players from teleporting away. Since Jace didn't care for PvP, he'd never had any use for one. Obviously, Damian had found a use for one.

Damian waved his hands, speaking arcane words. Jace hadn't heard the spell before but a wall of ice erupted from the ground behind them, cutting them off from the ledge. The dark elf laughed. "In case you were thinking of trying to kill yourself and respawn."

Jace swore and Damian laughed again. That had been precisely what Jace had been about to do. Now they were trapped. Damian had outsmarted them. He had outsmarted him.

As if reading his mind, Damian snickered. "Did you really believe you could think of something I wouldn't think of first?"

"Jace," came Diana's panicked voice. "What do we do?"

Not knowing how to answer, Jace stayed quiet.

Looking from Diana to Mika, Damian smiled. "You know. I've decided to kill you last, Jace. I'm going to make you watch me delete them first and then I'll kill you."

Jace growled but held himself back. There had to be something he could do. He brought up his HUD and scrolled through his spells and abilities. He saw the sword of light go from left to right.

"Eenie…" he heard Damian say and then moved the sword from right to left, pointing at Diana. The older woman whimpered and pushed back against the ice wall.

"Meenie…" the dark elf continued and moved the sword to Jace's otherside where Mika looked at him defiantly. Jace kept looking through items, abilities, anything that might help. But what would affect a person who was invulnerable?

"Miney…" the sword of light went to back to Diana.

"Mo…" Damian grinned and moved the sword back towards Mika. Just then, Jace's eyes caught sight of something.

Disarm
Swashbuckler Ability
Description: A special attack against an opponent's weapon that causes it to go flying.
Note: This ability cannot function when holding a weapon in your secondary hand and therefore cannot stack with Two-weapon Fighting.

Jace's eyes darted across the description. *Disarm* was an attack on the opponent's weapon. That meant it wasn't an attack against the enemy itself and maybe, just maybe, it would work. It didn't matter. He was out of time and he had to do something.

Activating the skill, Kraken's Claw slammed into the sword of light just before it hit Mika. The blade caught the crossguard of Damian's sword first, part of the weapon that was glowing but then slid off and touched the blade. His sword, which had served him so well in so many battles, exploded into fragments of light.

But it had worked. Damian's sword went spinning almost straight up in the air. All eyes followed the path of the sword as it went up and then back down. Jace and Damian looked at each other, their eyes narrowing.

The sword seemed to be falling back to Damian and the dark elf grinned. He started to hold his hand up to catch it when a primal scream surprised them as Diana barreled into the dark elf, knocking him to the ground.

Her attack hadn't hurt Damian, he was immune to damage as the admin. But it had done it's job. Jace stepped forward and caught the sword. Just as Damian pushed the shrieking woman off himself, Jace stepped forward.

"Goodbye Damian, rot in hell," he said and stabbed forward with the sword. He had no idea if the sword would affect the admin account, but he was out of options.

He had just enough time to see Damian's eyes go wide before the dark elf was engulfed in light and disappeared.

Chapter 54

Jace stared down at the spot where Damian had just been. There was no trace of him.

"Is he… dead?" Diana asked, sitting upright from where Damian had pushed her.

Reaching down a hand, he helped the older woman to her feet. Mika came to stand by him, putting her hand on his shoulder. He frowned. "No. Not dead. But if he was right, his character is gone. Wiped away."

He looked down at the sword in his hand, the blade glowing and crackling with some sort of energy. If the blade was really what Damian claimed, it was the most dangerous thing in the game.

Finding that he wanted to get rid of the weapon, Jace suddenly found he wasn't sure how to do that. He certainly didn't want to leave it lying around in the off chance that Damian was somehow able to log back in. Was it safe to put into his inventory? Wasn't that where Damian had pulled it from?

He closed his eyes and willed the item into his inventory, mentally flinching as he prepared to feel the sword disappear from his hand. Nothing happened. He opened his eyes and looked at the sword. It was still in his hand. He was about to curse when Mika spoke up.

"Does something seem… different to you?" Mika asked, looking around.

Diana and Jace both looked around, trying to figure out what she meant. Diana raised an eyebrow. "Is it me, or did things get really quiet in here?"

Jace listened. She was right. There was no sound. None at all. Before, there had been some ambient sounds and the low rumble of the volcano. Now, there was… nothing. Silence except for their own voices.

"That's weird," Jace said. "It's like some sort of silence spell."

Diana looked at the glowing sword. "Is it that thing?"

Jace shrugged. "Possibly. I can't seem to put it in my inventory, so I have to hold on to it for now."

"Just get rid of it!" Diana said, her face contorting into a mask of disgust.

"I can't," Jace shook his head. "If we leave it somewhere, Damian could come back and find it. I'm not about to make it easy for him."

"But isn't he… deleted?" Diana asked.

"Theoretically," Jace said. "But he was logged in as admin. It might have prevented him from being deleted."

Mika gave him a puzzled look. "Damian said that, and you did too. What exactly is admin?"

"Admin is a special account. It basically controls all the functionality of the game and has access to everything. And I mean: everything," he explained. "When you're in as admin, you can literally go in and change just about any aspect of the game and nothing can harm you."

"So, Damian could have turned us all into dung beetles?" Diana asked. "Why didn't he just do that?"

Jace chuckled and shook his head. "Even when you're logged in as admin, you're still bound by the rules of the game - the code. He would have had a special menu that allowed him to do anything within the normal rules of the game, like change a player race or class or level. But he couldn't change the code itself."

"So why didn't he do that?" Mika asked.

"I'm not sure." Jace shrugged and looked down at the sword in his hand. "I guess he wanted us gone permanently. The game rules wouldn't allow that, so that must be why he brought this thing."

Diana shuddered and even Mika's normally happy face looked sober. Jace understood. It wasn't every day you found out someone wanted to wipe you from existence - and had very nearly done so.

"Let's get out of here," he told them and began walking towards the tunnel. Neither girl objected and followed him up the tunnel and out into the island.

As they walked up the tunnel, he took a deep breath and decided to check on Luna. Jace hadn't been sure whether he had been able to dismiss her in time or if Damian had hit her with the sword. With a heavy heart, he went to bring up his HUD to try and summon her.

Nothing happened. His HUD didn't appear. He stopped, nearly causing Mika and Diana to run into him.

"What?" Mika asked. "Is something wrong?"

Jace tried to open his HUD again. There was nothing. It was just like when he tried putting the sword in his inventory. It just didn't work. He turned to face the girls. "Can either of you open your HUDs?"

Both girls stared into space for a moment before looking at him, their faces alarmed. "No. What does that mean?"

Jace had a suspicion but he wasn't sure and didn't want to share until he had more proof. "I'm not sure yet. Let's get up to the surface."

The group hurried to the entrance of the lava tube. As they stepped out of the mouth of the tunnel, Jace immediately realized his fears were well placed. Something was terribly wrong.

He could see the airship that had dropped off Damian. It was still hovering in the same place. Only, it wasn't hovering. It was frozen in place. The propellor-like engines of the airship weren't moving. Nothing was moving.

A terrible feeling began to come over Jace. He glanced out to the ocean and his blood went cold. The ocean wasn't moving. The waves were frozen as well.

Everything except them was frozen. He felt both girls move closer to him.

"Jace?" Diana murmured, her voice small and afraid. "What's going on? Why isn't anything moving?"

Even Mika had moved closer to him, her hand trembling as she gripped his arm. They were both afraid. So was Jace. He turned around to face them.

"I think," he started and then stopped as his voice cracked. He swallowed and tooth another breath. "I think we broke the game."

"Broke the game?" Mika said, wrinkling her forehead. "How?"

"I used the sword on Damian," Jace explained and they both nodded. "While he was logged in with the admin account."

The girls both looked at him with confused looks, not understanding what he was getting at. Jace bit and lip and tried to explain it in layman's terms."

"The admin account doesn't just give carte blanche access in and of itself," he told them. "The reason you have so much power when using the admin account is because it runs the entire game."

This time the girls' looks grew concerned. He could see them starting to connect the dots, so he continued. "When I used the sword on Damian, it didn't just destroy his avatar, it destroyed the admin account."

"And…" Mika swallowed, glancing at the frozen airship. "If the admin account controls the game…"

"… then what's controlling it now?" Diana finished, her eyes darting around the island.

Jace nodded. "Exactly. I think that's the reason everything is frozen. Without the admin account, the game doesn't work."

"What about us?" Mika said, grabbing Jace more tightly. "Are we going to freeze?"

Diana looked to him as well, her gaze almost pleading. "Are we?"

"No," Jace replied, hoping he was right. "A different account runs the players, at least, it runs their normal movements and functions. It's a safety precaution to prevent players from hacking the system."

"So, we won't freeze," Diana repeated, and put a hand on her chest. "If I were still alive, I think I'd be having a heart attack about now."

"What do we do?" Mika asked.

He looked around at the frozen landscape around them. He frowned. "Nothing. There's nothing we can do."

The girls exchanged looks and Diana opened her mouth to speak but Jace held up a hand. "There's nothing we can do but wait. Whatever needs to be done, WorldCog will have to do it."

Jace told them that, but he didn't know how they would replace the admin account. Not if what Damian had said was true. If the virus that the sword created did really seek out and wipe out all traces of something, even from the backups, he had no idea how they would restore the game.

And if they couldn't restore the admin account, then what? What would they do to the game? Would they shut it down? What would that mean for Jace and the others, who were a part of the game now?

Suddenly Jace dropped to his knees, a piercing pain in his head causing him to lose his balance. He squeezed his eyes against the pain, feeling them tear up. And then, just like that, it was gone. He blinked and saw a red blinking alert icon. He also saw that the girls were on their knees as well, hands on their temples, faces contorted in pain.

"What the heck was that?" Diana gasped, blinking.

"System message, I think," Jace croaked, still blinking the tears away.

"Are they trying to make our heads explode?!" Diana growled, wiping the tears from her eyes.

"Our sensation level is at max," he muttered. "To most players it was probably like a pinch."

"That was some pinch," Mika said, massaging the sides of her head.

Mentally clicking on the blinking red icon, Jace saw floating text in his vision. It wasn't quite like his HUD, but he could read it.

Adventurers of VEIL Online,

We are aware of the technical issues you are experiencing with the world. We are also aware that some of you cannot access your HUD and therefore cannot log out. Please know your safety is our top priority and we are working diligently to find a solution.

Until then, we recommend that everyone stay where they are and do not try to interact with the world, as this could have unforeseen consequences.

We will get back to you shortly.

Thank you!

WorldCog Support

Jace finished reading the message and then looked at the girls. Within moments, they were glancing at him.

"What does that mean, Jace?" Diana demanded.

"It means I was right," Jace replied. "The admin account must have been deleted and that caused all of this."

"Regular players are stuck in the game and can't log out?" Mika asked.

He nodded. "That makes sense. We can't access our HUDs. It stands to reason other players can't access theirs. And if they can't get to their HUDs, they can't log out."

"Now what?" Diana asked. "We just wait until they get back to us with another migraine message?"

Jace chuckled despite himself. Migraine message was a very apt way of putting those system message alerts. "I don't see that we have much of a choice. All we can do at this point is wait."

Chapter 55

Jace had no idea how long they waited. Like everything else in the game, his gnomish timepiece had stopped working, the hands frozen at the instant he destroyed the admin account.

They'd walked around the island, looking for any signs of movement but there was none. Even the smoke from the volcano was frozen. The whole thing was eerie and surreal. It was like walking around in a painting.

After what seemed like hours, they'd been knocked to their knees by another migraine message.

Adventurers of VEIL Online,

We have identified the issue causing the current problems with the game. Because of the severity of the issue and risk to player safety, we are forced to take drastic steps to correct it.

In 30 minutes, we will be doing a complete system restore. When this happens, you may experience drastic change in your environment as your avatar is returned to a previous state at a previous location. This is the normal and expected behavior of the system restore.

Once you return to your previous location, please log out immediately. We will begin to deploy emergency patches after the restore and will force logout at that time. All users should log off prior to this to prevent unforeseen issues.

Thank you for your understanding during these difficult times.

WorldCog Support

"What does this mean?" Diana asked after reading the message.

"I'm not really sure," Jace replied, still trying to get his head around it himself. To his knowledge, a full system restore had never been done before. At least, not since the game was in beta test. In fact, the game had never even been down. That was one of the big selling points of VEIL Online, it was up all the time.

"What will happen to us when they do this restore thing?" Diana asked.

"We'll probably just reappear wherever we were when they restore from," Jace told her. "Like teleporting or respawning."

"Oh," Diana sighed in relief. "That's not too bad."

"What about the emergency patches?" Mika asked.

Jace shrugged. "I'm not sure. It might just be a patch to prevent this from happening again. Maybe they'll create a secondary admin account and have the game run as a different account. Honestly, that's what they should have done before."

The girls lapsed into silence as they waited. After what seemed like longer than 30 minutes, the world suddenly went white. In the next instant, Jace was back in the volcano chamber with his back against the ice wall. Pain shot through their heads again but this time Jace was able to stay on his feet.

Adventurers of VEIL Online,

System restore has been completed. HUD access should be restored. Please log out now!

Emergency patch deployment will begin in 5 minutes. Forced log out will occur in 4 minutes 30 seconds.

Thank you for your patience.

WorldCog Support

He read the message before noticing he still carried the sword. That was strange. He would have thought the restore would have removed it from him. Once more he tried to put it into his inventory and this time, it disappeared. Checking his inventory, he saw the sword icon, but next to it was just the world NULL.

His headache gone, he scanned the room. Several feet in front of him, where Damian had been, was a large orange tabby cat. It was Luna. Without thinking, Jace rushed forward and wrapped his arms around the big cat. "Luna!"

The cat looked around in confusion but began purring as he hugged her and rubbed under her chin. The girls came over and gave Luna attention as well, the big cat soaking it all in.

Jace suddenly raised his head. "Do you hear that?"

The girls both perked up and listened. Mika stood up and looked around. "The sounds are back."

Diana looked at him and wrinkled her nose. "The sulfur smell is back too. That, at least, I could have done without."

Looking around, Jace frowned. "No Charlena or Mordred. And no Damian either."

"No big loss," Diana said.

"Does this mean things are back to normal?" Mika asked.

"Let's go find out," he said and gave Luna one more chin scratch before standing up and starting towards the cave entrance.

The group walked up the lava tube to the outside and immediately heard the sound of waves crashing against the island, as well as the whir of the airship's engines as it hovered a hundred foot above them. He looked at his gnomish timepiece and the second hand was moving again. Things did seem like they were back to normal.

"We're okay?" Diana asked from behind him.

"Yes, I think we are," he replied, grinning. "We just need to wait for the ship."

"What about that one?" Diana said and pointed at the airship.

Jace looked up at the airship floating above them. They still had some money. They could probably afford to pay them to get them all back to Nynymmost. He looked down at his timepiece. The patches were supposed to start any time now and he wasn't sure if it would be safe to be in a flying ship while they were running some sort of emergency patch. There was no telling what it might affect.

He turned to Diana to explain the dangers of doing that during an emergency patch, only to find that Diana wasn't there. He looked around. She was nowhere in sight. Then he noticed Mika was gone as well.

"Mika! Diana!" he called out. Were they hiding from him? It seemed an odd time to play a joke on him, but maybe Mika put Diana up to it.

There was no answer and Jace's heart did a flip flop. He yelled out louder, more urgency in his voice. "Mika! Diana!"

He glanced all around. There weren't any hiding spots in the immediate area and Jace was beginning to panic. "MIKA! DIANA!"

Once again, there was no answer he spun to Luna. "Luna, can you find Mika and Diana?"

Luna walked over to the spot where Jace had last seen Diana standing. The cat sniffed around for a moment before looking up at Jace. "Gone."

Luna loped over to the spot where Mika had been looking at the ocean and sniffed there for a long moment before turning her head to Jace. "Mika gone."

"Gone?" Jace said in disbelief. "How can they be gone?"

"MIKA!" he yelled out. "DIANA!"

There was no reply. Jace retraced their steps back into the volcanic chamber but there was no sign of them. Running back out, he searched the entire island before finally giving up. They were just gone. Walking back to the spot where he'd last seen them, he collapsed down on the hard ground and waited.

The airship had left a day later, apparently no longer willing to wait for Damian. Sunday evening, the Wyvern's Tail appeared off shore. Jace waited until the next morning and reluctantly rowed himself back to the ship.

As he climbed aboard, Colette was there to greet him with a frown. "Where are your two wives?"

Jace scowled. "I don't know. They disappeared."

Colette's eyes widened. "Disappeared? You mean by magic?"

"I don't know," he muttered. If they had respawned somehow, he knew where they'd be. "But I want you to sail back to Nynymmost. If they were transported somewhere, it was most likely there. If I can't meet you in a week, I'll contact you by raven messenger."

Colette nodded solemnly. "What about you, captain?"

"I'm going to stay here for a few more days," he told her. "I just need some more food."

"Aye, captain," the first mate said.

He went down to the kitchen and took several days worth of fish for himself and Luna. Going back to the side of the ship, Jace turned to climb down to the boat. He locked eyes with Colette. "If you find them, tell them to send me a raven message, letting me know they're okay."

"I will, captain," the first mate nodded and Jace climbed back down to the boat. This time, there were two sailors with him so they could row the boat back. Jace wouldn't need it. When he was ready to leave, he'd use the ring to get back to the gnomish capital.

***

Three days later, the girls had not appeared. Reluctantly, Jace decided to leave the island. At this point, he didn't think the girls would be returning. He was certain the emergency patch had done something to them. The timing was too coincidental.

He had an idea of what might have happened, but he needed to verify it. At least, verify it as much as he could.

"You ready to leave the island?" he asked Luna. The cat had been his only companion through the last few days but even she was getting stir crazy.

"Ready," the cat replied quickly.

"Me too," he sighed and took one last look around. Focusing on the ring, he activated the teleportation spell and chose Nynymmost as his destination.

The world blurred and bent around him and suddenly he was in the graveyard of the gnomish capital. He didn't hesitate but ran through the gates and back to the raven messenger office. He burst in the door, startling the gnomes in the office.

"I… need… to… send… a message," he managed, out of breath from his run. His stamina was low, but he knew it would regenerate.

"Oh, uh," the closest gnome seemed to come to her senses. "Of course. And who would you like to send it to?"

"Mika Knightly," he said, giving Mika's avatar's name.

The little gnomes eyes went vacant for a second before she shook her head. "I'm sorry, there's no one by that name."

Jace sighed. "How about Diana Knightly?"

Once again, the gnome's eyes went vacant briefly and then she shook her head again. "I'm sorry, there's no one by that name."

Jace frowned but then snapped his fingers. "How about Mordred Blacklock?"

"I'm sorry, there's no one by that name," the gnome told him.

"Alalorn Shadegazer," Jace said, trying to keep the bitterness out of his voice. He didn't really care about Damian, but if his avatar was somehow back in the game, Jace needed to know so he could watch his back.

"I'm sorry, there's no one by that name," the gnome told him.

Jace let out a breath and forced a smile. "Nevermind."

"Understood," the gnome said. "Come back again if you need to send a message!"

Jace walked out of the shop and leaned against the wall. All of their avatars were gone. Mordred and Damian weren't a surprise. Whatever virus Damian had created had destroyed both of their characters and not even a system restore had brought them back.

He also wasn't surprised that Diana and Mika's avatars were gone. If he were right, and he hoped he was, the emergency patch had sent them back to their original avatars. He couldn't remember if Mika had told him the name of her cat-kin character, but if she had, he'd forgotten. He had no way to contact her.

Diana hadn't had a character. She'd hopefully be creating a new one. He wasn't sure if she would get her money back but unless she reached out to him, he had no way of finding her either.

He was starting to feel down when a raven dropped out of the sky. He saw Luna tense, her tail twitching back and forth. He smiled and put a hand on her head.

"No eating the raven messenger," Jace told her and the cat actually pouted. He scratched behind her ears and lowered his voice. "At least, not until it delivers the message."

Luna perked up and narrowed her eyes at the incoming raven. The thing must have sensed the danger of landing too close to the large cat and it opted to land on the roof of the raven shop. The thing looked down at Jace and began to speak.

Message from Mimyeni Kohni

Jace,

This is Mika. I am in my cat-kin again! I have my former items but not my grandmother's money. I will make my way to Whitecliff as soon as possible but I must work on my faction. You know where! See you soon!

Love,
Mika

Jace smiled as he listened to the raven. As soon as the bird finished, it hopped away from the ledge and out of view of the hungry cat.

Turning to Luna, he dropped down and gave her a big hug. "They're alive Luna! They're alive!"

Chapter 56

Two months later, Jace, Mika, Diana, Charlena and his real self, were all in the Dwarvish Fork. Anyone who knew them from previously would only have recognized Jace and Charlena. It was a very different looking group now.

Jace had survived the system restore. He'd also survived the subsequent patch that reunited the players affected by Damian's hack with their original avatars. He wasn't sure exactly how he had survived. Had been because Damain had deleted any record of him? Was it because of the Null Sword, as he was calling it, that he'd taken from Damian?

Damian had said that the Null Sword was "outside" of the normal code. Was there some sort of polymorphic encryption that protected it, and possibly him, from the normal patch code? It was impossible to know for sure.

The real Jace and Charlena's avatars had been destroyed and irretrievable. They'd both lodged complaints with WorldCog but had to join the class action lawsuit that was currently underway against the company if they wanted any sort of compensation for the "incident" that had occurred.

Now, they were both playing elven rangers. Charlena looked almost identical, with her red hair and pointed ears. The real Jace, who was now called Mortolius Darkbow, had created a new elf avatar so the two of them could play together.

The real Jace had gone to the police about the attempted murder. After revealing to the authorities and WorldCog that he had been in a coma and that Damian had been the responsible person, an official investigation had started. Or rather, another official investigation had started.

When Jace had destroyed Damian's avatar with the Null Sword, it had destroyed the admin account while it was signed out to Damian. WorldCog had easily traced it back to the senior programmer and whether he panicked, or just decided to cut his losses, Damian had disappeared that same night.

There was currently a local and federal investigation into Damian for embezzlement, fraud, hacking, sabotage and a host of other crimes. All of his assets had been seized but they suspected he had a number of offshore accounts.

Mika, who was now a level 50 cat-kin, was snuggled up next to Jace as she purred softly. She looked very similar to her human body except slightly thinner. Oh, and there were the cat ears, little pink nose and the tail. Of course, Luna had instantly taken a liking to her. Go figure.

The cat-kin had set out for the good faction the day she's respawned in her avatar. She'd sent a raven message and then jumped on the first ship to the

Whitecliff she could find. She spent the next two weeks killing orcs and gnolls, building up enough faction to be able to walk into the city.

Their reunion had been steamy, especially once they realized that as long as Jace initiated the intimate contact, Mika could consent. That made their reunion much more enjoyable. It was one time when Jace didn't mind his sensory level at maximum.

Diana was no longer a human. She'd been able to create her elven character who wasn't quite as voluptuous as her human had been, but still a knockout. It had taken her two weeks to scrap together enough money to get on with a caravan that was coming to Whitecliff. Then it took another six weeks for the caravan to actually make it to Whitecliff.

Like Mika, Diana had none of her previous money, although WorldCog continued to let both of them know it was under investigation and how it wasn't the companies fault but the actions of a single individual, yada yada yada.

Neither of them really believed they would get their money back. Most likely WorldCog would find some legal loophole to get out of compensating them for their lost money. Not that it really mattered. None of them really ever had to work again. Least of all the real Jace.

After getting the message from Mika, Jace realized that all of the players affected by Damian's insert code had most likely been restored. As soon as he learned that, he took the money he had and two chests of holding and the fastest mount he could buy at his level.

He then rode as fast as he could to the swamp where the epic dragon had made its lair. It had taken him a week to get there and three more days to actually find the lair. When he did, he found something that startled him but made sense when he thought about it.

Scratched on the wall of the dragon's cave were the words "I am Big Cheese." Jace wasn't sure how, but that insane goblin leader must have died and hopped into the body of the dragon. That helped explain some of the dragon's bizarre behavior. He briefly wondered what would become of the insane player but then that was a problem for WorldCog to deal with.

The crazy dragon had collected an enormous amount of treasure and loot. Perhaps it had taken the loot from the towns it destroyed or perhaps some of it was from the raiders who had sought to kill him. Either way, there was millions of gold and dozens of magical items.

No other players came near the lair after the horribly failed raids, so Jace had the place to himself. He made several trips, filling up the chests and haversack each time and then dumping the treasure into his bank.

He had no idea how much treasure he had now, but he'd had to upgrade to the largest bank vault they had offered and it was filled. And that was after he'd divided most of it up between Mika, Diana, Charlena and his real self.

"What are you two going to do now?" Jace asked Charlena and his other self.

"I don't think we'll be in the game as much in the near future. With the money you gave us," Charlena said, glancing at her Jace. "We were thinking of traveling."

"Oh," Diana cooed, "I love travelling. Where are you planning to go?"

Charlena giggled and the real Jace grinned. "Everywhere."

"Good for you two!" Diana said and they all drank to that.

"We're also thinking about adopting this orange tabby cat," the other Jace said and looked at Charlena. "We're going to name her Luna."

Luna perked up briefly but then went back to eating her fish and everyone chuckled.

"How about you, Diana?" Charlena asked.

Diana shrugged. "I bought that vineyard I wanted and now I'm going to go and enjoy it. Thank you, Jace."

They all drank to that.

"With Bob," Mika said loudly when she put her mug down.

The older woman's face went beet red and they all laughed. Diana had let it slip that Bob had been restored as well and had run into her on the caravan. The two of them had hit it off and were now spending time together at her vineyard.

"What about you two?" Diana asked, looking at Mika and Jace. "What are your plans?"

Jace started to speak but Mika cut him off. "Jace needs to power level so we can adventure together!"

"Did you ever figure out why you stayed a beta character while everyone else reverted?" his alternate self-asked.

Jace shrugged. He was 99% sure it was the sword, but still didn't know for sure. "It must either have to do with the fact that I was inserted by accident and maybe Damian deleted the records of me. Or, something with carrying the Null Sword. Either way, I'm not complaining."

"Not now that Mika can consent," Diana teased and Jace and Mika both turned red.

"To Jace and Mika," Diana said, raising her mug.

"To friends," said Charlena, raising her mug.

"To brothers," Jace's real world self said.

Jace held up his own mug, "To family."

And they all drank to that.

Join the Adventure

To learn more about the adventures of
Jace, Charlena and Luna, or to learn of
his other books and projects, visit the
author's website at:

https://www.johnecressman.com

Or contact him via email at:

authorjohncressman@gmail.com

Acknowledgements

I'd like to acknowledge all the members of
the LitRPG Authors' Guild who helped me
in so many ways! Without your help, I
could never have gotten this far!

About the Author

John E. Cressman is an author, magician, mentalist, hypnotist, programmer, and longtime lover of roleplaying games and fantasy/sci-fi books.

As a teen, he wasted long hours creating D&D fantasy campaigns for his friends to play. He has tried several pen and paper roleplaying games from the original Dungeons and Dragons, Traveler and Star Frontiers to the new Pathfinder games.

He still enjoys computer RPGs and MMORPGs, with his current favorite being Elder Scrolls Online. He used to play Skyrim, but then he took an arrow to the knee.

John has published two books on hypnosis and is now trying his hand at the fantasy LitRPG genre with his new LitRPG trilogy, VEIL Online.